Promise of Purity

Gardens in Time Book Two

Marguerite Martin Gray

ISBN: 978-1-951839-83-3

Celebrate Lit Publishing

304 S. Jones Blvd #754

Las Vegas, NV, 89107

http://www.celebratelitpublishing.com/

For

My faithful readers and reviewers
from the very beginning with
my American Christian Fiction Writers
critique groups to
my early readers of my humble
pre-publication work.
You know who you are—my family and friends
near and far.
God bless you all!

Chapter One

East Molesey, England
March 1661

Kate Sinclair shuddered as she saw another soldier walk down the street. The uniform alone caused her heart to pound and her palms to sweat. Would this be the one to arrest her father, maybe her mother, or even Kate? Her position at the counter allowed her to gaze through the bakery window, hopefully giving her plenty of notice of any unusual activity.

For the past ten months her father had stayed in the back of the establishment during most of the day, in case royal guards saw him and wanted to question him. Many in her small village of East Molesey wandered in and out of secret rooms when rumors of officials abounded. In a few weeks the new king would be crowned, solidifying his hold and place of authority in England.

Anticipation accompanied bouts of anxiety. Would the king finally come to the palace? With the spring weather, the bakery saw more traffic and participated in its fair share of the gossip in the town. This Tuesday morning was no exception.

The Sinclair Bakery remained the most renowned bakery, located in the center of town, even though her father was a

Cromwell supporter and a Puritan. In the recent past many in the town shared his political and religious bent. It wasn't such a good thing now.

Today was slow since yesterday was the major delivery day. All that remained on the shelves were pastries, meat pies, and a few round loaves of bread. Slim pickings for the few customers or curious children peering through the window.

At the tinkling ring from the bell above the door, Kate turned her head in time to see Jane Washburn, her best friend, trip into the store catching herself with the support of the door knob.

"Are you all right? You could have hurt yourself." Kate leaned over the counter as Jane whirled around, pointing behind her in the direction of the closed door.

"A cavalier is in the village with a petition," Jane said, the strain of her news burning her cheeks red. "He's already come to Father's shop. He signed immediately."

Jane's father was the local butcher and had no problem relating to royalists, unlike Kate's father. Immediately, Kate understood Jane's staccato, breathless announcement pertained to Kate's father.

"Well of course he did. He never blatantly served Cromwell." Kate shook her head and frowned. No reason to hide her disappointment from her friend. "I don't know what Father will do. And if he doesn't sign, will he go to jail?"

Kate let her concern spill freely with her friend, the only one who listened without repeating or spreading Kate's deepest fear.

"I haven't heard of anyone who hasn't signed." Jane rounded the corner of the counter and glanced into the kitchen behind Kate. "Maybe he'll get a warning."

"Or perhaps he'll sign to protect his family."

Jane grasped Kate by the shoulders and made her look at her. Kate's thoughts spun. Her family without her father around? In Kate's twenty-two years she didn't remember being so unsure of her family's future, except perhaps about ten years ago when her father threatened to leave for America.

"I'll warn him. Thank you, Jane."

The girl hugged her and darted out the door, her bonnet hiding her flushed cheeks and wandering eyes.

So, the time had come. Kate tired of wondering what and when it would happen. Would the next few hours determine her family's fate?

Kate peeked around the corner into the kitchen. Her father kneaded the dough, preparing for deliveries on Wednesday. He pounded the mound in an exact rhythm as flour, combined with water and salt, produced a sticky, yeasty concoction all the way up to his elbows. She whiffed the hot buttery topped bread in the huge iron oven. She'd never tire of the aroma hovering over the room, in her hair and clothes. A few feet away her mother chopped mutton and prepared spices in a sauce for pies for local deliveries.

"Father, you might want to know there's a king's man in the village with a petition." She leaned closer to her father and whispered, "He's a few doors down."

He stared straight ahead and pounded his fist into the innocent mound of dough. She'd heard his tirades about the rule of Charles I and his problem with his son, the new king. Would her father voice his comments to the ambassador of the king?

Please, no. God give him wise words not heated ones. Can't he try to live in peace?

The middle-aged man with gray hair, stooped from the years of bending over a table, tried to straighten to his medium height.

"Clifford, what will you do?" Mother asked, the spoon dripping thick liquid into the pan.

Silence reigned, except for the fire roaring in the oven and a faint drip, drip from the stove top.

"I will know when the time comes. I won't be running or avoiding the talk."

"Father, please be careful and think about Robert and Margaret." Kate wanted to shake some sense into his stubborn being. He glanced at her through squinted eyes. Had she overstepped the line into his role of father? She didn't want him to forget her siblings' innocence. Margaret, twelve, and Robert, ten, had missed the turmoil of the Civil War, the devastating war between Cromwell and the Royalists. Kate wanted them to remain oblivious to hardships, and right now life without a father would be devastating.

Kate bowed her head and closed her eyes to the reprimand from his wrinkled brow and intense frown. His command to be quiet soared in her direction. She turned and bumped into the door frame as she exited, sending a jolt of fire through her body.

Although humility was taught in the church, Father lacked a godly share. Perhaps remembering the four other members of his family would startle some sense into him.

HOW MANY SHOP bells had he heard today? Peter Reresby disliked this part of his job. Surely, he wasn't as imposing as the townspeople's faces revealed. Big eyes, dropped jaws, and flushed cheeks accompanied fidgeting hands, slurred speech, and frozen stances.

One more inquiry at this bakery before he would retire for the noon meal. He'd go to the inn as a customer instead of a king's man on business.

"Excuse me, miss." A pair of dark amber eyes looked up from the counter, as the young woman closed a record book.

"Yes, sir." She recovered her dropped jaw quickly. Her scared rabbit stare revealed she'd guessed who he was. He gave himself away with his cavalier attire—crisp white jacket, red vest, shiny black boots, and the king's insignia on his shoulder. It begged authority but not anonymity.

"I want to speak to Mr. Clifford Sinclair, the owner of this bakery. Is he available?"

She tilted her head, nodded, and left. Her hair reached to her waist in a single braid. Was it the same shiny reddish-brown amber as her eyes? Even in the dim light her head glowed from the reflection from distant sun rays.

He shook his head. If he let his mind wander to a pretty girl, he must really need a break. He prided himself on being able to give wholly to his mission while on duty. Anyway, her attire showed the theme of puritanical staleness he'd seen in England over the last ten months. Peter caught his chuckle before he had to explain himself to any curious listener. The last thing he needed in his organized life was an interest in any Puritan. His mission for the king brought him close enough to the remaining rebels.

The scowl of the man entering the front of the shop dripped mistrust, anger, and annoyance. Peter had seen many of these today. He wasn't here for the man's story, only a signature.

"Mr. Sinclair, I'm here on behalf of His Royal Majesty, King Charles with the King's Petition. He desires to determine which citizens are willing to state their loyalty to his reign. Sign here if he can be assured of your support." Peter stood at attention hoping for an easy end to his morning.

The young woman, standing beside her father, and two customers behind him all sucked in their breaths emptying the room of fresh air. Was Peter in for trouble? In reality, nothing would happen to the man if he didn't sign. Peter wasn't here to arrest the village citizens, although he knew some like Mr. Sinclair clung to the old ways of Cromwell's rule. The man would probably rather be saying his prayers night and day in his dismal, dull prayer room or church pew.

Peter unfurled the scroll and laid it on the counter making sure the man could view the signatures of fellow East Molesey citizens. Each village wasn't subject to the same petition. But with the court moving to Hampton Court Palace soon, a heightened sense of loyalty seemed appropriate.

Mr. Sinclair grunted a "humph" and penned his name, adding a deliberate scratch on the page. It wasn't the first disgruntled Englishman he'd seen. Each one Peter found reminded him of his father, a powerful family man turned rebel. His own father died serving Cromwell in the Civil War.

"Anything else?" The short round man bore a hole in Peter's chest with his direct menacing stare.

Peter could think of a few warnings but chose silence. He glanced at the doorway to the kitchen and found a gentler pair of eyes staring at him. For a second his heart skipped a beat. Mistrust ran deep in Puritan families but her eyes held unanswered questions. A furrowed brow begged to be smoothed with his fingertips.

Oh no. I don't have the desire or time to spend straightening out an obvious Roundhead, Puritan girl. That could probably be as dangerous and unsuccessful as if she was a lady of the court. The extremes posed difficult and massive problems. Why couldn't he find someone to meet him in the middle? Were the only women left in England demure, unintellectual, and colorless?

Although amber eyes and rosy cheeks added natural warmth, color, and beauty to this girl's face, the fact remained no one like her would fit in the new England, not the one Charles planned to create.

The plume, jabbing into his hand, jolted Peter's attention to the man in front of him. Peter's six-inch height difference forced him to step back a foot to regain eye contact with Mr. Sinclair.

"I asked if there was anything else."

"No, sir. Thank you for your time. Good day."

After blotting the ink, Peter rolled up the scroll, watched Mr. Sinclair's retreating form, and nodded at the woman posing in the door frame.

She smiled and let air escape her tense cheeks. A sigh? "Thank you, sir."

"For what?"

"For being patient and kind with my father," she whispered. "He's not..."

Peter raised a hand for her to stop. "I don't need to know any details."

She lowered her head and fidgeted with the end of her braid hanging over her shoulder down the front of her stiff white apron. What horrors had she seen? While Peter had tramped all over Europe with the exiled heir to the throne, this woman stayed in a war-torn country. *Like my mother and sister.*

He wanted to touch this woman's cheek as he would his sister. "What is your name?"

"Kate."

"Miss Kate Sinclair." Pretty. His own sister, Rebecca, would be eighteen years old now and as pretty as Miss Sinclair.

"I'm Peter Reresby. Perhaps we'll meet again." Unlikely, but not so unpleasant.

He turned and listened to the bell punctuate his exit. His stomach warned him of the hour. The fresh, steamy, yeasty aroma from the breads at the bakery spurred him to relieve his hunger. He planned to focus on a hot meal instead of the plight of village girls. Yet, as he walked to the public house, the Crooked Inn, he tried to imagine his sister somewhere in this country, lost to him but hopefully safe and happy. Three years was a long time with no word. A seamstress in Cromwell's household, and then after his death, she had disappeared.

God, if You are still present, give me hope that Rebecca is still alive and whole.

Chapter Two

Kate twirled around with her basket on her arm, surveying the green lawn reaching down to the Thames River. The scene reminded her of a patchwork blanket with all the different families scattered about, enjoying the first gathering outside since winter began back in November. Sunday picnics ranked at the top of Kate's favorite activities.

Today, Reverend Turnard encouraged his congregation to delight in the spring festivities. Mother and Kate's siblings attended the Church of England but not her father. He favored the Puritan worship in the next town though he didn't attend often. Since the new reign, the pulpit in East Molesey once again was filled with a Church of England minister, and perhaps this outing as a church family would continue the healing.

Kate shook away the memories of religious conflict, hoping King Charles could bring order and peace. She'd leave the healing of hurting souls to God and the church. For now, Kate spread her basket's nourishment out by her mother. Fresh baked items with ham, meat pies, and strawberries enticed her to plop down on the edge of the blanket.

"Jane." Kate jumped up and hugged her friend.

"Careful. Don't dump my basket."

Kate pulled Jane down beside her and arranged the additional food items in a pleasing display.

"I'm so glad you brought your famous cheese puffs." Kate picked one up ready to savor the creamy mixture. As her mouth opened for the event, Edward Payne stepped into her view. She looked at the cheese puff and then at her friend. Manners won this time.

"Edward. It's good to see you. Come share our meal." Kate couldn't be rude. Edward followed her around like a lost puppy. He was sweet and had a liking for her, although she didn't encourage him. Edward would remain her friend. Her heart belonged to Richard Douglas. One time, one love, five years ago would be enough for a lifetime.

"Are you listening, Kate?" Jane punched her in the arm.

Listening? Not at all. "Something about a walk by the river."

"Yes. Later, let's go to the bridge." Jane talked with her hands, pointing and gesturing. While everyone filled their napkins with choice foods, Kate drew on memories of garden walks in the summer at Hampton Court Palace when the Protector resided on the grounds. Hand in hand with Richard, they planned their future. Although a stable boy, advancement in time promised a secure living.

Kate picked at her bread and cheese roll, making crumbs tumble to her skirt. Richard joined Cromwell's army, went to Ireland, and was killed in battle, making her heart a victim of war. She sighed and shook her memories to the side. This wasn't about Richard anymore but Edward. He would have to find someone else eventually. But today, she hadn't the heart to send him away from a harmless picnic with her family and best friend.

Anyway, Kate was past the marriageable age. At twenty-two she'd lost her dream of love, children, and happy hearth. The older men didn't look at her anymore. The younger ones like Edward, at twenty years, didn't seem to mind her maturity, but she balked at their lack of sense and wisdom.

What if I steered him toward someone else? Who, though?

She craned her neck and surveyed the lawn. Blanket after blanket of families and a few lovers. Perhaps a handful of eligible bachelors roamed around. But most men were married and a great number had died in battle, or moved to the continent or all the way to America. At least she wasn't looking for an exciting suitor for herself. Edward needed someone to concentrate his youthful efforts on who wasn't Kate.

Kate's head pivoted right back to her green-and-brown patched blanket, to Jane's sweet innocent face. Perfect. *Now how do I convince her to see him, someone I cast off, as potential husband material?* Her friend's nineteen years matched his better and a little courting wouldn't hurt either of them.

Focusing back to the reality around her, Kate knelt, with her skirt flared out around her, and bounced in place. "How about that walk to the bridge now?" Her mother, Edward, and Jane stared at her. She must have missed parts of a conversation or interrupted them.

Edward rose and held his hand out to her. "Yes, I'm ready, then I can come back and eat some more."

Kate ignored the gesture. So what if he thought she'd meant an intimate walk for two. "Come along, Jane. Mother, is it all right if I take Robert and Margaret with us? They do so love the ducks on the river."

"Be careful. Neither are good swimmers, at least not like you, and the water is still cold." Mother's permission regularly had added attachments. Well-meaning ones, but she still saw Kate as a child, not a responsible woman. How silly, since under different circumstances, she would have been married with two or three children of her own.

"I'll watch them." Kate bent to kiss the top of her mother's bare head. "Come on, you two. I don't want to miss out on the games later."

Edward offered his hand to Jane, which allowed the girl to

rise gracefully. Unlike Kate who practically had to push herself up awkwardly on all fours.

Not even a hand. I don't want to encourage Edward at all.

For a second Kate chastised herself for using her friend and siblings to stifle Edward's attention—but only for a second. The day was too fair to dwell on an uninteresting subject.

"Robert! Margaret!" Kate called across a green expanse full of children running and shouting. It took a couple of attempts before she coaxed them away from their game of chase.

"Where are we going?" Margaret tried to secure her hair and make herself more presentable for the older crowd. Kate wanted to tell her to stay a child as long as she could. Twelve was an awkward in-between stage. Margaret could marry in two years' time.

"We're going across the bridge. I want to see what's going on at the palace. Perhaps we'll see something exciting." Kate's curiosity had been high since the tall stranger came to the shop. His presence meant the king at least thought about coming to his palace.

"I wish we could walk through the gardens like we did before." Robert skipped ahead of them.

"Well, I wouldn't count on it. Remember this is a new king, and he might not like boys wandering his grounds. You're remembering a time when Father had special privileges." *That's changed. Just like the death of my true love, along with the carefree summers of the past.*

Jane claimed one side of Kate and Margaret the other. Kate smiled and released her breath as she observed her extended distance from Edward. If only she could find a way to leave these two alone. Would Jane mind?

"Are you sure we're even welcome at the gates?" Jane laced her arm through Kate's and held on.

Was she expecting Kate to protect her from gruesome giants? "Why not? We're just looking," Kate said. "Anyway, other kings have let the public in on occasion."

Edward crossed his arms. "But this isn't like that. The king is not even here."

Kate recognized a pout. Things weren't going his way. A wicked grin surfaced but Kate squashed any demeaning remarks.

"All the more reason for taking a peek. If we can, I want to see the vegetable and herb garden. I used to spend hours there growing and picking the sweetest spices and tangiest peppers." Kate's mouth watered as if a sweet pepper rested on her tongue.

Margaret and Robert ran ahead. When Kate caught up, their faces were pressed against the iron gate, their hands holding the vertical bars beside their heads.

"Look at those wagons. What do you think they're doing?" Robert jostled from foot to foot, up and down.

Kate's curiosity joined her siblings'. "My guess would be unloading valuable gilded chairs and ornate sofas preparing for the king and his court."

How am I any different than the younger ones? Her face, too, plastered against the tall gate, gave her a clear view of the inspiring red façade of the Tudor palace. Towers and turrets, ornate windows and doors set at the end of the long gravel drive. She'd only been in the inner courtyards twice. Once for the Lord Protector's first visit commencing with a procession of townspeople and ending with a celebration in the gardens through the courtyards.

Usually, her forays within the walls of Hampton Court secluded her in the kitchen or the many garden plots. But one other occasion had drawn her into the inner court—the public proclamation of victory in battle over Ireland. The inner courts filled with uniformed and armed soldiers on their massive steeds. Never had Kate been so close to so many fierce animals or men. Sharp prickles shot up her arms at the memory.

"Let's see if the side gate is open. I know a secret shortcut to the gardens. If anyone asks, we are just strolling and didn't know where we'd end up."

"You'd lie, Kate?" Robert's eyes bellowed disbelief.

Teach them the ways they should live.

"You're right. We'll just tell the truth. We want to see the gardens."

Robert's tense jaw and strained eyes relaxed. If he only knew the times she'd lied to get away from her stern, strict father. When the weight of his heavy hand almost suffocated her, she'd found an excuse to wander the river banks, walk the fields, or hide in the back of the church.

Kate had forgotten about Jane and Edward. Why hadn't they spoken up? She turned from the splendor of the palace to the road. Her hand went to her mouth to cover a giggle. Her friend, now a five-minute walk away, appeared to accept Edward's attention.

It didn't take him long to switch his affection. Kate marveled at the success of her tactics. Now she could concentrate on her mission. She grabbed a hand of each sibling, laced them through her arms, and aimed to find an entrance to the vast estate. Three abreast voided any hint of sneaking through the gates.

"TAKE CARE OF HIM. We've been through a lot together." Peter dismounted his white charger, Samson, and gave the reins to the stable boy. He rubbed the horse's neck and gave him a sugar morsel from his coat pocket. Samson had seen him through many long journeys across Europe and then back to England. His equestrian friend deserved extra care.

"Yes, sir. He'll get a good rub down and the best oats."

The locals put into positions at the palace worked hard and complained little. Some employed years ago like Phillip Payne, the master gardener, remained constant whether employed by Cromwell or King Charles. Peter headed in his direction right away.

Besides the ornamental gardens, Mr. Payne managed the

vegetable and kitchen gardens. Peter guessed the man didn't work on Sunday, but he could leave instructions for the week.

Peter shielded his eyes from the sun with his hand and surveyed the gardener's work. Neat rows filled eight plots. Walkways traversed evenly, making access easy and orderly. Spring herbs and plants poked their heads out of the fertile soil. But no Mr. Payne.

He followed the path to a row of cottages and took a paper out of his pocket displaying a map of the grounds. An "x" over the third dwelling denoted the master gardener's house.

Two sharp knocks on the door with the wooden block nailed in the center brought Mr. Payne out into the sunshine. By the look of him, Peter surmised the man took Sunday literally as a day of rest translated into sleep.

"I'm sorry to interrupt you on your day off. Do you remember me?"

The man scratched his scraggly chin. "I sure do, sir. You're the young man representing the king. You've come to fix up the old place. I've done what you said about the gardens. My boy and me worked hard to bring back to life what's been left undone these past years."

"I see that. Do you think you could hire a few more helpers from the village?"

"I surely could. My boy has some friends, and a few men my age have come back from war who need work."

"Good. If they do a fair job, there are permanent positions for a dozen of them. King Charles has a mind to turn this into a showplace to rival the gardens of France."

"France, you say?" Mr. Payne shook his head. "Why would you want old French gardens when you have everything you need right here on old English soil?"

Peter laughed. "You're right, sir. One other concern. Have you an ample supply of ingredients for the cook, Mrs. Downs?"

"That woman. Why does she need such fancy fixins? I put seeds out there, the ones she requested. There's no telling what will spring up. There's a girl my boy is sweet on who knows much about such tasty ingredients. Now she's the one who used to tend this garden and help Mrs. Downs on special occasions."

"And what's her name?"

"Miss Kate Sinclair."

Oh, the amber-eyed, strait-laced Puritan woman. "Yes, I've met her or at least talked to her."

"Mark my words. She'll come around soon just to check out my work." Mr. Payne yawned. Time for another nap?

"Ask her for advice. The king's household would appreciate your help. Good day."

The man reached for his hat but found he didn't have one on and bowed instead. The locals of the palace and Molesey didn't seem to hold any grudges against the restored monarchy, or sadness over the demise of Cromwell and the Commonwealth. Even a noted rebel like Mr. Sinclair signed the petition without outward anger or resentment.

He peered over the shrubbery wall surrounding the hidden gardens. Three figures entered from the left hedge opening. The middle person shrieked and dropped the hands of her charges. Her white bonnet hid her eyes. She raised her black skirt a fraction and skipped onto the path, stopping to gaze at each row of plants.

"Look at all the different herbs. Mr. Payne has been very busy."

"Do you know what they are?" a young voice asked.

Peter noted a younger girl about a foot shorter than the older, dressed in the same dark-colored dress with a long and high white collar topped with a white apron.

"Most of them, yes." The older girl stooped down and touched a short leafed green plant. "This is peppermint and this one is spearmint. In a few weeks the others will become more distinguishable."

The boy marched along the paths appearing uninterested in

the plants. He made a game of the straight walkways as if a soldier staking out his post.

What are three people doing in the palace gardens? They don't seem to be anxious about keeping quiet or getting caught.

The taller girl lifted her chin and eyes. Could it be? The same amber eyes that scrutinized him a few days ago, now reflected the sunlight and glowed like red gold. This had to be Kate Sinclair, the same mentioned by Mr. Payne.

As he gazed at the woman, the boy made his way around the shrub fence and stopped right in front of Peter. The bush separated the two. Was the child not scared of a stranger, of being caught on the king's property?

"And who are you, sir?" the boy asked.

Kate gasped and the other girl hid behind her sister.

"I am Peter Reresby, a caretaker at the palace. The questions really should be—who are *you* and why are *you* here?"

"Oh, right." The boy turned to Kate, and she nodded. "I am Robert Sinclair, and I'm here with my sisters, Kate and Margaret."

Peter smiled at the innocence of youth. Robert didn't process the implications of being caught on king's property as an offense. But shouldn't his older sister?

After the boy turned and skipped toward his sister, Peter cut through the opening in the hedges and approached the three. He didn't want them to escape before he procured an explanation from Miss Sinclair. If he could avoid her hypnotic eyes, he could concentrate on the situation at hand.

The lady, glued to the path, seemed to have no intention of fleeing. A mother hen with protective wings around the children's shoulders raised her eyes to his, challenging him to proceed with caution.

"Miss Sinclair, it's a pleasure to see you again."

She nodded with no smile. Her rigid stance showed no sign of relaxing. She exuded the same coldness as when he entered her shop. Was he such an enemy, an unwelcome entity?

He tipped his brown felt hat and bowed before replacing it. "Do you remember me, Peter Reresby, servant of the king?"

"Yes, well, I'm a servant of God." She paused. "And the king."

Margaret dropped her jaw and looked wide-eyed at her sister. Robert giggled and Kate smiled.

The purposeful reference to her true loyalty didn't escape Peter's notice. Her high collar and frill-less attire shouted her stern connection, if not commitment to the Puritan separatist church. He'd stick with servant to the king—someone he could see and trust.

"May I ask what you are doing here?" Peter clasped his hands behind his back.

"I wanted to show them the kitchen gardens. I used to spend lots of time out in these plots when the Lord Protector, I mean, the former..." She continued to stumble over how to label the previous ruler.

"Oliver Cromwell. I am familiar with the person." He preferred to keep her defenses up in order to detect her true feelings for the present sovereign.

"During that time the gardens were full of growth and delicious herbs, vegetables, and flowers." Kate let go of her siblings' hands and walked to a nearby plant. Peter had no idea what her fingers caressed until she stood. The potent basil aroma exhumed from her hand as she lifted it to her nose. Her closed eyes and upturned face made the scent stronger on its way to Peter.

"Basil, mint, rosemary." She gestured to all areas of the garden. "At one time plants like these were huge and numerous. We spent hours a day tending the garden in order to prepare feasts for the household and guests."

Peter felt she had forgotten his presence and entered a pleasant world of the past. Mr. Payne needed someone like Kate to bring the garden and kitchen up to a king's standard.

"Would you like to help Mr. Payne restore this section of the garden for the king?"

"Oh, yes, I would, sir. And Mrs. Downs, the head cook, would appreciate having the ingredients." Kate clapped her hands and brought them to her chin. Peter felt her contagious joy through her girlish excitement.

Robert stopped in front of Peter and pulled on his sleeve. "Is King Charles coming soon?"

Peter bent down to the child. *Was I ever so innocent?* Perhaps so. At Robert's age of around ten, Peter's world had not yet been rocked by the beheading of Charles I or civil war and exile. He wanted to wrap young Robert in his arms and beg him to remain pure and unscarred by the wounds of war.

"Yes, soon. He'll make a visit in May. Would you like that?"

"Oh, I would, sir. I've only seen a poster of His Majesty. There's one on the wall at the church. Does he wear ruffles and breeches with ribbons like you?"

"Robert, you aren't to speak of the gentleman's clothing," Kate corrected.

"It's all right. You will see much more in the way of ribbons and lace in the king's court."

"Will he parade through town on a fine black horse with his soldiers all around?"

"I'm sure he will." This boy needed someone to answer all his questions. After meeting Mr. Sinclair earlier, Peter doubted Robert asked his father anything about the restored king.

"Let us leave Mr. Reresby alone. We are trespassing and must return to the picnic." Kate gathered her chicks again.

"Miss Sinclair, I was serious about you working with Mr. Payne. Should I mention to Mrs. Downs that you have an interest in working in the kitchen?"

She peered at him from wide amber eyes devoid of scrutiny and distrust. "Yes. I used to bring baked goods from the bakery on special occasions."

"Good. I look forward to seeing you soon." Peter planned on

overseeing the gardens personally and hopefully encountering Kate.

"I'm sorry we trespassed, but I'm not sorry we met again, sir."

For her to feel a bit guilty, Peter must have broken through a layer of her coldness.

"From now on, you are welcome to traverse the gardens. Since Mr. Payne had just mentioned your name, I figured no harm had been done. Remember, though, this is a new reign with a court not familiar with your ways."

"Don't worry. I don't plan on having anything to do with the court. I've heard stories of the royal court. In a year the king's reputation for merry-making has given him the name Merrie Monarch. I won't mix with his crowd."

In more ways than one, she was right. Except for her exceptional eyes and chestnut thick hair, Kate would fade among court ladies. But out here in the sun, her natural beauty shone, casting a shadow over courtiers.

Please stay away from the glamor of the court. Peter had seen too many swept into the abyss of the court, never to emerge intact. He didn't want this fresh country maiden to add a fiasco in court to her battle scars.

"We'll meet again soon." Peter remained on the path and watched the Sinclairs disappear, taking a bit of the sunshine and breeze with them. If he were a man of faith, he would believe God sent them today for this encounter, but instead he believed the coincidence or chance meeting brought their lives together again.

He gave himself an invisible pat on the back. One hour's work secured a head gardener and one helper and an enthusiastic base for a well-run culinary establishment.

~

KATE MARCHED AHEAD of Robert and Margaret, hoping they stayed close behind her. The greater part of her being refused to check to see if Mr. Reresby watched them depart. Why did she have to get caught by the overseer? Why not Mr. Payne or someone else who knew her? Embarrassed by her childish meandering or trespassing, she huffed at her antics, releasing pent-up air from her lungs in a faint long whistle.

"Slow down, Kate. Why are you in such a hurry?" Margaret's heavy steps crunching on the gravel emphasized the child's extended effort to keep up.

"I'll slow down. I just wanted to find Jane and Edward." Kate turned and glanced over Margaret's head before connecting with her sister's red-faced stare. She sighed and relaxed. He was gone.

With the palace gate behind them, the return journey took on the pleasant pace of a stroll. The church steeple and the lawn by the river dotted with family blankets in sight, Margaret and Robert ran ahead.

Jane joined Kate along the bank. "We were concerned. What took you so long?"

Kate laughed for the first time since the incident. "We were caught by none other than the palace overseer or body-guard."

"Oh no. How can that be funny? I'm so glad we didn't join you."

Kate reflected on Jane's shiver. Did she envision a huge knight in armor pointing a sword at them yelling in a gruesome deep voice?

"You would have been fine. Do you remember the man with the king's petition?" Jane nodded. "He is the man in charge of the estate. Mr. Peter Reresby. He's harmless."

And good looking, interesting, kind…and a courtier in a wicked court.

"He even offered me a job in the garden."

Jane shook her head, blonde curls bouncing upon her collar

and hands on her hips. "I'm going to lose my friend once again to the infamous gardens behind the palatial walls."

"Well, if you don't want to come visit…"

"Of course, I will. While you toil, I'll admire the abundance of roses and lilies and flit away my hours in a cloud of perfumed bliss." Jane's nose pointed to the sky as her hands lifted her skirt an inch and swirled it from side to side.

"Now you're making fun of me. I'll have Mr. Reresby ban you from the premises." Kate threw her head back in laughter. When Jane put on airs, Kate could almost see her sashaying through the garden paths on the arm of a gentleman.

Kate and Jane sat on the blanket next to Kate's mother. The afternoon concert commenced before Mother could chide Kate on her absence. Would her parents let her go to the palace? It could mean more business for them. Would her father see only the image of King Charles and balk at any connection with royalty? He refused to go to the restored parish church. Instead, he worshipped with a priest and congregation separate from the Church of England. Would he draw the line at business too?

I'm twenty-two with a chance to help my family and add a bit of excitement to my days. I'll never have direct access to the wayward court or king. What harm would it do?

She'd talk to her father tonight. Kate sighed, leaned back on her arms, and enjoyed the fiddlers and singers. The hymns flowed into lively tunes as the young encouraged the ditties like "God of Winds" and "Tell Me No More." The adults slowly gained control of the concert and brought it back to the sacred level.

By the end of the afternoon the last pastry disappeared from the basket. Kate and Mother folded the blankets and mingled with their remaining friends. Edward resumed his place at Kate's side since Jane had left with her family.

"I hear that your father has been asked to restore and enlarge the gardens at Hampton Court," Kate said.

Edward crossed his arms and stepped in front of Kate,

blocking her advance. "Since when? I spoke to him this morning, and he said nothing."

"I think it just happened this morning. I saw the overseer, and he mentioned your father and plans for adding workers to help him, including me."

"Really? Finally, Father will receive more payment for his work and perhaps hire me back."

"I'm sure he will if you're willing to leave the Fletcher farm."

"We'll see how reliable this new plan is. Does it mean King Charles will bring his court here soon?"

"Yes. Won't that be exciting? All the carriages and pretty ladies and clothing and handsome soldiers and gentlemen." Kate noted Edward's frown. Was it her mention of the latter? Perhaps he wasn't as taken with Jane as she'd hoped.

"Don't you go get high hopes of catching a courtier's fancy. That would be no good at all." He shook his finger at her, which only made her laugh instead of taking him seriously.

Kate scooted around him, walking toward the main road and home. "So, I'm not good enough? I can bake the king's bread and till the king's soil, but I can't associate with the king's men." She added a pouting lip, making Edward squirm.

"Of course, I didn't mean that. You are fit to associate with kings and queens. But I don't," he paused. "I just don't want you to."

Kate touched his arm and cocked her head in his direction. "Don't worry. I have no desire to be taken in by the merry court." Although more time in Mr. Reresby's presence would entice her.

At the corner of Main and Court roads, Edward headed across the bridge and Kate to her house above the bakery. She didn't know how the events of the day would affect her daily life. She took the back stairs, avoiding the bakery and family rooms, wanting the privacy of her own bedroom.

The cabinet in the hall held the extra blankets. The picnic blankets fit neatly on the bottom shelf. She'd take the basket down later. Her room overlooked the back fenced-in yard and a row of birch trees. She'd chosen this room next to her parents instead of one facing the main thoroughfare through town. Here she could pretend her abode rested on a plot of land outside the direct comings and goings of the townspeople. She faced enough reality in the bakery every day to keep her dream as a dream.

Her shoes slipped to the floor as she swung her legs onto her bed, adjusting her dark full skirt around her legs. Wiggling her toes and flexing her fingers, Kate settled into her straw stuffed mattress and quilted coverlet.

Now to approach her dilemma and devise a solution, one her father could possibly approve.

Chapter Three

"But, Father, we could use the money and the exposure for business." Kate couldn't hold in her announcement and secret excitement any longer. At eight in the morning, she had burst out with the offer.

"You'd be working with and in a den of vipers. How could you even want to associate with the likes of those in the court of King Charles?" Her father closed his eyes and bowed his head. In prayer? Did he hope to dispel an evil spirit lurking in their midst?

"Father, I'd never even see the king or his court. I'd only work with the cooks and gardeners. Other household help, commoners like me."

He halted his pacing and faced Kate as she measured flour and sugar for the mid-morning sweet cakes. "And this overseer, Mister… what was his name?"

"Mr. Reresby. He was very cordial and complimentary of your bakery. You met him before when you signed the document of allegiance."

"Yes. A king's man all the way." His frown and scrunched up-eyebrows painted his opinion of the overseer.

Kate lost ground with every word she spoke. Perhaps fewer

details would be better to reach some form of compromise. What could she offer to bend his stubborn resolve?

She wiped her dusty hands on her apron, sending puffs of white clouds before her. Pulling in air tinted with the aroma of fresh bread and bracing her courage with her shoulders back, Kate drew on the advantages she had, beloved daughter and favorite child.

In front of her father, inches from his scowling face, she summoned her feminine wiles. "I promise to stick to my job and avoid contact with the decadent court. I want you to be proud of me. Please let me have this chance to share my receipts and experiment with herbs and spices."

His hands held her shoulders in a tight grip. "And if the court knocks on your door and collides with your strict morals, you will run from the devilish temptations?"

"Yes, all the way home to you."

He smiled, and she collapsed in his embrace. The feel of his strong hands on her reinforced her commitment to obey him. After all, she had joined him when he switched his affiliation with the established Church of England to the reformed church of the puritanical Cromwell. Now, he allowed his family to attend the local church because of distance and safety. So far, he hadn't asked too much for her to rebel.

"All right, my little pet. You may work at Hampton Court. Margaret and Robert can help a little more in the bakery. If you will give me your mornings 'til one, the rest of the time is yours. I expect you to keep the day of worship free. I have no idea if our worldly king observes the Sabbath." He shook his head from side to side and clicked his tongue as in a reprimand.

"I will do as you say. Thank you." Kate stood on tiptoe and kissed her burly father on the cheek. Her heart pounded close to bursting from her bodice. Did she really get released to pursue her dream of working in the royal gardens and kitchen? God answered her every prayer.

"Back to work. I assume you want to begin at the castle today."

Kate nodded and skipped back to her post. The morning baking floated in and out of the oven. Perfectly formed rolls, cakes, and loaves lined the counter shelves. By noon, the concoctions diminished as customers purchased their daily consumption.

The parish church bell sounded one o'clock. Kate's apron practically flew through the room to its hook in the hallway. Grabbing a small loaf of crisp bread, she waved goodbye to her mother and raced out of the single door fearing her father would call her back.

The garden gate squeaked as Kate stepped through the iron barrier. The ornate structure, topped with the image of a lion and a dragon, warned her that the premises were royal grounds. In her head she knew the soil was like any other soil in East Molesey, but in her dreamy state the fine rich soil held magic.

Kate leaned against the gate and surveyed the rectangular plots in front. They extended for the equivalent of three or four village houses. *Where do I begin in this vast territory?* A crate of seedlings sat by a plot a few yards away. She got on her knees to decipher what plans the gardeners had for the plants. Her outstretched hand seemed to have a mind of its own. She couldn't just start digging and planting. Her left hand physically pulled her wandering fingers back to her lap.

The shadow overhead drew Kate's sight upwards. "Mr. Payne. Hello. I'm here to help you."

He helped Kate to her feet and then released her elbow. "I'm so glad. We have our work cut out for us. As you can see, this area was too much for one man all these years."

"Put me to work, please. I know you have the rose garden, vegetable garden, and orchards to look after too. Do you have enough help now?"

"More every day. Edward should be back here full-time next

week, as well as four additional men. Mr. Reresby said to hire as many as I want. But I need to see the money first. Too many of us have worked for free in the past."

Kate bowed her head, embarrassed over his predicament. Cromwell had his following but at times no finances to support his plans. Was King Charles any different? In just under a year his reign gave signs of a flourishing prospect for England. But could he keep the country out of war and on a peaceful course laced with financial stability?

"You can start in the patch here with these herbs. I secured four varieties of mint, even one I hadn't heard of—chocolate mint." He bent down to bring the seedling in question closer for Kate's observation.

The seedling wrapped in a cloth ball of dirt at its base had a distinct rich smell akin to the cocoa beans she had held in the bakery. She'd never worked with the aromatic beans or tasted the delicacy but perhaps a nibble would come her way in the palace's kitchen.

"Does Mrs. Downs know what to do with these spices and herbs?" Kate set the plant back in the palette.

"Perhaps you can help her concoct delicious original receipts. I know you are good at that. Edward tells me of your experiments with pies and cakes."

Kate blushed and studied the gravel path. Admittedly, she loved the compliment, but she weeded out the other hidden message. Edward talked to his father about her. Why couldn't he center his comments on Jane? At some point Kate needed to put Edward straight for good. Didn't he see she was past the age of courting and silly dreams of romance? For some reason she couldn't settle for an existence of convenience.

"Thank you, Mr. Payne. I think Mrs. Downs and the court might be a little more particular."

"It wouldn't hurt to try."

"If I can get up the nerve."

The moist, dark soil sifted easily through her fingers. In the bakery she worked without gloves, used to the sensations of texture against her fingertips. Gloves were reserved for church and special occasions. At times she craved the feel of creamy lotion caressing her skin like the lavender cream from her city cousin that she kept under her bed used only on nights when a little indulgence soothed her callused palms and fed her dreams.

After placing the mint in neat rows and weeding the adjourning plot, Kate peered over the shrubs at the vegetable garden. Curiosity pulled her through the hedge opening. In a few weeks the court's pots would be full of fresh greens, onions, and carrots.

The red stone palace loomed to her left as she traipsed onward through the next opening. She missed the two steps and stumbled onto a gravel boulevard. Barely catching herself, she righted her form and brushed small pebbles off her hands.

The pounding of hooves shook the ground. She gasped and stepped back, avoiding a collision with a giant white steed. The massive animal appeared from dust and collided with Kate's vision as a dream. What a brute beast. She trembled and retreated bit by bit until her back pinned her against the hedge. She'd much rather feel the prickly sticks poking her than have the horse any closer.

After the dust settled, quicker than her rapid heartbeat, Kate faced the nose of the culprit a few yards from her. Her hands grasped the limbs of the shrub for balance.

"Kate, what are you doing?"

She ripped her gaze from the horse's flaring nostrils to find the grinning, dashing face of Mr. Reresby. The sun formed a halo of rays around his dark hair. She knew he was tall, but more like a giant on his horse. His green eyes begged for an answer, as she pushed herself closer to the shrub. Where was the opening to the garden?

"I was…" The horse seemed to get closer. She swallowed. "I was looking around and…" She shut her eyes.

"Are you all right?" Peter's voice sounded far away.

With eyes closed Kate shook her head. "No. I don't like horses."

She heard and felt the ground shift in front of her. Was she to be trampled by the animal?

Instead, she felt her hands covered by Peter's, and slowly her fingers uncurled from the hedge.

"Open your eyes. You are in no danger."

"But…" She obeyed and experienced a new fear as she saw herself in his sparkling clear eyes. So close. A new sensation to be held inches from a man, but at least he was between her and the horse.

"You're shaking. Does Samson scare you that much?"

"Samson? Is that your horse?" She peeked around Peter's shoulder to view the menace munching on grass, not quite the monster she saw earlier.

"Your fear is unwarranted. I had complete control." His thumbs covered her palms, sending tingles up her arms and jitters to her stomach.

She jerked her hands to her sides and pushed away from the bush, causing Peter to retreat a few steps.

"I don't like horses." She crossed her arms. Her peripheral vision convinced her that the horse wasn't a threat at the moment. He was almost like the docile beings she saw behind fences outside of town. She didn't mind them at a distance, as a dot in the picturesque field, no more than a sheep or a cow.

"Well, Miss Sinclair, perhaps I can help you overcome your aversion to the gentle beasts." Peter leaned against a flowering redbud tree.

He must think me a spoiled little ninny. Better that than a trampled one.

Peter clucked his tongue against his teeth and whistled for Samson. Kate stood still, no longer trembling as the animal lumbered toward Peter, the horse's head swinging to his steps.

"Here, I want you to hold out your hand, palm up and

fingers arched downward like this." Peter demonstrated the awkward pose. "I'm going to place a slice of apple on your palm for Samson."

Why she obeyed him she didn't know. Perhaps it was his soft articulate command, a tone used with a child or the image of the white head of Samson by Peter's shoulder. For whatever reason, Kate did as he suggested.

"Now don't move. He will nuzzle your hand and secure the apple with his lips. It will be wet but not dangerous."

Had Peter looked at the horse's teeth lately?

"Ready?" Kate nodded and Peter stepped aside and let Samson move forward. One step, two…and before she could scream or run, she felt a wet tickle against her palm. She stared at her hand—not one tooth mark.

Giggling as she wiped the slobber from her fingers, Kate wondered why she had continued with her fear of horses for all these years. Perhaps her lack of exposure to the animals explained her acute dislike.

"Thank you, Mr. Reresby, for not laughing at me. I do feel rather silly, now. Samson seems to be a fine animal." She rose up and down on her tiptoes and cast her eyes on the road away from Peter's gaze.

"Would you like to ride him sometime?"

"Oh, I couldn't." She eased her head up to meet his serious expression, eyebrows raised.

"Why not? I'd make sure you'd be safe."

She believed him but didn't trust herself on the back of a giant. "Perhaps later. I need to conquer one fear at a time."

"I quite understand."

"I must return now. Mr. Payne must wonder where I've been, and I need to see Mrs. Downs. Thank you, again."

Kate swiveled around as if being pulled against her will into the safety of the privet fence. Outside of it stood the palace, the vast property, and a handsome country gentleman on his huge daunting steed.

Yes. Inside the walls of the gardens is definitely my domain of comfort. I'll leave the outside world to the Reresbys of the terrain.

She straightened her black skirt and white apron and adjusted the straps of her white bonnet tied under her chin.

AIR WHISTLED THROUGH HIS LIPS, he hoped for his ears only. Samson's reins draped over Peter's shoulder. He stood still until the last inch of Kate's black skirt disappeared through the opening.

"What do you think, my friend?"

Samson snorted and stamped his hoof.

Peter had been around ladies of the court for ten years, beauties from several countries always outshining the one before in gowns of silk and satin and jewels. So, why was he in awe of a country lass in a simple black dress with a collar laced high on her neck?

He guided the horse beside him toward the palace. The early roses of red, orange, yellow, and pink shouted for his admiration. He tried to envision Kate in a gown of lavender or yellow. Either would draw attention to her slim frame and amber speckled eyes. What was wrong with a little color?

The bright, orange-petaled roses beckoned Peter to venture closer. He reached to pick the thorny beauty but hesitated, for he had no one to present it to at the palace. His sister had loved flowers as a child. He'd surprised her often in years past with bouquets of wildflowers or single blossoms. Orange was always a favorite color of hers from dresses and ribbons to flowers and fruit.

Where was Rebecca now? He feared he wouldn't recognize her eighteen-year-old form from the childish nine-year-old he left behind. The image of Kate's womanly figure startled him as he visualized his sister in a similar state. He couldn't picture the drab clothes on his vivacious sister. Black, gray, and brown ranked at the bottom of her favorite colors.

Perhaps Kate had no choice. From what he knew of her religion, they steered away from bright colors or anything that drew mankind's thought to the impure.

Looking back at the sunlit roses, Peter didn't see their colors as sinful. But he recalled many a lady in the courts of Europe who flaunted their bodies in dresses of vibrant colors like peacocks. And their sin ran free with no restraints. Even drab colorless garb couldn't stop it.

THE CLIP-CLOP of Samson's hooves jarred Peter to the present court of Charles. Would he want Rebecca or simple Kate in courtly attire ogled by every courtier and foreign onlooker? He knew too well of what courtiers were capable, especially in the lively court of the past year.

Kate had her father to look after her but who did Rebecca have? His father fought and died in the Civil War on Cromwell's side. All he knew of his sister came from two letters his mother sent over the past nine years. When Rebecca turned eight, she was sent to Cromwell's household as a companion to his daughters. As of two summers ago, Rebecca had disappeared.

He shook his head as he led Samson to his stall. He removed the saddle and buried his head on the animal's neck. Where could she be? Was life too horrible to return home? His mother pined the loss of her past—her husband killed, her oldest son Thomas hardened from war, Rebecca's disappearance, and Peter's attachment to the once deposed king's son.

It was time to visit his mother again. He dreaded the possibility of confronting his brother. At least for the past year, Peter had been on the winning side. Thomas didn't like it, but he pretended allegiance to Charles in order to keep his land and wealth.

Outside the kitchen Peter cupped his hands into a basin by the wall, scooped up some water, and doused his face to release the dust and refresh himself. He knew Mrs. Downs saved him something to nibble. So far, she surprised him with her enticing culinary skills.

Like one of the king's spaniels, Peter's nose whiffed a sweet concoction on the other side of the open kitchen door. He ducked his head and turned to his sense of smell and spotted a cobbler on the long table with one slice missing.

"What do you have here, Mrs. Downs?"

"Mr. Reresby, you gave me a fright." She put the ladle beside a big simmering pot of stew. "Go ahead and have a seat. That is a raspberry tart made by Miss Sinclair. It's a new receipt she made up using mint and a cinnamon crust."

Peter licked his lips and rubbed his hands together in anticipation. He'd spent too many years in exile scrounging for food. No part of him could pass up a sweet staring at him.

"Cut me a nice sized piece, please." He followed her knife from the cobbler to his plate. "Thank you very much."

The sweet yet tangy raspberry treat rested gently on his tongue and favorably with his taste buds.

"Tell me what you think of Miss Sinclair." Peter eyed the round woman already back at her post by the boiling pot.

"She's one of the best things this kitchen has seen."

"Do you think she could be of service when the king and his court arrive?"

"Do I ever. I think that girl could make even the king's mouth water. What do you have in mind?" Mrs. Downs faced Peter with her arms crossed across her large chest, cheeks flushed, ready to listen.

"Help with the menu adding interesting receipts, perhaps her own creations like this. She could be available to help you instruct others in the preparation."

"So, as my personal assistant?"

"Yes, but she has her other chores at her father's bakery that she can't neglect. I'll make a list of what the king fancies. You and Kate—Miss Sinclair that is—can find the receipts and write down items for the market."

The plan unfolded and spilled forth unrehearsed. "Then Kate and I will go to market to purchase the foods." He concentrated on his last bite and ignored his slip. For some reason he had a hard time referring to his new employee as Miss Sinclair.

Mrs. Downs opened her mouth to say something but closed it and raised her eyebrows instead.

"What?" Peter questioned.

"Oh nothing. If I didn't know better, I would say the king's man has a hankering for a young lass."

"No, thank you. The last thing I need is a religious puritanical woman in my life. The king's wishes take up my time, not the church, or a lady of any caliber."

"Humph. We'll see."

He pushed himself up from the table and swung his legs over the bench. His six-foot frame towered over Mrs. Downs. He bowed and kissed her flushed cheek. "Thank you again. I'll come by tomorrow to discuss the menu. Remember the banquet is two days after the king's arrival."

"Which is when?"

"Soon."

"WHY DID HE ASK FOR ME?" Kate fidgeted with the strings under her neck. The white hat was a nuisance. In Mrs. Downs' kitchen, she discarded it. A few loose curls wouldn't hurt the cook's opinion of her.

"He tasted your raspberry tart yesterday afternoon." Mrs. Downs looked at Kate between her lashes.

"And?"

"He devoured it. He's bringing by a list of suggested items for the king's banquet. Did you bring your receipts?"

"Yes. I keep them in this satchel." Kate unfolded the soft leather hide and displayed her stack of instructions, ones she'd copied over the years.

Mrs. Downs peered over Kate's shoulder. "Well, I'm not much for reading. I keep mine right here." The woman pointed to her graying head.

Kate reasoned Mrs. Downs didn't know how to read. Not many people saw the need. She found such freedom in the written word and was thankful her father insisted on her study. Even though her mother fought him about it, he won. She remembered his final words on the matter. "Kate needs to know ciphering and reading to get on with the business. And someone needs to know how to read the Bible if asked."

Her studies with the local priest, and nights of staying up late reading religious pamphlets and Bible passages, opened up a new area of interest in devouring all written words. Her father didn't know of her reading Shakespeare and Chaucer. Sonnets of love and loss permeated her imagination and took her out of the ordinary life of East Molesey.

"Excuse me, Mrs. Downs, Miss Sinclair. May I join you?" Peter folded his upper body under the top of the door.

The warm kitchen was even warmer by his presence. Kate brought her hand to her flushed cheeks. Why did his presence alter her body temperature? He was worse than a sonnet.

"Of course. You are always welcome, Mr. Reresby." Mrs. Downs backed away from the table and poured Peter a cup of water. "We were just looking at receipts."

"I brought some ideas about the king's favorite foods. Is it a good time to prepare a market list?" He directed the question to Kate.

She turned in search for Mrs. Downs. Had she faded away on purpose?

"Yes. I have the time." Kate scooted along the bench giving Peter more room to stretch his lanky legs. Next to her on the bench, Peter didn't seem so tall. She looked him straight in the eyes. In the afternoon light from the window, they shone a liquid green as in a fresh pool of water on the creek bed.

She jerked her head around so as not to swim away in his captivating gaze. Peter unfolded a cream-colored piece of stationary. *Kind of fancy for a scratchy menu.* Curiosity caused her to lean toward him almost shoulder to shoulder.

"Pheasant, venison, veal. Leeks, asparagus, cabbage. Lemon custard, raspberry tart, orange sponge cake." Kate paused. "No fancy French pastries or Italian pies?"

Peter smiled. "The king's appetite is not so hard to satisfy."

What wasn't he telling her? She guessed the king's appetite didn't just pertain to food. Some rumors tended to be true, and the king's taste for women, domestic and foreign, would fill quite a few menus.

"Do you think that gives you enough to work with?"

"It does." Kate fingered through her pile of written procedures, some on scraps of parchment paper from the bakery, others on pieces of stationary or newsprint.

Peter's breath tickled her neck. Did he have to bear down so closely? If she turned her head just a fraction, her lips would meet his. Instead, she forced her concentration on the receipts in hand.

"Here's one for pheasant, and I know just the spices for it." She placed it in his outstretched palm next to her elbow on the table.

"Rosemary and saffron." Peter smacked his lips as if tasting it already.

"Saffron might be a little difficult. But I could replace it with mustard powder."

Her fingers deftly found other suitable receipts. Peter nodded approval while confirming the choices with a smile reaching his eyes. The job became personal as she envisioned him partaking of the meal as well as the king.

"Yes, perfect." Peter shifted away from her space, taking the separated stack of baking instructions and details with him. "I'll write down these along with the other menu items and leave them here with Mrs. Downs."

"Perfect for you or for the king?" Kate teased. This gallant young man wasn't able to hide his expressions or intentions. If his smile didn't display his pleasure, his fidgeting hands and swaying body did. He appeared as a child in a candy store.

His eyes twinkled with mischief. "Will there be samples?"

"If you come by the bakery over the next few days, I'll let you taste a few of the breads and desserts. But I'm afraid you'll have to wait on the pheasant and venison since my family rarely feasts on that fare." Perhaps he understood her plight without more detail.

She laced and unlaced her fingers in her lap. "And when do you want to go to the market?"

"The coronation is next week on the twenty-third of April at Westminster. I will be gone for two weeks."

"When would the court arrive here?"

"The second Sunday in May."

"How about the second Saturday in May? Will you be back?" Kate didn't want to miss the parade and pomp. Perhaps King Charles would be a regular at Hampton Court Palace. She crossed her fingers, hoping his answer would comply with her wishes.

"Yes, that will be fine. On that next day, I'm to meet the party on the other side of Molesey and join the escort."

"How exciting." Was Kate missing an important link here? How could Peter sit at a lowly kitchen table, talking to a simple working girl and next week walk and dine with the king of England? His split identity confused her.

"Well, I've taken up enough of your time, Mr. Reresby. I'm sure you have more interesting things to do. I'll complete the list for the market and see you in a few weeks." She shook her head and released a giggle. She imagined Peter leaving his palatial room of comfort to mingle with servants in a crowded, loud market arena. At least her world remained constant—poor and simple.

Chapter Four

Early Wednesday morning before his thirteen-mile trek to London, Peter stood in queue at Sinclair Bakery. Kate's father had prospered in this small town. A stone dwelling with two chimneys and glass window panes complemented the busy thoroughfare. Somehow, he had maintained a fine business and home when others declined. Peter admired the man's prosperity even in difficult times.

At the moment Peter's appetite spoke volumes as he scrutinized the flaky items on the shelves. Slowly, the customers cleared, and he finally caught Kate's gaze. Did she belong in a modest home and shop or on a dance floor with the beauties of England? He shook the thought away. No, he wouldn't have given her a second glance if she was like all the other courtiers. For some reason she stood out among the other Puritan lasses.

In the two minutes of picking apart Kate's charming being, Peter was no closer to determining why he was infatuated with her. He really needed to get to London before he discarded all remembrance of lively entertainment and colorful characters.

"May I serve you, Mr. Reresby?" Kate's raised eyebrows made him wonder how many times she just asked him that question.

"Good morning. I must have been daydreaming about my trip. Yes, I want…" He paused and had no idea what he wanted in the area of food. "I'll take a loaf of oat bread, two raspberry tarts, a lemon treat and leaning over the counter, he whispered, "any special new treat for the road."

She placed his bread and tarts in his knapsack and added a flaky crusted roll. "It's filled with a gooseberry, pear filling, fit for a king."

He rubbed his hands together, knowing any concoction of Kate's held a finer quality. "I'll savor it."

As he placed his coins on the counter, he brushed her fingers. "I'll be back in a fortnight for our market date."

Kate blushed and pulled her fingers with the coins across the wooden space. "Yes, I'll be there early in the morning."

THE ROAD from Molesey to London teemed with carriages, merchants, peasants, and simple travelers. Samson, because of his sheer bulk, demanded passage. Could all these people be headed to London for the coronation? It reminded Peter of the triumphal entry a year ago when Charles appeared in London announced as king, and throngs of citizens cheered him on for miles and miles. Finally, almost a year later, he would be crowned.

Although Peter thrilled at the idea of Charles receiving the proper recognition and ceremony, a part of him dreaded the pomp. Could he avoid the excessive food and drink, rubbish and stench, and hordes of bodies straining to catch a glimpse? Once within the walls of Whitehall, he would experience the extravagant wealth and show, expensive perfumes, and lavish silks and satins. Where was a comfortable medium?

The Puritans missed the mark and the king's court overstepped it greatly. What did Peter want? Surely not the life of an exile. No, not that ever again. He'd choose to live in a predictable, comfortable environment instead of a campfire or hovel moving from court to court and country to country.

Charles expected him at the palace. Peter went through the guarded gates with no more credentials than the king's medallion, an imprint of the coat of arms, around his neck, the same emblem as over the door of Whitehall.

Handing Samson over to the waiting groomsman, Peter took the steps two at a time. For one who didn't particularly crave the opulent court life, he did desire the presence of the king.

"I believe His Majesty is expecting me." Peter walked to the big, double oak doors.

The guards opened them at once, receiving a nod from a gloomy secretary. Two toy spaniels raced out into the waiting room and circled Peter before returning to the grand hall. Peter followed them, knowing where they headed, straight to the feet of Charles.

"Peter, about time you arrived. Was your journey eventless?"

Peter bowed. "Your Majesty."

Charles jumped up and embraced Peter as a friend. "None of that, my man. Pretend we are huddling around a meager table. Haven't things changed?"

"I'd say."

Charles motioned Peter to an upholstered chair identical to his own. This one commodity Charles had favored in France made its way into every room in the palace.

Peter dropped his hand beside him as he sat on the red and gold gilded chair, only to have his fingers unceremoniously licked by a small red and white companion, one of many spaniels.

"Lady, down. They think they own this place, but I can't seem to prefer it any other way." The king laughed, and in effect Peter released the last hour's pent-up nerves. His friend was the same, although the addition of the long, curly black wig made Peter laugh.

"Ever wish for simpler times?" Peter crossed his arms and

knew, by taking in the king's elaborate apparel, wearing more material than he had owned in his entire wardrobe last year, that Charles wouldn't go back.

"No. God ordained me from birth to be king. My exile and wanderings prepared me beyond a doubt for this role." Charles dropped a tiny biscuit to the floor. The pattering and scuffing of tiny puppy nails resounded off the marble floors as the race began. It was good to see the king smile.

"Tell me of Hampton Court. Although I chose to make Whitehall my predominant residence, I must begin to spend time elsewhere to be among the people."

"It's in good shape. All it needs is a few of these fine chairs and the sound of your spaniels in the hallways."

"If I remember correctly, the palace does have narrow hallways and many old, odd rooms for them to explore. No sign of past ghosts like Queen Jane or Catherine Howard?"

"Well, not that I have heard, but of course, I'm not on the royal wing, either." Fortunately, courtiers were housed in a renovated wing off the front courtyard. His room faced the gardens. Gardens filled with vegetables, flowers and…Kate. Kate? Here he was in the presence of the king of England and the vision of Kate appeared. He would have to attend a ball soon to negate the homely image.

"The village is ready for your residence as planned."

"And I'll be anxious, too, for a change of scenery and pace. It seems this coronation has occupied the court's thoughts and agenda for six months."

"More like a year, ever since you stepped on shore."

"A year. It's hard to believe."

The scampering of puppy feet toward the door announced the entrance of the Countess of Castlemaine. Peter, as on every other occasion in her presence, willed his jaw to stay shut. Her blue-violet eyes and masses of auburn hair against alabaster skin captured Charles' heart last year in exile at The Hague and all his men with him. Her beauty surpassed any in the European courts and all of England.

Peter stood and accepted the hand she presented to him. He bowed and kissed her fingers. "Lady Castlemaine. It is a pleasure."

Her nickname spread throughout the court and stuck as her favorite. Duchess, Countess, or Lady, she in fact was Charles' queen, except by law.

"Congratulations on the birth of your daughter."

Charles believed the child was his, so Peter wouldn't contradict the fact.

She stood regally by the king with her hand on his shoulder. Her tall, voluptuous form begged to be noticed and placed in high regard. It didn't seem to bother Charles that the woman married the year before she became his mistress.

"You need to meet our little Lady Anne." Charles held the hand at his shoulder and caressed the huge sapphire ring on his mistress' finger.

"I hope to at your convenience." Peter didn't miss all the intrigue and dishonest liaisons, but after years of following Charles, Peter realized the lifestyle pleased the king. And until he married, the countess reigned.

"Peter was telling me of Hampton Court. I believe, my lady, you will be pleased. Although it is older and tends to be darker and damper than this place, the gardens and overall splendor are captivating."

Peter nodded in agreement with the king's words. Time would tell if the mistress approved. She was never one to hide her words or her temper. A closed door wouldn't block any disappointment she had. Once again Charles chose a vocal female companion to quasi rule with him. The previous mistress was Lucy Walters. Peter was sure to encounter the son of that union, James, the Duke of Monmouth, all of twelve years of age, very soon.

The rest of the afternoon found Peter at the stables. The royal horses represented the finest fare from all over Europe. But Samson's sturdiness and bulk surpassed them all.

I wonder what you think of returning to the royal mews.

Not like the open fields of Hampton Court. Samson whinnied as Peter stroked his brow and coddled his ears. There weren't many places to let the reins loose and run. A few paths, but no vast green hills. The hills where he planned to teach Kate to ride and cast her fears aside.

Peter shook his head like Samson and for the third or fourth time today banished Kate to the private recesses of his brain.

"I KNOW HOW FATHER FEELS, Mother. Anything to do with the new king is of the devil. But what do you think?" Kate stole a rare moment while her father was away in another town with a delivery. Without him being in earshot, Kate dispensed with her usual shallow comments to her mother.

"What he thinks, of course. The minister quotes from the good book every week about the rich young fool. That is our king." Her mother peeled a potato and dropped it in the pot.

"And what of Lord Protectorate Cromwell? How do you explain his power and riches? How was he any different from the present king?" Kate pounded the strip of beef more than usual, the echo in the kitchen calling her to task. Oh, the constant struggle between past and present, good and evil, interpretations of right and wrong. Rules and more rules.

"Now, Kate. I've heard your father explain this to you many times. Why do you still question it? Lord Cromwell was ordained by God to lead this country and set her on the righteous path to justice and salvation." Her mother quoted the standard reason.

"Through killing and murdering innocent citizens and taking their property and burning their crops." Kate attempted to keep her comment to a whisper, but the constant low hissing from the fire didn't cover her sarcasm.

With knife in hand, her mother turned red-faced to catch Kate's condemning words. Kate gazed at the knife in her pacifist mother's hand. Immediately, the woman laid the instrument on the table and wiped her brow with her sleeve. For a woman who didn't believe in fighting, she sure seemed to support the works of a fighter.

"I've lived through a fitful reign of a thoughtless king, his beheading, a civil war, and now this new king, all the time married to your father. Through it all he has had an unwavering faith and conviction that God wanted England to change."

"But, Mother, through killing and war? Isn't God a loving God of joy and pleasure too?"

"We never expected the horrific violence and death, but God's people have experienced it throughout history." Her mother resumed her work with the potatoes as Kate cut the meat into bite-sized pieces for a pie.

"What about now? Is it so wrong to enjoy a time of peace? Even the worship service has changed. It's almost as if more light has been released into the sanctuary. And I hear theaters and operas have returned. People are singing and laughing. And, oh, the dresses. I have friends who wear blue and yellow and the loveliest lavender for everyday frocks." Kate twirled her own skirt a bit, thinking of the light colors, reminding her of butterflies in the garden.

"Listen to yourself. That is what your father feared. You go off to the palace and soon you become a wanton, misguided heathen." Her mother sniffled.

Do I cause her that much grief or does her life with Father make her shed tears?

Kate placed the meat in the pie crust, washed her hands, and walked to her mother's side. Ever so gently she wrapped her arms around the smaller woman.

"It's not like that at all. I'm working with God-fearing men and women. No harm will come to me. I've not even ventured into the palace beyond the kitchen. I will be honest. I do enjoy the vast colors that God created in the flowers and produce. And occasionally, I want to spread that color to a skirt or ribbon or a hat, making me smile and enjoy His world to its fullest."

Her mother squeezed her hand. "I have noticed your smile and your singing. I thought perhaps it was a young man, Mr. Payne's son?"

The young man Kate envisioned wasn't Edward but Peter. She could never share that tidbit with her mother or anyone she knew. "No, I'm hoping Edward and Jane like each other. I'm staying out of the way. He's more her age. Anyway, I had my chance at love, and war swept it away."

"But, my girl, don't give up. A few young men will return."

"And marry the younger girls. Not many would settle for me when a youthful beauty of seventeen is around. It's all right, Mother. I have the bakery, cooking, and gardening. I'll enjoy others' good fortunes."

"You just wait and see. Someone is out there for you."

"Yes, somewhere," Kate whispered, walking to the waiting pie. The sliced onions, peppers, sauce, and spices filled the crust. The someone she imagined dined on fine court food in the heart of London, and as her father called it, "the den of thieves." Her respect for her father stifled her yearning for freedom and change. *How do I follow what I think God is calling me to do when Father sets the rules?*

One more week. If Peter remembered they would meet at the market to prepare for the king's banquet. After two weeks of sampling royal fare, would he still consider her work acceptable?

Chapter Five

London filled to the brim. Not a room could be found. Once again Peter thanked his circumstances for his shared quarters with other knights and courtiers, many old friends from exile. Westminster glowed and shimmered with the thousands of candles reflected off the gold chandeliers, candlesticks, throne, jewels, and paintings.

Peter stood with other close friends of Charles, titled and untitled, but strangely fashioned as his longtime faithful entourage. The time of exile sealed Peter's fate with Charles.

Opposite the aisle gathered the king's mistress, his son James, his brother James, and many relatives and royalists of the realm. Peter surmised some of the guests to be recent converts to the present monarchy, flitting from King to Lord Protector, back to King. In general Charles knew who they were and maintained a careful watch over them. The thirty-one-year-old king's smile didn't mean he trusted the recipients.

Charles Stuart wore the crown attached to his birthright. Peter had staked his life on this moment and hoped never to see battle again. The peace over the land was more of a shadow than a blanket of warmth and security. As long as Cromwell's parliament men lurked around every corner at every meeting and function, Charles had a battle to fight, whether physical or mental.

"His Royal Highness the King of England, Scotland, Wales, and Ireland." Sitting on his throne with scepter in hand, no one would see the wandering exile except an exile himself.

The darting dark eyes, never quite still, combined with sharp keen hearing alerted Charles to the hunter, the enemy. Peter knew this for he lived it at all times. Creaks in the night, uneven footsteps, punctuated his nights as he always anticipated an attack.

In London his instincts perked up. At Hampton Court, Peter relaxed enough to realize perhaps in the future he'd have a normal existence. But he still had too many dreams of his wandering days left, prohibiting him from slipping into any semblance of a predictable life.

Whitehall returned to all its former opulent grandeur, as nobility and faithful supporters and military with wives and leading ladies filled the corridors, ballrooms, and every gilded hall. Peter managed to escape the direct circle of the king onto a balcony. The real beauty and splendor rested in the manicured gardens below chiseled out of neglected tombs of ancient bulbs, vines, and plants. It reminded him of Kate's work. Inch by inch, territory reclaimed to offer its intended beauty and value.

He turned his back to the gardens and surveyed the crowd. Jewels and fabric mimicked the rich tapestry of the April gardens. Not one plain black or gray dress in the bunch. Kate would never fit in this setting. Nothing about her screamed admittance to the court. Why did he think of her here? Her puritanical ways and beliefs attached to her dress and manners banned her from his world.

"Why so pensive, Reresby?" Young James, the king's son, approached Peter. Pensive? Peter quickly uncrossed his stiff arms and replaced his stern frown with a smile.

"Thinking of another world. How are you enjoying the festivities?" The lad was a miniature of his father except with a blonde curly wig, no moustache, but yards of velvet, fur, silk, and jewels. Lucy's son filled a place of high position as Charles' offspring.

"Father says I can stay up all night and sit with him at his table."

Peter elbowed the child. "And what do you think of the young girls in the court?"

"Ah, Mr. Reresby, they're all older than I am. Although the one over there in yellow seems not to mind. Perhaps at the ball she'll go around with me."

"Perhaps, after all, you are the newly crowned king's son."

James, the young duke, stood straighter. In time he'd gain Charles' height and strength. James held an important place, though Peter knew one of the next items to be conquered for the king was a royal wife and legitimate offspring.

"And what about you? What lady will you pick?" James asked.

"I'm not going to participate. I'll just watch from a safe distance."

James scrunched his eyes up at Peter. "Really?"

How could he explain the overall distaste Peter had for the flamboyant, promiscuous females lurking on gentlemen's arms? He'd have to know much about the lady's virtue before he gave even one evening of his attention to her. At least with Kate, he knew what to expect, a pure heart and body. But was that enough?

Bereft of any company for a moment, he supposed his body, and soul perhaps, had enough of parties, banquets, and coquettish prattle to last him the rest of the year. In a bit over twenty-four hours, Peter would saddle Samson and be gone from the coronation festivities.

One more look around the crowd. He still expected to catch a glimpse of his sister among the guests. Part of him longed to find her in any position or status, as a court lady or a mere servant in the halls. But no one knew of Rebecca Reresby. Probably because she was long gone to America or tucked away in a farmer's cottage. His mind knew that but not his soul. If only she had escaped the war in a small town like Molesey and befriended a girl like Kate.

He clucked his tongue. What kind of assurance was that? Somehow, he conjured up an image of a rosy-cheeked child in a flowing yellow dress picking flowers by the river without a care in her life.

Not so, he feared. The war left few in that whimsical state of being.

Rebecca, where are you?

Chapter Six

"Kate!" her father yelled from the kitchen before the bakery opened for the morning.

What now? She'd been the object of his disdain for days. "Coming." She darted from the front counter to the work table in the steamy kitchen. Sweat already ran down her father's cheeks and neck.

"I have a few words for you. Listen closely, child." He kept his back to her as he plopped a spoonful of dough on a pottery tray.

"Yes, sir." She could guess the subject, the king's banquet and even the object of the lesson, herself. No one else in the household received the reprimands and warnings. She hadn't done anything wrong, yet.

"You have placed yourself in the devil's way, and I don't want any harm to befall you. The Bible says to flee Satan. I've warned you but you insist on placing yourself right in his den. Also, the Bible says be pure and holy. I don't want any daughter of mine labeled impure by association with the unruly ways of the court."

Her defense was always the same. "I will obey you, Father." But today she wearied of the repeated, rehearsed words. At some point her father had to trust her. The gardens within the palace grounds, the kitchens within the palace walls, and Peter within the palace court hadn't caused any harm or blatant disregard for her beliefs.

She hung her head, prayed for patience, and stood still, awaiting dismissal. The red-faced man glaring at her demanded her acceptance.

"I am your dutiful daughter."

"Good. We'll see where you stand when this town is turned upside down. Go see to our customers."

No worse than usual. She unlatched the front door and let the cool April breeze sweep over her. Perhaps the aroma of fresh bread would awaken the town and purse strings. Kate set aside a special raspberry mint biscuit, another attempt with a new receipt. Any day Peter could step back into the bakery, smacking his lips together like a child for a sample, or more likely he could forget this small town against the appealing background of royal residences. Still she labored with her receipts and produce from Hampton Court.

Margaret took Kate's place as Mother asked for help with a tiered cake. If not completed quickly, the sugary glaze hardened in a lumpy mess.

"Thank you. Four steady hands are better than a few clumsy ones like your sister." Mother crinkled her eyes. "She certainly didn't receive the gift of baking."

"But she can sew and sing."

"Her children will be the best-dressed starving angels," Mother said.

Kate marveled at the difference between Margaret and herself. Perhaps Margaret would sew for the king's family and work with the finest material. Not such an out-of-reach idea with the court just over the bridge. To create the most elegant gowns and never wear one. At least Kate could sample the court's savory food on occasion without dining at the table.

"Kate, there's someone here to see you!" Margaret yelled.

Couldn't the child use her normal voice instead of always rattling the furniture in the kitchen?

"All right." Kate received a nod from her mother to leave.

She searched for a familiar face like Jane or the minister's wife, Mrs. Turnard. Instead, she faced Peter in the king's livery.

"Hello, Miss Sinclair."

"Mr. Reresby, welcome back." She bowed her head as he tipped his hat.

His huge grin lit the dim room. Leaning over the counter his gaze traveled the width of the counter and back.

"Are you looking for something?" she teased, glad now that she'd set aside his treat. Like a stray puppy, he had to return one day.

He licked his lips, a habit it seemed in the bakery. "Perhaps."

"Could it be this biscuit right here?" She reached onto the bottom shelf and returned with the sweet, fruity delight.

"How did you know I'd be by today?"

"I didn't. But I haven't stopped experimenting just because you've been gone. My family has taken up your slack. Anyway, I knew you had to return before Saturday." Or did he forget their shopping rendezvous?

He stepped to the side so Margaret could take care of customers, even as she stared at Peter. He did look handsome in his fine coat and breeches.

"Yes, Saturday." Crumbs tumbled to the floor and gathered on his lips. Kate was tempted to brush them away, but laced her hands stiffly in front of her. He wiped his lips.

"That was delicious. Now about Saturday. My day is clear. We'll meet at the market at six before the crowds."

"I wouldn't count on beating the masses. This is the big market of the month, so everyone will want to find the best early." Kate wrapped two more biscuits in a cloth.

"Right. I better be going. I'll see you around the gardens or at least on Saturday." He skirted the line of customers, his plumes and flashy attire gaining the eye of every lady. The comments didn't cease with his exit.

Peter is back. I'm glad. I want to know all about the coronation and all the pretty costumes and…

Each worldly, out of reach detail. All the ones far from her simple and pure life. The colors of his world contrasted to the grays and shadowy shades of her life. Wasn't there a recent sermon on being careful envying the riches of others? It was easier for a camel to go through the eye of a needle than a rich man to get into heaven.

But the colors, and the music, and the laughter. She prayed for contentment and let the ordinary day at the bakery bring her back down to ground level.

FOR TWO DAYS in a row Peter stopped by and sampled Kate's treats at the bakery. He forced himself not to return twice in one day. With the palace running smoothly, the stables in improved condition, the grounds transformed into classic beauty, and the workforce hired, Peter had time on his hands. When his mind was free, he thought of Kate. Sitting at her table at home most likely would remind him of his family years ago, possibly laughing and singing and talking about events of the day.

Although his father was a gentleman with property and means, his family enjoyed being close. Until Cromwell split their seam down the middle. Civil war hardened men who before were gentle and kind. His own father died, while Kate's father carried the scars of rebellion on his being through sharp words, deep frowns, and furrowed brows.

That image changed Peter's mind. He couldn't sit at Kate's table ever, regardless of social status. Her father would thrust him out the door in a wordless gesture. He would forever remain a king's man on the customer side of the counter.

Even that picture caused Peter to whistle his way to market

early Saturday morning. He left his horse in the palace stables, preferring the freedom of entering the townspeople's realm without the trappings of royalty. Although not of royal birth himself, his association and closeness to Charles gave him rank and privilege. His attire for the day, though not torn or dirty, resembled others in the market. Tan breeches with a darker tunic over a laceless shirt tied with a leather belt. His boots laced instead of buckled. Not a hint of silver or gold adorned his costume.

A head above most people, Peter quickly spied Kate at the first stall, turned toward him. She waved and stepped forward. Today, her white apron covered a gray dress. A yellow rose pinned to her bodice was the only color other than her rosy cheeks.

"Good morning, Miss Sinclair."

"Mr. Reresby." She slightly dipped her body in a curtsy. He wanted to grab her elbow and prevent the motion but thought the contact would embarrass her.

"Ready?"

"I have the list."

He admired her neat penmanship, impressed with her spelling. A compliment would insinuate his continued surprise at her accomplishments. Perhaps one day he'd ask her about her education. Not many ladies of the court knew how to read and write.

"Sir, would the king expect you to purchase food for his banquet?"

Peter laughed. "During exile each of us including the king obtained food however we could. Many times, I took the money bag and bargained at town markets for our next few meals."

"Certainly, that didn't apply for the whole nine years."

"Of course not. At times the courts of different realms prepared banquets and feasts before sending us on our way. The fickle political scene determined our acceptance and hospitality from the people. Some days we went to sleep on the ground with empty bellies."

She held her basket in front of her. "It's hard to imagine our king in that condition." Her usual twinkling eyes clouded on the subject. Perhaps she did care about Charles and could be a loyal subject forgetting the rule of Cromwell.

"Today, Charles has no need to fear lack of sleep or food. He's safely tucked in his castles and palaces with plenty of nourishment. Yet, he still hasn't tasted your unique blend of ingredients."

The mass of people didn't equal his experience in Paris or London, but for the small village of East Molesey the numbers surprised him.

Kate started with the spice merchants. Her long slender fingers gently touched the fine powders or caressed the tiny seeds. Her nose did most of the work.

"Does the king know most of his vegetables and herbs were planted under the watchful eye of Lord Cromwell?" Kate ran her fingertips over light yellow peppers and cocked her head towards Peter.

Was she trying to bait him into badmouthing the former ruler? "And I take it you had a part in cultivating the royal gardens. For the king, I thank you for your dedication and care until the true owner returned."

Her jaw dropped as did her eyelids. No one could question his loyalty. Anyone living in exile for years with the heir to an abolished throne had to be a faithful committed servant.

"One thing I can say about Cromwell is he took care of the palace and the grounds until his death two years ago. Rumor has it he enjoyed Hampton Court more than any other abode. Would you agree?"

"There was no abuse here. For a few years the village prospered, work could be found, and I had free access to work in the gardens."

As they wandered from stall to stall, Peter had Kate's orders sent to the palace where the vendor would collect his payment. Kate kept a running total on her folded list with tick marks from her gray flint chip.

"Have you ever prepared for a hundred guests?" He gently guided her by her elbow through the center of the market away from the butcher stalls and the strong smell of fresh blood. The pheasant, venison, and veal for the banquet would come from the estate so there was no need to tarry at those stalls.

"No, but thanks to you I only have to multiply the ingredients and supervise the cooking. I have a couple of surprises just for the king and his closest guests."

Peter leaned closer, hoping to be included. "And me?"

"Well, that depends. You either have to be sitting by the king or sneak into the kitchen for your treat."

"Give me a hint, please."

"Lavender and mint."

"To eat?" Peter raised his hand to his throat, mimicking choking.

Kate laughed, bringing tears to her eyes and almost dumping her basket of packaged spices. "And you say you've traveled in France. These are herbs used to enhance the flavors of custards and sauces."

"Speaking of food, are you ready to stop for a morning break? We could buy a few meat pies and eat by the river."

"I'll meet you there. I have two more items to pick up for the bakery."

His hand immediately missed the feel of warmth from Kate's arm. She disappeared in the direction of the cheese vendors. He secured their meal along with a flask of lemon and sugar water, and then exited the market. Since he had no blanket, he chose a stone placed as a bench beside a shade tree. At this mid-morning hour most of the citizens would be at home with chores or at the market. He and a few squirrels and birds were the only occupants by the river.

In the near silence with the faint gurgling of the Thames,

Peter took his reed from his pocket and played a ditty, one that made his heart swell. The memories danced across his vision of a peaceful furlough in Holland. Charles and his entourage camped outside the walls of an ally duchy. The exiled king reposed on the ground with a rock for his head.

"Lad, teach us a local tune." Charles enjoyed music of any variety. Peter and a few fellow travelers had filled the king's anxious circumstances with lively songs of the realms.

Today, Peter's audience consisted of a few skittish rodents and birds that could outplay him anytime.

"What tune is that?" Kate appeared from behind and joined him on his stone perch.

"An old folk song from Holland about a lad leaving his lassie for adventure."

"How sad. Did he return?" The golden specks in her brown eyes begged for resolution. Should he lie and make it to her liking?

"Yes, he returned with stories to tell, but she had married another."

Kate jumped up and placed her hands on her hips. "I knew it. Men are all the same, seeking adventure and war and excitement, and at the same time expecting your sweet little lassies to stay at home pining."

Where did that fire come from? Experience? Kate fumed as if she were the girl in the simple song.

"Not all of us do that." Peter smiled, needing to gain a little respect for his gender.

Her wall of fire cooled a few degrees as her hands dropped to her sides. "Are you telling me you didn't leave a string of girls all over Europe with promises to love them forever?"

"Not one, though I had many offers."

"Oh."

Did she believe him? What did it matter? The rest of the troupe gave their love freely and often. Once or twice, he was tempted, but he knew Charles would move on to the next post. When Peter fell in love, it wouldn't be for one day only.

Peter tucked his reed back in his pocket. "Let's eat."

He handed her a pie. Their fingers touched briefly, but Kate pulled away quickly and placed her food in her lap. She bowed her head and closed her eyes. Peter stared at her as she gave thanks to God.

All Puritans were the same. Peter had no use for invoking God in his everyday life. The Puritans beheaded the previous king and put Cromwell in charge. The mess that continued for ten years had no sign of God's intervention. God provided little comfort for Peter. His confidence had to be in himself and the king.

But Kate seemed to believe strongly in her ways. Even away from the watchful eyes of her father, she remembered to give thanks.

"You are different from what I imagined a courtier to be." She nibbled on the pasty, letting the crumbs drop to the ground.

"I'm glad. I have no title or money, so I have no reason to play the part of courtly prince. What I do have is the ear of the king, an honorable position, and dreams of a better England."

"For England? What about for you personally?" Kate wrapped up half of her pie in a cloth and placed it beside Peter. He watched her swallow a sip of lemon water and wipe her mouth on her apron.

What should he tell this village girl of his long-term dreams? He hadn't told the king, his mother, or close companions. The flirtatious court would laugh and his mother would shun him. What would Kate say?

"My plans?" He clasped his hands together with elbows on his knees and leaned forward, mesmerized by the flowing river. "A cottage outside of a small village with pastures and stables for breeding and training horses."

The words hung above him. He'd never verbalized this out

loud even to himself. He almost wanted to suck them back inside. Did they sound silly to Kate?

She touched his arm and sought his eyes. Kate wasn't laughing or belittling him. The words still rose above him, intact, as a possibility.

"That seems perfect for you. Your gentle ways with horses and people are evident with how you handled me with Samson."

He covered her fingers and held tight, anticipating the pull of her hand in retreat. "Thank you. I've never told anyone. And it's only a dream."

"Dreams are fine as long as you can still live in reality." She managed to slip her fingers out of his hand.

"And your dreams?"

"Maybe some other time. My reality is getting back to the bakery."

Kate stood, straightened her dress, and shook the crumbs on the ground.

"Kate." Her head jerked to the side, staring up the slope right to her father's glaring face. "I want you home this instant."

"Yes, sir."

"Is he angry?" Peter gathered the remaining items, flask, and Kate's meat pie.

"Don't worry about Father. I'll think of something." She took three or four steps up the bank. "Thank you for this morning and your time. I feel better about the task before me."

Peter's two strides brought him to her side, but he pushed back in case Mr. Sinclair lurked behind a bush. From what he had witnessed, the man most likely stomped his way home. Should Peter walk her home and make sure she didn't receive abuse from her father?

"Is it only me or would your father be upset with any male he saw you sitting with?" He stopped, hoping that she would too. The open market wasn't the place to carry on a personal conversation.

Her basket, carting cheese and a few spices, rested in her grasp in front of her and occupied her attention. She sighed and cocked her head before looking up. Tiny wrinkles touched her eyes as she smiled. "Father has his ways and means well. Honestly, he isn't confident that I can withstand the influence of the court. You aren't a local boy with a reputation of goodness within the church and community."

She leaned in closer and whispered, "You are a mystery to him, and he doesn't like anything outside of the convention of the church or his domain. To answer your question, his dislike of you is wrapped in distrust."

"Oh." He straightened and stepped back. "You, my dear lady, have presented me with a challenge. And I accept. I will strive to win your father's trust personally and for the Crown."

He placed his hand over his heart and bowed. Kate giggled and covered her mouth with her free hand.

"Do you not believe me?"

"I do, sir. I do. It seems you plan to be here a while."

"At your service."

"Which at present includes making sure Cook is prepared for the king's wishes. You handle the palace, and I'll take care of Father."

They skirted the center of the market and parted at the bridge. Peter wouldn't mind spending the rest of the day at the Sinclair abode. Although there was plenty of activity at Hampton Court, no one caught his attention like Kate. Perhaps she'd spend time on the grounds later. He leaned against the post on the bridge and contemplated the bewitching Puritan in her swishing black skirt and white collar. The magnetism definitely wasn't in her attire, which he would gladly replace with brighter colors, but in her demeanor, one of purity, of course, but also determination and adventure. Underneath the trappings dwelled a spirited, lively, intelligent woman. He had an inkling he'd only seen a chink of the real Kate.

Chapter Seven

Upon entering the bakery, her father said two words as warning to Kate. "Be careful."

Careful of Peter? She decided to be thankful the excessive amount of bakery orders, keeping Father thick in flour and dough, prevented a long lecture. His concise sentiment covered a litany of already-spoken and overly rehearsed fatherly concerns. The two-word sentence had a sermon length form too.

If he had voiced more, would she have defended Peter? If she thought there was real danger in associating with him, she felt God would pressure her and prick her heart to resist. Yet, she never considered her time with Peter as an indiscretion to avoid.

Elbow to elbow with her father and mother in the sweltering kitchen, the next few hours filled Kate's mind with details of Molesey citizens' reactions to the king's visit. People her own age speculated with excitement and wonder. Her parents and customers hesitated, curtailing any jubilation. Were they remembering the last king beheaded in their lifetime?

"We can expect this number of orders every day for a few weeks, Laura. When does the new girl start to work?" Her father riveted his eyes for a half second toward Kate. Because of her work at the palace, they hired an extra hand for a few weeks. A little guilt lingered around Kate's slight frown.

"Tomorrow, and not an hour too soon. Don't you worry, Clifford. We're all doing our part, even young Robert. You'll make a baker out of him yet. That or the strongest, fastest sprinter in town."

"If I had known," Kate said, "I would have turned down Mrs. Downs' offer."

"Now, don't go thinking any of this success, and therefore extra work, is your fault. We're thankful for the surplus." Kate knew her mother answered before her father could interject his negative return.

"Humph." A deep grunt from the floured figure, standing by the table with ten loaves of rising bread, sealed his opinion. The animal-like sound reminded Kate he heard every word.

LATER THAT AFTERNOON Kate inspected the herbs and placed them in her basket for her receipts. The actual baking would commence tomorrow after morning church, at which point she would retrieve the herb cuttings. The smell of thyme lingered on her fingers as she couldn't resist releasing the aroma with her touch.

Mr. Payne approached her from the back gate. "You best hurry, Kate. Mrs. Downs already sent someone out here to find you."

"What's the emergency?"

"It seems the first of the king's entourage has arrived."

"Oh. Did she not have any warning?"

"Don't know. I think she's more concerned about the banquet than feeding today's guests."

Kate knew Mr. Payne had a different set of priorities for the king's visit—the presentation of the gardens, all in his domain, except for the groves of fruit trees and oaks. Anything that encircled the palace saw his command.

The kitchen door stood open, and Kate heard the demanding voice of Mrs. Downs. Feet flew across the pavement in and out of the large enclosure. Kate squeezed in without bumping into a busy servant. Even with all the activity, the kitchen was in order, everyone in his place with room to spare. In Kate's quick glance, she noticed a half dozen or more new faces. A taller round version of Cook convened at the pantry with Mrs. Downs. The king's personal cook?

Kate waited her turn, enjoying the hustle of the moment, indicating something exciting around the corner. A dark-haired girl with big round green eyes stepped down into the kitchen with a serving tray of refreshment items. Her glance of uncertainty caught Kate's attention. They both shrugged, not knowing where to set the tray. Kate took the few steps to the girl's side.

"I really don't know where it goes. I don't work here often, but how about putting it over there on the small cutting table. I'll tell Mrs. Downs in a minute."

"Thank you, miss." The young lady didn't dress or speak like an ordinary servant. Her dress of light blue swished as she walked through the kitchen, the softness of the material begging to be touched. Kate saw the barest hem of a satin petticoat peeking out from the ribbon fringe as the lady set the tray down. She rubbed her hands down the plain gray of her flat, dull skirt. Kate couldn't be much older than the beautiful girl, but she felt ancient and lifeless in her presence.

"Are you new here?" Kate ventured as the girl returned to the steps.

"Yes. I arrived today with the court's seamstress. My name's Betsy."

"Nice to meet you. I'm Kate, the daughter of a baker in town."

Betsy's eyebrows rose in question.

"And, I'm helping with the king's banquet on Tuesday."

The young woman's hands clapped and rested, clamped together under her chin. "A banquet with a ball. I love seeing all the pretty dresses and beautiful courtiers."

"Do you attend the ball?"

"No, never." Betsy giggled and her eyes sparkled with the anticipation. "But I do watch from a staircase, balcony, or window. Many of the ladies are wearing the costumes I have helped create. It is like watching a theater production."

"Much like my creations in the kitchen. Before they are served, their display is a masterpiece of delicious, exotic tastes and aromas."

"I haven't thought about it that way. Once we get our supper, the presentation has diminished, although the taste still lingers."

"Do you like gardens?" Kate admired this newcomer and her closeness to the court, though on the outskirts.

A frown replaced the girl's pleasant smile, erasing her dimples. "Yes. My family had beautiful gardens before the war. Now I don't know if anything is left."

"Where is your family?"

"I don't know. My parents gave me to Cromwell's household as a sign of their dedication when I was only eight. My father and one brother went to war. My other brother ran away. Mother wrote for a while but lost track after years of war and moving around. They might be dead or have fled the new regime."

"Oh." So many questions Kate desired to ask. How did Betsy escape Cromwell's household and land in the restored king's employment? What a difference in lifestyles. Puritan to moral freedom. Her clothes shouted a complete transformation. Under no circumstance would Cromwell have allowed a low neckline, ribbons, color, and shimmering buttons and bows.

Kate would love to show the new girl around the gardens. "Meet me in the rose garden in about an hour. It is right around the corner of the palace."

"I'll see what I can do. I have a little free time since the king and Lady Castlemaine don't arrive until tomorrow."

"Fine, until then." Kate didn't feel as jealous now after Betsy's sad story. Even though her own father clung to his Puritan ways and discipline, Kate realized he loved her. Also, she had her mother and siblings. Betsy had no one.

THE PALACE HALLS filled with trunks and servants. Peter wished for the days when Charles had one small chest and a handful of close friends instead of fifty trunks and a court full of guests plus a mistress, a young son, and a dozen toy spaniels. Peter assigned the rooms and the servants delivered and unpacked the trunks. The stable was in excellent condition to house the king's horses, carriages, and groomsmen.

Out of a second-floor window, Peter longingly surveyed the grounds, especially the rose garden. His wandering glance came back to two figures gliding down the paths stopping to smell the new blooms. The taller graceful form had to be Kate with her plain white bonnet and auburn loose tendrils and gray skirt and white apron. The other shorter woman, in light blue with long dark hair, was most likely a new arrival. Since the court hadn't arrived, she had to be a servant, a well-dressed one.

Part of him wanted to abandon his duties and stroll the parks with Kate, preferably without her additional acquaintance. Yet, just as he fell into his daydream, a footman asked for directions.

Peter laughed at the youth's confusion. "Be sure to study the map on the round table in the great room. These halls are numerous and connected in illogical designs. In a few days, you won't get lost anymore."

"Thank you, sir."

Hampton Court Palace, a gift to Henry VIII from Cardinal Wolsey, boasted countless rooms, four courtyards, and two thousand acres of grounds. Although the Tudors loved the place, Charles told Peter it hadn't been one of his favorites. The king preferred large open spaces, bright corridors more in the style of the French. How often had Peter reminded him that now he was in England and needed to embrace the English architecture and way of life? That was one reason he asked Kate to prepare the menu and add new English receipts. No reason to bring the king's French chef everywhere.

Peter bent closer to the window, but the women had disappeared in his momentary sidetrack. Better to concentrate on his work at hand anyway. The kitchens, though in excellent hands, drew him below.

He entered through the stairs from the Great Watching Chamber. Not one head turned to acknowledge his entrance. Pausing on the last step with his hands braced against the stone entrance, he surmised the staff had tripled. Even so, the huge kitchen once serving one thousand two hundred meals a day was more than ample for feeding a hundred guests.

"Mr. Reresby," Mrs. Downs called from her work table piled high with produce. He wove through the servants to her side. "All the items arrived, and I'm sorting through them now."

"You think you can handle so many meals a day?"

"I've fed more. Once with Cromwell there were upwards of seven hundred soldiers. Mind you, I didn't have to prepare any feasts or banquets."

"Well, it should really help now that servants aren't fed at the king's table. Since the king pays wages now, your workload should remain bearable."

"That's fine on a normal day, but not with the court in residence. All the additional courtiers and servants have to be fed."

"Maybe you'll make a few friends." Peter looked around, hoping to find a friendly, familiar face but met with bent heads concentrating on sorting, cutting, and preparing vegetables and meats.

"Oh, they're a good lot. It's still my kitchen, so they need to ultimately make me happy."

Peter laughed. "I knew you could do it. Have you seen Kate today?"

"Yes, she inspected the ingredients and is ready to begin work tomorrow."

"Will all these people listen to her?"

"Mr. Reresby, surely you have other things to worry about. Kate will do fine. You trusted her for a reason. Your instincts are good."

He bowed his head and picked up a stalk of celery and broke it. He saluted her with the piece before biting into the crunchy stem.

"If you want to see her, she went to procure the herbs and hang them to dry."

That explained her absence in the kitchen, but not her meandering in the garden. "I saw her in the gardens earlier with a young woman. Do you know who that was?"

"Curious lad. Let me see. I didn't catch her name, but she is a seamstress for His Majesty's mistress. I'm surprised you don't know her."

Seamstresses were not his domain, even though the court employed many of them. "When with Charles, I have court duties, no time to visit with household workers, although I would rather their company than dukes and earls."

Mrs. Downs' eyebrows shot upward, crinkling her forehead. "I suppose you have a special lady arriving with the court tomorrow?"

He shrugged. Madeline hadn't been in London for the coronation due to her mother's illness. He wouldn't say he missed her much. Truthfully, she fancied him, and he sought her company to avoid others. There wasn't an understanding between them.

"Not really." He waved his celery stick at Mrs. Downs and whispered, "I have to be very careful not to become bewitched by damsels at court. Their sticky webs have caught a few unsuspecting gentlemen."

"Oh, Mr. Reresby, are you telling me that there is truth to the rumors?"

He placed his hands up, palms out in innocence. "My lips are sealed. I'm confirming that I'm not easily entangled."

Another stalk in hand, Peter exited through the kitchen courtyard and Seymour gate to the tree-lined avenue. Outdoors again, where he felt most comfortable, he breathed in the fresh flower-perfumed air, closed his eyes, and determined his path through the garden gate.

Destination? Kate. *I mean the vegetable garden. Careful.* Peter had just claimed not to be entangled. The only thing worse than a lady of the court could possibly be a Puritan from the village. Except that the woman, Kate Sinclair, was much more than a Puritan or a commoner.

"COULD you please hand me the rosemary, Edward?" Kate posed on the step ladder, adjusting the string already full of fresh herbs drying in the green house. It wasn't often Kate worked alongside Edward. Unfortunately, he still hinted at courtship. Didn't he understand when she threw Jane's name in conversation so often that he could transfer his feelings to her?

"Here you go." He knew his plants, not surprising being the son of Mr. Payne. The older man spoke many times of relishing the fact that his son was back on the property full-time.

Edward moved aside as Kate stepped off the ladder. "What do you think he'll be like?"

"Who? The king?" Of course, no one spoke of anything else. She wiped her hands on her apron and shook her head. "I don't know. We'll see tomorrow. I'm sure the whole village will cram the streets for a peek. I expect His Majesty will stand out in the parade with his famous plumes and flamboyant attire."

Kate wondered more about the ladies and their fancy clothes, but she didn't discuss that with Edward. Betsy shared many details to spike her interest. The girl surprised Kate with her elegant but humble ways. From her childhood, Betsy knew how to read, a favorite pastime with her family, and often she read to the ladies in waiting in the long hours at Cromwell's court, which lacked formal entertainment—no games, no dances, no celebrations. She mentioned the Bible and approved books on history and religion as her sources. Kate anxiously waited for a time to ask Betsy more personal questions about her family.

Not much different from me. Father doesn't know I've read some of Shakespeare and Marlowe.

Edward took the empty basket outside, while Kate admired the many strings of herbs dangling from the beams. She threw her arms out, wanting to embrace the fresh herbs. The mixed fragrances let out a heady strong aroma with no one dominant scent.

"I heard you were here." Peter interrupted her awkward imaginary dance with the herbs. "But I didn't know it was for dancing." He laughed.

She could only wonder what she looked like. Her father would chastise her if dancing were her objective. "Oh, I wouldn't call it dancing. Perhaps giving the herbs a little attention." That sounded worse. She needed to clamp her jaws tight before more foolishness escaped.

Peter stared at her with his arms crossed leaning on the door post. Her hands went to her cap and found her loose hair instead. Waves of unruly locks had escaped their prison as her cap barely hung on down her back.

I could frantically stuff the mess into my cap or act as if it didn't matter. She chose the latter and ignored his continued stare.

"Did you need anything, Mr. Reresby?"

"Hmmm. I must have. Let me recall." He placed his fist under his chin and grinned, providing some comic relief. "Yes, everything seems to be under control for the banquet. I merely want to know if you need any more supplies."

"No, not for my part."

Kate touched the dark green leaves of a potted hyacinth. What she needed he couldn't give. A yellow dress like Betsy's or a lazy row down the river or a stroll in the pond garden at sunset. Such silly ideas brought on by the lush colors of spring and a world outside the bakery and her father's eye. To be Betsy for one day. The girl offered to let her try on some of her dresses. Father would never know, but God would.

Kate shook her head, releasing more of her curls, reminding her of her disheveled appearance. During her daydream, Peter had moved closer, admiring the purple blooms by her hand. Startled, she jerked her fingers away and braved an upward glance.

"I look forward to seeing you every day. That way I know everything will turn out all right."

"Why do you trust me so? I could make horrible chaos out of everything."

"I've watched you work, at the bakery, in the garden, with other people, and even with a newcomer in the rose garden this afternoon."

"You saw us?" *Me in my drab skirt and Betsy, a flower in yellow. I wonder who he prefers.*

"Yes, you distracted me from the mundane distribution of trunks and lost servants. I was envious of your leisure."

"Leisure? I guess it was for a few moments. The girl is new and waiting for the court to arrive. She's part of the court staff and seemed to be lonely. I might have found an unlikely friend."

"Why do you say that?"

"Well, look at me, a common village girl, compared to her, a courtly young lady."

"I think she has very good taste making you her friend."

Kate looked at her dirty skirt and apron and the weeds in misshapen mounds around her feet. Although she cherished every minute in the dirt, an occasional foray on the grounds in a fresh day dress would be a threat.

"If I ever have a pretty dress, I'll not be digging in the dirt in it." Kate stood and discarded her gloves on the gravel walk. "Did you need something, Mr. Reresby?"

"Yes. I need you to call me Peter."

"But…"

"But you can. We seem to be spending a lot of time together."

She tucked her chin and looked at her boots covered with a dusting of dirt. Kate knew their time would be limited, and he'd disappear with the court in a few weeks. It wouldn't hurt to call him Peter at least in private.

"All right, Peter, how may I help you?"

"I actually want to offer my services and see if there is anything you need for the banquet."

"Not unless you have the power to split me in two to be in two different places at one time." She giggled, releasing a bit of anxiety about the event. "Don't get me wrong. There are plenty of helping hands but few creative minds. We'll do fine, Mrs. Downs and me. We've done it before except not for this king. Will he be agreeable?"

Kate noticed Peter holding one hand over his mouth, trying to cover a huge grin.

She pulled his sleeve dislodging his hand from his chin, triggering a pent-up laugh from his throat. "What's so funny?"

"Charles is the most affable man I know. I wish you could meet him around a campfire roasting a rabbit. He will appreciate any morsel you place before him. But I will say his praise increases with the quality of the delicacies. I have a feeling you'll receive high praise."

Her cheeks warmed as Peter showered compliments and encouraging words. Responding to his grin, Kate's wide eyes probed his handsome face and challenged him with her raised brows.

"Do you think I'll be able to see the king? Will he dance at the ball? Will you be a part of the dancing that night?"

For some reason Peter broke his gaze and replaced his smile with a frown. Shoving his hands in his pockets, he studied the palace walls before turning back to Kate. Why the hesitation?

"The king loves to dance and will be the leader in many drills all night. As for me, I'll try to stay on the sidelines. I don't particularly enjoy being part of the show."

Kate wondered what pieces of information he failed to divulge. A man in his position surely flowed in the court with ease as a fish in water. If she had to guess, she'd say he was the center of many ladies' dreams. So why the frown?

She closed her eyes and swayed to imaginary music. It appeared the images that made him frown made Kate smile. "I'll probably join the servants, sneaking peeks from the balcony or stairway. I've never seen anyone dance. Nothing like that happened when the Protector lived here."

"Careful with your musings. Court life has two sides fused together. It's hard to exist in the glamor without the consequences. Don't let your pretty head waste too many minutes in a deceiving picture of grandeur." He leaned closer. "Let the court keep its secrets."

He ducked his chin, catching her amazement at his words, and caressed her cheek with his thumb. Did he always communicate with mystery? Why didn't he just come out and tell her all the troublesome details? Because he must see her as a plain, boring, village girl excited about anything having to do with Hampton Court.

She backed away from his closeness, taking the heat of his touch with her. "Well, perhaps I'll have to find out a few of those secrets on my own. Betsy will help me. She's been a part of court life and survived nicely."

"Has she truly? You've known her all of an hour?"

Why was he so adamant about her distance from the court? Hands on her hips, she projected her chin, fixing her eyes firmly on his steamy green ones. "I see no harm in seeing our Merrie Monarch and his court in person. Maybe the rumors are true or maybe not. I don't think your job, Mr. Reresby, is the same as my father's. I'm old enough to make a few decisions myself." She dropped the personal "Peter" in her anger.

He sunk his hands deep in his pockets and looked at her

through thick lashes. "Please accept my apology. Is there a way we can be friends again? I'll do better in keeping my opinions about the court to myself. But before that subject closes, I want you to know I'm looking out for your purity. It is a treasure in this new time."

Peter bounced slightly and extended his hand. Kate placed her gloveless hand in his and nodded. "Forgiven. And yes, we can be friends...Peter."

She didn't doubt his sincerity or his words of warning earlier. But did she need another adult telling her what to do or not to do? Her desires were harmless—a glance of courtly men and women in beautiful garments, enjoying an entertaining dance. That was all.

Chapter Eight

"Mr. Reresby, sir." A page ran on the garden path toward Peter. "I have a message for you."

"Thank you." Peter received the missive and turned it over in his hand, then lifted it to his face. As he smelled the letter, he closed his eyes for a second.

Could he tell who it was from by the smell? Kate had heard of scented paper. Would he tell her?

He popped the seal with his finger. His lips moved slightly as he surveyed the message. His sigh brought his eyes to Kate's.

"Bad news?"

"I'm afraid so. It's from my mother." He folded the paper and placed it in his jacket pocket and sighed, running his fingers through his hair. "She is threatening to move to America to join my aunt and uncle. After Father was killed, she had the same notion but didn't go because of my sister. Now since Rebecca has disappeared, she wants to leave the memories behind."

Kate shook her head not understanding a mother leaving her children, however old they were. "But she has you and your brother."

"Right. A son returned from exile and a discontented Puritan turned Royalist." At the last statement Peter peered sadly at

Kate. "I'm sorry. There are many like your father who've signed a piece of paper but whose loyalty is really elsewhere."

"Don't worry about my family. You seem to have enough to figure out. What will you do?"

"After the week of celebrating at Hampton Court, I'll go try to convince her to stay." He pasted on a partial smile. "If only Rebecca would come home and give Mother hope. I think her heart is broken."

Kate reached for Peter and ran her hand down his arm and squeezed his hand. "I'll pray for all of you. God still listens and heals." Did Peter even believe in God's power? In this situation Kate believed only God could fit all the pieces back together.

Her family had faced similar decisions, but her parents pulled together instead of separating. America had been an option as it was the destination of some of East Molesey's citizens. At least three families uprooted.

"Kate, I didn't mean to burden you with this. Please forget it and concentrate on your own work and concerns. I'll see you later."

"Bye." Kate noticed the Peter who left her walked with heavier steps than the one who greeted her half an hour before. It wouldn't be easy for her to disregard his burden. She'd just incorporate it in her prayers.

WHY NOW? Peter had enough to occupy five minds and now his mother decided to escape her pains by running away. Perhaps that was what Rebecca did a few years ago. Just had enough of conflict and disappeared.

As he entered the Great Hall, he looked up at the hammer beam roof with the elaborately braced trusses. Each pendant, royal arms, and badge above him represented a family from the past. How had they conquered their problems?

Peter chose the route of exile while others fought. Many in

Henry VIII and Elizabeth's time never got the chance to leave before they were beheaded or imprisoned. At least he didn't face that option. He breathed in the rich oils being applied to the doors, walls, and furniture preparing for the king's arrival tomorrow. He ran his fingers over the ornate tapestries making sure they had been thoroughly dusted. Quickly, he had to figure out a way to concentrate on his immediate duties and relegate his mother's announcement to another compartment.

Continuing into the Great Watching Chamber, Peter stopped in the doorway and surveyed the area. The before sparsely furnished room now held long tables with gilded chairs along three of the walls. The fourth wall housed the tables for the food.

Mrs. Finn, the king's personal kitchen mistress from Whitehall, approached him. "Mr. Reresby, I hope you find everything to your liking or should I say to the king's liking."

"Yes. All my instructions seem to have been followed. Personally, I'm glad the court will remain small for this visit. You've planned for a hundred total—correct?" Peter noted the stern stance, smile-free face, and gray attire of the thin lady. He wanted to stand on his head to make her laugh, but doubted his success. This was how he always saw her.

"A hundred plus a few extra," she said. "I do appreciate not having to feed the local servants."

"That was a clever move of the king to distribute wages instead of feeding a thousand like former monarchs."

"I expect His Majesty and entourage by early afternoon. Of course, the big banquet is Tuesday afternoon."

Mrs. Finn cleared her throat. "I still don't see why I wasn't in charge of the menu and preparation for that event." She sucked in her breath, causing a hiss of discontent.

Jealousy in the kitchen? "I knew there would be additional guests, and thought you'd enjoy a little less stress." *And I wanted the king to experience Kate and Mrs. Downs' fare.*

"Well, I guess I can relax a little after all, Mrs. Downs is in charge of the kitchen here."

"I appreciate you working with her. There are many palaces belonging to the king with no cooks or less accomplished ones."

"Yes, you're right. Now, I must get back to work."

Peter stared at the straight-backed figure rounding the corner to the kitchens. Hopefully, he appeased her pride and saved Mrs. Downs a few offhand remarks. It sure was much easier killing their own meat and roasting it over a campfire.

Peter ended his inspection in the cellars. He tapped a few barrels and calculated the number of days. Possibly, the king's weeklong visit wouldn't outlast his ale. A memory of an almost empty cellar last year made him chuckle. Things had changed from the Protector's reign to the Merrie Monarch. Peter would never switch his loyalty, but he would prefer fewer barrels of ale and more courtiers in control of their actions, speech, and dress. The extremes boggled his senses at times.

Obviously, Mrs. Downs had complete control of her kitchen. As Peter entered the main arena, she appeared as a general in her crisp white apron with twelve cooks and assistants lined up in a straight line in front of her at attention. Peter stood at full height, too, out of respect and a bit of fear.

"You are dismissed for the day, but I expect you here ready to fulfill your duties by six in the morning. Understood?"

"Yes, Mrs. Downs," almost in unison, resounded off the pots and pans and around the overstocked shelves.

Peter felt dismissed and decided to try to get some extra sleep after he said goodnight to Samson with the hope of possibly clearing his mind during the cool walk down the avenue.

KATE STRETCHED LONG AND DEEP, awaking from a dreamless sleep as far as she could tell. Her hands reached for the ceiling and quickly returned to her sides pushing her to a sitting position.

Oh my. How could I forget about today? Not only the Lord's day, but the day the king arrives. She dizzily sprung to her feet and made several circles around the floor not seeming to know where to go.

"Stop, Kate," she said out loud. Why the hurry? She had nowhere special to go at dawn on Sunday morning. No customers. No chores. In her excitement she confused this morning with every other one.

Now that she was up, she claimed her favorite perch on her window seat, although used very seldom. It supplied her with a view of a fresh spring morning, clear skies, and a low mist over the fields and river in the distance. She pushed the window out and breathed in the fragrant moist air, a mixture of dew-covered grass, gardenia, and honeysuckle ascended.

Today, she would see the king, not face to face but from a controlled distance. Would he wear his royal robes and his crown? And what about the rest of the court? Would she catch glimpses of their glittering attire?

"I'm looking out for your purity. It is a treasure." Peter's words startled her memory. Her purity was not at stake, not by seeing a few pretty dresses. Didn't he know she was protected from the evil of the world?

With my whole heart I have sought Thee: O let me not wander from Thy commandments.

Kate closed her eyes and lifted her face to the heavens. The words of Psalm 119 comforted her. God's word and her commitment to Him would shield her from temptation.

Thy word have I hid in mine heart, that I might not sin against Thee.

What Peter beheld as purity, Kate labeled as her desire to live a righteous life. Her eyes shot open. Who was he to warn and scold, for he lived in the midst of it all and appeared to be unscathed? She'd let her conscience covered with years and layers of sermons and Scriptures be her guide, not a courtier.

I'll look at all the pretty dresses I want from a distance. It's not as if I'll ever touch one, much less wear one.

The sun coming up over the river touched her heart and returned her vigor for the new day. Before the first flamboyant petticoat graced the town, Kate had to break the fast with her family and attend worship service.

Her pressed white collar stared at her from the tall hutch in her corner. White and black as on every Sunday. She smiled and thanked God she didn't have to rummage through numerous dresses and make a decision. Her parents and years of practice determined her attire.

"Father, I can't believe you want to miss the king's procession." Robert bounced in his seat like a four-year-old as Kate walked into the breakfast room off of the kitchen.

"I've seen plenty of processions in my time. Hampton Court has always been a favorite of kings." Her father placed his satchel containing his lunch over his neck and shoulder.

"Are you sure you're not going to the Puritan church just to avoid the king's arrival?" Looking over her cup of tea, Mother voiced what Kate assumed as true. The four mile walk to the next town in the opposite direction of London guaranteed Father would not have to witness the royal party marching through the town in front of their house.

"I know I can't prevent you from watching, but I don't have to participate." He ruffled Robert's hair and patted Mother's hand. "Just don't let the gold and trimmings pierce your hearts. There's not enough room for God and gold."

The same lecture as Peter's except Father's held a spiritual edge. What was it with these men? She knew most of the husbands and fathers, boys and young men, would be pressed in to see the sparkle and glitter. Like Kate they would then return to their black and white world. Color was slow to return to East Molesey—a little green, a little blue but no yellow, orange, or purple like she expected to see today.

Reverend Turnard shared his wisdom to a full church this morning. Kate felt a live pulse of anticipation run through the congregation in smiles, handshakes, and embraces. The hymns lingered and hovered instead of dissipating once sung. Kate stole glances around the parish sanctuary hoping to name what was different. The dress and outward appearance remained the same, so it had to be the extra sway, bounce, or smile people added.

Kate stopped her wandering eyes by the end of the priest's sermon, long enough to hear his parting words from First Peter.

"Seeing ye have purified your souls in obeying the truth through the Spirit unto unfeigned love of the brethren, see that ye love one another with a pure heart fervently; being born again, not of corruptible seed but of incorruptible, by the word of God, which liveth and abideth forever. Amen."

Purity and love. I need to copy that scripture for myself and for Peter. Lord, I am determined to remain pure in thought, word, and deed.

PETER SADDLED SAMSON HIMSELF, adjusting the breast plate with the king's arms. His horse lowered his chin trying to see what Peter added. "Only for today, my boy. You have to look your best for the parade, just as I do."

Today, Peter wore the livery of the king—black boots, white breeches, red jacket, and all the gold trimming, ruffles, and lace. He preferred his daily work clothes, ones he could move freely in through the stables and gardens. But he knew Charles' love of triumphal entry included the costume of his court.

"Ready? Let's go meet the king." Peter and Samson passed the parish church. By the sound of the voices joining in a hymn, the place had to be full. He didn't know what drew them there week after week. Church had never added much to his early life, and now he had all he needed. What could God give him that he hadn't obtained for himself?

Family. Peace. Hope.

He turned in his saddle. No one followed him. Must be his

subconscious working out his dilemma about his mother and his concern over his sister. Well, perhaps his life didn't contain all he needed.

About five miles outside of Hampton Court on the road to London, Peter pulled Samson in for a rest under an oak tree beside the well-trodden road. At least this section wasn't full of holes nor had it been washed away into the Thames.

He stretched his legs by standing in the stirrups. Shielding his eyes from the early afternoon sun, Peter saw a moving dust cloud in the distance making a turn in his direction. He knew Charles enjoyed every minute of the journey outdoors. The lords and ladies in the carriages probably didn't share the king's enthusiasm for travel.

Samson pawed the grass as the entourage led by the guards approached. "Soon enough, boy. Are you sure you want to share your stable with these royal steeds? Although you are just as royal, I think you've enjoyed the peace." He rubbed Samson's ears before sitting tall in his saddle.

Slowly he advanced not wanting to trigger the guards' defense. The breast plate on Samson and Peter's own regalia should pass as a friend of the troops.

King Charles on his black charger broke from the procession and loped toward Peter. Nose to nose, the horses raised and lowered their heads and pricked their ears.

"Your Majesty." Peter bowed in his saddle.

Charles extended his hand. "None of that. I'm Charles, remember?"

Peter laughed as he shook his friend's hand. "You are a version of the Charles I know. But you must understand, you are also my sovereign."

"Yes, yes, but really the only difference is I sleep in a bed and not on the ground."

A myriad of memories flashed in Peter's mind. So much had changed for the better. After all, Charles' rightful place on the throne was their goal during exile. Power and wealth replaced their freedom.

"Are you ready to face your subjects and claim Hampton Court once again?"

"I wonder if it holds the ghost of my father from his imprisonment here along with Anne Boleyn and Catherine Howard's phantoms." Charles adjusted his position and grinned. "Any sign of spirits running through the halls?"

"None at all. I think you'll enjoy this palace."

"I hope so. Let's proceed. I want you to follow Lady Castlemaine's carriage. Keep your eyes open for potential troublemakers."

"I think you'll find a devoted crowd here. They anticipate a glamorous entrance. I don't feel they'll be disappointed." Peter would love to see the procession through the innocent eyes of Kate or even young Robert. The gold and glitter offered no surprise to him now.

Samson and Peter fell in behind the gilded carriage drawn by black geldings matching the king's stallion. Lady Castlemaine leaned out the window and reached her gloved hand to Peter. He bent down and held her fingers briefly. A royal lady—always beautiful and in control of all within her small realm, including the king.

What changes will she bring to Hampton Court? It could use a feminine touch but Peter realized that the overhaul of the palace put in her hands would be extravagant and expensive, changing the whole aura of the residence.

About a half mile outside of town, the citizens lined the road. Some waved banners and handkerchiefs, while others threw flowers and handed bouquets to groomsmen on horseback and ladies extending their hands through windows. Peter hoped Kate would view the royal entrance from her doorstep.

Even the king veered out of the procession and reached down to accept a bouquet. Peter received two bouquets and gave one to

Lady Castlemaine, who refused to extend her hand to the commoners. While the king relished the attention of the villagers, his mistress desired the attention of the court alone. Peter didn't remember her ever venturing out into the public even with the king.

Once inside the town, Peter's senses honed in on the presence of one person. Surely, she attended the event. Logic dictated she'd be in front of the bakery. His legs itched to stand up in the saddle for a better view. Yet discipline kept him seated. A courtier didn't crane his neck and make a spectacle of himself just to find a person in the crowd.

He found her anyway. Her amber eyes focused on him. Kate. He waved and bowed his head in her direction. Her smile was enough to make him pull out of his place in the parade.

"LOOK. HERE HE COMES." Jane bounced on her tiptoes and waved her white handkerchief.

Kate leaned into the street, straining for a peek. "Oh, I see him. He rides like a king—doesn't he? His long black hair draping over his shoulders looks like a fur cape. Is he handsome? Can you tell?"

"Too many people in the way." Jane lowered her arm and settled back, nestled between Kate and Margaret.

"I wish Betsy were here, but she had to wait at the palace for her mistress." Kate took over Jane's stance and used her tiptoes for an extra few inches. Where was he? All she could see was the row of guards and the top of the king's head. Wouldn't Peter as a friend and member of the court ride in the procession?

Jane giggled and cupped her mouth and said for Kate's ears only, "Wouldn't it be strange if your mistress was actually the mistress of the king?"

Kate thumped her friend's shoulder in reprimand. "You shouldn't say that."

"Well, you know it's true. I haven't heard one person deny it. I think she's probably in that carriage following the king."

"Oh, I hope so. I want to see her." Not that Kate approved of the king's immoral meandering, but Lady Castlemaine was considered royalty in the court's realm.

Cheers rose and flower petals from upper windows on the other side of the road rained down on the king as he passed in front of the bakery. His black steed pranced to the beat of the drums.

"Long live King Charles." Many voices blended together.

Kate's eyes shifted from the king to the green pull of Peter's eyes. Her smile appeared to be attached to his by a string, for as he grinned, she did too. She let the gilded carriage pass without even a glance inside. While Jane waved to the occupant, Kate took a step toward the street while locked in Peter's gaze.

It's a silly notion, but it seems Peter was looking for me.

Samson, the gentle giant, stopped in front of Kate. As Peter reached out his hand to touch Kate, she forgot to be scared of the animal snorting close to her shoulder.

Peter leaned down and kissed her fingertips in his grasp. "Miss Sinclair."

No words escaped her lips. As Peter moved on, she realized the Peter she knew she could have talked to for hours. With this new Peter, in his royal uniform and position of prestige, she remained speechless.

"Did he just kiss your hand in front of all these people?" Margaret stared big-eyed at Kate. "Just wait until I tell all my friends."

Kate grabbed Margaret's sleeve. "Don't you dare. He was only thanking me for all the work I've done at the palace."

From her other side Jane said, "That didn't seem like a thank you gesture. In the middle of a parade?"

Kate crossed her arms and ignored them. Four more carriages passed along with many gentlemen and guards on horseback before the pomp disappeared across the bridge, leaving the street littered with flowers and handkerchiefs.

"Now, they'll be locked behind their gates with few to venture outside their court for a week." Jane sighed and laced her hands in front of her.

"But," Kate said, "I deliver baked goods daily, and I might need some help."

"Count on me," Margaret chimed.

"And me." Kate guessed Jane didn't want to miss a glimpse of a courtier.

Kate failed to mention her additional forays on the fringe of the court with the banquet and ball. That one day would give her enough fodder for quite a few tales of merriment. Fabulous food and fashion awaited Kate over the next few days.

"BUT I CAN'T, BETSY," Kate protested.

"Sure, you can. The dress is one of my older ones. I'll not miss it. And it's not as if you are wearing it anywhere important. Please try it on."

Today, Betsy wore a simple lavender dress with tiny white flowers on an overlay. She carried a hamper now extended toward Kate.

"All right. I guess it wouldn't hurt. You watch and make sure no one enters."

Kate stepped into a small room within the larger storeroom by the gardens. The dress was the color she always had in her dreams—yellow. The soft cotton gown felt feathery light on her body. The full skirt reached to her ankles at just the right length. Kate pulled at the sleeves expecting them to touch her wrists, but they landed just below her elbows and the remainder was inches of lace extending to her hands. Kate felt naked without her full collar, for the bodice dipped down and rounded below her neck.

"Oh." She supposed it looked like the ones Betsy wore, which were a medium cut. She enjoyed not feeling strangled, and the breeze on her neck enticed her to raise her chin to the sky.

"Ready?" Betsy asked.

"All right, as long as no one else sees me." Kate pushed the squeaky door open and stepped into the light beaming through the window.

"You are beautiful, Kate. Twirl around." Betsy clapped and praised Kate's performance.

Kate raised her hand to touch her sleeve and felt her curly hair also. "I must have lost my bonnet in my haste."

"Perhaps that is why you are so stunning."

Looking down one more time, Kate memorized the feeling, the textures, and the color before changing back into her gray and white dress.

She rolled the dress up neatly and placed it in the hamper and gave it back to Betsy.

"No," Betsy said. "I want you to keep it here. When you feel the urge, you can put it on. Everyone needs something nice."

If only Father believed that too. Kate ran her hands over her hips down her coarse skirt and adjusted the white apron in front. For a second, she didn't know who was the real Kate—the one dressed in sunshine or this one all plain and nondescript as a gray cloud.

"Thank you for that experience. I'll put the hamper in the loft above this room." Kate carried it up five steps on the ladder and pushed it to the wall. Safe from any curious hands. If she ever needed a tangible item to raise her spirits, she had one.

Betsy turned to the door. "I must go. There's probably a pile of clothes to repair with buttons or lace detached. I'll see you tomorrow. Let's meet during the ball in the north cloister. Then we'll find a place to view the celebration." Betsy clapped her hands. A few days ago, Kate's new friend was quiet and almost sullen. But now she beamed with a new interest.

"I'll see you there." Kate watched Betsy skip down the path

to the palace's east wing, her lavender skirt billowing in the wind.

As Peter walked through the garden hedge, Betsy turned again and waved to Kate.

"Is that your new friend?" Peter asked.

Suddenly, Kate felt insecure compared to Betsy. "Yes. She's a lovely young lady. I'm sure you would like her."

"As I said before, I'd like any friend of yours." Peter kicked at some pebbles on the path. "What may I do to help you? The big banquet is tomorrow."

"As if I'm not nervous enough." Kate squatted to pick a few springs of mint and some basil across from it.

"Don't be. It's only one hundred of the king's closest friends. He left the majority of his following, including ministers and Parliament leaders, in London. This crowd is more casual, here to enjoy the hunt, the grounds, and a calmer life. And a week will be long enough for most of them."

"Hmmm." Kate turned, holding her sprigs to her nose. "Peter, what did you decide about your mother?"

"I'm going home when the king leaves to convince her to stay. And, after talking to you about family, I've decided to double my efforts and try to find Rebecca. The more I think on it, the more I'm convinced she doesn't want to be found."

"Who wouldn't want to be found by a brother like you?" Kate lowered her lashes, wondering if she sounded too enthralled with him as a man.

"But, remember, she doesn't know me. Not really. Three years is a long time to an eight-year-old. I could be an ogre in her eyes. To her I deserted the family once. Why would she want to come back?"

"Oh, Peter, she must know you care. I'll pray that you find her."

"This will take more than mere words released to the heavens. I'll have to use every wit I possess. My cunning and detective skills will lead me."

They reached the garden gate, the one leading to the rose garden. Peter indicated for her to go before him.

"I don't think I should. What if the king or his mistress is strolling in here?"

"Don't worry. I have free range, and I can walk with whomever I please."

Fear and a renewed sense of lack of position clung to Kate over her plain garb. She stepped backwards onto the herb walkway, her domain. "You go ahead. I'm going to the kitchen."

She ran in the opposite direction from Peter. He belonged in the cultivated rose gardens for a leisurely stroll with a pretty lady. Kate knew she existed for the kitchen and servants' quarters.

Peter's "Kate, come back" faded as she neared the kitchen door. Stopping to catch her breath and tuck her loose curls under her bonnet, Kate glanced once over her shoulder. No one followed her. She hadn't run from a person but rather an idea, a deflated dream as well as a yellow dress, a rose garden, and a handsome courtier.

Chapter Nine

Because of her nerves, Kate anticipated a sleepless night, but her early hour labor in the bakery the day before, and extended hours in the gardens and kitchen of Hampton Court, claimed her body, priming it for exhaustion and a deep sleep.

She barely looked in the glass in the morning before descending to the already warm kitchen downstairs. Her father had to hire additional hands for the palace's needs for the week, especially for the banquet. The profits on the bulky orders pleased her father, although he commented over and over about the extravagance of the court. Since bread was a staple, he didn't see his role as contributing to the gluttony of the participants.

Tying her apron, Kate entered an efficiently run organization. No idle hands at six in the morning here.

"Good morning, Kate." Mother was the captain of this scullery ship. "Edward just arrived with the cart for all the items. Once we load yesterday's breads, you will be ready to go with the first round. At noon the second load will be ready."

"Thank you, Mother. I feel guilty for not helping here this morning. I just have…"

"I know, you have so much to do at the palace. We'll rest after the next order is filled." Her mother smiled. Could she be enjoying the drama of the court's visit?

Margaret stood with her hands on her hips. "Why can't I go with Kate?"

Mother pulled in a deep sigh. "We need you here to handle the everyday customers. We each have our place, so no more whining."

Kate knew Margaret wasn't jealous of the work awaiting Kate, but of the potential of seeing a knight, prince, or lady-in-waiting. If only it was that kind of carefree day.

Margaret advanced with the wonder of a child in her eyes, a curiosity of anything new. "Please, Kate, tell me all of the stories."

"Stories of the kitchen? Of my receipts?" Kate asked, trying to cover a giggle.

Margaret slapped at her upper arm. Kate deserved the physical outburst. "No, silly. Of the ball, the banquet, and the dresses."

"Oh, those stories. I don't know how many I'll have, considering I'm the kitchen help."

"Please try."

"All right, for you. I'll try to get a peek, but no promises."

As Margaret returned to her post, Mother rolled her eyes. "That child has a flare for the flamboyant."

I do, too, it seems. Did her mother wonder about or ever desire a pretty yellow gown? Actually, her mother told stories of before the war when she was a girl. Then she had a few church dresses of various colors, not one of them gray or black. But that was before. This was now. Her mother kept them in the black and gray world, even as changes happened all around them.

Edward stepped through the side door into the kitchen. "You ready?"

Kate's father turned and motioned Edward to the two large baskets. "Start with these, son. Do you need Robert to help you?"

"No, sir. I have Jane right outside the door with the cart."

Jane was here? Kate stepped to the street. "I didn't know you were coming. I'm so glad. How did you talk your father into it?"

"I only have a few hours, but I didn't want to miss an opportunity to get closer to the court."

"The kitchen is hardly close to the court."

"Yes, but what if some of the guests are walking in the gardens or strolling in the front drive when we walk up?"

"Well, don't fall out and faint. Edward and I have lots of work to do. I thought perhaps you just wanted to spend time with Edward?" Kate raised one eyebrow in question. What was taking her friend so long to attach to him?

Jane shrugged. "I'm not sure he still doesn't have eyes on you."

"Don't be silly. Try a little harder to be interested in his work or whatever it is girls are supposed to do to attract a man. I'm out of practice and don't plan on attracting one."

"You should. Richard has been gone a long time, and you're not getting any younger."

"Thanks a lot. Anyway, Richard took all romantic notions with him." Kate shook the melancholy cobwebs away. "Come inside to help with the baskets. They're heavy, and I don't want Edward dropping one and flipping it over."

The girls scooted inside. A few minutes later the cart, filled with fresh baked goods, rumbled over the bridge to the palace entrance. Edward lowered the cart to rest his arms. Kate used the time to survey the grounds. As expected not one soul roamed the drive at the eight o'clock hour.

Kate noted Jane's pouting lips. "Your wish of seeing a countess or duchess is not going to come true."

"Perhaps when I leave in a few hours."

"Perhaps."

The trio entered the side gate left open for deliveries. They could have found the kitchens blindfolded by following the aromas of every pot boiling, every oven lit and stuffed with pies and simmering meats.

"Thank you, Edward. Jane, take one side, and I'll get the other of this first basket. Ready? One, two, three." Together Kate and Jane heaved the basket up and over the low side of the cart. A long table against an inner wall in the first kitchen held the breads. Since the large basket belonged to the palace, the girls didn't have to unload them.

"Good morning, Mrs. Downs." Kate waved at the red-faced, alert woman at one end of the room. Jane followed Kate in that direction. "You're managing a small army in here." About twenty servants manned the ovens and tables.

"Yes. Thank you for relieving the additional preparation of the breads. That was an idea from heaven."

"We'll bring the second large basket and the smaller ones, then I'll get to work on my receipts."

Mrs. Downs nodded toward another room. "I set you up in the smaller kitchen, leaving you the oven facing the outside window."

Looking around, Kate gave thanks that she had her own assignment and wasn't trapped in the large kitchen with cooks she didn't know. And she had a large open window looking out over the gardens—a breeze and a view. "All right. I'll retrieve all my items from the larder."

Edward had all the smaller baskets arranged on the table. Now, he flirted with one of the new servants, a very young one chopping mushrooms and celery. Jane was prettier than the little girl, perhaps all of fourteen years.

"Edward, don't you have something to do in the gardens? Why don't you show Jane around before you get back to work? You'd enjoy that wouldn't you, Jane?"

Her friend shrugged her shoulders, miffed probably at Edward's wandering eyes. Kate placed Jane's arm through Edward's and pushed them out the door. "Be gone. I have work to do."

The last Kate saw of them, they were still arm in arm, winding through the paths with Edward pointing here and there. Her matchmaking accomplished, Kate had serious work to complete and only about six hours to finish it.

Mrs. Downs narrowed Kate's assignment to five of her special receipts: lemon chess pie, raspberry cream puffs, almond ginger cake, gooseberry pie, and orange pudding. Also, she only had to make enough for the head tables, about twenty guests including the king and Lady Castlemaine. The pressure to impress the king rivaled her desire to prove to Peter she could tackle the court's palate. He believed she could, but how could a king who had traveled to many royal European courts be impressed with her simple fare? Possibly through the unique spices and blends of flavors.

Mrs. Downs sent in two helpers to arrange the finished products on platters and to clean all the messes Kate continued to make. Always one to clean up after she baked, Kate disliked the fact she didn't have the time.

Covered in flour and ingredients smudged on her face, arms, and hair, Kate glanced out the window and came eye to eye with Peter. His smile and clean-shaven face under a felt feathered hat caused Kate to forget her project momentarily.

She'd desired to see him all day, but knew the court activities upstairs required his attendance. So how did he get away? Some beautiful lady would be missing him right now.

"Hello, Kate." He leaned on the window sill, arms crossed under his chin. She watched him survey her table where the last of the cream puffs waited to be filled.

"Tell me how the king likes the palace and all of your work." Kate had yet to look away from the green pools with thick black lashes casting shadows on his cheeks.

"At present the king is surrounded by many guests in his apartment. Every room has been opened to accommodate the attendants. We walked around the gardens, letting his spaniels sniff the roses and hedges and chase all the birds and squirrels away. I spared the vegetable and herb gardens from possible destruction."

"I've never seen one of his popular spaniels. Are they as special as I've heard?"

"They are cute, but I don't know if they are any better than another species. But Charles practically worships them. He brought four adult dogs and their puppies."

"Where do they stay?" She imagined a royal pen, perhaps by the stables.

"In the apartment with the king."

Kate's floured hand went to her mouth. "Oh." She failed to cover a laugh. "You mean in his bed?"

"Sometimes, but mostly on pillows at the foot of the bed. They are housetrained but with a new place it takes a few days to adjust, if you know what I mean."

Kate had no experience with dogs, but assumed an inside cat was the same.

Peter straightened and stared at her lips and then at her hair and bonnet. She wanted to smooth out the wrinkles and make sure her hair was neatly tucked away, but she knew her messy hands would only add a new dimension to her disheveled look.

"Kate," his voice shook, "I wish you could sit with me at the banquet. I feel more comfortable with you than anyone upstairs."

"Oh, Peter, you are a dreamer. I would never be invited to the king's banquet. You need to go back to your circle of friends or your young lady, or ladies, and have a merry time. And please, enjoy the food."

"I will. But it won't change my desire." He broke his stare and pushed away from the window sill. "I'll see you later, Kate. Thank you for doing this."

"You're welcome. Bye."

His words and actions confused Kate. Why would he want a plain servant girl sitting at a banquet with him? Did he think she'd want that?

She rolled her shoulders back and shook her arms out, releasing tension.

"Miss, will there be anything else?"

Kate blinked, barely noticing the girls in the doorway. "Just these last puffs." Kate glanced at her work displayed on the table on China plates and silver trays. Works of art. "Thank you for helping me." Both girls smiled and left for their next assignment.

Kate would love to be finished, but she had to check the herbs and spices on the leg of mutton, venison, duck, and pheasant. Each had a special combination of herbs to bring out their juices and individual tastes. She grabbed her spice bags from the larder, each labeled for the different meats.

The large kitchen was hot and stuffy with every oven fired. Mrs. Downs walked with Kate as they went to each position. Kate sprinkled the spices generously over each juicy concoction. "That ought to do it."

Mrs. Downs patted Kate's arm. "Thank you, child. I wish I could say the court will appreciate it, but we'll never know. At least you know, I do." *And Peter.*

Kate nodded. She didn't do it for approval. She enjoyed just knowing she could do it and that someone recognized her ability.

~

THE GUESTS at the king's head tables resembled a family ensemble. Charles chose to keep politics on the outskirts of the banquet by drawing in his closest friends and family— his brother James, his son James, Lady Castlemaine, and his remaining court from exile, including Peter.

Between the laughter, music, and numerous platters of delicious pleasing entrees, Peter kept his ears tuned to the king's mood and comments and his eyes on the faces of the guests. He caught Madeline batting her eyes at him several times. His gut had warned him she would be here, especially after their encounter in London. Sighing, he resumed his savory experience with his food. Thoughts of Kate in her gray dress and apron in the kitchens replaced the sparkling pink-satin attire of Madeline.

Venison stewed with carrots, onions, and garlic cozied next to oysters and flounder and rare fricassee. He cut the duck with his fork and let the different spices awake his enjoyment. If only Kate sat next to him to elaborate on the various mixture. Did the other guests care about the skill and expertise needed for the cuisine offered tonight?

Charles clapped his bejeweled hands once. "More wine and the desserts."

Servants scurried, clearing the king's plates and refilling his goblet. Peter followed the line of sweets with his eyes as they appeared from the side holding rooms. The first items delivered to the king's head tables would be composed of Kate's special receipts. As Peter licked his lips in anticipation, he trusted her gourmet treats would satisfy the king too.

When presented with sweets, Charles reverted to a child and took one of each from the platters. Peter noticed he discarded his fork and brought a cream puff to his lips and smacked them together in pleasure. He raised his second bite in Peter's direction and nodded. The king approved of Kate's work and expected Peter to pass his praise along.

Before the ball began while tables were cleared away, Peter weaved through the holding rooms down the stairs to the kitchens. His courtly attire turned heads and instigated curtsies as in a domino effect. If he had realized his influence, he'd have entered through an outside door closer to his destination—Kate. Somehow, she had found time to fix her hair, clean her face, change her apron, and replace stress lines with smile creases.

On impulse Peter hugged her and twirled her around. Her fists lightly beating on his shoulders warned him to set her down.

She struggled to stand straight and grabbed his upper arm

for balance. "Peter, what came over you? Too much ale has messed with your senses."

"The banquet was a success and more importantly, your sweets surpassed the culinary attempts of Europe. I so wanted Charles to find another thing to appreciate about England. He compares much to the continent, and when England falls short, it frustrates his cause and hope. So you see, you have helped the nation."

He placed his hands on her blushing cheeks and dipped his lips to hers, grateful for the vacant kitchen and Kate's friendly presence. The light pressure was a mere second or two before he stepped backwards still caressing her cheeks with his thumbs. Her eyes closed and lips posed for another kiss, and Peter realized he'd crossed the line of their friendship. Kate wasn't one to be kissed on a whim, her innocence invaded.

"I'm sorry, Kate." He dropped his hands slowly to his sides. "I missed you, and believe it or not, I felt alone in the banquet hall."

Kate shook her head from side to side and shivered as if shaking off a bad thought or a pesky spider. Her cloudy amber eyes searched his face and darted to the door and back. Did he give her a scare? *Please, Kate, understand my intentions to be honorable.*

"Thank you for your kind…words." She looked at her boots peeking from her skirt. Head tilted with her smile and twinkling eyes back in place, Peter breathed easier.

"Shouldn't you be changing for the ball?" she asked.

"I will. How about a walk in the gardens for a few minutes?" He expected a "no" answer.

"You know what I'd like to do? Show me the horses, if you could, and the carriages."

"I can do better than that."

"How?" She rose up on her tiptoes as a child ready for a surprise.

"Wait and see."

Chapter Ten

W*ait and see.* What was she thinking, going with him after his display in the kitchen? Or was it her starry-eyed actions? Either way his kiss left her questioning its meaning. Did he think she allowed just anyone the privilege?

No one expected her anywhere for another two hours. Betsy would finish dressing her mistress and her ladies by then. She'd convinced Kate that peering at the guests at the ball was appropriate activity not punishable by anything other than embarrassment if caught.

"Let me retrieve my clean bonnet." Kate discarded her tight scullery cap. Her long hair cascaded in bouncing ringlets down her front and back, having come loose from any form of restriction. Her back to Peter she wondered what a mess she appeared. Quickly, she tucked her hair in a bun and secured her bonnet under her chin. What a relief to have a little more movement around her ears and neck.

She turned with a bounce. "Ready." She followed him through the Seymour Gate down the boulevard behind the palace to the stalls on the west side of the grounds. Her nose crinkled before she ever saw a horse. The presence of staunch manure from the numerous horses assaulted her senses, more potent than what she used in the gardens.

Hesitation cut her motion forward short. With Samson she would be a bit comfortable, but fifty or more the same size as Peter's steed would frighten her. What was she thinking about making this request?

Peter probably knew it would take physical presence to advance her through the stable entrance. "Take my hand. I promise all the arrivals are secure in their stalls or out to pasture. No harm will come to you."

The snorting and pacing from several horses echoed off the rafters and through the hay loft. Peter's hand guided her like a child to a stall at the end of the stable. "This is Annabelle. She's gentle and a perfect size for you to ride."

"Oh no, not me." She stepped back as Annabelle poked her nose toward her.

"Think about it. When I return next time, we'll go for a ride."

"I don't think my opinion will change before then. Anyway, I can't ride a horse from the royal stalls."

"She is to remain here, so yes, she is royal but more of the country variety—pure pleasure, not show."

"As if that makes a difference to her strength." *Or her gentleness or my fear. A horse is a horse.*

"Trust me like you did with Samson. Here is a carrot for her. Remember, palm out and let her muzzle your hand with her lips. Harmless."

Palm out, carrot positioned. Kate let the tickling begin, and this time her hand remained steady. Timidly, she reached out for Annabelle's forehead and adjusted her forelock. *Maybe if I come every day she'll remember me, and I won't be as scared.*

"Now for your surprise." He led her to another stone building beside the stables and with both arms, he swung the massive doors open. Kate followed him on a cobbled drive to cubicle after cubicle of carriages, gilded with crests and coats of arms. Varying sizes and shapes, some square, others round, but all fairy tale symbols of wealth and royalty. Fit for princes and princesses and kings and queens.

Peter stopped by a solid gold carriage made to seat four. He unlatched the door and bowed to Kate. "Your carriage awaits, my lady."

Playing along, Kate in her innermost being knew the carriage was not for commoners. No way would this brief encounter give her airs of false hopes. Born a common village girl, she would remain one. One who had the experience of sitting in a carriage.

"Thank you, sir."

He helped her into the leatherback cushioned seat complete with pillows and ornate curtains. Peter stepped in after her and sat beside her with them both facing the view outside the doors —the palace and the beginning of the orchard.

"Where is our destination, Madame?"

"London, of course." A dream for her but nothing to him. What big city or country hadn't he seen? Glancing around the elaborate gilded cage, Kate compared her stark gray skirt to the beauty of each pillow and tassel. Where did she fit in this picture? *Nowhere.*

But Peter in his richly trimmed breeches, coat, and feathered hat belonged in the golden world. Fidgeting, she tried to unlatch the carriage door to her right but couldn't even figure out the latch of such a refined contraption.

"Ready to go so soon?"

"I don't really belong here, Peter." She ran her fingers over the satin-covered pillow. "Although I do thank you for the experience."

"Well, I don't belong here either. I belong on a small farm outside of a small village raising horses, with only a practical carriage to transport my family to town."

"And to church." She could imagine his dream fitting more her common status. Anyone in the kingdom could possibly achieve that much.

"What is keeping you from that?" Surely, he had the means and the connections.

"The king. He feels he needs me, and I can't cut the strings yet."

"But you will?"

"We'll see. Our years in exile have a hold over me. I want to protect him and support him as best I can."

"He must admire your dedication. I do." She waved her hands out in a circle. "And, you have access to all of them."

"Humph." He rubbed his fingers along the gold rim of the window. "Gold and jewels. You think that every courtier desires that? Not so. One or two of us want a simpler life."

She raised an eyebrow at his proclamation. How simple? Would he live over a bakery? In a village where the local entertainment consisted of market day and a church picnic? His image became hazy as she substituted a live performance at the Globe or a worship service at Westminster. Why trade that life for one in a place like East Molesey? He couldn't possibly give it all up.

"And where would you live if you had a choice?" Peter's voice snapped her to her present still settled against satin pillows.

"Not on a dusty thoroughfare for sure. Perhaps in a stone cottage by a brook with a view of Hampton Court. To see but not touch that life."

Peter perked up placing his finger on her chin pulling her attention to his playful smile. "What if you could have both worlds?"

"Impossible. I have access to one world only."

"Well, I hope to have a life outside the court one day and still be a friend of the king."

"I hope you are able to do that. As for me I have a destination in the village." Kate pinned her body deeper into the pillows, closed her eyes, and memorized this moment of suspension from reality.

Light fluttery puffs of air made circles on her neck, cheeks, ear, and hair. She refused to open her eyes and spoil her reprieve. So what if Peter was toying with her senses, taking advantage of her dreamy state. In the end, she'd step out of the carriage a plain daughter of a baker.

HER RELAXED NECK was as inviting as her rosy lips, but it was the serene and pure aura of her face causing him to stop at a few whispers of his warm breath on her skin. The sudden duplicity of his reason, good versus evil, do versus don't, drove him to take her hand instead and pat her until she descended from her dreamy state.

"We must go, now. Obligations await me." He wanted to follow up with his wish that she could come to the ball, but some desires needed to be suppressed.

He hopped out and kept her hand in his until she touched the ground. Walking in silence, they looked at the other carriages before exiting the carriage hall.

"Thank you, Peter. I enjoyed my surprise."

"Where are you going now?"

"Betsy's meeting me. Perhaps I'll spy you later." Her innocent smile warmed him. The prospect of searching for her curious eyes from the dance floor offered a pleasant diversion. If only Madeline would attach herself to someone else.

He left her by the spiral steps off the kitchen. Even in her indiscreet garb, Kate lit up the stove alcove. Hopefully, Betsy would introduce Kate to a gentler side of court life. For all he knew, her new friend might be the sort knights and gentlemen talk about around a late-night table.

The king's apartments hosted a hallway full of dozing servants in the corners and guards at the doors. He considered the work waiting behind the doors, spanning from entertaining the puppies to dressing the king. Where his role fell, Peter was soon to find out.

After knocking on the door, the guard in the inner room ushered Peter into a large sitting room. Not a female in attendance, Peter joined six other gentlemen lounging about the area.

"Where have you been? The king asked for you." Geoffrey, a comrade in exile, led him to the king's inner chamber before Peter answered with a made-up excuse.

Charles lounged in a huge bed with coverlets, pillows, and curtains of satin, silk, and sheer gauze with a spaniel under each arm. "Peter, come here. I need your opinion on a few ideas."

"Of course." Peter pulled a chair closer to the king's bed. Charles always had an idea, or a plan. And on occasion Peter added to the scheme or the implementation of it. Their friendship allowed him to be honest, most of the time.

"Lady Castlemaine would like a new apartment complex added on here at Hampton Court for her use." Charles, black wig skewed a bit, accenting his black eyebrows, trained his gaze on Peter for a response.

"At this palace, sir? Does she plan on remaining here much of the time?" Other questions lurked. Having the king's mistress here would mean a more permanent staff and years of projects.

The king scratched a dog's head. Peter could never remember the pooches' names or the favorites. They all looked the same to him.

"I'm willing to indulge as long as it makes her happy. Anyway, it will occupy her time this next year."

"You must mean your upcoming engagement."

"Exactly. As the official engagement creeps closer, she wants more of my attention and demands restitution for my impending marriage. This old house will benefit from her lavish demands." Charles flexed his jeweled hands in front of him and sat up straight, swinging his legs over the edge of the bed. "Tomorrow, we'll talk of the gardens and the addition. Now, I must dress to entertain this crowd. Gone are the days, Peter, of lounging under a shade tree in a faraway dale."

Peter stood with his arms crossed. Looking around at the satin, furs, and yards of expensive material dressing the windows and bed, he noted nothing could be more opposite their abodes in forests and valleys. "Do you miss the lush ground?"

The king ran his hands over his satin dressing gown and glanced out the window. "I can't miss something I tried to escape for ten years, can I? In ordinary circumstances, Peter, I would have spent my youth in peace and tranquility in my father's court. For better or worse, I can't have our carefree existence in exile and my court and kinship. I have accepted that fact. And now you need to also."

Charles placed his hand on Peter's shoulder and grinned, using the same smile that saw him through court after court, mistress after mistress. Of course, Charles was born to this way of life. But not Peter. He couldn't accept that he'd never have the rolling hills and simple life again. Not as an exile but as a country gentleman. Would Charles understand Peter's desire when and if the time came?

Bowing as he exited, Peter made his way to his quarters, avoiding a group of playful puppies. Before he could dream of a different life, he had to mingle in this one.

Chapter Eleven

"I want you to have this, Kate." Betsy pulled out a yellow silk shawl with slivers of gold thread dispersed throughout. The edges contained tiny tassels of yellow and gold threads.

Kate eyed Betsy's trunk full of colorful items. It felt strange being in this part of the palace, in Betsy's alcove, a place she shared with many other girls. *And just below us is a magical world of royals and wealth. Jane won't believe me when I try to describe all of this.*

"Oh, I can't. It is too extravagant." Kate held it against her face for a second. So soft, but so forbidden. She pushed her hand out toward Betsy, ready to release the treasure.

"No, I want you to have it. I have so many nice things. Please keep it. Here let me drape it over your shoulders."

"Only for tonight." Although Kate couldn't see herself, she felt different, prettier than usual. If only she could let her hair down like Betsy and wear a bright dress. What was happening to her? She had sat in a gilded carriage and now wanted a golden dress.

Betsy motioned to Kate. "Come, there is an opening." Kate followed Betsy to an open panel looking down on the

Great Hall. The music filtered to the rafters and surrounded Kate.

She looked around the walls to the ceiling, expecting to see other servants peering through cracks. Every few yards faces vied for a view of the courtiers.

"Do you see those colorful figures on the rafters and the eaves?" Betsy pointed to little cherub-like creatures in human form perched or hanging over the eaves of the ceiling and walls.

"What are they?"

"Eavesdroppers. They are placed there to watch over the activities of the courts. Like little spies. A bit superstitious for me. But it might make some think twice before acting foolish."

Kate giggled and glanced upward one more time, feeling the one with the green cap and big ears watched her. She wasn't here to look to the sky but to the dancing floor. All the tables had disappeared. Velvet-covered chairs graced the walls and a red velvet throne sat at the far end in front of Kate's view. Two smaller straight-backed padded chairs perched on either side.

"Where's the king?" Kate asked.

Betsy poked Kate's arm. "Silly. He has to make his grand entrance. But I'm sure it's soon."

Where was Peter? Kate didn't know where a man in his position would stand. And what was he wearing? Her angle wasn't the best for seeing faces. The green eyes would give him away and his stature.

Betsy leaned into Kate, trying to figure out her object of interest. "Who are you looking for?"

Could she share with her new friend her acquaintance with Peter? But what would she say? *He's my employer, my friend, my confidant. Someone I am starting to like and depend upon. Not one of those descriptions sounded right.*

"Someone I met in the garden."

"A gardener, in here? I don't think so. It is strictly courtiers. And this is actually a small crowd compared to the king's usual gatherings."

"You're right. Tell me who you recognize since I know no one."

Kate studied the ones Betsy pointed out in the next few minutes—the ladies in green satin and red silk, blue hues and simmering yellow, gowns with jewels and lace. Diamond tiaras, gold brooches, ruby pendants.

A hush hovered over the crowd and a guard hit his staff on the floor, sending an echo through the chamber. "King Charles and Lady Castlemaine." The hush turned to "ohs" and "ahs" and whispers as the couple greeted the guests and proceeded across the empty dance space to their royal posts.

"Enjoy yourselves." Charles nodded to the orchestra. "Maestro." His additional nod signaled the guests to begin dancing. Violins and flutes commenced in a heart pumping fashion.

Kate's jaw dropped in awe as the king led his mistress in the first dance. Such grace and poise from the couple but especially from the king. "Where do you suppose he learned to dance?"

"The French court, for sure." Betsy swayed with the music, a lively *branle,* where many couples held hands and danced in a line, then a circle.

Notes twisted and twirled around Kate. "I've never heard so many fiddles at one time."

"The king loves the violin and has many in his court. See the two musicians to the right of the violins? Do you know the instrument?"

Kate poked her head out a bit more at just the right angle. "No, I've never seen one. What is it?"

"The guitar. And the king's most skillful performer is Francisco Corbeta from Italy."

Kate closed her eyes and concentrated on his graceful style. "I can see why the king likes it."

"Already the instruments have gained in popularity like the violin, or fiddle, as you call it. If the dance follows the usual pattern after the *coranto,* we'll see the lively and boisterous courtly dances."

"Does the king dance all of them?" Kate had expected Charles to take a seat at any moment.

"Many of them. Lady Castlemaine will tire and step aside. He'll choose a few other damsels to join in the French dances."

"I'm tired just watching them." Kate let her eyes roam from the brilliance of the king to his courtiers. Where was Peter? She might hope he was without a partner, but no one of his stature and looks would be alone at the ball.

Only after a brief sweep of the room, she spotted him in his black velvet jacket and golden breeches with a voluptuous young lady with golden hair braided in ropes resting on her shoulders. Kate forgot to breathe and almost choked before quietly pulling air into her lungs.

"What is wrong? You are holding your throat as if you can't breathe. Who do you see down there?" Betsy's curiosity followed Kate's stare.

"The man with the lady in the green dress. He's the king's right-hand man and my employer, Peter."

Betsy gasped. "Well… he is handsome and dances well. I'm surprised I have not seen him before."

"He's been here a while and from what I gather, he doesn't like court life and keeps busy for the king elsewhere."

Perhaps that satisfied Betsy for now since the questions stopped.

What a perfect couple. Peter chose a beauty, or did she choose him? Kate was certain either one could have had anyone of his or her choice. True members of the court with their glitter and finery. The lady's emerald dress swirled against Peter's legs as they touched hands, arms, and waists during the intimate steps of the dance.

Kate blushed, realizing how closely the couple molded to each other during the dance. *Should I even be watching this? Perhaps Father and the Puritans are right—dancing with men is a sin.* But she would set aside those teachings for just one dance with Peter.

Yet even as he danced, he never met the young lady's eyes. He touched her as required, but he searched the room for someone else or something else, straining his neck above his partner. As he lifted his eyes to the next level, he caught her gaze and smiled as if seeing her brought pleasure that dancing didn't.

Don't be silly, Kate. He has one of the most beautiful women, a virtual princess, in his arms. And I am a servant still behind a panel.

Kate returned his smile, wanting to clap at his superb performance. Each time he twirled in the opposite direction, his eyes determined to return to her stare. Mesmerized, she explained her reluctance to pull away from her view. Just this one dance. *I'll pretend I'm in his arms, and he only has eyes for me.* It worked until the music stopped.

"I must go, Betsy."

"It is getting late." Betsy seemed very quiet and pensive. "Will I see you tomorrow?"

"I'll be in the garden in the afternoon as usual. Thank you for this experience."

Betsy gazed once more at the myriad of colors below. "If only we could have gotten to the dance floor."

"Oh, no. Not me. My senses couldn't have survived." Kate laughed. "Goodbye."

"Bye."

On the way home through the garden gates, Kate let the music surround her soul a little longer. Even as it faded, the images of color and light remained just in sight, almost able to grasp. *Thank you, God, for this evening, for the whole experience from the garden to the cooking, the beauty of vibrant color to this shawl on my shoulders.* She pulled the garment down over her bodice as a shield in front of her, flying in the wind. On the bridge the line between her two realities disappeared, leaving her stranded in the one of a country baker's daughter. Even so, no one could take her memories away.

Thank you, Peter.

She looked back at the palace wondering about the hours Peter had left with his pretty mistress of the court.

Thank you for my job, the time in the carriage, and the glimpse of you at the ball. I can't forget Betsy, my precious friend, and her gift of the shawl and showing me a window to another world.

Careful, Kate.

Turning a complete circle, she saw no one. The words didn't scare her but coaxed her to listen.

Remember, Me first. Hold loosely to the world.

Her fingers gripped the shawl, released to barely a touch, just enough for it to remain secure. She could keep the material without allowing it to keep her in its grip.

I understand, God.

She folded the dainty scarf in her room and put it in a corner of her trunk. Beauty and purity could exist side by side in a proper place of order. Worship of God required purity of purpose. Beauty existed for His pleasure and man's. But worship was for God only, a holy and loving act.

Help me see where You are in the beauty of people and things. It can't all be a sin, for You made the butterflies and flowers in every shade of vibrant color. I want to be seen as an object of Your creation, beautiful and pure.

Chapter Twelve

"Kate, wake up. It's past seven." Margaret sat on the edge of Kate's bed, moving and shaking like on a ship.

Her eyes refused to open. "Stop. Just a few more…"

"All right, but Father will be angry."

Margaret still sat there making the straw mattress tilt, threatening to deposit both on the floor. "Is it really so late?"

"Yes. What time did you get in? What was it like? Did you see the king? What…" Margaret strung her questions together as in one.

"Let's see. Midnight. Lots of food, music, and bright clothes. And yes, I saw the king."

"I'm so envious. Do you think I'll be able to go someday?"

"Not unless you get downstairs and cover for me."

"Will you tell me every detail later?" Her sister rose and rested her head on the door, dreamy eyes focused on Kate.

"Yes." Perhaps not every detail. She'd leave Peter out. If anyone knew her personal thoughts about him, life wouldn't be the same. "Now go so I can dress."

Why was she so tired? She hadn't danced or exerted any energy unless her heart pounding double time counted. Perhaps her early morning mind wondering about Peter, and the beauty on his arm or in his arms, contributed to her fatigue.

Cold water on her face spurred her senses to join the daylight creeping in the window. She paused, using seconds she didn't have, to rest her elbows on the window sill. The grass on the field in the distance glistened with the sun rising to the east. It would be one of those days she'd want to be outside not in a hot kitchen.

Her head shook as she pulled herself away. If she didn't get to work, her father wouldn't let her venture outside the door of their home at all today.

As she raced down the stairs and crept into the hallway, grabbing her apron and bonnet, Kate pulled in an extra measure of air and added a prayer.

Who should she connect with first? Mother or Father? Both were busy at their work tables. Why was she worried? Had she done anything wrong? No. They knew she'd stay out late at the palace.

"Good morning. Sorry I'm late."

Her mother looked up and winked at her. "So how did you sleep?"

"Fine. I didn't wake you, did I?"

Her father grunted but didn't glance from his kneading.

Mother snickered and patted Kate's hand on the table. "Your father hears everything except his snoring."

"Where do I need to start today?"

"Right here." Father pounded his kneaded dough on the center work table. "This is part of a dozen round loaves for your palace friends."

Kate caught his eye. He wasn't smiling. Did he feel he was losing a battle, and she was the pawn? On impulse she stepped beside him, kissed his floury cheek, and took her position at the table. His next grunt wasn't as gruff.

For the next two hours she gave details of the banquet to her mother and Margaret, when she had a lull from customers.

Robert and her father appeared to be uninterested, although Father never left the kitchen. Did he close his ears to anything dealing with the king and his court?

"Tell me about the ladies and their dresses?" Margaret clapped her hands and rested them under her chin anticipating the details.

The gruffy tone returned from her father. "I don't want to hear any of these stories in my house. Margaret does not need to know about the goings on at the court and neither do you, Kate. I told you the glitter and sparkle of the king's ways would influence you. So no more painting pictures for your sister."

"Yes, sir." Kate felt relief that she didn't have to lie and cover up her true feelings about the brilliant colors and lively dances and faces. Later, she would water down the details for Margaret, leaving her sister innocent of the true merriment of the court. In truth Kate saw very little of the wayward actions of the Merrie Monarch. Her few minutes from her high perch revealed splashes of color and fancy footwork but no lewdness or drunkenness.

She stopped her meandering thoughts before she speculated about what went on behind closed doors or between the courtiers, between Peter and his lady, and the king and his mistress.

A servant from the palace retrieved the bread around noon, so Kate's walk to the gardens bounced light and free, a stroll without the heavy basket. After she crossed the bridge, the sun's rays dancing on the river beckoned her to the banks. A small side gate let her amble down a path to the edge of the Thames.

She sank to a grassy carpet under a shade tree, reaching its limbs out over the water tumbling over the stones along the river's edge. Scanning the area to her right and left, she breathed deeply.

A high-pitched whine pierced the air. Kate snapped her head to the left and rose to her feet. A white drenched ball of fur clung to a rock and whimpered a low throaty sound. When it caught Kate's attention, the big brown eyes begged for help.

"Hold on, little puppy. Please don't be scared. I'll get you out of there." How much trust would a small animal have of a stranger? *Please, God, help him stay put.*

She eased into the shallow water, stepping on the stones. The whimpering stopped but not for a second did those soft brown eyes leave her face. With one swift move, Kate scooped the trembling, wet puppy into her arms and gingerly retraced her steps to the dry grass.

The small, white puppy with red spots shivered in her arms, not from the cold but most likely from fear. Kate sat for a few minutes and wrapped the near-drowned creature in her apron, soothing him with her sing-song words.

"Hush now. I'll take care of you." She rubbed his damp head. His floppy ears didn't remind her of anyone's dog in the village. "Where did you come from?"

Looking around, all she encountered was the gated grounds of the crown. Across the river the village loomed. Well, he didn't swim across, for he would have been carried down river and died.

"You must belong right here. I'll take you to Mr. Payne. He'll know what to do."

By this time the puppy had snuggled into the crook of her arm, resting his head close to her heart. No whimper or whine. His eyes closed. Kate prayed he was asleep not…no, she felt his heart beating against her arm.

The path from the banks to the upper grounds seemed to go on forever. Before she arrived at the entrance to the gardens, pages and guards raced out of the main palace entrance followed by a tall figure calling "Rollo. Rollo." His frilly shirt flopped in his hasty turns and spins. His wigless head revealed short cropped dark hair. Could it be?

The puppy slept on as the voice pulled Kate forward directly in the path of…the king. He placed his hands to his mouth again.

"Rollo." This time the puppy opened his eyes, whined, and wiggled.

"Rollo?" Kate smiled as the squirmy puppy responded by licking her hand.

Kate curtsied as best she could with her burden bouncing in her arms. "Sir, Your Majesty, I think this must be Rollo."

Charles stood still with hands on his hips, towering in front of Kate. "Well, well. I believe you have our missing little prince."

His ringless hands reached out for the puppy that jumped into the powerful arms and licked the king's face. Kate watched in wonder, forgetting the protocol not to stare at the king.

Puppy and king turned to Kate, both sets of dark eyes focused on her. One smiled ear to ear while the other extended his pink tongue in repeated jerking motions.

The king placed one hand behind his back and bowed. "And who is the fearless rescuer?" His eyes twinkled gently.

"Kate Sinclair, sir." Surprisingly her voice didn't shake or stutter. Why would it in front of a gentle, soft-spoken man?

"Where did you find this rascal?"

"Hanging onto a rock in the river." The king's eyebrow shot up, and Kate smiled, realizing trespassing was not a notable characteristic.

"I work here, sir, in the gardens with Mr. Payne. I was on my way when I stopped on the banks and saw…Rollo."

"I see. To us you are an angel." Rollo seemed to nod in agreement. "Please come in. I want to reward you."

"Oh, no, sir. I would have done it for anyone's puppy." Could she tell the king "no"?

"Well, at least come meet Rollo's mother, who I'm sure misses him greatly. And if you like dogs, you can come visit them often in the courtyard."

The courtyard. The king's courtyard. In the walls of the palace. This she could not refuse.

"I would like that, Your Majesty."

As she followed the king and his guards, Kate compared the

picture in the parish church of the king and her glimpses last night to the man strolling in front of her. Without his long curly wig and heavily jeweled coat, Charles II appeared as any other man, yet still regal in his manners and speech. The love of his puppy threw her off a bit. She'd heard stories of the King Charles spaniels but had never seen one up close. The first King Charles introduced the breed to court. From what she witnessed, the small dog loved people, especially the king.

As she stopped under the arch of the red-brick entrance, passing the statues of lions and dragons, Kate ran her hands down her apron, now muddied with her river bath from Rollo, hoping to better her appearance. She consciously criticized her black worn and scuffed boots, peeking from under her gray skirt.

Touching her white bonnet hiding her long unruly ringlets, she caught the eyes of ladies mingling in the back court talking to gentlemen. They bowed in the king's presence and stared at the unlikely entourage of disrobed king, common villager, and contented puppy. Kate felt the scrutiny of her garb against the lavenders, yellows, and greens of the ladies' attire.

I shouldn't be here. Could I turn now and run? Can one run from the king? No, I am invited, simply dressed and humble, into the courtyards by His Majesty himself.

Her gaze left the faces of strangers to the windows and elaborate balcony in the first court, while cobblestones led them further inward. Kate remembered to turn around once in the middle of the next courtyard. High above the arch, the old clock of Henry VIII sat between two turrets flanked by statues of two emperors. She forgot who they were. Perhaps one was Augustus. But the other? She shielded her eyes to get a better view.

"Emperors Virellius and Augustus," the familiar voice of Peter whispered close to her ear.

She wasn't startled, half expecting him to be present in this environment somewhere. "Yes, I tried to remember." She turned to Peter who captivated her more than the elaborate clock.

"What are you doing here?" What a silly question. He belonged here.

Peter laughed. "I have the same question. I was searching for the king, and I found him here with you. So, am I correct in concluding that you found the missing Rollo?"

Kate bowed her head and twirled her bonnet strings around her fingers. "Poor thing. He was drowning in the river holding on for his dear life. If I hadn't …" She didn't want to voice what might have happened to the much-loved animal.

"As you can see, Charles is very enamored with his puppies."

After skirting a huge elaborate fountain, they passed under yet another arch into a green courtyard to find the king surrounded by fifteen to twenty spaniels. Kate saw him bend to the ground and place Rollo next to a slightly larger red and white version—his mother. She smiled as the scene reminded her of the biblical shepherd who left his ninety-nine sheep to find the one lost sheep. To any other, one missing puppy out of so many wouldn't matter. But to this king, Rollo symbolized his deep love and concern for God's creatures. Did that apply to mankind as well?

A tear rolled down Kate's cheeks. "How can such a powerful man care for something so small and insignificant?"

Peter shifted his gaze from Kate to the king. "Last year he lost a brother and sister to smallpox. He's seen his father beheaded as well as family members and friends. He lost country and countrymen. Believe me, he cares. Underneath his robes and crown, this is what is real. You and I may not give love so freely without moral bounds, but he does—for dogs, women, whether royal or common. Life is for him a celebration."

Conversation halted as the king, wiping his hands on his white lacy shirt, approached. "Peter, I see you've met our heroine. Kate has done the court a great service." He draped his arm around Peter's shoulder.

Peter smiled. "More than you know. This young lady also coordinated the banquet last night and prepared the pheasant and venison with her own special spices as well as the delicious tarts and custards."

The king leaned back and let his laughter resound off the courtyard walls. "How ever did you find her, Peter? Is there any way we can whisk you off to London to show my cooks a thing or two?"

Kate shook her head. "Oh no, sir. My father would never approve." Her hand went to her mouth regretting the words. He could question his or her loyalty if she wasn't more careful.

"Have no fear. I'd never take you from your father's home or this village. I'm happy here, as is my court." He leaned in closer. "Promise me when I'm here you'll continue to present your delicate fare."

"By all means, Your Majesty. I'll also make sure your gardens contain the best herbs and spices."

"Indeed. A cook, gardener, rescuer. An emblem of something pure." The king's gaze roamed from her head to her toes. "Don't let this one go, Peter."

"Uh. Yes, sir. I'll do my best to keep her close at hand." Peter stuttered. Was he embarrassed by the king's praise of her skills? She certainly was.

"Good. Good. Now, I must change for a game of tennis. I'm afraid these courts haven't been used in decades." Charles chuckled. "Maybe since the robust Henry built them. Put them on your list, Peter. I want courts to please any in Europe."

The king with his shirttail hanging to his knees released Peter and walked toward the inner court trailed by four puppies. "By the way, Lady Castlemaine has some changes to the gardens to promote. Perhaps you and Miss Kate could meet with her tomorrow morning."

Peter bowed in answer. Kate's gaze darted to Peter who covered a huge grin with his hand. Hopefully, he didn't just answer for her. Her list of excuses grew as the seconds ticked by.

I have to work. Father would forbid me. I have nothing to wear. And why would my opinion matter to the mistress of the king?

After she was certain the king had disappeared, she jabbed Peter in the ribs with her elbow. "He wasn't serious, was he? I can't meet the Countess or Duchess or…his Mistress." She whispered at the end. "Someone here is mistaken or crazy, and it's not me." She crossed her arms, emphasizing her resolve to stand firm and avoid surrender.

The snickering from the courtiers stopped, and Peter stepped in front of Kate, casting a shadow over her, allowing her to meet his green gaze without shielding the sun. The crinkles by his eyes showed he was still amused, although his deep smile retreated. He mimicked her pose, arms crossed, feet firm, shoulders stiff.

"Do you think I had anything to do with that? The king didn't even know you existed before today."

"But I promised to not become involved in the court. You have to refuse for me."

His hands went to her shoulders, drawing her gaze farther into his as if to hypnotize her. "Let me guess. Your father told you the court, and perhaps the king's mistress, is a den of vipers ready to entice its prey with its evil ways to a sure death."

"How did you know? Those were his words almost word for word."

"The Scriptures. I have been to a service a time or two."

She tried to shake free of his intense stare, but his grip and firm words drew her back. "Then you know I can't go into that kind of place."

"Look at me, Kate. I'm not evil or dead, and I'm part of the court almost daily."

"How do you deal with the impurity all around you?"

"My thoughts aren't impure. In fact, I look at the lifestyle of the courtiers and royal family and shudder. I have decided I can live in their world without it consuming me. If I had more influence or power, believe me I would change it. It's not all bad. You saw the king and his simple love for his dogs. And you've made a new friend in Betsy. I've learned to find the good. And you can too."

"So, you're not going to tell Lady Castlemaine that I can't meet with her?"

"Not unless you beg me. I think you can add some glimpses of purity to her otherwise extravagant life."

Kate glanced at her dark skirt and simple overall attire. A giggle sprouted from within her jumbled midsection. "I'll probably be the first simple Puritan-clad girl in her presence, actually summoned by the king."

"And the prettiest creature in all Hampton Court." He caressed her cheek with his palm and thumb. Could he feel the heat of her blush ease under his touch?

"You're just saying that to make me say yes."

"It's true in my eyes."

"Well, you haven't seen Betsy. And I saw you with your lady last night. Honestly, is there even a comparison?"

"You are right. No comparison at all. You shine far above Madeline and any of the others."

"Madeline. A pretty name."

He guided her to the edge of the courtyard by a large tree and tilted her chin up, catching her gaze. "Pretty on the outside doesn't mean pretty on the inside. You, by the way, are pretty inside and out. Pretty and pure. And I can't let this court take that from you."

As he bent his head to her and coerced her face closer to his, Kate imagined his kiss as from a prince, the one in her dreams. Before contact, she pulled away from him, putting his charming face a good foot from hers.

"I'm sorry, Kate. I thought…"

She adjusted her bonnet and swiped the edge of her eye, catching the lonely tear involuntarily escaping. "You weren't thinking of me. When you closed your eyes, I'm sure you saw another lass. But no harm done."

Peter coughed to clear his throat. Hanging his head, avoiding her gaze, Peter confirmed by his actions what Kate knew as true. He was embarrassed by his *faux pas*. She turned away before he once again captured her affection.

"Right." Walking beside her around the back of the palace toward the kitchen, Peter lightly squeezed her elbow. "I will talk to Lady Castlemaine and schedule a meeting for tomorrow at eleven in the morning. Do you think you can get away?"

"I'll work something out with as little detail as possible. After all, it does pertain to the gardens, so I won't really be lying."

"I'm sorry if this is awkward for you. But the project itself will be amusing. The chance to form a special garden fit for a king."

Kate smiled at Peter's enthusiasm. He was as excited as she was to confront this adventure. Though they probably differed in the degree of nervousness and uncertainty.

"I do look forward to it, at least the part after the initial meeting with the king's mistress. If only I could be behind a screen or send Betsy in to talk for me."

"You'll do fine. I'll be right beside you."

"Yes." *Making me more nervous and more conscious about my attire.* Peter would be the perfect image of a courtier and Kate the epitome of a simple country lass. When would her heart rate retreat to its normal strong continual beat instead of this stopping and starting, rapid then breathless? This might not be a den of vipers to Kate, but it definitely was an unpredictable den of surprises.

"I must leave you here for the moment." At his words Kate jerked her head in the direction of the privet entrance.

"I don't know yet if I should thank you for coming to my rescue in the courtyard. Your presence has landed me in more trouble." Her smile assured him that trouble had a possible pleasant outcome.

"Then thank me later, when you see the results."

"Yes, perhaps."

Peter brought her hand to his lips and brushed her fingers with his warm kiss.

Once through the opening, Kate hid behind the wall of shrubs and forced her rambunctious heart to slow. It wouldn't do to have Mr. Payne question her flushed cheeks or stilted words. Already she'd have to explain her muddy apron and tardiness.

Before she left for her home at dusk, Kate dropped a note off with Mrs. Downs for Betsy. Kate's mind had steadied with her concentration on the clipping of some overgrown vines by the hot house. Her quickly jotted note read:

Please meet me in the kitchen if you can in the morning at half past ten. I am to meet with your mistress and need some advice. Thank you, Kate.

Someone needed to tell her how to act and what to say to an acting queen. Peter wasn't much help since he was one of them. She needed the help of a servant and a female. God sent Betsy to her, knowing all of this would come to pass. But Kate questioned why God wanted her, Kate, the daughter of a baker, to set foot in a palace. She might never understand her Creator.

She realized more and more her activities centered around the person of Peter. Ever since he walked in the bakery door, their paths continued to cross. Whether it was part of God's plan or not, Kate seemed bound up in the life of Peter for now.

The yellow, orange, and red of the setting sun reflected off the river running under the bridge that lighted her way back to her village and abode, her true place under the protection of her father. As long as she divided her existence into reality and dream, she could face the discrepancies. Her reality brought safety, love, comfort, consistency; whereas her fantasy world across the Thames delivered excitement, frights, uncertainties, hopes, challenges, and false promises.

Chapter Thirteen

What was Peter thinking? If only he had stayed hidden in the alcove of the courtyard and watched Kate from a distance. But her presence with the king drew him from the shadows. Why he thought she needed protection, he didn't know. It was obvious she could take care of herself just by being the sweet Kate he'd come to cherish.

He paced his square room with hands stuffed in his waistband. The meeting with Lady Castlemaine proved she really did have plans for Hampton Court. The details would spill forth tomorrow when Kate arrived. His big mouth succeeded in drawing Kate's innocent being deeper into the court. The thing he loved about her—her simple pure inner self—he kept exposing to the thing he disliked most—the deceptive, materialistic court. Hopefully, he hadn't unwillingly destroyed a truly good creature of God.

He sat at his desk and by candlelight composed a brief letter to his mother—the second in a few days. He planned to leave in two days for his visit. Setting his plume aside, he held his head between his hands, closed his eyes, and racked his jumbled mind for solutions. All women in his life were positioned on a cliff with danger lingering. His mother fought the will to continue her life on earth. His sister had to feel abandoned and unloved, lost to her family. Madeline continued to pressure Peter for a deeper dalliance in the sinful ways of court life, ready to become his mistress. And Kate. At one point miles from the court, she stood inches from the line. One step, a new dress, one taste of this life, one kiss, one wayward courtier, and she would forever be changed.

How could he juggle all these concerns? The priests in his life said, "Give your problems to God." The same priests beheaded a king, fought in the civil war, and now embraced a new king and a renewed church. What did they know?

After making a list of priorities for Geoffrey, the overseer for the month of Peter's absence, he tried to sleep. Despite the awkwardness of the meeting tomorrow, Peter smiled, visualizing Kate in the presence of make-believe and temporary beauty. He already knew who would shine at the presentation.

THE GIRLS MANAGED to keep their mother at the breakfast table. "Please, let Margaret come with me, Mother. Betsy wants to meet her, and Margaret has such an interest in sewing as does Betsy." Kate had devised a plan based on truth, although also a cover for her early hour at the palace. Betsy *did* want to meet Margaret, but not necessarily today. Kate needed an excuse to meet Peter and keep her appointment with the king's mistress.

"What kind of girl is Betsy? Where is her family? Who could place a girl in the king's court and leave her?" Her mother had valid questions. Ones that Kate held a curiosity but hadn't asked. Somewhere under her friend's shiny exterior was a story.

"She's the same as any other eighteen-year-old girl. Full of life and hope and dreams. She's a servant, Mother, not a princess or a duchess." Kate failed to add that Betsy dressed in brilliant colors and fabrics spun with fine threads and also served as a lady-in-waiting to the number one woman in England.

"I could learn a lot from her, and it might help me when I open my own dress shop." Margaret sat as still as she could, adding a little bounce every few minutes.

"You're dreaming, child. Do you think this village needs a dressmaker?"

"Yes, and if not this village, then another one." Margaret's harsh words startled Kate. Her twelve-going-on-twenty-year-old sister usually guarded her words a bit more.

"Give her a chance, Mother. Anyway, she's the only one of us who has any talent for sewing."

"All right. Go meet this seamstress. If you like her, Margaret, you can spend a few afternoons here with her. But I can't allow you to dwell at the palace for any long amounts of time. Your father won't allow another one of his daughters to enter the gates of Hampton Court often."

Margaret jumped from her seat with enough force to make the bench teeter. Kate righted it before it tumbled, alerting Father to the excitement. "Thank you, thank you." Margaret covered Mother's face with kisses.

Releasing her daughter from her embrace, Mother stood with hands on her hips. "Enough of that. You both have two hours of work before your meeting. Go, before I change my mind."

Kate saw a woman with a loving heart struggling to do the right things for her daughters. *Please, God, help us not to be a disappointment. Give me wisdom in my dealings with the court to please You and my parents.*

Arm in arm Kate and Margaret entered the gardens and wove their way to the kitchen. Mrs. Downs and Betsy had their heads close together in a whisper. What could a cook and a seamstress have to discuss?

"Good morning." Kate put her question aside, remembering Margaret by her side. "I'd like you to meet my sister, Margaret."

For once Margaret was speechless. Kate wondered if her decision had been right. Margaret stood as tall as possible reaching Kate's shoulder. Their clothes were identical as well as their caps but nothing else. Kate turned to her freckle-faced sister flushed from their walk. The large blue eyes against rosy cheeks stared at the other women.

Betsy broke the spell and rushed to Kate's side. "Oh, Kate, what a pleasant surprise." She took Margaret's hand in hers. "Kate has told me about you. We have a lot in common, I think. I always wanted a sister like you. But I only had brothers."

"I have a brother too." Margaret regained her voice and smiled at Betsy.

"Please sit down and share a piece of cake with us." Mrs. Downs touched Margaret's elbow and guided her to the long table. "We were just talking about you, Kate."

"I saw your heads together and wondered."

Betsy reached on the bench beside her. "I made something for you, for your meeting this morning with my Lady."

"For me?" Kate wiped her hands on her apron before accepting the gift. She unfolded a crisp light-blue apron trimmed in a delicate white lace and a cap of the same soft material and color.

"Why, Betsy, they are beautiful."

"Lady Castlemaine appreciates beauty, and I thought this would complement your hair and eyes."

Kate touched her cap with the thick tresses within. Betsy didn't wear a cap and let her hair flow down her back. *I could never do that.*

"Here, let me show you what I was thinking." Betsy removed Kate's cap and a long braid tumbled down as well as shorter pieces around her face. With swift gentle fingers, Betsy placed a new cap on Kate's head and left the braid down her back. From the corner of her eyes, Kate saw wisps of hair remaining outside the cap, the strings of the bonnet tied at the back of her neck rather than the front.

Margaret clapped and untied Kate's apron and placed the

blue one over her gray frock. The softness of the fabric reminded her of a fluffy kitten, not one coarse spot, only a smooth surface. "I would never work in this. Betsy, it is beautiful."

"Yes, on you it is. And you are right—it is for show not work. Every girl deserves something pretty every so often."

Kate remembered the dress she had hidden in the loft. Would she ever have a time to dress for "show"? Now was a time, although even in the new apron she felt unworthy.

"Betsy, what do I say to her? I will be speechless. She couldn't possibly want my opinion."

"Just listen at first. If an idea comes to your head, present it slowly, giving her the opportunity to accept it or reject it. She has spoken of the gardens before, so she has her own ideas."

"Yes. And I have the overseer with me. He'll do most of the speaking."

Betsy widened her eyes and raised her eyebrows before turning to Margaret. "Would you like to come with me to see where I work? Kate had asked me earlier, and I think it's a wonderful idea. My mistress will be busy with Kate."

Margaret sought Kate's permission. She nodded approval. "I only have an hour, but I would love to see anything you can show me."

"Who knows? Maybe we'll make this into a routine." Betsy shrugged her shoulders and winked at Margaret.

"Mother said we'd have to meet at my house in the future."

"I've so wanted to go to the village to see where Kate lives."

"You never told me that," Kate said. "It is ever so small and unlike what you are used to."

"But it has family and noise and all the things I miss."

Was it her imagination or did Kate glimpse puddles of moisture in Betsy's eyes? If she did the evidence disappeared as her friend, swinging her head around, took Margaret's hand and promised, "I'll keep her safe and send her home in an hour."

Margaret didn't even hesitate or wave goodbye. Was Kate

right in letting her be swallowed up in the belly of the court? Whether a right or wrong decision, Kate's prayer followed them and hung over Margaret in Kate's absence.

PLACING his hand on the door frame, Peter ducked his head before entering the kitchen. The breeze from the oak trees near the palace served to lift the heat from the kitchen. He didn't know if Henry designed it that way or one of the later monarchs. Whoever included the high ceilings and many windows saved Mrs. Downs many stifling days in the heat.

"Hello." Peter poked his head into a smaller chamber where he found Kate and Mrs. Downs sharing a piece of pie. Caught with spoons in their mouths, they both looked at him wide-eyed. "Now you have to share with me."

Kate pushed her chair back and walked to a cabinet to retrieve a saucer. Something was different about her. He put his finger on his chin. Her thick auburn braid resting on her back seemed to be woven with golden strands. When she faced him again, he pinpointed the difference.

"Kate, you have a new apron and cap and..." He stopped before he said anything more personal about her golden laced hair caressing her forehead and cheeks.

"Do you like them?" Her grin reached her eyes as she swung her hips ever so slightly.

"Of course. And who convinced you to add this colorful adornment?"

"Betsy made it for me for meeting Lady Castlemaine."

"You look very nice." Peter sat, before he made a fool of himself and reached out to touch the delicate lace on the trim of her cap. Diverting his eyes to his gooseberry pie, he studied her from a safe distance between bites.

"I don't know if I agree with you taking Kate in to meet the mistress," Mrs. Downs whispered. "Surely, you can go on your own."

Kate sat across the table, facing both of them. "But, Mrs. Downs, I want to go, just to satisfy my curiosity."

"Look at her, Mrs. Downs. I can't argue with her and the king's mistress." Peter laughed at Kate's changed attitude since yesterday. Fear might lurch under her skin, but her outward façade reeked of determination. He had a feeling if he didn't take her, she'd go herself.

"Are you ready, Miss Sinclair?"

"Yes, Mr. Reresby."

He offered his arm as part of their resumed formality for the austere occasion. This everyday occurrence for him was indeed an important milestone for Kate. Her innocence and purity beckoned him to protect her even in this low-profile situation.

Peter determined to make Kate's experience as memorable as possible. As they entered the Great Hall, he slowed his pace and halted, for he had lost his companion. No one else was around this morning, probably sleeping off a late night's activity. Kate twirled around on her toes with her head thrown back.

"I saw all of this from above," she said between breaths. "Now I'm one of the dancers."

Her weaving and flying across the room resembled a waltz, perhaps of a butterfly. Peter added his hand on her waist and captured her hand in the air. The least he could do was offer her the dance she didn't have at the ball. For someone who had never danced, Kate displayed light feet and a willingness to follow his lead.

As the imaginary music stopped, Kate let out soft giggles as she pointed to the ceiling. "Look closely at the eaves. Do you see the funny creatures staring at us?"

Peter focused and saw colorful, playful statues peering down at them. "I have never noticed them."

"Betsy said they are eavesdroppers, spying on the humans

below. Now they have something to tell about us." Her hands covered her flushed cheeks. "Do I still look presentable?"

"Yes." He stared and stepped back. "We need to keep going in order to make our appointment." *And to prevent me from continuing this intimate dance.*

He kept Kate close in the numerous hallways. House servants and ladies in waiting, pages and manservants dotted the passageways, waiting for their masters and mistresses to summon them.

"Lady Castlemaine's rooms are straight ahead and to the left. Personally, I think she has the best view of the grounds."

"Of course, she would, Peter. Who else would be entitled to the grandest rooms?"

"The king?" he joked. Even the king would give up his pleasure for hers. "Anyway, she has plans for a new wing, leaving the Tudor structure for other guests."

A guard let them enter the hall to the suite of rooms. Peter scratched on the door. He prayed Madeline wouldn't open it. She didn't. A pretty young girl smiled up at him, curtsied, and ushered them inside.

"Come in, Peter. We're expecting you." Lady Castlemaine sat at a large table covered with what he surmised as plots and maps of Hampton Court and the gardens.

He bowed with his right hand in front and gestured with his left for Kate to do the same. Since he heard the shifting of her feet and the crinkling of her skirt, he guessed she had been in a curtsy before his suggestion.

"Rise. Rise. Bring your little beauty to me."

Kate took his outstretched arm and placed her hand on his for her introduction. No sweaty hand or hesitation in step. In fact, Kate didn't look at him at all. Her smile and attention rested solely on Lady Castlemaine. *Another one under her spell. I'm ready to peel her away if she's pulled in too much.* Did he trust Kate to know when to pull back? Innocent enough now on the part of the Lady, but with future encounters, he wasn't so sure.

"My Lady, I'd like to introduce Miss Kate Sinclair of East Molesey."

Lady Castlemaine stretched her hand out for Kate to touch.

"My Lady."

"Such a sweet-looking young lady. What a surprise to find her here. Peter has told me a bit of you. He seems to think you can work miracles. Is that true?"

Kate laughed, breaking the spell, to Peter's delight. If Kate could be herself around Lady Castlemaine, perhaps his worries were for naught.

"I doubt they are miracles. But I do like to restore and rescue neglected plants and revitalize forgotten ones."

"Perfect." The woman clapped and spread her hands over the charts on the table. "I have a project for you then. The Privy Garden appears like this mess on the table—chaos. I want order and restoration. I've walked the grounds and think there is promise, perhaps a chance to regain a bit of its purity and simplicity."

Peter realized the comparison was accurate. The papers in front of him had no apparent order or purpose—no neat stacks or symmetrical leanings. But he knew each sheet had a purpose if only an artist could find it.

Kate stood at the edge of the table scrutinizing all that Peter saw. "I can try, My Lady."

"It's a pretty day. Perhaps we should stroll the garden and let you see for yourself. I just hate to think it is hopeless." Lady Castlemaine raised her hand and snapped her fingers. Very quickly, a maid ran to her side. Grabbing the back of the chair, the shy girl released her mistress from her seated position.

"Follow me. Elaine, you may let two, and only two of the dogs, go with us."

Peter snickered and caught Kate's eyes, wide with unasked questions. At the door he whispered, "The king's mistress only tolerates the king's spaniels. I think she's a bit envious of their unregulated access to Charles."

"Oh."

They followed as an entourage down a private staircase out into the Privy Gardens—the neglected grounds of a once regal garden.

SO MANY QUESTIONS. *Am I allowed to ask them? How can I help if I am silent?*

"Lady Castlemaine, may I ask you a few questions as we walk?" The woman walked about two yards in front of Kate.

The lady halted and turned to Kate. "Of course."

"Do you want to keep the basic layout of plots, terraces, and walkways?"

"Yes, and I want to add little cabinets in the brick walls with seats in the shape of little towers. Places of seclusion along the path. But that is for the architects to decide."

For a moment the king's mistress spun in circles with the two puppies chasing her slippers. She lost her royal façade and existed in a make-believe place or at least a place not yet created.

"Charles has plans to build a wing for me overlooking the gardens with a balcony. Therefore, I want this area to be spectacular."

"I think I understand." Kate walked to a plot built up and outlined with timber posts. She parted the vines and found the dirt. Very few bulbs and plants could break through the thick foliage but with much work the original gardens could flourish again. "The soil is good and most of the vines are on the surface, easy to clip away. Once they are removed, I think you will find some plants wanting to burst through again."

She stood and checked a few shrubs and trees. "The same applies to these trees. A good pruning and clearing of debris will give them new life."

Lady Castlemaine clapped her hands once. "That's what I want to hear. You may have as many servants as you need to complete the task. I want the best rose bushes and bulbs. The paths need to be cleared and new gravel added."

The group continued to walk as the determined woman gave her orders. Kate hoped Peter, who remained unusually quiet, took notes. How could Kate possibly remember everything?

The lady faced Peter with straight, serious lips. "Young man, this bower is a necessity. I want you to organize men to turn it, shape it, and relieve some of the weight from the years of neglect. We'll have royalty from all nations walk through our gardens. I want them finer than any in Europe."

"Even Versailles?" Peter questioned.

"Yes, Charles has plans for canals, and I want a vineyard. We have plans for a summer house, orchards, and more gardens. It can be done." A dramatic pause ensued before she added, "It will be done."

Kate shook her head and for the first time doubted her role in the lady's scheme. Peter must have seen her shake, for he came to her side and patted her arm. "Have no fear, Kate. Your role is with the Privy Garden, not the whole estate."

"Oh yes. This is an intimate endeavor, the most personal and important. Here is where your magic will work." Kate felt Lady Castlemaine meant to encourage her, draw her away from refusal.

"Just like it has in the herb and vegetable gardens." Peter's words reassured her, for the other gardens had been transformed with many hours of labor and many hands. Kate wouldn't forget God's role in the process either.

Kate sighed and pulled in a deep breath. "All right. I'm committed to do my best. I've heard the beds were full of strawberries, roses, mint, sweet Williams, carnations, and primroses. I see hints of wild ones amidst the brambles. Do you want those to remain?"

"Yes, in abundance. More than any queen of Henry VIII imagined. And…" Lady Castlemaine strayed off the path searching for something specific. "Peter, I've heard there are twenty brass sundials scattered throughout the garden. Have you seen one?"

Kate searched alongside Peter, lifting vines from the surface of the beds.

"Here's one." Peter cleared the tangled weeds away from a tarnished sundial. "With some polishing they could shine from the roof tops like the stories said they did a hundred years ago."

Lady Castlemaine ran her hand over the brass structure. "This will be our gift to the king. The restoration of this garden will be a symbol of his restoration."

Kate thought it was a lovely gesture, but the amount of funds needed for this project shattered her reasoning. Where would the Lady secure that amount of money? Kate remembered when Cromwell brought in statues and fountains and started projects at the palace but never had the funds to pay the workers or artists. Would it be the same?

Somehow Peter read her mind. "Lady Castlemaine, how much of this does Charles want to do now? In other words, is he willing to pay for the extensive labor?"

Kate's opinion of Peter rose even higher when he blatantly confronted the king's mistress about financial affairs.

Lady Castlemaine laced her arm through Peter's and continued on the walkway. Kate and the others followed, able to hear every word the woman said.

"Have you heard about the negotiations the king is having with Portugal about his bride's dowry?" Kate heard the Lady spit the word "bride" out with a strong gust of venom, a hiss.

"Yes, Catherine of Braganza will come with many financial benefits."

"Hmmm. And His Majesty has promised my position will remain intact. Believe me, this revitalizing of Hampton Court is only part of what he'll give me. Catherine of Portugal might give him Tangier, the Seven Islands of Bombay, trading privileges in Brazil and the East Indies, and two million Portuguese crowns, but I have to only give myself for his love. I have the better deal —wouldn't you say?"

Kate noticed he didn't say anything. How could the position of mistress be better than the godly position of wife, established by God? Lady Castlemaine made it sound as if her sinful life was the proper, pure way to live, giving the king children while married to another man and building rooms and gardens to welcome more courtly pleasures. Kate didn't begin to understand or want to for that matter.

Yet, she desired to be a part of the recreation of the Privy Garden to show off God's glory, not man's.

"Elena, have refreshments brought to my chambers and take these puppies with you." Lady Castlemaine shooed the dogs away from around her skirts while Elena dangled biscuits to capture their attention.

With a flip of her hand in the air, Lady Castlemaine motioned for Kate to come beside her. "You will join us for refreshments?"

"I beg your pardon, My Lady, I must join Mr. Payne in the gardens for a few hours. I appreciate the challenge you have extended to us." Kate made sure Peter knew he had a share in the endeavor. Leaning forward she spied him on the other side of the woman, and he returned her glare with a wink.

"I'm sure you and Peter can work out the specifics. I'll give him a detailed drawing of my plans."

Upon entering the courtyard from the back of the palace, Kate planned her departure. In the middle of her curtsy, Betsy appeared from a staircase.

"My Lady." The girl bowed and walked toward them. When she reached them, she linked her arm with Kate. Lady Castlemaine and Peter bowed their heads at her.

Kate wanted to leave immediately with her friend to a more familiar society. Betsy tugged on her arm and stopped for a few seconds locked in a stare with Peter. Did she know him? Should she introduce them? Before she could open her mouth, Betsy jerked her away. Her touch changed from a soft nudge to a forceful pull.

"Slow down, Betsy." Once they rounded the building Betsy released her. "At least I said goodbye before you dragged me away. What is the hurry?"

With arms crossed Betsy asked, "Who was that man?"

"That's Peter Reresby. Haven't you met?" Perhaps that was the problem. She either didn't like Peter or didn't like Kate knowing him. It made no sense to Kate.

"No. Is that the overseer you talk about?" Betsy fidgeted with the seams on her skirt.

"Yes. We met with your mistress. What's made you upset?"

"Oh, nothing. Don't worry about me." Her frown changed to a forced smile not reaching her eyes as her hands stilled by her side. "I wanted to tell you about Margaret. We had a lovely time. She's a great student. If your mother approves, I'm going to come by your house and show her some more of the latest skills with the needle."

When Betsy mentioned Margaret, tension left her face, releasing a genuine effortless grin.

"I'm so glad. Mother will enjoy meeting you. She feels she knows you already."

"I don't know how that could be good considering my place in the court."

"She'll get over that like she did with me working in the palace gardens and kitchen. And perhaps we'll avoid my father. Wear something plain, and you might blend in with us." Kate looked down at her apron, expecting to see her usual white one. Instead, the soft-blue lacy one caught her eye. "By the way, I thank you for this creation. I felt a little more acceptable with Lady Castlemaine, and Peter commented too."

Betsy's shoulders snapped back. "You're welcome. It's a pleasure sewing for you." Her words were quick and clipped as if she wanted to move onto another subject. Did Peter's name evoke fear or disappointment?

Kate stepped toward the larger kitchen. "I must go to work now. I'll see you soon."

"All right. Margaret is to send word when I can visit your home."

"Soon, I hope."

Kate joined Mrs. Downs for a light luncheon after she retrieved her own old apron from the kitchen peg. She certainly couldn't wear anything so fine in the garden on her hands and knees.

"What is that, Mrs. Downs?" Kate pointed to a large, prickly golden-brown skinned item with thick green leaves on the top set in the middle of the table.

"A pineapple."

"And what do you do with it?" She touched the hard thick shell.

"I don't know. It was a gift to the king from a guest. All I know is it's a fruit from the Indies. There are three more by the window."

"May I pick it up?"

"Of course. If you can figure out what to do with it, let me know. I sent word with a courtier to ask the king what he wants done with them." Mrs. Downs set two plates down with ham, rolls, and cheese for a light meal.

Kate poked at the pineapple before picking it up, judging where the prickly points were harmless. With two hands she brought it to her nose. "It smells sugary and fresh, definitely a fruit. I wonder what color it is on the inside."

"It could be purple for all I know."

"No, the aroma is like sunshine and flowers, so I'm guessing orange or yellow or pink."

"Now you're dreaming. Set it down and eat your food."

Each time Kate brought her hand to her mouth, the mysterious fruit essence circled. It probably tasted good just by itself, but her mind wrapped around using it in a custard or cake.

"Let me know when you get it open, Mrs. Downs. I have a suspicion it will be quite tasty."

The rest of the afternoon loomed uneventful. It needed to be for Kate's sanity. As she weeded and pampered the plants, the morning's events rolled through her mind. From Peter to the Privy Garden to the pineapple, Kate prayed for continued peace and purpose.

Chapter Fourteen

At Charles' request Peter delayed his visit to his mother. Although he was not one of the king's ministers, Peter often found himself alone in the king's private quarters discussing issues of state. The plush velvet sofas and chairs replaced the crisscrossed logs by a campfire. How many battles had they fought with their stories and imaginary conquests? If all their dreams had succeeded, Charles would be king of half of Europe with mountains of gold and hundreds of palaces.

"What do you think?" Charles handed Peter the parchment with the details of the dowry he requested from Portugal at his marriage to the Portuguese princess. One hand held a goblet and the other petted the spaniel sprawled at his side and over his lap.

Peter braced his elbows on his knees and leaned forward. "The most important part of this to me is the transfer of the Bombay Islands to England. The access to trade with India could be a financial boon for us for years to come."

"That's what I like about you, Peter." The king laughed, shaking the spaniel's head in his lap. "You think of the future. Here I am dwelling on the present, the actual funds I'll get soon, and you look beyond to even the next generation."

"I can do that because I'm not the one managing or spending the money."

"That reminds me. You haven't seen the portrait of Catherine." Charles reached behind him, set his goblet down, and procured a framed portrait. "Tell me what you think. Will all this wealth be worth marriage to her?"

Peter hoped he could be honest, hoped the girl held true beauty, hoped she would please Charles. He held the image in front of him and could honestly say, "Yes, Charles, she is a beautiful princess. You shouldn't have any qualms about her being at your side."

But could she take the place of Lady Castlemaine? The young princess had an innocent, sweet beauty; whereas, his mistress boasted a wild, desirable rare beauty seeping into her actions, words, and grace. Peter wondered how the new queen would fare in Lady Castlemaine's presence.

"I'll sign the official marriage treaty the last week of June. I need you to return here after your journey and take care of Lady Castlemaine's designs for the palace. She'll return to London in early August."

"I think we can make much progress on the gardens and the addition of the wing."

"Good. Also, the architect will start renovations for Catherine and our honeymoon here."

"Here? I'm glad you like the palace so much. The area is growing on me too." Enough to put down roots? Peter hadn't had roots in over ten years. Could he stay in one place, tied to one piece of land? He could if…if what?

If I had a wife and a reason to stop, a purpose other than court life?

"I'm glad because I need you at Hampton Court for the next year or two. Since it's so close to London, you can be of service to me in both places. The urgency now is to make this place fit for a queen and a mistress." Charles laughed and shook his head. "Could be an impossible feat."

"I'll try to meet the wishes of your present mistress right

away." Peter wouldn't trade places with his friend. Better to deal with a few physical building projects than the emotional turmoil Charles might face.

Charles leaned his head back and closed his eyes. "I think she'll be happy as long as there is some progress. Anyway, it will keep her out of the city during the sweltering sickness season. And it's good for little Anne too."

Peter had no complaints being relegated to the area. Days spent in close proximity to horses, wide-open spaces, and…Kate. Lazy summer days talking and walking and perhaps even riding with Kate in the fields along streams.

Peter rose shaking a sleeping puppy off his boot. "I need to check on the orders for the Privy Gardens. I hope to depart in a few days from now."

"I'll not be dallying long after you. As soon as the last of the guests departs, I'm headed to London." Charles remained, lounging on his couch. "Send my scribe in as you leave."

Even though Peter felt the strong friend and brother bond with Charles, the fact loomed that he was king. Bowing, Peter backed to the door. Clarence, the scribe, waited at the door with his box of utensils.

"Your turn." Peter patted him on the shoulder. The older man had supported Charles in exile and remained faithful.

"And the mood of the hour?" It always helped to know, although Clarence like himself had witnessed all the king's dispositions.

"Pleasant." Peter smiled as he made his way through the halls, down the steps, out into the fresh air. It would be hard to stay inside today. The gravel pathway through the rose gardens deposited Peter in the vegetable gardens. Without any preplanning, he knew what he wanted to do with his afternoon.

Looking over the hedge into the herb plats, Peter spied Kate, diligent as usual. An orange cat weaved back and forth over her feet.

As she picked herself up, she grabbed the cat in her arms and brought it close to her face. "Sunshine, you are going to get hurt crawling all over my feet. Go find Nettles to play with you." He meowed when his paws touched the ground before running toward the green house.

"Do even cats obey your orders?"

Kate turned to Peter's voice. "Only that one. He's taken a liking to me."

As have I.

"What would you say to a riding lesson this afternoon?" He stepped two feet closer to catch her reaction.

"You want to teach me to ride a horse? But I can't. I'd be no good at it. Surely, I'd waste your time." Her fists clenched and unclenched and finally rested at her sides.

"Whoa, Kate. I wouldn't have asked if it was a problem. Also, we need a chance to talk before I leave."

"Right. I hadn't forgotten about our project."

Not quite what I had on my mind.

"Meet me at the stables at three. I'll have Samson and Ginger saddled and ready to go."

Kate grimaced. Her big amber eyes shot rays of doubt and fear, yet her voice maintained a calm acceptance. "Until then."

"WHAT WAS I TO SAY, Betsy? He asked so nicely and he doesn't mind my fear." Kate shared a bench with her friend by the green house. Betsy seemed to be the only person she could talk to about this.

"From what I've heard, he knows much about horses. I think you'll do fine." Betsy looked off with a faraway stare at the orchards. "I grew up with horses. My brothers and father raised them."

As Betsy switched her gaze to her hands, Kate brought the talk around to a safe topic. "Peter wants to have his own farm and breed fine horses. I'm afraid love of horses comes natural to some, and I'm a hopeless case."

"Not at all. You can learn something new." Betsy adjusted her pose to sit on her hands, contemplating the grass under her slippers.

For a few days Kate noticed her friend's spurts of silence, staring as if considering a serious dilemma. What could be overshadowing Betsy? Could Kate help her? If not Kate, then surely God could solve anything.

"Do you want to tell me anything? I'll listen."

Betsy shook her head. "No. At times I think of my family, and I drift away to the past."

"Do you not have anyone?"

Her friend forced a few tendrils escaping her braid back behind her ears. "My family left me, deserted me years ago." A single tear raced down her cheek.

"I'll be your family. I'm not going anywhere. Every time the court comes back, you'll have a friend here." If only Betsy didn't have to travel to London.

Betsy's chin lifted. "My mistress says we are to stay the summer, so I have a few more months."

"Hopefully, you can spend some time at my house, go to church with us, and fairs and markets and…" Kate rejoiced at the gift of fast friendship.

"Do you want to come with me to the stables?"

"Not now. I have work to do, and I don't want Lady Castlemaine to send out a search. You go and try to have fun." Betsy gave Kate a little push toward the main path.

Fun? Since when was an encounter with a huge mammal an enjoyable occasion? Perhaps with Peter, her concentration would be divided between his handsome face and the riding experience.

The snorting and whinnies directed Kate to the two horses tied to a post with Peter tightening Samson's girth strap. Ginger was true to her name, a light reddish brown and from

Kate's point of view about half the size of Samson. The dark eyes with long lashes blinked at Kate, pulling her in with her charm.

"She's beautiful, Peter."

"Come closer and run your hand down her neck, scratch behind her ears, and let her see you and nuzzle you."

She'd never thought a horse would appreciate her eyes being rubbed like a cat or a dog, but Ginger even put her head down lower for Kate's continued ministrations.

After Peter explained her side saddle and the function of the reins, she used the two steps and Peter's guidance to arrive at her destination on top of the horse. She adjusted her skirt over her boots and turned to sit as ladylike as possible.

Peter rolled his shoulders and leaned his head from side to side. "Relax. If you keep that rigid pose, you'll feel sore for a week. Go with the fluid gait of the horse. We'll not go fast."

She mimicked Peter's actions with her shoulders and head. He led Ginger around in two big circles. The gentle sway became a part of Kate's body and relaxed her fear to a healthy cautious level.

His hand covered hers as he gave her control of the reins. "Follow my lead. Ginger will follow Samson. Are you ready?"

She wanted his hand to stay on hers. The absence left her unsure of herself, advancing her lack of courage. But then, Peter's smile and confidence in her spurred her forward. If he thought she could do this, then she'd try not to disappoint him. "Ready." She patted Ginger on the neck, secured the reins in her hand, and willed her body to settle into the steady motion of the horse.

Kate turned once to watch the red-brick palace sparkle in the sun and slowly fade into the horizon. Even though the mid-summer solstice officially appeared in about three weeks, the land didn't know that summer had not begun. The sun, green fields, leafy trees, and abundant wildlife acted as if the lazy days had truly blossomed. Kate slacked her firm hold on the saddle horn, reset her shoulders, and let her body soak in the delightful warmth.

Samson halted beside her, and Ginger followed suit without instruction.

"Look to your right by the stream, a fox and two of her litter," Peter whispered and pointed.

As Kate gently turned her head and surveyed the land, she caught the alert gaze of the red-brown fox. Kate prayed they would be spared in any fox hunt. "I hope the king doesn't have a fox hunt scheduled before he leaves."

"No, his hunting comrades left yesterday, so our friends here are safe for a few months."

"I always feel sorry for the fox. How would you like two dozen dogs chasing you?"

"Unlike the deer and boars used for food, I feel there is little value in the death of a fox. A few fox tails don't seem like enough of a reason."

"Do I detect a soft spot for the little creatures?"

"Unashamedly. And for the big ones, too, like horses. I despise abuse of these resourceful, pleasant beasts." He bent down to rub and pat Samson's neck. Kate mimicked his action on Ginger and received a nod of thanks from her brown-eyed mount.

Her forehead wrinkled in concern. "You don't consider placing your weight on a horse and riding for miles and miles an abuse?"

"Not at all. Horses need exercise and a person's weight is light compared to the ton of a horse. The plow, wagons, and carriages are also acceptable with the proper care for the animal like rest, water, and food."

"And battle?" Kate stayed by Peter's side as they continued their ride through the field, quite a distance from the palace. Kate traveled unfamiliar turf with the landscape and with Peter.

"An unfortunate necessity. Our giant friends have gone

beyond duty in many battles as have men. Both lose their lives in mostly unnecessary events."

Kate had trouble understanding men and their battles over land, riches, religion, laws, and even women. Compromise in Kate's opinion could cover as much peace as any battle. But that would take listening and time—something men forgot in their haste.

"See that line of trees in front of us? I want you to hold onto the pommel and loosen your reins. We're going to canter. Ginger will follow, if you give her a little encouragement with your heel."

Kate's one hour in the saddle hadn't given her much confidence, at least not for a full-scale run. "She won't race, will she?"

"No, we'll save galloping for another day. Find your rhythm with the horse and her motion and relax. You're doing fine."

Deep breath. She let her empty lungs fill again with courage. One more pat applied to Ginger's neck and the canter began.

The scenery sped by faster than in a wagon. Kate had a clear view with no hindrance of ruts and bouncing. In fact, her saddle was more comfortable than any wagon seat. Perhaps the golden carriage would supply more cushion, but still the bumps and ruts would affect the ride. This definitely was her preferred way to travel. She wanted to close her eyes and let her arms fly out from her sides like a bird, but fear reminded her to stick with the instructions from Peter for the time being.

Peter pulled up at the trees and settled to a walk. They had followed the stream, which now bubbled in front of them. "How is this for a rest? The horses can drink and graze while we, too, drink and eat."

His hands on her waist, Peter helped her down. She placed her hands on his strong shoulders and didn't want to let go, even when her feet touched the ground. If Peter hadn't removed his hands long seconds later, she would still be standing hypnotized by his gaze and touch.

"You choose a big rock or log for our seat, and I'll take the refreshments from my saddle bag."

As she walked and forced her legs to cooperate, she straightened her skirt and untied the strings of her bonnet. A huge boulder by the stream offered a place of rest. The breeze from the water and the shade from a nearby oak tree convinced Kate to complete the refreshing experience by taking off her bonnet, if only for a minute.

Closing her eyes, she listened. No voices, no evidence of palace life, no commands. But not silence either. The stream babbled over stones. The birds argued in the trees. The horses snorted as they ate. Her breath flowed in and out and soon was joined by Peter's quiet breathing.

His presence pulled her from her reverie without breaking the peaceful music of their surroundings. Between them he placed an uncorked bottle of lemon water and four tarts.

"Let me guess. Mrs. Down's lemon and raspberry tarts."

"How did you know?"

"Well, the raspberry is your favorite, and I can smell the lemon."

"Oh."

Did she know him too well? Had she crossed a line? Perhaps not, for she knew the same details about Jane and her siblings. He just happened to be in her life a lot.

She glanced at her cap in her lap. "Oh, I forgot."

Before she could raise the item to her head, Peter captured her hands.

"Leave it for now. Your hair is beautiful, especially the way it curls around your face." He reached for a long piece, curled it around his finger, then placed it behind her ear.

"Eat up, for I have one more thing to show you before we go back."

How can I eat when I only want him to look at me and touch me? But the gnawing in her stomach spurred her to bite into a lemon tart. The concoction satisfied her hunger in a few more bites.

Peter slid the last tart her way. "And the other one?"

"I can't. I'm afraid I'd be too full for the ride back."

"Then I will." Peter never shied away from sweets. Fortunately, his job kept him active, otherwise, he'd be as plump and round as Kate's father. Perhaps not, for Peter stood a good six inches taller.

Peter sliced an apple as Kate packed up the bag. While he talked to the horses, Kate quickly untied her boots, slipped off her stockings, and stepped to the stream. Lifting her skirt a few inches, she placed one bare foot at a time in the cool running water.

I could do this for a while yet. She tipped her face to the sun, relishing the freedom of her hair, neck, and chin from the constraints of her bonnet. *I really should be a farmer's wife away from the village with my own stream and the occasional lazy afternoon.*

"No bonnet—now no shoes. What have you done with Kate?"

She kept her face bent up toward the sky and peeked at Peter through one eye. "She's still here, exploring a bit of an afternoon of leisure. Just for a bit, I'm letting my daydreams come true."

As she lowered her head, she stepped from the cool stream, feeling like she left a part of herself behind. Peter munched on a slice of apple and watched every move she made. Yet, like a gentleman he remained by the stream as she replaced her stockings and boots.

Her fingers hesitated on the strings of her bonnet. It was time to cover her head and resume her wholesome role. Peter walked toward her and stopped her hand from tucking in the last of her curls.

"Leave that one." He pulled the end and it bounced back around her face.

"Now I want to show you my surprise."

They mounted the horses and cantered along the stream. At a bend in the banks, Peter pulled Samson to a halt. Shielding her eyes with her hand, Kate followed Peter's head, and her view swept over rolling hills with clusters of trees and shrubs. Few walls marred the pastureland. In the distance a lone house perched at the base of a hill facing the stream.

She sighed. "How did you find this place?"

"Long rides while surveying Hampton Court lands."

"Does all this belong to the king?"

"No, his property line is behind us with the high wall."

Kate turned and pushed herself up in the saddle to see for herself. "So, who owns all of this?"

"A man who moved to London. He wants to sell it."

"How could anyone sell a piece so lovely?"

"Exactly what I thought. But he's getting old and can't take care of it."

"Sad." The house now appeared lonely instead of welcoming. "Is this your surprise? The beautiful view?"

"Not entirely. I'm thinking about buying it, and I want your opinion."

"My opinion?"

"Yes. Do you think it's an insane idea?" He clicked for Samson to move forward. "I could have grazing for the horses and some cattle, maybe some sheep. Build fences and pens for the breeding and training of horses. The cottage, although adequate for me, could be enlarged in time for a family. There is a road on the other side of that hill." Peter pointed to the distance and rose up in his saddle as if to get a little closer. "It connects to the main road through the village and Hampton Court. It's private, but not too far from people."

His dreams spilled over into Kate's imagination. She saw him on Samson roaming the land, checking on his horses and livestock. A large vegetable garden appeared behind the house surrounded by apple trees. The front of the house pulsed with color from flowering shrubs and blossoming beds of roses, petunias, and lilies. For an added touch to the picture, she placed a little girl and a boy running around the house chasing a toy spaniel.

A giggle escaped, and Kate's hand covered her mouth.

"What's so funny?"

"I can't tell you." She shook her head, letting the images fly away. "I think it is a great plan. What will the king say?"

"I haven't asked him, but he knows my life goal is not to remain in court. And I don't like London. I don't think he'll be surprised if I choose to serve him at Hampton Court."

Peter pointed to the wall behind them. "The property goes all the way to the back wall of Hampton Court. I could easily access the palace through a gate."

"I'm happy for you, Peter. You have a dream, and it looks like it will come true."

He slowly opened and shut his mouth. What did he want to say? Why couldn't he tell her? She had yet to understand why he shared any of this with her.

"I must get you back. Mr. Payne wasn't overjoyed with me taking you away."

"Let's race." From deep within Kate confidence emerged. She let Ginger carry her across the fields back onto the king's property. Surprised at the ease of her lead, she laughed as Peter pulled beside her. "You let me win."

"Samson let you win. I think he realizes you're a good friend to have." They walked to the stables, letting the animals' breathing return to normal.

"Well, what do you think of your first riding lesson?"

She let her arms spread out as if to embrace the experience. "It was perfect. I'm just sorry I've lived so long with a fear of these amazing animals." She leaned down over Ginger's mane and tried to wrap her arms around her neck. Ginger's snorts and slight nods reassured Kate of the horse's sentiments.

Peter dismounted and handed Samson to a stable boy. He appeared at Kate's side and lifted her down. The boy led the two horses away, leaving Kate in Peter's arms. She pushed but held on to him at the same time. He took a step backwards but didn't release her.

"I had a wonderful time. I'll miss you when I'm gone."

"Oh, Peter. There are hundreds of girls like me, probably one in your mother's house."

"You are mistaken. I've traveled all over Europe and England and I promise you—no lass is like you."

Something was wrong. He couldn't mean that. His words were just sweet talk to a servant girl. No courtier would truly fancy a village girl.

"I probably won't see you, at least not like this before I leave. Will you give me one kiss for my dreams?"

"I don't know…" She was going to say "how" before he placed his hands on her face and tilted it up so her lips touched his.

"Yes," escaped as she felt the warm pressure from his soft lips. The warmth covered her entire body in the few seconds of his kiss.

When he pulled away still caressing her cheeks, her eyes drifted open. She shook her head not to release his hands but to clear the image of the dream. Well, he was definitely in front of her so the kiss was real and her hopes a dream.

"That will hold me until I return." He dropped his hands from her face and led her, as a bewildered child by his fingertips at her elbow, into the afternoon sun to the garden path and her world.

"Thank you, Peter, for everything. Goodbye. Be safe."

As she turned, the golden hue on the red bricks of the palace engulfed Peter, embedding him in the palace wall. He bowed and pivoted toward the palace and his world where he belonged. And behind her the gravel paths and plots of dirt held her captive. Her feet appeared rooted to the spot—her sphere of earthly grandeur overshadowed by worldly opulence.

Goodbye, Peter.

"HELLO, MR. RERESBY." Kate gravitated to Margaret's greeting.

Kate missed the step up into the shop and stumbled her way to the counter, grasping the cabinet to hold herself upright.

"Peter…Mr. Reresby…I didn't expect to see you."

Their parting yesterday seemed final. Kate's lips tingled as if just released from his kiss.

"I had to have a pastry or two for my travels and a fresh round of bread for my meals. Mrs. Downs gave me cheese and ham, but refused the bread. I wonder why?" His grin admitted he knew the answer.

"She must have needed her loaves for another purpose." Or did she want Peter to see Kate one more time? The cook carried a soft spot for Peter and possibly threw him in Kate's path to keep a friendship growing. *If only she knew about the kiss.* Kate's fingers pressed against her lips for a moment.

Looking down at her floured apron, Kate almost ran her hands over her skirt and blouse to release any lingering powder, but she remembered Peter had seen her dirty and messy before.

"How long is your journey?" Margaret asked.

"Three days, weather cooperating." Peter pointed to five different pastries. Margaret put them in his napkin, and he placed them in his bag on top of the round loaf.

Kate moved to the end of the counter after he paid. Privacy wasn't an option with her father in the next room and customers waiting in line.

"Take care, Peter," Kate whispered. "There are bandits on the highways."

He placed his hand on the counter close to Kate's. "I can handle a few highwaymen."

Glancing at the close proximity of the customers, Kate didn't dare touch his fingertips. What was she thinking? He probably didn't even notice.

"When does the king leave?"

"Later this morning. The courtiers are not early risers. Soon you should see the wagons with the trunks and a few servants pass by. And since Lady Castlemaine and her ladies are staying for the summer, the exit of the king will be tame and calm compared to earlier."

"I'm so glad she is staying because I'll see more of Betsy."

"Don't forget to be ready when the mistress has questions about the garden. She won't wait until I return. Already the men are in place to begin the project."

She clasped her hands and brought them to rest under her chin. "I will be there every day just out of curiosity."

Peter stared, smiled, and remained silent.

"What?" She leaned toward him.

"I'm going to miss your spontaneous enthusiasm."

"Oh." *And I'm going to miss looking at you, riding with you, talking, sharing, and seeing you almost every day.*

"Goodbye, Kate."

"God's speed, Peter." Their whispered adieus and slight nodding of heads formed an anchor in Kate's mind of a time in the future when they would meet again, God willing. The bell on the door sounded his exit.

"Kate." Her father called from the kitchen. That sound sealed her present fate. Her normal days from two months before would never return, the days before Hampton Court and Peter. No longer would she anticipate his voice or footsteps. Instead, she would envision him in the garden they planned, the stables, the kitchen, the new receipts she created, the river's edge, the market day. Peter might physically be absent, but Kate had him lodged in her heart and head. Reality demanded he remain a memory for all time even when he returned. Perhaps in time she would cease daydreaming about him and carry on as if a kiss never happened.

Chapter Fifteen

"Come on, Jane. I promise it will be fun." Kate sat at Jane's kitchen table with a cup of lemon water. What was holding Jane back from spending a few hours in Betsy's company? "Anyway, I need the company. Betsy will be teaching Margaret complicated stitching techniques. I'll need you to talk to."

Jane traced the worn lace doily on the table with her finger. "Well, when you put it that way. If I won't be in the way."

I need to get to the meaning behind her pouting. Have I done something? Is it Betsy? Or possibly Edward and his procrastination?

Jane crossed her arms on the table and finally looked straight at Kate. "You see a lot of Betsy, don't you?"

"A few hours a week. Does that bother you?" Could Jane be jealous?

"No." She laced her fingers together. "Oh, I don't know. It just seems you and Edward see so much at the palace, things I'll never see stuck here with Mother in the house. I think you enjoy her company more than mine."

In an instant Kate exchanged her seat across from Jane to the bench right next to her. "Look at me. You are my dearest friend and no one will take your place. That is why I'm asking you to share this with me. The same way I ask you to come to the gardens. My world might be expanding a little, but I want you in it. Please come over tomorrow."

"All right. I'll bring the dress I'm working on, and perhaps I'll learn something new." Jane's smile reached her eyes this time.

"Now that's the Jane I know and love. I'll even make us some raspberry tarts, the same as I made for the king."

Jane giggled. "To think I'll be eating like the king." Jane's laughter joined with Kate's, vibrating in the room.

An hour later Kate shook her head over the bed of lavender, smiling at Jane's silly jealousy. But if she really felt that way, Kate would have to be careful how much she talked about Betsy until all three of them became better friends.

"Kate." Mr. Payne's voice carried over the hedge from the rose garden.

"Over here, sir." She continued to till the soil around the sweet-smelling plants.

"I'd like you to meet someone."

Kate pushed herself from her knees to her full height. Hadn't she met all the gardeners, except for the ones recently hired for the Privy Garden?

Turning, she faced Mr. Payne and a middle-aged man with a prominent pointed nose, dressed in the latest fashion of the court with buckles and lace and plumes in abundance. He had to be extremely hot out in the sun in mid-afternoon.

"This is Monsieur Mollet, the Master Gardener of His Majesty's English Gardens."

She curtsied as the gentleman bowed. "Monsieur, it's a pleasure. I've seen your plans for the gardens. I'm honored to meet you."

"*Enchanté*. According to Lady Castlemaine, I should be the honored one. If you have managed to catch the attention of the king and his mistress, then you have my support too."

Why did he want to meet her? What could she possibly add to his expertise?

"If you can spare the time, I'd like to walk through the Privy Garden with you. You are familiar with the soil and the hardy plants of the area. The king enjoys my work in the French royal gardens, but he respects the thoughts and wisdom of local gardeners too. He realizes the climate and landscape are different."

Mr. Payne nodded to Kate, releasing her from her chores. She hoped he would follow them. Anyone familiar layered her confidence.

"I'd like your presence and opinions, too, Payne."

Thank you, God.

The tour didn't take long. Already the landscape had transformed as sprouts escaped years of coverage and native vegetation dared to seek the sun. She wanted to run the length and width of the garden checking on each plot, but the presence of Monsieur and the many windows from the palace halted the progression of her imagination and impulses.

"Like every true gardener, you are wanting to run your fingers through the soil and touch the emerging plants. Go on, I can talk while you explore."

Monsieur's words released her urge. He truly did understand. As her fingers roamed and rearranged the soil, she pointed out her finds, and at the same time she didn't miss a word of his detailed plans.

"As you see need and can spare the plants and time, I want you, Miss Sinclair, to fill in as many beds as possible with your flowering seedlings, herbs, and any mature plants, mostly perennials, that will complement the bulbs, shrubs, and trees."

"Yes, Monsieur. Lady Castlemaine approved of some ideas, and I've picked out a few plants ready to transplant."

Monsieur Mollet pointed to two plots close to the palace in view from the windows. "These are the most important ones.

We've decided to keep the statuary here, although the pieces were originally from Whitehall Palace and St. James's Place. The king likes them and doesn't think the other palaces will miss them."

Kate tried to recall what Peter had mentioned about Monsieur Mollet when reminiscing about his wandering with the king in Europe. The man was from a long and distinguished family of French royal gardeners. Kate curtailed her giggles as she visualized Monsieur in the gardens of Versailles. The pictures she'd seen of French gardens made Hampton Court gardens seem minuscule and wild. At least he was willing to blend his ideas with the uniqueness of the English soil and climate.

Monsieur left Kate and Mr. Payne at the Privy Garden entrance with a bow and a pivot.

Mr. Payne grinned. "I see you are going to need more hands, Kate, and more hours in the day." His positive suggestion didn't lessen the challenge ahead for Kate.

"What do you suggest? I'm already arriving an hour earlier than before. My father has kept the extra help for the summer."

"As I understand it, Mr. Reresby suggested additional workmen would be employed for the Privy Garden."

"Yes." Just the mention of his name triggered the reality of Peter's departure. "At least I won't be planting the garden by myself."

"I'm going to lend you Edward for a few weeks until the bulk of the transplanting occurs."

"Thank you, Mr. Payne." Kate would rather work with someone she knew and liked, someone like Edward, than a stranger. The only problem was Edward's continuing notion about Kate as his future wife. Perhaps her time with him could be used to influence the transfer of his affections. Was Jane willing to get her hands dirty?

~

MOTHER PACKED her sewing into her wicker box and stored it under a corner table. "That should give you girls plenty of room now."

Kate reached from the settee to her mother's sleeve. "I'm so glad you agreed to this. It's good for Margaret. Also, Betsy misses her home and indicates the time away from the palace will be soothing."

"And Jane?" Her mother ran a cloth over the nearest shelf. Kate didn't expect her to find any dust.

"I hope she finds Betsy to be a normal, unintimidating, possible friend. Jane's view of the palace and its occupants is a bit skewed."

"She's not the only one who holds that view. I believe you when you talk of Mrs. Downs and Mr. Payne and even Mr. Reresby, but all the others, I'm not so sure."

"You mean the king and Lady Castlemaine."

Her mother placed her fingers under Kate's chin to lean her head back capturing her attention. "Not quite the image of purity I want my daughter to see. And the other courtiers too. You still have to be very careful."

Her mother's smile contained wisdom and sincerity as it creased the corners of her piercing gaze. "You've changed, Kate. Not in a bad way. You are more confident and curious. Offering your talents has allowed you to experience close proximity to a realm just outside your reach. I don't want you disappointed or hurt."

Kate stood and embraced her mother and her loving words. Did she need to promise again and convince her mother that purity was still one of her goals? For some reason Kate did not mind the petit lecture. She grasped the acceptance and interest her mother offered. In a way her mother gave her permission to explore and expand her world while emphasizing the boundaries and limitations of her freedom.

"Thank you, Mother." Kate released her before the tears pricking the edge of her eyes trickled down her cheeks, marring her complexion. As her mother left the room, she patted Kate on the cheek.

Kate glanced around the room. What would Betsy think of the small room lacking upholstered, high-backed, gilded chairs and velvet curtains?

Fidgeting with her long braid hanging over her shoulder, Kate took pleasure in the fact of her head being uncovered for the afternoon. So often, Betsy's hair was free, framing her face with loose tendrils. Kate wanted to try the same approach. Her mother didn't mind since the girls remained inside. What dress would Betsy wear? If only Kate could wear the dress Betsy had given her. There the boundary and the limit struck her. These walls demanded her simple dark attire with her white apron. The dark colorless blue couldn't wipe the smile off her face as she thought of the afternoon's occupation.

BETSY ARRIVED first with a large wicker basket swinging from her arm. Kate took the treasure from her friend and laced her right arm in Betsy's. "Mother, we will be upstairs working. Direct Jane when she arrives, please."

"You girls have fun. I think Margaret is waiting for you."

"Margaret has been waiting for hours," Kate added. "She's been bouncing all over the place, startling the customers with her energy."

"Well, I must put her to work then."

Betsy followed Kate into the family room. Margaret had already claimed one end of the table, her scissors, threads, and fabric ready for transformation into a masterpiece. Kate suspected not much visiting would transfer if Betsy didn't get Margaret occupied with a dress pattern. The material, though plain in the eyes of the court, contained the slightest hint of a design as faint blue lines crisscrossed a pale-yellow background. Mother approved, while Father questioned the choice.

"Good day, Margaret. I see you are anxiously waiting." Betsy stood by Margaret's chair as Kate set her basket on the table.

"Yes, what do I learn today? Something to dazzle the court?"

"No, not today. How about I show you the stylish cut of the bodice where it attaches to the skirt?"

Margaret clapped her acceptance. Kate knew anything new pleased Margaret. Not that she would have any place to wear a new dress besides church, if it were simple enough.

Kate found her own basket of material pieces and settled in a chair close by. Her talent, or lack of, was better used on an unpretentious underskirt.

"Hello," Jane announced her entrance.

"I'm so glad you are here." Kate pointed to the seat next to her. "Come join me over here, unless you would rather a table."

"Oh, Jane, you must want to see what Betsy is teaching me," Margaret said.

Betsy looked up as Jane walked toward her. "Good day, please join us."

Kate wanted her friends to become friends. Perhaps they would bond over a sewing lesson. The fewer words from Kate the better. Jane joined the girls at the table, leaving Kate to her solitary work. *Give me a garden or a kitchen anytime.* She giggled.

"What's so amusing, Kate?" Betsy asked.

"Just how precise you three are with your sewing, and how sloppy I am."

"You're not so bad. Anyway, no one will see your stitches," Margaret said.

Jane bent her head to her work. "What did you tell your mistress about this afternoon's escape?" Jane copied Betsy's pattern and stitches. Her fabric was of a medium green hue. The cream lace would emphasize the new waist connection without drawing too much attention. Jane's parents, although a little more open to the modern dress, still preferred the subdued color tones of the past decade.

"This afternoon is my free afternoon. Anyway, Lady Castlemaine likes her ladies to spend time in the village to catch the latest gossip."

"Well, you won't hear any of that here, unless you share some palace stories." Jane put down her work and leaned forward. "Will you tell us anything about the king or the palace?"

"Let me see. The king and his court are back in London. It is a lot calmer now, not as animated or as much entertainment."

"What does Lady Castlemaine do all day?" Margaret asked, not even looking up from her stitching. "Does she sew? Sing? dance?"

Kate hoped Margaret's continuous questions didn't wear Betsy down.

"Yes, to all of those. She is working on an elaborate tapestry highlighted with gold thread. And some of the court musicians and dance instructors remained for the summer. There is a lot of eating, sleeping, and walking in the gardens."

Kate wondered about the Lady's true impression of the Privy Garden. Would Betsy be privileged to an honest assessment? "Does she like the gardens?"

Betsy put her purple bodice aside and turned to Kate. "How could she not? Every day she strolls through the Privy Garden with Monsieur and discusses each new inch of progress. I admit I don't know anything about the plants, but she knows so many. I listen from a distance as we walk. Don't be nervous, Kate. She is pleased. At times she watches you from the window, clasping her hands in front of her, smiling."

"I'm so glad. Mr. Payne and Monsieur seem to be pleased. Edward is a huge help. But we need more hands." Kate had a small chance to get Jane involved. "Would you be willing to help some, Jane? If your parents could spare you a few hours a week. I promise wages are being paid on time."

Please say yes. For Edward's sake.

"Edward asked me the same thing. Mother says a few hours would be fine."

"Why didn't you tell me, silly? When can you start? Tomorrow we are putting in a bed full of herbs. Please come help. Edward and I can show you exactly what to do." Or perhaps only Edward.

"All right. By the way, have you heard from Peter?" Betsy's head shot up at his name. Jane didn't know about Betsy's disdain for just the word "Peter."

Kate looked at Betsy. The same faraway stare and grimace faced her. "It's too soon. He should have arrived by now and seen his mother and brother."

"Betsy, what is wrong?" Jane asked.

"Nothing. I pricked my finger, that's all."

I must find out what Betsy knows about Peter. I can't imagine a problem he might have caused. He's too sensitive and caring to have said anything hurtful. Or did he have another side?

THE HEAT of the day failed to deter Kate from her mission with Edward and two under-gardeners at her command. More like the beck and call of Monsieur and Lady Castlemaine.

"We'll start here with the herbs and move to the seedlings next." Kate surveyed the newly cultivated plot with its eight equal sections. "Thyme here. Sage there, then rosemary, basil, oregano, mint, dill, and parsley. That should spice up any meal. But I think the plot here is for scent and viewing, not taste."

Edward laughed and pulled the wagon of healthy plants closer. "If Mrs. Downs finds out these herbs are going to waste, she'll sneak in at midnight to pilfer some."

Kate showed the two boys precisely how to treat the plants and where to place them. Symmetry was a requirement for the lady.

She set the first rosemary plant in its hole, stood, and shaded her eyes against the sun. Turning a full circle, she took in the whole garden. At the gate to the vegetable garden, Jane waved and called to Kate.

"Come on in. We just started working." Kate met Jane half way and took her hand. "What do you have in the basket?"

"My gloves and a few treats for the workers."

"You mean for Edward." Kate winked at her friend noticing her blush under the rim of her straw hat.

"Oh, is he here?"

"Right over there." Kate followed Jane's glance. Edward waved his soiled glove in their direction. "If you're ready to work, I have the perfect spot for you."

Next to Edward while he planted thyme, Jane secured the mint. Kate opted for the delicate job of planting seedlings around the edge of the rose bush plots. Occasionally, she'd hear their laughter or catch a glimpse of them talking. Jane didn't seem to be sharing her treats with anyone but Edward. Kate witnessed his mouth full a few times.

Thank you, Lord. This might work. Your creation, Your beauty, and maybe a young man for Jane.

"Kate, is that you?"

Kate squinted and gazed up to see the shadow of Lady Castlemaine peering over her. "Excuse me, My Lady. I didn't hear you approach." Kate curtsied as she stood.

"I like to admire the progress of my little garden. What are you planting? They look like weeds to me."

"Oh, no, Madame. I have cosmos, aster, poppy, and carnation. I promise they will bloom in abundance given time." Had Kate messed up? Was her vision of border flowers a mistake?

"Don't be nervous. I approve of anything you and Monsieur decide. I must admit I am ignorant of flowers and herbs. I do want to learn though." The beautiful woman in her light muslin dress trimmed with the finest lace and gold tassels could have been an elegant shining statue in this garden. When she smiled, she brightened the cloudiest day and the most disheveled garden.

"I can show you the herbs, if you like." Kate gestured to her left where the four others worked.

Lady Castlemaine nodded.

As they approached, Jane, Edward, and the two boys stood at the back side of the plot bowing and curtsying. Kate didn't know if she should acknowledge them or introduce them to the Mistress. Betsy said she liked knowing the names of her servants.

"Who do we have here?" Lady Castlemaine saved Kate the trouble of a decision. "Robert, Jane, Mark, and Willie—My Lady."

The ladies with the mistress giggled as the young boys bowed, almost touching the ground. Kate hoped Jane wouldn't faint. If she did Edward would save her with a romantic ending. Kate smiled. Matchmaking lightened up any serious situation.

Lady Castlemaine turned to the bed. "You were going to tell me about these herbs."

"Oh, yes. I will put markers in each of the small plots for future reference. Each herb has a distinct smell, like this one, rosemary." Kate broke a small end of the stem and handed it to the lady.

"A powerful scent. I recognize it from the rosemary chicken served here." She passed the leaves on to her ladies to smell and discard.

"All the others you have heard of too. Thyme and dill with basil and sage. Over here are oregano and parsley. And my favorite peppermint. We have other mint varieties in the large vegetable garden like lemon." Kate made herself stop, for she could talk of plants for hours. But Lady Castlemaine was not Mr. Payne nor Mrs. Downs.

"Thank you, Kate. I'll let you continue your work. By the way, when is your young man, Peter, returning?"

My young man? Should she contradict Lady Castlemaine?

"I don't know, My Lady. At least a month."

"I'm sure it will pass quickly."

Her entourage followed her the length of the garden stopping at statues, sundials, and fountains. Kate stared, hands on hips. Did anyone else hear her insinuation about Peter? Why would she call him her man? She'd need to ask Betsy later what her mistress said about Peter and Kate.

Hours later, Edward gathered the tools in the wagon. "Anything else for today, Kate?"

"No, it is beautiful. Thank you all for your help. Jane, I knew you would enjoy the work. At least I think you did by your smile and dirt smudges."

Jane raised her hand to swipe imaginary dirt from her cheeks.

Kate giggled. "I'm only joking. Your face is fine."

Edward remained close. "If you don't mind, I'm going to walk Jane home after I store these items." He whistled as he went into a hot house.

"Of course. I have a few things to do in the kitchen. You two be gone."

Kate had the Privy Garden to herself. The breeze lifted the scent of the roses, honeysuckle, and herbs as a light screen around her.

God, You created all of this beauty. Thank you for letting me be a part of it. And bless Peter on his mission. Bring him back home safely.

Home. Was his home with his family or here in the palace or even at his future cottage? Or was his home wherever she was?

Chapter Sixteen

The further Peter traveled from London, the territory he knew as a child sprung forth from the landscape. Talk at the wayside taverns convinced him the people supported the new regime, at least for now. He wondered about a few years later when Charles' extravagances asked for a larger portion of the citizens' products and proceeds. For now, the smiles and cheery toasts to the king sustained his dreams of a restored country under an able sovereign. After all, he had sacrificed his youth for this renewed nation. As many people as possible should be enjoying it, including his mother.

Sheffield, situated about 150 miles north of London in the West Riding of Yorkshire, came into view after three days of travel. With only Samson to think about, Peter's journey ended with no delays. Reresby Manor and grounds spread out south of the township of Sheffield amongst the valleys and woods.

Nothing could possibly be the same as fifteen years ago when his father lived peaceably off the land, doing his duty as a conscientious landlord and personage of his country. Then, Thomas, Peter, and Rebecca lived in peace and comfort as a family with prospects of education, social events, marriage, and continued wealth.

The only ones left, besides the ghosts of the past, were his widowed mother and older brother, Thomas. Both were bitter, having emerged from the war scarred and broken. The parameters of Peter's role loomed sketchy and vague. Thomas never wanted a royalist brother just as Peter didn't understand his father and brother choosing Cromwell and civil war.

"Well, Samson. This is home for a few weeks. I'll try my best to remain faithful to my cause."

Reresby Manor's gray-stone façade spread out in front of him. Recently trimmed shrubs revealed the new pane glassed windows on the ground floor. The upper levels still had the old shutters. Peter acknowledged the improvements and investments his brother had made. It couldn't be easy to hang on to the house and make a profit. But his story mimicked other landlords pardoned from their roles in the Civil War. Charles wanted livelihoods and lives to find some normalcy, even if a new healthy normalcy only vaguely revealed the past.

Peter tied Samson to the hitching post and decided to enter the front door instead of the side after such a long absence. The new butler took his name and announced him to a solitary person sitting in the front parlor.

"Peter." His mother stood by her chair and stretched her arms to him. Her black dress hung on her loosely.

Peter touched her black hair, streaked with gray, and her pale cheeks. "I'm filthy from the dusty ride." Yet, he folded her in his arms. Even through all the pain of the past, they remained mother and son, loving and dear.

"I expected you today, just as your letter stated. Always on time. Always with a plan." She guided him to a place on the couch next to her. The butler brought in refreshments—tea and biscuits. As Peter bit into one, he remembered the incredible tastes of Kate's pastries. Mother would enjoy a better variety and change of nourishment and vista.

"You know why I am here, Mother."

"Yes, son, you have a plan to convince me to stay in England, in this lovely house instead of going overseas to a new life." The note of sarcasm oozed in comparison to her recent letter about the house as her prison.

"You know me well. How about a change without leaving the country? You have your children here, Thomas and me. And… and Rebecca." Why did he bring her into the conversation? The loss of her only daughter drove her to this state in the beginning, not the death of her husband. Peter understood that his father was not coming back, but Rebecca could.

"Yes, Rebecca. We sent her away, but only for a little while, I promise." The tears of a broken heart, an unforgiven soul, dampened her handkerchief.

"I know. I've thought a lot about her. For some reason, an instinct, I feel she is alive and living a good life." He had to believe that or he would carry around blame and remorse for his years abroad.

Her blue eyes met his, pleading through dark wet lashes. "But why won't she contact us?"

He had his opinion, one that would hurt his mother as it daily had confused and hurt him. Was she strong enough to hear the truth, his version of the truth? "Perhaps we can discuss this later."

"Now, Peter, while Thomas is out. I need to know what you think and feel. I need help." She squared her shoulders, wiped away her tears, and showed the tough features he knew she had.

Peter paced the room, touching old familiar pieces of furniture, crystal and ceramic objects, and books. What lifeless objects when compared to an eight-year-old child. A child no longer, but a young woman. He would give away all of it to ease his mother's pain and have Becca back.

The nagging feeling in his gut begged to be released. Since he had mentioned this to no one, perhaps this chance could soothe the gnawing strain and tension. He traded the cushiony couch for a hard wooden seat—his dismal meanderings and a comfortable seat didn't mesh.

Putting his chair directly in front of his mother, Peter clutched his hands together and braced his elbows on his knees.

"This is how I have come to explain Rebecca's disappearance. As a child she did your bidding, worked in Cromwell's household, became a member of the family. She saw you very rarely. In time, she substituted her old family for the new one, the one feeding her and housing her, possibly even caring for her."

His mother shook her head in denial. "But we loved her. We wanted her back. Your father thought to advance himself in Cromwell's eyes by placing her in the ruler's household. He did the same with your brother, and he would have with you in time."

"That doesn't make it easy or right for a small child." Peter remembered the tears and the screams from Rebecca as his father put her in the carriage and drove her away from her home and her mother.

"My theory applies to Rebecca as a thirteen or fourteen-year-old. The country was in war. I had left. Father and Thomas were fighting, and you left her with Cromwell's family. She must have changed her name and identity in the chaos and disappeared into a safe place, possibly as a servant or nursery maid or a baker or a seamstress. She could have even married by now. We wouldn't know what she looks like as a woman, not really."

"Why doesn't she come home now?"

He ran his hands over his weary eyes and face. "Don't you understand? This is not home. We are not her family, if my opinion is correct. She gave up on all of us years ago."

His mother sat up straighter with eyes alert and seeking. "What can we do?"

"Pray." Where did his answer originate? He looked around as if the voice wasn't his.

Pray, Peter. Pray.

"Pray? I think I've forgotten how since your father was killed and the war raged all around. How do I begin again?" She asked

Peter, one who only recently thought of prayer as a resource, an answer at least for someone like Kate.

If Kate were here, she'd know how to pray, the exact words, the ones that brought peace to her life.

"I've forgotten, Mother. But I've become friends with someone who speaks to God daily. My words might not reach to God's ears, but I'm going to try. My words might be simple, but they are from my heart." He bowed his head and found words from deep within. Some source that Kate spoke of often. "Father God, I don't know how to ask or what to say. Please protect Rebecca. Keep her safe from harm. Somehow let her know her family loves her and misses her." He paused. "Amen." He hoped God would accept his plea. Perhaps daily communication was the answer for him too. It certainly couldn't hurt.

"Amen." His mother smiled, an honest response to his sincere words.

"Now, no more tears. I'm going to find Thomas after I wash my face."

"And I'll speak to the cook to make sure there's an extra-large portion for you tonight."

"Don't go to too much trouble. I could eat anything."

Peter found Thomas in the stables. Like Peter, Thomas had good horse sense and took a special interest in the animals' well-being. The war decreased the Reresby stock, leaving a mere ten head of high-bred horses.

Peter saw his brother in the last stall, his sleeves rolled up as he groomed a roan mare. "Thomas."

Thomas rested his arms on the stall door. "I heard you were coming for a visit."

Was Peter welcome? Years on the opposite side of the war grafted a strained relationship. Peter was on the winning side but at what cost? His father's life? Alienation from his home and brother?

"Just for a few weeks. I wanted to talk to Mother."

"Good luck convincing her to stay. She has her hopes set on the colonies."

"I have a few suggestions."

Thomas hung the brush outside the stall and latched the door. The scars on his neck and his hand spoke of a war Peter had avoided when in exile with Charles. If only Thomas had chosen the other side. If only Charles I had not been beheaded. If only Civil War had never existed. But there was no magic formula to change the past.

The brothers walked toward the house. "Why are you really here? Are things not going well with Charles?"

"Honestly, I'm here to check on Mother…and you."

"I'm fine. I've even found a girl who actually wants to marry me, scars and all. She's given me some hope, a reason to stay and make something of this place."

"Congratulations. I wish you the best."

Thomas smiled. "Her name is Constance. I'd like you to meet her, although your approval is not needed."

"Don't worry, big brother. The time for judgment is over. Acceptance and healing are more important."

"And you? Anyone in the merrie court or do you have a dozen ladies lined up?"

"It's not really like the gossip says. There is one lady who wants more than I'm willing to give her. I need someone to share my dreams and plans, which do not include the court."

"Seriously? I thought you had become a flamboyant courtier. It almost sounds like you'd give it up for a small house and a plain wife."

"You're not far off." Peter had already tried to discard his golden-haired beauty, but Madeline hinted of her availability at every chance. No way would she inhabit a cottage instead of a palace. And would she give up the court and the vast activities? It was time for her to move on to another of Charles' new courtiers, the ones with titles and political ambitions. Most of Charles' close friends and former comrades in exile wanted a calm, stable existence. Ten years of roaming was enough for Peter. And Madeline failed to understand his preference for the countryside.

Only Kate approved. Yet in all fairness, he hadn't told anyone else or showed the property to another soul. Charles would have to know soon enough. Anyway, that was the only approval he needed. And if Charles let loose of the strings, Peter could concentrate on his farmhouse. He didn't need a wife to begin his venture. There tended to be enough confusion already. The first thing, his mother.

"Do you think Mother has her mind set on America?"

Thomas stopped on the gravel walkway to the manor. "The house gives her no joy. Until recently, before Constance, I would mope around in her presence when I wasn't struggling to secure the land and tenants once again. Her friends are gone, having to find other places to live, with their friends and family. I can't force her to stay."

"She does have friends relocated to London. I'm going to suggest she spend some time there. Or there is a small manor I could rent outside of Hampton Court close to a small village. Since most of my time will be spent there in the near future, she might consider it."

Thomas kicked at the gravel, his arms folded and brow wrinkled. "She might consider that plan. It's not as if she has booked passage yet."

"I appreciate what you have done for her. I don't regret my decision to follow Charles. But my guilt at leaving Mother, and Rebecca, weighs heavy."

"We all made our own decisions and our own mistakes."

"Could we leave that behind and accept each other again, as brothers and friends?" Peter put his hand out, and immediately Thomas grasped it and pulled him into an embrace—a clasp of forgiveness.

"Now let's go in and have dinner. Perhaps the nourishment will provide some answers."

Peter, not familiar with the new cook, devoured the meal, pleasantly surprised at her culinary skills. "Mother, where did you find your cook? Mrs. Downs at the palace would love this artichoke pie receipt as well as the burdock roots. I have a friend who makes the most delicious pastries and desserts." Talking between bites limited Peter's conversation. "Orange pudding, shell bread, gooseberry pie."

"Son, you haven't even finished your leg of mutton, and you are on to desserts. Someone has bewitched you with sweets." Mother laughed—a sound Peter hadn't expected to hear.

"If anyone could bewitch me, it would be Kate with her magical receipts."

"Kate?" Thomas and Mother said together.

Peter held his fork in mid-air. "Oh, yes, Kate. Kate Sinclair is the daughter of a local baker, and she works at the palace with the cook, and also with the gardener."

Thomas raised an eyebrow. "The cook and the gardener?"

"We spend a lot of time together since I'm in charge of banquets and now the renovation of the gardens." *And because I try to be with her every moment I can.* Would Mother and Thomas understand? Not now. Even though Peter had just shared with Thomas about leaving judgment behind, he didn't want Kate involved in any questionable remarks from his family.

Thomas looked up from his plate with his wrists resting against the edge of the table. "So, your duties are varied. I pictured you reclining on a cushion all day, lounging in the chambers of the king with few responsibilities."

Peter almost choked on the mutton. The raspberry wine saved him. "Never has my time with Charles been one of reclining and lounging. Only in the last year have any cushions been involved. I prefer being busy and involved with the outdoors far from court drama. The kitchen and the gardens are safe."

Safe except when Kate could be around any corner. When he'd rather spend his time with her than doing the bidding of the king or Lady Castlemaine. What would happen if Charles knew of the amount of time Peter would like to spend with Kate?

Mother nodded to the servant for the plates to be cleared and the desserts served. "I see you are daydreaming about your courtier life. When do you return?"

Peter twirled his crystal glass by the stem, mesmerized for a second by the red liquid. "I have a few weeks. Long enough, I hope, to convince you to cast aside your desire to sail away. Will you at least listen to a few suggestions?"

His mother surprised him as she sat back in her chair bolstered by the strong wooden slats. Hands clasped in her lap, she seemed prepared to listen, even if she wouldn't adhere to the advice. "I'm listening."

Peter received a nod from Thomas. He wished he could see or hear approval from God to continue. But since he hadn't actively involved Him to this point, except a few hours ago, he hesitated asking Him now.

"I know that Mrs. Bradbury and Lady Malcolm have both moved to London and each reside in a smart neighborhood. They are safe and flourishing even without their husbands. Society has accepted the wives of fallen rebels with or without titles."

"I see. And the expenses?"

"Thomas and I have ample means to support you moderately in London."

"Thank you. And you have another suggestion?"

"Since I am working at Hampton Court for the next few years with my projects for the king, I could rent you a small comfortable manor close to the palace in the small village. It is peaceful without the high society pressures of London. You could even spend part of the year in both places."

Her head dropped as one hand raised a handkerchief from her sleeve to her eye. "I don't know what to say. I've been so lost here without your father. I need a change and a purpose. Who knows? One day maybe one of you will give me grandchildren. Could this truly work?"

Peter joined his mother on her side of the table and took her hand. "I think so. If you allow us to help you, this could be a new start."

"Perhaps I will find someone who knows of Rebecca. Possibly, I could see her in the London streets or in the markets."

Peter's head nodded. "There's always that possibility. I am certain she is prospering, and soon she will have a change of heart, a heart of love and forgiveness."

The arrival of tea and desserts broke up the teary wonderings. His mother opened to Peter's ideas. Now, he had two weeks to contact her friends and get everyone's participation.

After dinner he spent time writing to Kate. The proper way to send it was probably through Mrs. Downs or Mr. Payne, not her family. Peter wanted only Kate's eyes to read his words. If only he could talk to her face to face about changes and plans in his life.

Chapter Seventeen

Her basket of vegetables appeared heavier than usual. The June crop supplied a great variety for Mrs. Downs. Kate set her goods on the long kitchen table in the almost empty kitchen. Early afternoon tended to be a respite for the scullery staff. "I brought a few fresh items for you." Kate peeked through the door not wanting to startle anyone. Mrs. Downs had a pot of water boiling as well as a large stew pot hanging next to it ready for the meat of the day.

"I'm so glad you came. What did you bring me? I hope onions, carrots, and potatoes."

"Yes, and greens, artichokes, and green apricots."

Mrs. Downs reached in her deep pockets and pulled out a letter. "For you. It arrived today."

"For me? Who's it from?" Kate held the neatly folded paper with a bold blue wax seal for a few seconds. It wasn't often, only twice before, that she had received a letter addressed to her. This was a monumental treat: *Hampton Court Palace, Attention Miss Kate Sinclair, Care of Mrs. Downs.*

"The return address is Mr. Peter Reresby." Mrs. Downs grinned, causing Kate to blush.

"Did he write you too?"

"No, my dear, only you. Now open it up before I die of curiosity. It was heavy in my pocket, waiting on you."

Kate pried the seal up with her fingernail. She started to read it out loud, but decided to read it first just in case it contained something personal. Like what? Secret admissions of endless love, loneliness, sleepless nights. Peter wouldn't ever say these things, not to her. Probably anything he said Mrs. Downs could hear.

Dear Miss Sinclair,

I hope you are well. I am certain palace life is tedious and uses a lot of your time with Lady Castlemaine in residence. I picture you in the Privy Garden, working your magic with the plants. Do you have enough help? Mr. Payne for sure is looking out for you. Have you visited Ginger or rescued any stray puppies? I think of your delightful smile and open amazement often.

I've only just begun my campaign to convince Mother to come to London or East Molesey. I will need a good dose of luck and courage to succeed. My brother Thomas and I have repaired our broken relationship, somewhat. He will marry soon. The house and grounds are stable and fruitful once again in his hands with the pardon and encouragement from the king. If Thomas continues his loyal commitment to the new realm, he will prosper.

Know that I miss you. Pray for me and for my mother, for your prayers are as pure as are you.

Your friend,

Peter Reresby

Kate set the letter on the table and met Mrs. Down's eyes. She would have loved to read the kind words again in private.

"So, how is Peter? Good news, I hope."

"Yes, he's safe. He asks for prayers for his mother and the decisions to be made." For some reason that answer sufficed. Mrs. Down's chose not to question further. Once she thought about it, Kate didn't feel the letter was overtly personal. The remarks corresponded to their friendship, the things they shared. She was right to understand any secret admission of love would never be.

"Would it be appropriate to write him back? Would it arrive before he left?"

"I don't see why not. A courier could have it there in less than a week. I could send it with the royal correspondences for quicker, reliable service."

"I should do it now, then. Do you have any paper?"

"Not fit for a letter. But I'll send for paper from Betsy. I'm sure there is something in a desk drawer at her fingertips."

"Oh, thank you. And maybe she will deliver it herself."

"Perhaps." Mrs. Downs jotted down the request and disappeared into the inner hall to find one to carry the missive. She returned chuckling.

"What is it?" Kate felt like laughing while watching Mrs. Downs.

"Those men, all sitting around tables playing backgammon or chess, not a care in the world while the king is away. Why, if the palace were in danger, they'd be useless. But I guarantee if they catch word of her making her daily round in the halls, not a game would be found. Oh, to have a life of leisure!"

"Do you know how to play chess or what was the other one, back-something?" Kate had never had the opportunity. Her father certainly would see it as a waste of time and possibly sinful.

"Backgammon, my dear. And no. I have played cards, but never one of these games. When would I have time?"

"You could set up a board in here and play when you had a few minutes."

"I'd rather catch a few winks."

"How about a cup of tea? Someone should be down soon."

Kate helped Mrs. Downs and pondered what she would tell Peter. Of course, she'd share the progress on the garden, and perhaps the new friendship between Jane and Betsy. It might be fun to add the so-so advancement between Edward and Jane. As long as her personal sentiment about Peter stayed in check, she'd enjoy the correspondence.

Betsy skipped into the room, not her normal entrance style. In fact, Kate had never seen any of the servants skip, run, or jump in the palace, even though the long hallways and vast halls begged for a little informality.

Jumping up at her appearance, Kate met her halfway in the kitchen. She hugged her courtly friend. "I was wondering if you could get away."

"Lady Charlotte, one of my mistress' ladies in waiting, gave me permission and shared this lovely paper with me. I can guess to whom you are corresponding. Is it Mr. Reresby?"

Kate felt her cheerful tone was edged with disapproval. "Yes. He wrote me a letter, addressed only to me. Can you imagine that?"

Betsy released the paper into Kate's hands. "Just be careful. You can't always trust men of the court."

"All men or just Peter? I wish you would tell me what you don't like about him."

"I will, one day. When does he return?"

Kate caressed the folded letter on the table in front of her. "In about three weeks. He has to take care of family business."

Betsy sat across from her as Mrs. Downs brought in the tea, three cups, and biscuits. Mrs. Downs joined Kate on the bench. "Do you have time to join us for some tea, Betsy?"

"Oh, yes, this is a treat. My Lady doesn't care for tea, so it is never offered in her quarters." Betsy sampled one of the black-currant biscuits.

Mrs. Downs poured the hot amber tea. "I know, she always asks for lemon water or a fruit drink, recently raspberry."

Kate added honey to her cup. Moments like this made all her hard labor worthwhile, being with a good friend and with a second mother.

Betsy lowered her eyes, concentrating on her tea. "What news do you have of Peter's family?"

"Thomas, that's his older brother, has managed to reclaim the property and make a profit. He might even be getting married soon. Mrs. Reresby has almost consented to moving to London or outside the village here."

Betsy's cup hit her saucer with a heavy clink. "Here. Why would she want to come here?"

"I assume to be close to Peter." Kate looked at Mrs. Downs for guidance. "Betsy, you best tell me what you know."

"Nothing. I don't know anything at all. I'm sure she is a nice lady, and Peter is a nice man. I need some fresh air."

Betsy pushed away from the table and ran through the kitchen door. Kate stood ready to join her, but Mrs. Downs placed her hand on Kate. "Let her go. She told you she'd tell you. She needs to work it out for herself."

Kate understood the need to be alone at times. Personally, her own emotions and problems overwhelmed her often. She couldn't share her secret affections with her mother or her best friends. Fear stopped her from divulging too much. Fear of disapproval, of her imagination, of loneliness.

Chapter Eighteen

A brown rabbit hopped in front of Kate, not something she wanted to see so close to the flourishing herbs in the Privy Garden. Hopefully, the thorny rose bushes and prickly, flowering thistle plants would deter any wayward bunny. The cats and dogs did a fair job of forcing the rabbits to burrow elsewhere.

Today, she worked alone in the Privy Garden, a nice reprieve from the constant bombardment of questions. The other gardeners, scared of making mistakes, asked her tedious questions, although their judgement was right and on target in most cases. The potential wrath of Lady Castlemaine triggered their concern. So far, Kate had no encounters with her to cause worry. Ultimately, Monsieur Mollet was the authority.

Pondering a recent sermon of the possible damage produced by a fiery tongue, Kate prayed never to be guilty of the sins attached to a loose tongue. The silence surrounding her reinforced the beauty of few words, even if only for a few minutes.

Kate heard before she saw the intruders of her peace.

"So, he's finally signed the treaty." The lady wore a flowing loose gown of turquoise, one that allowed her to twist and turn as she flayed her arms and hands in every direction. "I suppose the king received everything he demanded."

Kate stayed on her knees hidden by a large oak tree. Betsy, two ladies in waiting, three courtiers, and a messenger in Charles' livery, walked along with her, or rather trotted to keep up with her irregular pace.

Abruptly, she stopped and pivoted to face the messenger. "Read it out loud, slowly. I want to hear every word."

He held the scroll in front of him, gold tassels hanging from the rods. The gentlemen cleared his throat.

"On this the twenty-third day of June, 1661, in the reign of Charles II of England, Scotland, Wales, and Ireland, King Charles II and Catherine of Braganza enter into a treaty of promise of marriage. Upon marriage Charles II will receive for his realm Tangier, the seven islands of Bombay, trading privileges in Brazil and East Indies, and two million Portuguese crowns. Signed: King Charles II and King Alphonse VI."

Lady Castlemaine, the first lady of the realm in all but name, the mother of Charles' daughter, the mistress of Hampton Court, wrung her hands and made a large circle on the lawn. Kate imagined her trying to determine a course of action, but there wasn't one. For Kate there never would have been a dilemma. Lady Castlemaine should not be the king's mistress, for she was married. Charles should not seek a mistress, only a wife. Baby Anne should be the child of Lady Castlemaine's marriage.

Lord, nothing is as it should be. This is the life my parents and You want me to avoid. Help me keep my beliefs pure, even in the midst of this drama.

How could Kate feel sorry for a woman who openly, blatantly followed an immoral path? But she did. She had seen firsthand the love Charles had for his mistress. He continued to lavish gifts on her and give her all her desires. This garden was for the lady, not the king. The new wing on the palace was being built for the lady to her specific design. Yet, Kate saw a woman in distress. Even though Charles gave her most of her wishes, he could not give her marriage.

The lady stood still with her elegant hands on her hips. "Does it say when the marriage will take place?" The diamond and ruby weighted fingers sparkled in the sunlight, emphasizing her importance and wealth.

"In May of next year, My Lady." The messenger rolled up the scroll and put it back in the leather carrying tube.

"Good. By then I will have delivered the king his son." The lady stretched her fingers across her belly.

Kate noticed that Betsy and the other ladies glanced back and forth. Even her close companions didn't know this news. If she told the truth, yet another child would be born into the king's household. Royal but with no claims.

As Lady Castlemaine and her party headed back inside, Betsy noticed Kate as she popped her head out from behind a tree, catching one last glimpse of the mistress. Betsy joined Kate for a moment.

"I assume you heard all of that."

"Yes. Hard not to." Kate stood, a little wobbly after being on her knees so long. "Are you surprised?"

"By the treaty or the baby? The treaty was bound to happen soon, but the child?" Betsy shook her head. "That indeed will be a feat only Lady Castlemaine would think of supplying just months before the marriage. And if the child is a boy, the king will have another illegitimate heir to reconcile to the realm. It's too much for me to comprehend."

"How do you do it day to day and not get pulled in by the lifestyle?"

"I pray, and I keep hoping there is still a decent gentleman for me somewhere."

Kate swung her arms in a circle. "There is. I know there is. Please don't give up and give in to the glamor of all of this." She spoke to herself too. *I promise, Lord. My promise of purity.*

Chapter Nineteen

The annual summer festival in East Molesey fell the first week of July. All of the neighboring parishes joined the festivities, camping out along the Thames for a few miles. The event brought needed trading and extra income for the townspeople. Rumor had it that this year the king might make an appearance, if only for a few days. London and Parliament had kept him locked away at St. James Place. But having a large group of his citizens together could entice him to partake of the country life.

"I'm so envious, Jane," Kate commented when her friend showed up at the bakery the first day of the festival. "Your parents are allowing you to wear this new dress. I wonder why?" Kate winked at Jane as she pulled at the light weight pale yellow skirt.

"I think since Edward has been coming around, they decided a little color and modest style might help keep him around."

Kate placed the soft fabric, creamy in texture, next to her own sleeve. "Perhaps your mother could talk to mine. At least they let me wear this white airy blouse under my sleeveless bodice. I don't feel quite so restricted. Anyway, I have no one to impress."

"You had Edward but gave him away."

"I gave him a little push in the right direction. And both of you couldn't be happier. Right?"

Jane hugged Kate. "Thank you."

"You're welcome. By the way, I'll be helping at our booth for a few hours, but I'm free after eleven. Let's meet and explore together. I want to watch the boat races."

Jane's eyes widened. "Boats?"

"Yes. I heard from the palace that local lords and squires along the river are having a friendly show of their boating skills. The king enjoys boating and yachting. Who knows? He might even participate."

"I'll find you for sure. Having Hampton Court open again does have its benefits." Jane left Kate for her meandering with Edward. Although Edward was probably Kate's last chance at marriage, she believed her friends had a love match that would thrill Kate for her lifetime.

Her father's booth held a prominent position, one of the first at the edge of the village where all had to pass for entry to the numerous ones set up along the river. The main thoroughfare out of town followed the river. Since she volunteered to help organize the event, Kate assured her father had first pick of location. It helped in the carting to and from the shop with fresh baked goods.

As far as she could see, booths faced each other with a wide walkway between them. She had not found any time to wander the path and peruse the merchandise. Father had his family very organized, baking for days. Awake early this morning, Kate's limbs anticipated their overuse from many hours of running back and forth and standing. The customers were nice enough, and the clinking of coins in her pockets spoke of profit. But the whole time she knew behind her, the activity along the banks beckoned young and old, visitors and townspeople, and courtiers to partake of the summer activities, food, and meeting of friends.

Would eleven o'clock ever arrive? And possibly even then the booth would be too busy for her parents to handle. Robert and Margaret had left an hour ago to explore and join their friends, both promising to return to relieve Kate. Her eyes followed Edward and Jane down the pathway as they sampled wares and stared into each other's eyes.

"Your day will come, my dear." Her mother handed Kate coins from a customer.

"I don't think so, Mother. But I am ever so happy for Jane." She clasped her hands over her heart. "I think they're in love."

"Don't be silly. Love doesn't come so quickly. But I do believe they truly like each other."

"Oh, Mother. Have you never heard of romance? Shakespeare wrote many plays about love between a man and a woman."

"How do you know that? Have you been reading his works? Don't let your father know. Anyway, that sort of romance is only for literature and drama. Marriage is practical and works best with like beings with the same goals."

"Like you and Papa." Kate wanted to see in her mother's face a sign that her parents did possess some romance, but her mother turned aside and rearranged the loaves of bread.

"Yes, exactly," her mother whispered.

Kate was not convinced marriage had to be a series of accomplished goals. What did it matter to her? She'd keep her romantic views and read her volume of Shakespeare's plays to support her opinion.

When Kate saw Margaret and Robert run toward their booth, she untied her apron and handed it to her mother for safe keeping, since a bit of the proceeds remained in the deep pockets.

Robert arrived winded, speaking between puffs of air. "You have to see the boats. There are fifteen of them. I counted. All of them have flags with coats of arms. The king's flag has a red lion like at the palace. He's sure to win."

"Is the king here? Did you actually see him?"

"Sure, at least I think it was him. Go see for yourself. All the court is on the opposite side of the river." Robert finished off a sausage on a stick before taking the wagon to the bakery for more goods.

Kate sidestepped to Margaret. "Is he telling the truth?" When did her sister begin to grow so tall? Before long, she'd surpass Kate.

"I sat on the bank and watched all the pretty people across the way. The king hasn't left his yacht yet. I did see Betsy walking with a young gentleman. She had the prettiest dress of them all. It was new, I think. The underskirt shone a bright yellow and the outer skirt was green and yellow strips. The whole dress was shining as if touched by the sun." Margaret's stare into the blue sky confirmed to Kate that her sister's head was full of romantic notions.

"All right, Margaret. Come back to our world." Kate tied an apron around her sister's gray skirt.

"One day, Kate. One day I'll be on the arm of a nice young man."

Yes, you will, Margaret. You have the time that I don't have. I had Richard briefly, and now I desire one I can't have.

Perhaps, Jane, Margaret, and Betsy could find true love or at least like her mother, companions for life.

Kate adjusted her bonnet and felt for her coin purse attached to her skirt in her pocket. Her stomach growled. In the busyness of the morning, she hadn't even taken a bite of a pastry. She bought a hand-sized beef pasty from a local vender, wrapped it in a cloth, and headed to the river, hoping to see Jane and Edward.

"Over here, Kate." Jane waved. Her friend had a blanket on the bank under a huge birch tree. Edward lounged next to her propped up on one elbow.

The cozy domestic scene made Kate want to refuse, but they were her friends and wouldn't mind her company for a little while. If she and Peter had a blanket to themselves, would she call her friends to join? *I hope I would be open to friendly intruders.* She giggled…if Peter…she was as starry-eyed as Margaret.

Jane sighed. "Don't you wish we could walk on the other side and mingle with the court?"

"Well, I walk over there every day as does Edward. And you, Jane, can come as often as you like. The gates are open, especially to you now that you are a regular," Kate said as she arranged her skirt around her ankles.

"You know what I mean."

"Yes, I do. From here it is like watching a play. We are being entertained, and we could make up scripts and dialogues for them. For example, see that older man with the long white wig and the royal blue coat? He is an earl seeking a very young lady's attention. He's a widower who needs an heir. The lady he's spied is Lady Agnes, the daughter of a duke."

Jane sat forward following the plot line. "Which one is she?"

"The one in silver and white."

"Of course, she's beautiful and so young and surrounded by many young courtiers."

"Yes, well, we'll see who remains. The earl is walking toward her. The young men part and leave her standing alone."

"Why did they do that?" Edward sat up, caught up in the charades.

"Oh, Edward. They know they are no match for the earl with his lords and money. Those young men are only members of Charles' court out of some request made by their parents. Watch, he takes her hand. 'My Lady, you are the fairest of all. Would you like to stroll with me and feast your eyes on my humble little yacht?' His is the one by the king's just a fraction smaller with the blue falcon flying. 'Yes, I would, and I'll of course marry you.'"

The three laughed, grabbing their stomachs as the fits of abandonment racked their torsos.

Jane blurted out between giggles, "You should be a writer,

Kate. Either that or your imagination is being infiltrated by whatever book you are reading now."

"It's nothing but court intrigue. Nothing seems to be real or to have a high moral value." Kate replaced her laughter with a forced smile. Indeed, the *Merrie Monarch* preferred a court of liveliness and lewdness. She hoped it did not trickle down through the kitchen and gardens and out into East Molesey itself.

Kate ate her beef pasty in silence. She waved to Betsy across the river. The gentleman, in brown breeches and a mustard hued coat, reminded Kate of Peter. He had dark hair, about Peter's age, and definitely one of the established courtiers. Betsy didn't seem to mind his attention, as her hand draped through his arm. No one forced her to attach herself. Kate had no drama or dialogue for them. Betsy had no title or wealth, only beauty and wits. To Kate, Betsy herself should be enough for any young man.

Please be careful, my friend. Courtiers are not known for their patience or high moral calling, except maybe Peter. Guard yourself, Betsy.

A bugle sounded, possibly a half mile down the river. As if predetermined and practiced, the crowds on both sides of the Thames stood and formed rows three to four deep to view the races. Kate and Jane managed to get a front row position with Edward behind them. Soon Robert and Margaret inched their way toward them and finagled their shorter bodies in front of Kate.

"I wonder how much money has been wagered on this race." Edward bent his head between Jane and Kate. "I heard the king's yacht is not part of the race, which might make it fairer."

"Look, here comes his boat all by itself," Robert said. "I think that is the king sitting on a large chair at the front of the boat."

"I believe you're right." Kate placed her hand on his shoulder and used her other as a shield against the sun.

A wavelike ripple began on both sides of the river where

court and townspeople curtsied and bowed as the boat passed. The king wore his signature long, curly black wig, and a lightweight beige coat trimmed in purple. He almost appeared to be enjoying an afternoon cruising the river, except for the constant wave and bowing of his head. Lady Castlemaine sat behind him, outshining the king with her brilliant purple robe embroidered in gold designs.

The common citizens approved of the king's thrift in clothing. Peter had told Kate that Charles did not want to repeat the mistakes of his father. At one point the royal dress had the power to make a monarch. Charles felt the lavishness and expense of his father's court in regard to clothing was one reason for his downfall. His citizens accused Charles I of valuing his clothing more than his subjects. Charles II adopted the suit—a coat, with no ornate doublet, and breeches. Even though he had lived with the fashion of Louis XIV's court, he did not adopt it, nor did Charles II make any decree regarding what people could and could not wear.

Peter had said, "Charles realizes he is no longer the absolute monarch with absolute power. Instead, he rules by paying a nod to the power of the people and Parliament. Since he doesn't yield as much power as before, he didn't need the clothes."

Before he crossed under the bridge, the king's boat pulled into an inlet and rested there. Kate watched as the king had his chair turned to face the oncoming boats.

"It looks like they are racing in threes," Edward commented.

Robert clapped. "I like it that way. Five races instead of one."

"Make that six with a final among the top three to five." Edward seemed to have valuable information or creative insight.

Kate admired the strong oarsmen as they swiftly conquered the current of the Thames. The smaller boats seemed to have the advantage.

"Your earl's boat with the blue falcon appears to be struggling," Jane said.

"Sometimes, bigger isn't better. I'm secretly pulling for the less ostentatious ones." Kate eyed a small, highly polished vessel. "I'm guessing that one will win this round."

Edward shifted his gaze to Kate's choice. "You might be right. It could possibly win overall. Watch how consistent the rowers are, not missing a stroke."

"It's easier to coordinate six than twelve." Kate continued to support her choice. The livery and flag were from a region farther north. Could Peter possibly know the owner? Peter could enlighten her on many things. If he were here, he'd be on the opposite bank with Madeline on his arm. In her dreams, he would be with Kate on either side, for she'd be in a cream-colored dress with light blue trim, her hair down, and her arm in his. On various levels her picture was not possible.

In the end her chosen boat received second place. And her dream, relegated to the back of her mind, took last place.

BY THE THIRD day of the festival, Kate missed her work in the garden. Baking and serving customers consumed her time. Today, Betsy sent a note wondering if Kate could steal away for an hour or so, and meet her over the bridge by the river. Mother approved. The line of customers would diminish by mid-afternoon in preparation for the games later.

Kate lifted her light skirt in order to walk quicker. She valued her time with Betsy. Stopping in the middle of the bridge, Kate spied her friend on the bank.

Betsy stood and advanced in her direction. "I'm so glad you could come. I feel you are the only true friend I have. Who can I trust in My Lady's circle?" Betsy held her hand briefly as they found a place on the river's edge.

Kate settled comfortably on the sloping bank. "Believe me. I needed the break too. Tell me how things are progressing at the palace with the king in residence again."

"After the first big one-sided shouting match about His

Majesty's marriage treaty, My Lady calmed down to enjoy the king's company. He's leaving tomorrow."

"That is one good thing about being close to London. He can quickly travel here." Kate passed Betsy a blueberry pastry. "Try one of these. I used a bit more sugar, so they aren't as tart."

Betsy took a bite. "Hmmm. Delicious."

"Tell me about the young gentleman I saw you with the first day of the festivities."

"Geoffrey. He was a companion in exile with the king. He's now in charge of the king's quarters here at Hampton Court, and in his free time when the king is gone, he works in the stables and oversees the upkeep of the carriages."

Like the one Peter showed me, forcing me to dream of another life.

"You looked very comfortable on his arm."

Betsy lowered her face, blushing. "I do enjoy his company." She raised her head and shook her curls as if trying to rid herself of something annoying. "Kate, I need to tell you something. It's been weighing on me for a month. It's about Peter."

Kate caught Betsy's stare. Fear? Anger? Uncertainty? So, the time had come for Kate to hear the worst about Peter, for someone to destroy her image of a true gentleman.

"All right, if you think I need to know, or if I can help."

"I feel there's nothing you can do to help. I'm alone in this situation."

The girls faced each other. Betsy picked a dandelion and blew the delicate pieces heavenward. Kate prayed as they reached upward that her prayers for Betsy would too.

Give me strength, Lord, to have the words to say, to accept what she has to say without misunderstanding or misinterpretation.

Pulling in a deep breath, Betsy let her shoulders settle. "Please have patience. You'll see the connection at the end. Some of this you already know but I need to say it out loud for my own placement of the memories and facts. First of all, you have heard from me mostly negative statements about my family. For eight years, I was a *princess* in a loving family and environment. I could not have asked for anything more perfect." Betsy smiled and stared out over the blue-black river.

"My parents laughed a lot and my brothers played with me. My every wish was granted, although I really had none, since my days contained endless hours of learning, freedom, and existence among my family. As a child I worshipped my father and my older brothers. When I was six years old, I stood between my parents blindfolded. When it was removed, my brothers presented me with a white pony of my own. I called her Dandelion, Dandy for short." Absently, Betsy picked the nearest dandelion and held it still in her lap.

"Kate, I'm not lying when I say I had a perfect life. One of my favorite pastimes was making dresses for my dolls. I had eight dolls, one for each birthday. Their dresses matched mine, for Mother always gave me the scraps—satin, velvet, silk, the softest fabric in all colors. I spun my dolls around in our new clothes." Betsy threw the flower aside. "Then it all stopped."

Kate was scared to hear the rest, although she knew part of it. "What stopped?"

"I remember the day clearly. I was on the floor at Mother's feet, playing with a kitten. My brothers were playing cards, and Mother and Father were laughing and talking. A messenger came from Oliver Cromwell. He asked Father to join with the newly formed government. Realize, I knew nothing of politics except that Charles I had been killed for doing some bad things."

Kate remembered the confusion of a beheaded king and a new leader who wasn't a king and a war and a new religion. The list continued and only minimally cleared up years later.

She still didn't understand those years. "I understand your confusion. We were only children when that happened. We believed what our parents told us."

"Yes, but you weren't offered as a token of your father's support and loyalty. He offered me as a sacrifice, to live and work in Cromwell's household as a servant. I went from a *princess* to the lowest member of a household." Tears flowed as

Betsy gathered and released her skirt in her hands. "I didn't understand. Father and my eldest brother became soldiers and my favorite brother, ten years older than I, went into exile with the beheaded king's son. I remember screaming as the carriage took me away. My family stood there getting smaller and smaller until eventually nothing was left. And in my heart that is what happened too."

Tears pricked Kate's eyes as she saw a beloved child misplaced and seemingly discarded. "But surely you got to see them."

"Yes, twice a year for the first five years or so."

"Then what happened?"

"Father was killed and Mother couldn't bear to travel and see me. She abandoned me forever. The bright part of my existence was sewing, yet the style and colors disappeared, replaced by…"

Kate spread her hands over her skirt. "Black, gray, dark blue, like this."

"Yes. The sunlight and life were taken away, forbidden. But you are not like that, Kate. You still smile and liven up my life no matter what you wear." Betsy sighed. "So, you see, since age thirteen I've been alone. When Cromwell moved from his London residence, I was placed in a nice family as their seamstress. I changed my name."

"You what?"

"I set aside my former identity and became Betsy."

"What if your mother or brothers wanted to find you?"

"They couldn't. Remember, they left me. I never wanted to leave them."

"But it's been years. They must think you are in trouble, or dead." As much as Kate might disagree with her family, she didn't think she could cut off all ties. But then again, she wasn't discarded as a child.

"Don't worry about me. My life improved after Cromwell was overthrown. I landed a nice place in Lady Castlemaine's court. Even without her patronage, I could set up my own shop in any village."

"Yes, you could."

The silence enveloped the girls. Strange nagging nuances caught Kate by surprise. All of Betsy's confession started with Kate's questions about her friend's dislike of Peter. Peter, who left for exile, whose father was killed, who had an older brother. Kate stared at Betsy and placed her hand under Betsy's chin, turning her so that she was directly in her view.

"You have the same eyes. Why didn't I see it before? Betsy, are you Peter's sister?"

Betsy's head dipped before she hardened her features. "Yes, I am. Rebecca Reresby by birth." She shrugged her shoulders. "That is what I wanted to tell you before you guessed or he guessed."

Kate shook her head, confused. "So why doesn't he recognize you?"

Betsy—Rebecca—jumped up and twirled around. Her womanly body and poise and long full dark hair looked nothing like an eight-year-old.

Kate giggled. "I see. And given the fact that you always quickly disappear when he's around, there would be no time for him to study you."

They walked to the river's edge, sober again not flitting around. Kate stopped and pulled on her friend's sleeve. "Betsy, Peter is a fine young man. I think you would like him. He must be hurting for his lost family too."

"Do you think so? How do I walk back into their lives? They abandoned me."

Give me words, Lord.

"You forgive them. Please pray about it. God can surely guide you. Do you want your family back, faults and all?" Kate thought of her own family—her strict father set in the ways of the past ten years, her mother balancing the desires of her husband and the changing times for her children, Robert and

Margaret facing childhood and youth under the new rule of a flamboyant king. Kate knew the struggles she faced living within a family caused worry and concern, but the love held them together. She'd forgive them anything. Even leaving her in a strange household as a child? That had to have been a difficult decision for her parents. Perhaps they thought she would be safe there.

Tears streamed down Betsy's cheeks and tumbled on to their clasped hands. "When I saw Peter, I wanted to run to him as if I were eight again, and he could do no wrong. And I've seen your family, disagreements and all, and want that again. I just don't know how."

"I'll help you and so will God. As for Peter, his heart will open and embrace you. He's suffered too. His decision displaced him for ten years apart from his family."

"Yet, it was his decision. I had no choice. I wanted him to come for me."

Stroking Betsy's hair Kate let her cry on her shoulder. Ten years of pain and hurt, not just for Betsy but for Peter, his mother, and his brother. The war tore this family to pieces. Peter, who confessed to being an alien in his family, now had a chance to reconcile with his mother and brother. And Rebecca? That would be the greatest miracle of all. Could he forgive his parents and Cromwell and most importantly himself? Kate believed in him. The pieces were already welding together. Perhaps if his mother came to East Molesey the process would be complete. But it wouldn't be easy. Betsy hadn't said if she would even meet Peter, much less her mother.

"Betsy?"

"You can call me Rebecca or Becca when we are alone. I haven't heard my name in such a long time. It will be our little secret."

"Little secret? This is huge…Rebecca. When will you tell Peter? In time he will figure it out. You must have a plan."

"I can't tell him." Betsy paced five feet of river bank and

turned around wearing down the grass again and again. "And you can't say a word, either."

"I've never lied to Peter." *Except about my feelings for him.* "He'll know if I do. That is one of the things he likes about me. Honesty."

"If he never asks you, then you don't have to lie. It's not as if he'll say 'Have you seen Rebecca?'"

"But if he guesses, I will tell the truth: that he needs to talk to you."

Betsy stopped trampling the grass, shook out her skirt, and placed her fists under her chin. "All right. When he returns, I'll tell him and will see if there is any hope of acceptance."

"There is always hope, my friend. I have a suspicion God will honor your honesty."

"While I'm at it, I want to tell him a few things about Madeline. She is not the right girl for him. Her image needs to be wiped from his mind." Betsy started up the embankment.

"I'd take one step at a time. Don't attack his love life just yet." Why would Kate endorse Peter's involvement with the beautiful blonde? Because he was entitled to love and happiness.

Betsy's smile lingered in contrast to her red-rimmed eyes. "Mark my words. I will tell him just where he needs to be looking, and it's not in the court."

On the bridge Kate faced Hampton Court. The red-brick walls held secret stories. Now Betsy added another. Kate prayed this one would be revealed and not because of a ghost in the many hallways.

Betsy placed a finger in front of Kate's lips. "Thank you. You are the only person in this whole realm who knows my secret."

"I'll be quiet. But remember your promise. I respect Peter tremendously and know his role in your life is about to change. Give him that chance."

Chapter Twenty

His mother limited her traveling trunks to three, which pleased Peter and the carriage driver. If she stayed away longer than a few months, Thomas would send the rest.

"It's not as if I'll need a great many dresses."

"Lady Malcolm might change your country ways and entice you to attend balls and fashionable teas and dinners," Peter suggested.

"Who wants the company of a bunch of old widows?"

"Label them pretty and entertaining ones, and then quite a few gentlemen would come calling."

His mother stood straight and regal in the center of the salon surrounded by her luggage. "Peter, don't you think you are going to marry me off."

With that look Peter knew his mother could change her mind in a moment, and all his hard work would disappear.

"Do not fret, Mother. Lady Malcolm has no intention of finding a husband for you or for herself. She says London life suits her widowhood lifestyle. You, too, will find a place and purpose. And remember there is still that manor in East Molesey if you prefer the country life again."

Two field hands arrived and carried the trunks to the carriage including his one large travel bag. Thomas waved them off, promising to send word of his marriage and confirming that the house was always home for Mother.

Peter had scouted out comfortable ale houses and hostels on the secluded rural roads. Since Charles' return and the restoration of order began, the inns improved profoundly. The ones he found had cleanly swept brick floors, crisp linens fragrant with lavender, snowy lacy curtains, comfortable and restful. Not the standards of home, but safe with ample food and drink. For his mother's comfort, Peter extended the journey to London an extra day.

Lady Malcolm sheltered his mother under her wing and roof, leaving Peter free to conduct his duty to the king. London didn't draw him as home like Hampton Court. Out of all the places in the last ten years, the palace gave him peace and hope. He understood the peace because court intrigue mostly remained in London, although bits and pieces followed the king and Lady Castlemaine wherever they went.

The hope resided in his future home and life work. Home—a wife and children. Or would his home be by himself with only his horses for company? He'd need to talk to Charles soon to finalize his purchase and his exit from fulltime courtier. For now, a wife posed intangible and untouchable, existing only in his dreams. Even his dreams eluded him and became wrapped in a haze.

In order to find the king, Peter followed the yapping of a bunch of spaniels through the halls of St. James Place. Charles preferred this palace to Whitehall where he last saw his father before he was beheaded right outside the Whitehall windows.

The king was in the Great Hall where many tables supported various projects: paintings, science displays, fabrics, books, games, a regular bazaar for Charles' eyes and desires.

The king raised his hand toward him. "Oh, Peter, you're back. Come look at this spy glass. I can see all the way into the next room. Have a glance." Charles handed Peter the glass and picked up a chart of the stars.

Impressed with the magnified images, Peter examined the scope. "I've heard of these. We could have used one or two on the continent."

They wandered from table to table where Charles touched everything and asked questions, interrupting any conversation with Peter. The only table that interested Peter was the one of books. Many nights passed effortlessly with a good book. One volume caught his eye, bound in leather. Someone had taken four Elizabethan plays and bound them into one volume: *Doctor Faustus* by Christopher Marlowe, *The Duchess of Malfi* by John Webster, *The Shoemaker's Holiday* by Thomas Dekker, and *Volpone* by Ben Jonson.

"You seem very taken with that book. Put it on my order and let's move on," Charles said.

Normally, Peter wouldn't make a purchase while with the king, but this rare find was a gift for Kate. She loved Shakespeare. Why not these other playwrights? He tucked it in his coat and patted it in anticipation of presenting it to her.

Charles picked up one of his puppies and ran his hand over the slick coat. "You know about my marriage treaty?"

"Yes. How did Lady Castlemaine take it?" Peter could imagine the rehearsed dramatic confrontation.

"I survived. At least she'd had warning for months." The king placed his arm over Peter's shoulders. The king's loose-fitting frilly white shirt, untucked over his breeches, suggested he had not any immediate state appointments. Peter was better dressed than the king at the moment.

"I have another project for you, Peter. You need to prepare Hampton Court for the honeymoon next summer. Any renovations fit for a queen. New draperies, floor coverings, furnishings in the quarters next to mine. I hope the wing for Lady Castlemaine will be finished soon. Right?"

"It is on schedule for the fall." How was the king going to

handle his mistress and his queen on the same property? Air escaped in a whistle as Peter shook his head. His words wouldn't change a thing.

"Don't worry, my friend. This is a juggling feat I will have to perfect. How to keep two women happy. And you are to congratulate me again. My Lady is to have a child in January. And she promises me it is to be a boy."

"But, sir..." Peter halted his reprimand. He didn't understand Charles' moral code when dealing with marriage and illegitimate children. These children deserved a father who could legally recognize them. Peter didn't doubt the king's love for his son Richard or his daughter Anne or the new baby, but what of his queen and Lady Castlemaine's husband? He rolled his eyes, for he could not straighten out this dilemma.

"Any news of Hampton Court?" The dust from his recent voyage still clung to his boots, but he longed to be on the road again to—home.

Charles placed his hand in a silver bowl of loose gems and let them cascade through his fingers. Peter surmised it could be time for another gift for his mistress—a string of red bobbles to appease her perhaps. "I spent two days there during the festival. I tell you that the villagers know how to entertain even while trading. From my yacht I waved to hundreds of my subjects. And I feel they enjoyed the boat race of the peers."

"I'm sure they did, sir." The king didn't give him the information he wanted. "And the Privy Garden?" And Kate?

"Oh, yes. The jungle has been tamed. Lady Castlemaine is well-pleased. Your little Puritan has worked miracles."

"Did you see her? Miss Sinclair?"

The king's attention returned to the gems. He chose five of the glittering rubies and handed them to the jeweler. "Make these into a necklace on a gold chain." His hand fluttered in front of the man's face. "Oh, you know what to do, something fit for a queen."

"For your bride?"

Charles chuckled. "Oh no, Peter, my present queen." His joke mimicked what the realm believed—Barbara Villiers the Countess of Castlemaine as queen. Did the citizens question Charles' fidelity to her? Peter knew others would catch his eye if not his heart. Would one of them be his betrothed Catherine of Braganza?

Peter's original question unanswered, he'd have to find out in person how Kate faired during his absence. How would a sweet, innocent woman hold up under the demands of a court icon like Lady Castlemaine? At least she had Mr. Payne and Mrs. Downs and even Betsy. He wished he knew more about Betsy. For all he knew she could be just like the other court ladies, seeking a position of advancement by whatever means possible —like Madeline.

Gaining Charles' attention with a pat on his shoulder, Peter ventured a request. "Do I have Your Majesty's permission to leave for Hampton Court within a few days?"

"Why the hurry?" Charles flung his long curls to his back. "Oh, I know. It must be that girl, the one you asked about. Be careful—her charm might be deceiving. Even under her Puritan dress, she is like all other women—secretive and mysterious. That is what makes the hunt exciting. I don't think I'll ever understand one woman, much less the whole tribe."

"I'm not on a hunt. Kate is not like that. Anyway, she is a friend and a very needed person around the palace," Peter defended.

"I see no problem with you leaving. I'll make sure you carry the new plans for the renovation with you. Make sure they get into the hands of the architect. Discuss the urgency of My Lady's quarters being completed and the commencement of the honey-moon renovations."

In his chamber Peter removed Kate's gift. He compared it to the extravagant jewels the king showered on his mistress. He had no doubt Kate would cherish his simple gift. A necklace of rubies would fail to improve on her simple beauty as she tilled the earth, bringing forth real rubies and diamonds in the perfectly created roses and daisies. They were her adornments sparkling in the sunshine.

THE FIELDS of wheat swayed in the wind on either side of the dusty road. Occasionally, a cottage or farmhouse with vegetable plots or small orchards dotted the scenery. The Thames serenaded Peter as he anticipated the tree-lined entrance to East Molesey and the steeple rising above the village.

"Samson, we're almost home." His faithful companion nickered as if he too was looking forward to their sojourn's end.

Since it was mid-afternoon Peter passed the Sinclair bakery without stopping. Chances were Kate would be at the palace. And what would her parents think or the townspeople if he rushed in to see her before he did anything else? Also, the action could confuse Kate. His only intention was to greet a missed friend.

The afternoon sun painted the red-brick palace walls golden, an illusion for even this king could not afford a palace embossed with gold. The drive was void of carriages and visitors, hopefully meaning Lady Castlemaine did not entertain guests today. Lazy summer days at Hampton Court would be a reprieve. As he entered the stables in the rear, he heard the sounds of construction—hammers hitting nails, workmen yelling orders. Perhaps not lazy for some.

A young stable boy appeared with shovel in hand. "I'll give you a hand, Mr. Reresby"

Peter slipped off of Samson. "Stephen, isn't it?"

"Yes, sir."

"I'll unsaddle him while you spiff up his stall with fresh hay on the floor, feed, and water too."

Samson shook his sweaty body, rid of his heavy load. He raised his head up and down, snorting as Peter brushed his damp hair. "I'll give you a rest, my friend. No long journey for a while." Samson led himself to his stall, ready for his familiar home. Actually, Hampton Court had been their longest furlough in years.

Geoffrey entered the stables from the carriage house. "Peter, it's about time you returned."

"Only a month. Surely, you didn't get bored in that short amount of time."

"I found a few things to occupy my time." Geoffrey's wink announced his entertainment included one or more of the pretty ladies. He never remained without a girl on his arm for long. They joked that Geoffrey would have a hard time settling down if he had to choose just one.

Peter smiled and shook his friend's hand.

His comrade's smile lacked the usual insincere, lazy element. Serious? Geoffrey? "It's not like that. I might have found a girl I could wrap my life around."

Folding his arms in front of him, Peter squinted at the stranger. "You're serious. Where did you find her, in the village?"

Geoffrey stepped forward and whispered, "No, here at the palace. I almost missed her because she's not a flirt like the rest of the mistress' ladies. But her green eyes caught me."

"You sound smitten."

"We'll see. Lady Castlemaine keeps her very busy, and when she's not in the palace, she's with your Kate at her house in the village or in the gardens here. I have lots of competition."

My Kate? "I wouldn't call her my Kate. We work together—that's all."

"I know that. What would Peter, a Kingsman, need with a village girl? You have the pick of the court."

"And you've already picked through them."

"Not Madeline."

"You can have her, but I think she is after a title and wealth.

And the last time I looked our knighthoods didn't come with anything but Sir."

"Don't you believe Charles will honor his word about land and wages for our years of service?"

"Yes, I've asked him recently about a piece of land nearby."

"And?"

"He's not ready to let me leave his service completely, but I am to procure the piece of property in my name by the king's authority. I have enough set aside to remodel the cottage. The elderly owners are happy with the purchase amount. Charles is thrilled that the property borders Hampton Court, and I can finally see a future beyond the court."

Geoffrey clucked his tongue. "I didn't know. I don't think I'm ready to leave court. After years of poverty, I like the liveliness and perks surrounding Charles."

While the two walked into the inner courtyard, Peter hit his gloves against his coat and breeches, releasing loose dirt and dust. "I've about had enough of the lively and oftentimes lewd court scenes. I do understand the relief of the people and the relaxed, carefree atmosphere is an attempt to return to normalcy."

His friend patted him on the back. "Did you hear what the Earl of Rochester said? It made it to the papers. 'We have a pretty witty king/And whose word no man relies on,/ He never said a foolish thing,/ and never did a wise one.'"

Of course, Peter stayed on top of the ditties about the king, unofficially part of his job. "Yes, Charles told me his response to the upstart earl. 'That's true, for my words are my own, but my actions are those of my ministers.'"

"I had heard something like that. Do you think Charles will keep his popularity?"

Peter's shrug meant… what? *Would he?* "He's been on the throne a year. If he can offer some meaningful solutions to the religion issue and work with Parliament on foreign affairs, he has a chance. And I do not think he'll fall into disfavor like his father, who never listened to Parliament. This is the first king who realizes without Parliament he would have nothing to rule."

"Let's drop the heavy predictions and find some refreshments. I'm glad you're back. You brought a little sense back into my life here."

The Great Hall of Hampton Court differed from the London palaces mainly because the king was not in residence, but also, because this palace held the reputation of being a country home away from the high political profile of London. Perhaps that was why Peter liked it better. And for the gardens and the acreage. Without the gardens, there would be no gardeners and no Kate. Now was not the time for honesty, not walking into a group of courtiers playing games and eating.

JANE PLOPPED DOWN BESIDE KATE, setting her basket between them. "He's here. I saw him riding through town. I couldn't mistake the great white horse."

"You mean Peter?"

"Of course, silly. Who else have you been missing?"

Hopefully, no one else noticed Kate's overt attention to who entered the village. "I'm glad. For his safety, of course." Jane teased Kate often about Peter but she didn't know Kate's deepening feelings about him, and she certainly didn't know his relationship with Betsy. That layer of intrigue added a new level of nervousness at seeing Peter. What if she revealed too much? She didn't want to hurt either one of them.

Kate tucked her loose tendrils in her cap. "I doubt he'll seek me out today."

"Here, let me get the dirt off your face." Jane laughed and reached out as Kate angled her face for the cleaning. "Just joking. You are as pretty as always."

Kate chuckled and grabbed a fistful of dirt intending to

harass Jane. Her friend placed her hands in front of her face. "Now, I'm just playing. Anyways, you might run into Edward and a dirt-streaked face would never suffice."

They worked side by side for a half hour. Their terrain for the day was the Privy Garden under the windows of Lady Castlemaine's quarters. The roses bloomed profusely with the detailed care of the gardeners. Kate spent extra care in the beds seen directly from the palace. While Jane checked on the rose trellises around the garden, Kate gathered her tools, content with her afternoon's work. She bent for her basket and connected with a hand instead. Startled, she reversed her action.

"Oh, Peter. You surprised me. I thought it was one of Jane's pranks."

"Only me. I wanted to surprise you, and it appears I succeeded."

She straightened her bonnet and her skirt, checked her shoes and apron. Dusty and dirty, of course. But Peter still smiled at her disheveled state. She didn't notice anything out of place with his attire. Obviously, he had changed from his travel clothes and looked like he could stroll into any king's court. Could she be any farther from him in dress and appearance?

"Let's sit in the alcove over there." He pointed to one of the new seats in the garden wall with a rose trellis giving it some privacy. He set the basket at her feet and placed his hand over hers in her lap.

His thumb caressed her fingers. "Did you miss me?"

"Well, yes, we all did. Thank you for your letter. I assume you worked everything out with your mother."

"As much as she'd let me. She's in London at a friend's house. The next move might be a house close to here. She prefers the country life."

"And the rest of your family?" Thomas and Rebecca? She wanted him to confide in her, yet then she'd have to confess her knowledge of Rebecca. She had promised to give Betsy time to confront Peter.

Peter stared at Kate's hand in his. "Thomas has established himself as a reliable landlord, farmer, and even horse breeder. He'll regain the family's position soon enough. And…" he hesitated.

"And what, Peter?"

"Uh…he's getting married. Yes, that's it."

Kate let him think his delayed response was normal. *Give me patience, Lord. You guide him in the right path.* She tried to pull her hand out from under his.

"Wait, please." He looked up from her hand, using the green depths of his eyes to captivate her. "Do you believe God can forgive anything?"

"Yes, I do."

"Can a person forgive another person for a wrong action or word?"

"Yes." She placed her other hand over his. "Yes, Peter, a person has that capability." She tilted her head and forced a smile. *He's struggling.*

"Good. Now don't look that way. All will be fine. I just have a few decisions to make." He released her hand and cupped her chin with his fingers. "You have given me courage to pursue an aggressive course of action."

"Not dangerous, I hope."

"No, not in the physical sense. I need some vital information."

Perhaps he was ready to find Betsy. *God, open his eyes.* Already too much time had been lost in their lives. If they couldn't bring it to pass, maybe she could. But she had promised Betsy to keep her secret. There had to be a way to honor that promise and to get them together.

Smiling, she walked beside Peter out of the garden into the sunlight on the open vegetable garden. She touched Peter's sleeve. "I'm glad you're home."

"I have something for you. When do you have an afternoon free?"

"This Sunday."

"Would you like to take the horses for a ride?"

Kate clapped her hands and smiled. "I have missed riding. I'm ready for another lesson. I'll bring a basket of refreshments."

"Meet me at the stables at two o'clock."

Kate turned toward the green house. Looking back at him, she waved, letting her fingers fall to her skirt. With renewed hope Kate prayed Peter would find the answers to relieve his turmoil.

WALKING through the palace the next day, Peter observed that the construction and renovations on Lady Castlemaine's suite of rooms had progressed even in his absence. Normally in the absence of an overseer, workers would not feel compelled to stay on task. But with Lady Castlemaine hovering in the halls, appearing like a mist, and demanding instant progress, Peter concluded construction had not suffered and could possibly be ahead of schedule.

Her rooms lacked the dark closed-in effect of Henry VIII's time. The chambers were larger and open with lots of outside light from the large paned windows. She had chosen a light-grain wood panel for the walls, opposite of the dark somber tone of the rest of the palace. Bright tapestries would line the walls devoid of angry wars and battles.

Wood chips and dust covered the floor. Peter crossed his arms in front of the windows without glass. A faint breeze unsettled the dust swirling it into tiny whirlwinds before landing at another site.

"What do you see, Peter?"

He stepped aside and bowed. Lady Castlemaine's sudden appearance confused him. "My Lady, I didn't expect you in this dusty chamber."

"I find I'd rather be in the midst of the creation from time to time where I can determine any mistakes before it's too late." Even as she lifted her scarlet skirt off the floor, Peter noticed the trail her train had made. He admired a woman who didn't mind a little dirt and grime in order to see a project to the end.

The regal woman posed with Peter, peering down into the Privy Garden. "This is what I was previewing from the heights. I'm impressed."

"This is where I'll have a window seat, always a view of the elegance, but also of any figures using the garden as a secluded venue."

For spying. The voices of anyone below would most likely carry up through any open window. He stored the piece of information in case he sought the garden for privacy. Indeed, it was not meant for secrets.

"Monsieur Mollet has pleased you?"

"Remarkable talent and wit. He prances around with his French airs but has to bend to the English command." She leaned toward Peter and whispered, her ringed fingers half covering her mouth. "I only argue with him for amusement. I really do like his designs and trust his judgement partially because he consults Mr. Payne and the little gardener, Kate. She is prettier than any flower out there."

Yes, she is. The lady cut her eyes toward him. He refused to submit Kate to the gossip of the court. Somehow, Kate's innocence and natural goodness had to remain intact. Had he already subjected her to too much scrutiny by befriending her? He couldn't protect Rebecca but now he had a need, an obligation to guard Kate. But it seemed Kate became a permanent necessary addition to the Hampton Court family with the ones who would care for the grounds with or without royalty within the walls. Her friend Betsy presented more of a threat with her access to the lady, her clothing, and her courtly ways. Influence could happen either way. Perhaps the girls could meet in the middle: Betsy bringing light and color and Kate sharing goodness and purity.

Later in the afternoon Peter spread Charles' rough designs for the renovation on the mahogany table in the king's antechamber. The architect, Mr. Jameson, leaned over with his monocle in place. Peter drummed his fingers on the parchment. "King Charles is adamant about the renovation being completed by March. It will greatly increase the new queen's comfort and acclamation to court life and her status."

Mr. Jameson's hot breath brought discomfort into Peter's space, as did his words. "Will he have the coinage to pay for all of the labor?"

"For now, the purse strings are generous, for Parliament supports Hampton Court as a first-class resort for the king close to London. And where the marriage is concerned, anything the king can do for the new queen is desirable. You will be paid and your workers too."

Peter was not hiring anyone he couldn't pay. So far, the king's interest in Hampton Court had helped many townspeople secure work. Reports from across the kingdom showed the restoration and distance from the war created a canopy of genuine happiness and prosperity. For the present, Charles as the Merrie Monarch was an appropriate moniker to settle years of hatred and despair.

Still the casualties of Civil War rested heavy in Peter's life. His sister's disappearance, his father's death, and the Puritan strain on religion and moral codes left wounds to heal. Although the Puritan beliefs meant nothing to him personally, they permeated Kate's life in her father's strictness, her dress, and her outlook on class. Were these barriers rigid or pliable? If Kate were the only one he had to consider, the answer would be easy and his course set. But she had a family, even a whole village, to convince. He didn't know if she saw him as a possibility.

Chapter Twenty-One

Sunday morning, his doubts plagued him. Religion seemed to bring comfort to others. He found himself in the small chapel at Hampton Court with other courtiers, Lady Castlemaine, and household servants. He kneeled in the back pew far from curious eyes. The stained glass dispersed colorful patterns on the stone floor, the saints dancing in the light. He felt so distant from the saints of history. Only just recently had he started to pray again. On his journey Peter believed God had supplied the answers for his mother. His relationship with his brother mended after years of doubt and separation.

Leave your burden here.

Peter searched for a long-ago knowledge. He'd heard and believed that before. Why not now? He'd been through too much turmoil.

The priest read the scripture from his raised podium: "All ye that are heavy-laden, I will give ye rest."

If I leave my concerns behind, how will I find answers? Can You send Becca to me or open Kate's heart to me or bring Mother contentment?

Peter bowed his head. *I'll happily give them to You. Yet, I'll be talking to You often to remind You.*

He filed out, trailing Lady Castlemaine and her ladies. One turned her head toward him. Betsy. He noticed her green eyes shaded by her lace cap. They had shared few words in the past, but both Kate and Geoffrey held her in high esteem. What was it about her that made her different? He dipped his head in recognition of her stare. The moment passed.

After the luncheon Peter placed Kate's book in his coat and headed to the stables. Young Stephen sat on a bale of hay, weaving straw into stick figures, a child's army.

Peter placed his elbows on the hay. "Do you want to help me?"

The scrambling youth reminded Peter of all the times he'd jumped for the chance to work with horses.

Stephen stood at attention like the stick soldiers he'd made. "What do you need, sir?"

"Saddle Ginger with a ladies' side-saddle. Do you know what that is?"

"Mr. Geoffrey showed me. I practiced before Lady Castlemaine rode one day."

"Fine. I'll saddle Samson. Make sure you brush Ginger's mane and tail."

"Who's the special lady? Is she the one that visits Ginger once or twice a week?"

"Well, I don't know, Stephen. Her name is Kate, and she usually has a long braid and a white bonnet and possibly an apron."

"I know her. She always brings an apple for Ginger and a pastry for me." Stephen licked his lips. "She hasn't been here since you've been back."

Peter laughed. "Well, she'll come today." For someone who had never touched a horse before her encounter a few months ago, Kate showed a soft spot for the creatures, at least for Ginger.

Kate swung her basket as she forced herself to check her pace, settling between walking and skipping.

Ginger nickered upon her arrival, her head pulled against her tie, up and down. Kate reached in her basket for the apple slices Ginger knew.

"Here you are, girl." Kate ran her hand over Ginger's face and neck.

Peter led Samson from the far end of the stables. "I hear you've been bribing Ginger."

"I have some for him, too, if you don't mind."

"Not at all."

"Where's Stephen?"

"Did you come to see everyone but me?"

She blushed, not knowing how to answer. A grinning Stephen poked his head out of a stall. "Are you responsible for preparing Ginger?" Kate asked.

"Sure am. Her strap is tight, her bridle in place, and brushed to a shine."

"Thank you." She pulled out a gooseberry tart. "I think this is your favorite."

Stephen bowed in thanks and climbed on top of a bale to consume his sweet.

Grinning from the encounter, Peter leaned against the stall with his arms crossed. "You've made a friend for life."

"Who? Ginger or Stephen?"

"Both. And me, too, if there is something in there for me."

"You'll have to wait." It was easy being with Peter. Her treats could never hurt. She handed the basket to him to strap to Samson's saddle.

With a little experience behind her, Kate used the steps with grace and confidence. Peter made sure her boot fit securely in the stirrup. Her new light-blue skirt draped over her boots. Betsy persuaded Kate to ask her mother to consider the lighter material for the sleeveless bodice and skirt with her white blouse. Surprisingly, her mother conceded. The style was simple, no lace, ribbons, or bows, but a lively color. Betsy approved of the new look. For today Kate wore a cap instead of a bonnet with strings. More of her hair framed her face. No shadows on her cheeks or brow.

Peter patted her foot and looked up at her, his eyes a dark green in the stable light. "Nice."

"What's nice?" Kate was confused.

"Everything. Your boot in the stirrup, your attire, you." He laughed. "The basket, the day. I could go on. I'm glad you are here, Kate."

"Me too." *When he looks at me like that I should probably dismount and go home.* Did she have any reason to go with him besides pleasure? A purely selfish reason. Yet, that frivolous understanding didn't force her to leave. She had to see this through. This opportunity could be the one to help Peter confront his past. She didn't know her role. Hiding away wouldn't reveal it. Perhaps a lovely ride and a shared meal would.

The mid-summer heat contrasted with the cool spring breeze the last time she rode. Peter kept their path under the shade of the trees. The tall, green grass rippled in waves in the meadows. An occasional rabbit or squirrel stirred the stalks changing the patterns. Birds in flight cast shadows over the green canvas. Kate rarely saw such undisturbed scenery.

A lone tree graced the top of a hill. Kate recognized the terrain, although last time they'd approached from the river instead of the woods.

"Is that the hill facing your house? Is it your house yet?" She assumed he had convinced the king of his plans.

"Yes. I'll race you to the top. Ready?" Samson took off with Ginger close on his tail.

The speed surprised her. A little more warning would have been nice. Then she could have said no to the racing. All she could do was hold on and trust her mount. Luckily, she still had the reins in her grip. As Samson slowed, so did Ginger. Kate was more winded than the horses.

Peter and Samson faced Kate. Were they both laughing at her? Samson opened his mouth, revealing several large teeth, and snorted. Peter's deep rumble resembled a stifled snicker.

"Give me warning next time."

"Would you have accepted the challenge?"

"Maybe not, but next time I will win."

After dismounting, Peter took Ginger's reins and led them to the large oak. He placed his hands around Kate's waist and swung her to the ground. She wobbled before finding her equilibrium again. For those few seconds, Peter held her in his grip until she pushed against his chest with her fingertips.

"Thank you. I think my legs can work now."

The horses grazed together on the hillside untethered. Peter retrieved the basket and a large table cloth. With Hampton court behind them hidden by the forest, they faced Peter's future home.

Kate folded her hands in her lap. "Where are your property lines?"

"From this hill to the river and the woods, past the house around the bend in the river. About a hundred acres total. Everything behind us belongs to the king as part of Hampton Court."

"So, this is all yours."

"It will be in a few months. I'm in no hurry. I'm in no hurry, since I'll have to renovate and furnish the house. Anyway, the Hampton Court projects need my daily attention now." Peter opened the lid of the basket and peered in like a child tired of waiting.

"Go ahead. You are as bad as Robert."

He unwrapped cheese, a loaf of bread, strawberry jam, slices of ham, gooseberry tarts, and a jar of apple cider. After tearing off a piece of bread, he cut a piece of cheese and added ham.

Kate watched the crumbs fall to the cloth and fought the urge to brush off the few around his mouth. The scenery did its best to keep her wandering eyes entertained.

He reached inside his coat. "I have a gift for you."

"For me? Why?" She rarely received any gift from anyone much less from a gentleman. Should she accept it? What would Betsy do? Or Jane? "I can't accept your gift."

"Why not? I saw it, and it begged for me to give to you."

"Peter, gifts don't talk." She giggled, sitting on her hands in order not to reach out overzealously for the item now hidden behind his back.

"This one did. Do you want it or not?"

She dropped her chin and tucked her loose hair behind her ears. "I do. I do." She sounded like Margaret, eager to see something new.

He placed a small almost square object in her hands. Wrapped in brown paper and tied with a string. Kate guessed by the weight and size that it was a book. Her eyes met Peter's as her two fingers prepared to release the string.

"Go on," he encouraged.

The paper fell away revealing a leather-bound book. She ran her fingers over the black embossed words on the cover. "*Four Elizabethan Plays*. Peter, it's beautiful."

"Open it. I think you will like these plays. I know you enjoy Shakespeare."

"Marlowe, Webster, Dekker, and Jonson. I've heard of Marlowe and Jonson but not the other two. Are you sure this is for me? It looks like something for your mother's library or yours."

"Please accept it, Kate." Peter enclosed her hands and the book in his. "It will give me pleasure to imagine you reading it. They are full of intrigue, wooing, murder, espionage, and wit."

"Have you read them all?"

"Yes. I even committed to memory the 'Month of May' song from *The Shoemaker's Holiday*."

Kate sat up taller on her knees. "Please recite some. It will be like going to a play. Have you been to many performances?"

"In exile we saw many in the French court. In London the theaters have been open for less than a year. I've seen a few, though not many new ones. Mostly, they are Shakespeare's and ones like these." He stood, cleared his throat, and looked to the distance poised as an actor.

"O the month of May, the merry month of May,
So frolic, so gay, and so green, so green, so green."

Peter gestured with his hands to the green meadows. Kate smiled and clapped her hands on her knees. His voice took on an accent worthy of the stage.

"O, and then did I unto my love say:
'Sweet Peg, thou shalt be my summer's green!'"

He stared at Kate as he spoke of Peg. Could he want her as his summer's green? The words were not his own. Spoken to her would be unrealistic. She forced herself to concentrate on the characters and to not place herself in the song.

"Now the nightingale, the pretty nightingale,
The sweetest singer in all the forest's choir,
Entreats thee, sweet Peggy, to hear thy true love's tale;
Lo, yonder she sitteth, her breast against a brier."

He bowed. Kate bounced up and clapped. "That will be the first one I read. Well done. Perchance you missed your calling. You are an exemplary actor."

"Merci, Mademoiselle. Perhaps we can discuss the plays after you read them."

"Yes, I'd like that. Thank you, Peter. It's the nicest gift I've ever received."

They returned to their perch on the hill. Kate had much she wanted to ask him. Why didn't he mention his sister anymore? Months ago, he briefly spoke of her. Did it hurt too much or had he forgotten her? One day soon it would all come out. She hated keeping secrets from him. Looking away from him, she focused on a hawk circling over the distant trees.

"Kate, what are you thinking?"

"Of family, of friends, and our lives here." She faced him, his green eyes wide and curious. "You never mention your sister, Peter. Have you given up hope?"

Now he searched the sky. She could have told him no answers were there in the clouds or the hawk's flight.

"Rebecca is always present in my thoughts. More so now that I have spent time with Mother. In London I walk the streets, hoping to see her but I have no idea what she looks like at eighteen. I look into the faces of children and have to remind myself she is not small anymore." His voice cracked as he spoke of her.

She found his hand and held it on her knee. "I'm praying that when you find her, you will be reconciled and healed."

"So, you believe she will just show up one day." He shook his head, his wavy curls covering his eyes. She brushed his soft hair aside.

"Yes, I do."

"I do too. That is why I still look."

In silence holding Peter's hand, Kate believed God could reunite Peter and Rebecca. It would be soon, but how many hurtful words would be said? Could they just meet and release the past?

Peter stood, forfeiting the conversation to the breeze. "Let's clear away the crumbs and call the horses before they eat all the grass."

"When you buy all your other horses, they will have help."

A few clicks of his tongue and the horses arrived at his side.

Kate hoped horses remained a safe topic. "Will you be able to keep Samson?"

"Yes, he's mine. I'll be using some of the thoroughbreds in the stables to start a high pedigree line. In time I'll be able to supply the king's men with fine horses."

Peter used his cupped hand to boost Kate onto Ginger. "A few more outings and you will be an experienced rider."

"I would like that. Do you think I could ever take Ginger out alone?"

"After a few more lessons. I need to show you how to fix a saddle and a bridle in case you have to adjust things on your own."

"I'm willing to learn."

"What happened to your fear, Kate?"

They headed back by way of the river, staying close to the trees lining the water. The sun still reigned over the vast meadows.

"I decided Ginger and I could be friends with help from apples and carrots, and encouragement from young Stephen."

"As I said before, bribery."

They laughed while Kate shrugged. "It works."

The orchards, well-groomed and well-tended, provided shelter from the imposing sun and seemed as a path to the palace. When Kate tried to explain to her mother, Margaret, or Jane about her impressions of the grounds of Hampton Court, she couldn't do it justice. She felt grounded in the land and gardens not the walls and its furnishings.

Kate dipped her head before rising to meet Peter's eyes. "Before we get back, I want to thank you for the outing and the book."

"My pleasure. But really you supplied the greatest gifts, this basket and yourself."

How do I respond to that compliment? She felt her cheeks warm as an undisciplined blush formed. Silence enveloped them as their journey ended in the stables. Peter's strong hands circled her waist to help her dismount. Too many possible eyes emphasized their reason to part from the embrace.

Peter tied the horses to posts and handed Kate the basket, empty except for the book and jar with a few sips of cider. Jerking his head around at the sound of a bucket hitting a stall wall, Peter whispered, "Stay here. I'll check it out." He peered into a stall. "Geoffrey? What are you doing in there?" He paused. "Oh, I see."

Peter turned his back to the stall and rose and fell on his toes, staring at the ceiling with a grin.

Kate had not moved an inch. Within seconds Geoffrey stepped out, holding the hand of Betsy. Her friend had hay sticking out of her hair and clothing. Betsy tried to pick it off. At first she hid behind Geoffrey, then she boldly stood at his side.

"I…we…" Geoffrey shrugged his shoulders.

"I understand. No reason to fret, yet," Peter said.

Kate was embarrassed for her friend and stepped forward to come to her aid.

PETER STARED AT BETSY. Why did this girl let Geoffrey take her to the stables? Then he shook his head. He had taken Kate here and to the carriage house. His intentions weren't on quite the same level, although he did steal a kiss. The more he looked at Betsy the more her green eyes questioned him. What was she asking? Kate was now at her friend's side, but his eye contact with Betsy deepened.

Betsy blushed and took two steps toward him. "Peter?"

Those eyes, her dark hair, her height, and her age. Why didn't he see it before? "Becca? Could it be little Becca?"

She stopped and nodded. The young woman didn't run and embrace him nor did she flee. No smile. Only a few tears overflowing. She quickly wiped them away and raised her chin, never breaking eye contact.

The silence seemed to last for minutes not seconds. Peter tried to process her admission and what it meant. But he failed. Instead, he saw Kate's rigid stature, her arm laced in Betsy's… Becca's, her brow wrinkled not in surprise but anticipation. Had she known? Had she hidden this from him? Just an hour ago she had questioned him about his sister. And Becca, how long had she known? Since he met her two months ago? Why the deceit? Geoffrey leaned against a post, staring at the girls and then Peter. He guessed Geoffrey didn't know her identity or he would never have brought her here under Peter's nose.

Kate was the first to break the silence. "Peter…I…"

"Don't give me any excuse or lie, Kate. You knew I wanted to find my sister." His anger at Kate was a new emotion. So much for innocence and purity. Try lying and manipulating.

"But…" Kate changed her mind for no words followed. She lowered her head and dropped her defense.

"Rebecca, why didn't you tell me?" Peter stepped forward, but Rebecca stepped back releasing Kate's arm.

"You let me go ten years ago. You heard me scream and cry out when I was taken away. You didn't try to find me and take me away. You, like the rest, forgot about me. I was left in a stranger's house for years."

She circled behind Kate, causing him to search Kate's face. Tears escaped her thick lashes and dropped to the ground. She had known but the secrets had been difficult and against her nature to keep. He knew her well enough to drop his suspicions of vindictiveness.

Rebecca discarded her temporary hiding place, now pacing the stable floor. "Don't blame Kate. Unlike you, she recognized that there was a connection, some reason why I disliked you."

Running fingers through his hair didn't release the tension or clear his muddled brain. "Rebecca, I didn't know it was you. After you left, I joined Charles in exile. In a different way, I lost my family too."

Her fist pounded her chest. "But it was your choice. I had no choice. I was a pawn to appease Cromwell. After five years I changed my name and gave up on my family. I decided to find a life and existence I could claim as my own. I've done well."

As Peter expected, she had made it difficult for anyone to find her. At the moment his young sister was a picture of strength and beauty in her cream-colored dress, long curly hair, and familial green eyes. She lacked a smile and contentment. Compared to Kate, Rebecca lacked the simple joy of living. Peter didn't blame her. It was his fault, and he planned to change that.

"I won't give any excuses for our parents in what they did. Father paid with his life during the war. Thomas struggles with his battle experiences. Mother is heartbroken over the loss of you and your childhood."

He advanced a few paces and stood wringing his hands in front of his sister, her arms crossed as a protective wall. He ached to embrace her. Would that day ever come?

"When I returned a year ago, I tried to find you. There was not a trace. I described an eight-year-old girl who lived in Cromwell's household. I've never stopped looking, although I realized you were eighteen and most likely had changed your name. Mother wanted to stop living, thinking that you were dead or in some compromising situation. I never gave up hope. Each young girl I saw in London, I expected to be you. For some reason I didn't notice you here at Hampton Court. I'm sorry." Tears pooled in his eyes, barely containable. When he dipped his head, they escaped.

Rebecca stilled, her voice barely a whisper. "I didn't want to be found, Peter. I made sure we didn't spend much time together. I'm not the little sister who followed you around and worshipped you. The only reason I have let down my guard now is because of Kate."

Peter watched as Kate, her perfect mouth slightly open ready to speak, turned toward Rebecca. But her restraint prohibited any words. What influence did Kate have on Becca?

His sister's hands disappeared behind her back, giving her a less harsh aura. "Kate had only positive things to say about you. Glowing reports of your gentlemanly ways, your dreams, your looks, your dedication to king and country. The picture of the brother I had come to regard as nothing more than a deserter was a prince in her eyes. Kate couldn't understand my caution around you and my discouragement toward her relationship with you. So, a few days ago, I told her with her promise not to tell you."

Peter peered at Kate, trying to understand. Her cheeks were heated and her eyelids heavy over wide amber spheres. She clasped her hands in front of her, feet apart apparently steadying her pose. When she nodded, Peter knew Becca told the truth. Or did he know all along that keeping a secret would not have been Kate's idea?

Continuing the dramatic disclosure, Becca smiled through the delicate tears. "Her promise had conditions: that I would tell you soon, and that she would not lie to you if you figured it out. I don't think she broke her promise or lied to you. But it has caused her pain."

His sister walked over to Kate and embraced her. Both young women cried in each other's arms. Peter felt like an intruder, especially with his sister's apology.

"Kate, I'm sorry I asked you to carry the burden of my secret. You have been a dear friend to both of us," Rebecca said.

Then Rebecca opened up one side of the embrace and motioned for Peter to step into the circle. His boots seemed heavier than usual as he took three steps and was immediately in the arms of Rebecca and Kate. He kissed his sister's forehead and squeezed Kate's ribcage. Could anything be more complete?

Becca turned her green eyes to Peter. "I don't know what any of this means, Peter."

"We'll figure it out."

Geoffrey cleared his throat and looked hesitantly at Peter. What should he do with this man who thought it proper to kiss his sister in the stables?

"I'll deal with you later. For now, my sister is off limits. No more rendezvous in the stables or any place else. I will determine any future meetings with Rebecca." Peter took his brotherly role seriously, not concerned if Becca acknowledged it or not. Geoffrey would, or else.

Thank you, God, that I can be a brother again to Becca.

Geoffrey left the stables like a disciplined child or a wayward puppy. Peter knew Geoffrey would do the right thing, and their friendship would stay intact.

Becca backed out of the circle. Peter felt the void and hoped for other ties of closeness. "I'm going to leave you and Kate alone now. I have lots to think about and a mistress to please."

"About your place with Lady Castlemaine," Peter started.

"We'll discuss that later. I think you have enough on your hands."

As she left, Peter felt he would collapse, but Kate was beside him to support his weakness. He had made a jumble of things. Having rehearsed this episode many times, he always assumed he would be the one in charge with all the answers. Right now, it appeared his sister and even Kate had the upper hand, and he looked like the chastised party.

Kate did not shy away and try to fade into the background. In fact, she had not moved. The circle, comforting for a few minutes, now was broken, leaving Kate by his side, too close for him to think. He stepped away and paced back and forth in front of her, looking at the dust he kicked up with his boots.

Laughter echoed off the high beams, startling Peter at first until he realized he was the one laughing.

"Peter, what is so funny? You are scaring me." Just her voice calmed him, reining in his laughter to heavy sighs. How could he explain his joy and his fear? He wanted to laugh and cry. And Kate was right in the middle of his frustrations.

"Do you realize the utter relief and joy I have because Rebecca, my little Becca, is found? She's alive. And I laugh." For a moment he saw his sister and her new form standing in front of him, not Kate. In his imagination Rebecca smiled at him. Then the image shattered when she ran from him like she'd been running for years.

"Then I battle with fear. Fear that she will not forgive me. Fear that she is so embedded in the court that she's lost forever, fear of hatred, scorn, of punishment. What do I do, Kate? What answers can I find?"

His anger at Kate for her secrecy dissipated, for he needed her comfort and presence devoid of hate and judgment.

She walked toward him, her skirt as dirty as his attire, her braid loosened with long tendrils falling down the front of her bodice, her cap discarded in the basket. Beauty and purity, untouched by the court, gliding to his rescue.

Taking his hands in hers, she halted his pacing. "You are a good man and a faithful brother. Rebecca cannot see that now, but in time she will comprehend your hurt and pain for the years lost. If you truly want to know how I feel, I'll tell you."

He nodded.

"I see God's plan unfolding before us. He has protected Rebecca all these years. Yes, she is part of the mistress' court but she has remained wholesome and remarkably untouched by their ways. God placed her here, and you here, in order to find each other. Since He has done that, He will continue the reconciliation. He is a God of forgiveness. Rebecca and you and your mother need to accept that from Him and from each other."

Kate cupped his cheek and stroked his skin as if comforting a child. With her touch he didn't feel like a little boy but as a man loved by a woman. But this was Kate. Could she possibly love him, a man faced with difficult decisions attached to a far from perfect family? A terribly broken family.

"I'll do whatever I can to help," Kate promised. "She trusts me and knows my family. If she needs a place to stay, I'll happily share my room." She dropped her hand, paused, and bit her bottom lip. "But, remember, she has been independent for many years. She's guided her own life decisions. She won't easily give up that freedom to a big brother, well-meaning or not."

Peter let out a heavy pent-up breath and lowered his shoulders in acceptance. "So, you are saying I cannot order her to leave Lady Castlemaine's service and to never see Geoffrey again."

She giggled. "Exactly. About Geoffrey. They have been friendly for a while. It could even be love. Tread carefully please. I'd hate for you to leave her with a broken heart on top of all the confusion."

He cocked his eyebrows. "Since when did you become an expert on love?"

"I've been known to make a match before."

"And yourself?"

"Once, a long time ago." Peter noticed she wasn't sad, just honest. "Anyway, this is the time for Jane and Rebecca to fall in love. I had my chance. So, Peter, don't mess it up."

"I'll talk to Geoffrey and make sure he does things properly, not like the fiascos in court life."

"Good. One more thing." He would grant anything with those amber eyes, peeking out behind long lashes. "Forgive me."

"I already have. You acted as a friend should."

"She knew it wouldn't be long before I told you, for you are my friend too."

He bent and kissed her cheek as a friend. Her lips would have to wait. The obstacles and unanswered questions made a road block between Kate and him. For now.

While she replaced her cap and picked up her basket, Peter wondered what would have happened if he hadn't found Rebecca and Geoffrey. Would he have received the kiss he wanted after a pleasant afternoon? Somehow, he had to convince Kate she hadn't lost her chance at love.

Chapter Twenty-Two

Kate plunged her hands into the tepid water, found the rag, and began to scrub away the bits of flour and accumulated ingredients from the day's work. A window faced the side alley where a lone lilac bush grew. She wondered where the week had gone since she last saw Peter. She dared not search him out, and he certainly didn't seek her.

A few days ago, Becca had approached her in the Privy Garden under the shade of a willow tree where Kate planted a variety of ferns. The sun rarely reached the ground on that corner of the garden.

"That's the smile I like to see," Kate said.

Rebecca plopped down, crossing her legs before spreading out her flowered skirt.

Her friend picked a few clover flowers and began to string them together. "I'm tired of being gloomy. I figure I've faced the past, well, part of the past, and now I have to determine how to proceed with the future. I'm going to choose happiness."

"I'm glad to hear it. So, you and Peter are friends now?" That was Kate's prayer since the encounter in the stables.

"Can a brother and sister be friends?" She sighed. "He still wants to rule my life. Don't tell him, but some of his ideas I do like. I'm just not ready to give him my approval."

"I won't tell him. I haven't seen him this week."

"Oh. I wish he would take his attention off me and give some to you." She placed her clover chain around her wrist. "He even hovers over Geoffrey and me when we try to talk in the Great Hall. I want Geoffrey to tell Peter to leave, but he won't. I think Peter has laid down the rules with him."

"Now you know what having a family does. They look out for you, and in this case, Peter thinks he is making the best decision."

Her memories aside, Kate put the scrubbed bowl in the rinsing tub and then on the mat to dry. Through all this drama with Peter's family, Kate appreciated her family more, even her strict father. Lately, his words were few when she chose to leave her bonnet off or wore her light blue skirt instead of her dark ones. A simple "humph" let her know he noticed.

"Let me help you. I'll rinse." Mother joined Kate for the chore. "You've been around the bakery more this week."

Kate lifted the heavy pan and handed it to her mother. "Well, things have slowed down. The summer vegetables are coming to an end, and the Privy Garden is progressing to the point where planting is decreasing and the other gardeners will take over the upkeep."

Her mother looked up at Kate, emphasizing the few inches difference in height. "Is that what makes you sad?"

"I don't think I'm sad. Actually, I am very happy for a few friends. I've been waiting to tell you, but…"

"I know. You are no longer Margaret's age where every detail of every event spills over. I respect your privacy, yet I want you to know you can still share your life with me." Her mother touched Kate's wet hand and squeezed.

"I didn't mean to shut you out. I'm going to tell you about Peter and Betsy."

"Don't tell me they are courting now."

Kate laughed, shaking water on her skirt and the floor. "No, Mother. They are brother and sister."

Mother raised her eyebrows and opened her mouth in surprise. "This is a story I have to hear. Let's have some tea and biscuits. I don't want to be working when I hear this."

Smiling for the first time all day, Kate dried her hands and sat at the kitchen table with her mother. As the story unfolded, Kate felt relief, now that her mother knew something personal about her.

"I knew how close you and Betsy…Rebecca…had become, but I didn't know you felt so intensely about Peter."

She didn't mean to reveal her feelings for Peter in her story telling. Did she say anything to give her mother that idea? "But, he's only my friend, my very dear friend."

"I think this *very dear friend* has taken part of your heart. Does he feel the same way?"

"Oh, no. Not at all. He spends time with me because I listen. But he is part of the court and has ladies there, one in particular, Madeline." Her words streamed together at a rapid pace until her mother took her hand to calm her.

"I understand, as long as you know fantasies about Peter cannot become reality. Someone else will come along for you. Someone from the village. Just be patient."

A few deep breaths later, Kate nodded, affirming her mother was correct. Peter had no intention of including her in his dreams. How could he?

"Now that you know about Rebecca, would it be all right if she stayed with us for a few days? She's missed out on a family for a long time."

"I'll see what your father says. It's about time he realizes everyone connected to the king or his mistress is not evil. Rebecca and Peter are a good place to start."

"Thank you. Forgiveness can go a long way in healing past impressions and mistakes. Perhaps King Charles' reign will show people how to love and forgive, and therefore, live in peace."

Her mother reached for Kate's hand across the table. "Perhaps one family at a time." Hope pumped through their hands to Kate's misguided perception that things might never change. If she could help her friends reestablish their love and trust, then she could help her father too. She did not want to live in fear of what he might say or think. Honesty on her part could open up that gulf between them, and in time, perchance, the next man she took a liking to would pass her father's judgment. Although Kate believed there would not be another man for her. Yet, for Margaret the hope existed.

At that moment her little sister hopped into the kitchen, threw her apron on the counter, and blurted out her request. "I'm ready to see Betsy again. When can she come over for a sewing lesson or just to talk?"

Kate shook her head. Her sister's youthful actions lacked poise and patience. But Mother laughed and held out her other hand to Margaret. "We were just speaking of…Betsy. I think that suggestion is a good one. I'll leave you and Kate to discuss the details."

In the space of a few minutes, Kate told Rebecca's story again. Each time it became clearer that Rebecca and Peter had a unique opportunity to turn a terrible mishap into something beautiful and permanent.

"So, I have to call Betsy 'Rebecca' now?"

"Yes, but she's the same person. I think she likes coming here because we're a family."

"She likes our family, even Father?" Margaret released some of her pent-up energy by circling the table with skips and twirls.

"If you can sit for a few minutes, we'll write a message to her and invite her to come her next free afternoon." Kate knew Margaret enjoyed Becca's company, but would she like her staying here for an extended period of time? "Suppose Rebecca wants to stay with us for a few days or even longer?"

"Here? I'd love it. I'd learn so much."

"Yes, you would, but remember she wouldn't be here to be your personal tutor."

The girls laughed and with Kate's prompting, Margaret wrote an invitation to Rebecca. Kate would deliver it tomorrow.

As others' lives advanced, Kate wondered what was in the future for her. With the Privy Garden almost finished and Lady Castlemaine's court most likely moving to London, Kate's daily life would revert back to her hours in the bakery, a few in the vegetable garden, and hours to think about things that would never come to pass.

She pushed herself away from the table and away from the negative thoughts. God would give her new dreams and purpose.

HIS DAYS WERE A BLUR. Peter had envisioned summer days of wandering the countryside, checking on his future home and property, leisurely talking with Kate, along with his daily conversations with Lady Castlemaine, Mr. Payne, or the architect. No one could have convinced him a few days ago of the added task of caring for Rebecca.

Daily, they spent time together, both trying to establish a healthy relationship from debilitating pasts. The time he would have spent with Kate in the gardens, Peter used instead to capture Becca's attention and pull her away from her mistress' side.

"Let's walk in the garden," Peter suggested. The halls of Hampton Court seemed congested and smaller than usual.

"Are you hoping to see Kate?" Becca wore a light-weight orange dress, perfect for a stroll. Peter remembered his sister's favorite color was orange. As a seamstress she could design beautiful garments for queens or ladies. It pleased him that she chose a more modest attire for herself, although of fine fabric.

The cut of the bodice and lack of excessive frills would even have been appropriate for Kate.

He winked at her insinuation. "I haven't seen her all week. Someone has taken precedence in my mind and with my time."

As they entered the Privy Garden, Peter picked an orange rose and gave it to her. "Your favorite color as a child."

"And now too." She tugged at the waist of her skirt and swayed. "Out of all the colors I work with daily, orange still grabs my attention and makes me happy."

Peter led her to a bench in the wall. "We need to talk seriously for a few minutes."

She sighed, leaning her back against the pillar and facing him. "I'm listening."

"I have to go to London for a while at the king's request. Soon Lady Castlemaine and her court will be returning to London for the season. While I'm gone, I'd like you to stay with Kate if her family permits it. You could still work here during the day until the mistress leaves. Then we can rethink the situation."

Peter wanted her to say "yes" with no questions asked, just to trust his decisions. The court was not the place he wanted his sister to remain.

"Are you afraid I'll sink deeper and deeper into the sinful den of iniquity, never to return to the good life?" She giggled as she made her hands dance like hypnotizing snakes.

"Yes."

"I'm not opposed to spending time at the Sinclair's. I'm surprised you think a village home is the proper place for me."

"It is for now. A little wholesome simple fare might counteract the opulence you exist in now. It's not forever. I have a few more plans in the works."

"Can you tell me?"

"Not yet. For now, I need to know you are safe for a few weeks."

"Do you want me to tell My Lady or do you get the honors?"

"I'll handle Lady Castlemaine after I talk to the Sinclairs. I need to know that you are willing to try my experiment."

"And this keeps me away from Geoffrey."

"It helps." Peter smiled, knowing that in his absence he would not be able to keep his eye on them. Perhaps Geoffrey was willing to act as a proper gentleman from now on.

Young Stephen ran through the garden and delivered a note to Rebecca. "It's from Miss Kate." He turned and skipped away.

Peter surmised Kate worked in the kitchen or the other gardens at the moment. Would she let him walk her home?

"Margaret wants me to come over on my afternoon off to talk and teach her something new. She is a dear child, always chattering and full of questions. She's so very content and secure in her family. I feel she knows she's loved no matter what." She folded the note and placed it on her lap.

"It should have been that way for you at age twelve." He understood but couldn't take away these last years.

She patted his hand. "I'm going to sit here for a few minutes. You go take care of your concerns and of Kate. I'll be in shortly."

He hesitated at the garden entrance, debating whether she wanted him to stay or not. With women he never knew for sure if their feelings matched their words. This time he determined that Rebecca needed time alone to work out her past.

Taking the path toward the palace's summer gardens, Peter spied Kate talking to Edward. Her wide-brimmed straw hat hid her hair and her face. She waved as he approached.

"Do you have a moment, Kate?"

Edward bowed and resumed his work at another plot. Kate raised her amber eyes to Peter's. Had it really been almost a week? Seeing her in the sun among the flowering shrubs and vegetable plants made Peter feel a part of her vibrant life. She belonged out in the beauty of creation, not behind a bakery counter. Perhaps not digging in the dirt, but strolling through the Privy Garden or orchards. She was by far the most beautiful of God's designs.

Careful. I have too many things to accomplish. Placing Kate permanently in a garden is not one of them right now.

"I've missed seeing you," Peter said.

"Me too. You must be overwhelmed with your newly found sister. I'm happy for you."

He knew his smile did not do his immense joy justice. "It is still a bit unbelievable." Peter presented the flower he hid behind his back to her. "Do you think I could walk you home today?"

Kate's fingers brushed his in the exchange as she met his gaze and bounced on her toes. "I would like that. I'll be in the kitchen with Mrs. Downs, trying out a new receipt with mint, lemons, and strawberries."

"Will I be able to sample some of it?"

"Of course. Does Mrs. Downs ever say 'no' to you?"

Laughter surrounded Peter's otherwise serious challenges. Why had he stayed away from Kate so long? And now he had to leave again at the king's command.

"YOU LOOK FINE, dear. No more flour on your pretty face." Mrs. Downs approved of Kate's clean dress after removing the apron. "Don't forget your bonnet."

Kate planned on carrying her bonnet in the basket with Peter's samples from the kitchen. The tart was sweet and tart in the same bite. They decided on mint in the crust and strawberries mixed in with the lemon custard. Kate wrote everything down on the back of an existing receipt.

Ducking under the kitchen door frame, Peter sniffed like a hound-dog searching for a treat.

"Kate has your sweet in her basket. You can eat it on your way." Mrs. Downs handed Peter the basket and shooed them out the door.

Once outside, Peter asked, "What's her hurry?"

"She doesn't want you sampling the dinner." Kate knew Mrs.

Downs really wanted them to have a leisurely walk home and not to be waylaid by small talk.

Outside the gardens, Peter opened the basket and took out a round tart, still warm.

Kate stood still, wanting his approval. "Careful. It is a bit messy since it hasn't cooled."

"Just one bite." The lemon custard managed to remain in his mouth without a dribble. "Excellent. I knew it. You wrote this one down?"

Kate tucked a stray hair behind her ear and stroked her bare head, wondering if her usually confined mane was too unruly. "Yes. It will be easy when the fruit is abundant."

At the bridge he stopped to face her. "You were right earlier, guessing at how busy I am. I need to ask you again if you would mind Rebecca staying with you for a few weeks. I'm going to talk with your father now." The ducks on the banks of the Thames quacked at the disturbance of human voices.

"Of course, I would welcome her. I've talked to Mother, and she sees no problem. I don't know Father's answer."

"I'm ready to plead my case. He has managed to rear a most recommendable daughter. Perhaps he could pass on his fatherly advice to my sister for a few weeks."

"You realize he is very strict. Although he won't lock Becca in a room, he will want some rules to be followed. He is a bit lenient to me because of my age, but he does have to keep a tight house for the benefit of Margaret and Robert."

He continued to the main road to town. "Don't you see? That is what Becca needs. I pray that she can let loose of the court a little at a time. I know she can't regain the innocence of childhood, but perhaps looking at life through the eyes of a family would anchor her desires to a simpler lifestyle. I certainly don't think it could hurt."

"You can't expect Rebecca to change overnight. Anyway, why would you want her to be like any of us?"

"Not just anybody. Like you."

"But Peter, I have changed. I'm not the same as I was months ago. Being around Becca, the palace, and you have shown me a new way to look at life. A life with color and laughter, with activities and foods."

Peter touched her arm, encouraging her to look at him. "Yet you are still warm, lovely, and pure."

Kate didn't want to break the intimate moment, the depths of his green eyes, and the tone of his deep, quiet voice. But...they were in the middle of the road one shop down from her house.

She regained her mental abilities and her arm. "This isn't about me. Let's see what Father says." Enough about her loving and pure demeanor. The same characteristics had led to forbidden kisses and embraces. How pure would her father think his daughter?

They used an alley entrance avoiding any last-minute customers. At this five o'clock hour, her father would be enjoying a pre-supper cup of lemon water or a cup of tea if he needed something stronger. Kate found him in the family room going over lessons with Robert. While Peter remained in the entrance to the room, Kate advanced and placed a kiss on her father's head.

"Father, Mr. Reresby would like to speak with you." She moved aside so he could see Peter. The two had met a few times after the petition signing, but never as formally as this.

"Sir." Peter bowed his head and took a few tentative steps. Kate covered a giggle. What did Peter have to fear? He'd met kings and princes all over Europe. Here was a common baker. Yet, Peter respected him as a business owner, a father, and a strict moral man.

Her father stood. "Please have a seat. We were just discussing Alexander the Great."

"A fine topic." Silence.

She stared at her friend. "Peter… hmm… Mr. Reresby, has a question to ask. Right?" Why didn't he speak and take hold of the conversation?

Peter left his trance behind and physically shook his head. "Yes. Right. I need your assistance if possible. I have a sister, Rebecca. I think you know her, sir, as Betsy. Well, I have to go to London, and I want her in a safe place while I'm gone."

"Is the palace not a safe place?" Her father countered in sarcasm. All along he had stated his concern about palace life.

"She is not in danger. But since I have found her, I've kept an eye on her. To be honest, sir, in your household, I know for sure that she will be well cared for and looked after. She needs a father or a brother, looking out for her."

Her father's lack of height didn't hinder his menacing presence. "And you figure I am such a model?"

"Yes, sir. I know you are. Look at Kate, she is far from harm, safe in your protection."

All eyes seemed to land on Kate, making her nervous during the critiques. How would she fare in the scrutiny?

Her father tsked. "Even she has escaped to the palace and the charm of the court."

Thrusting his shoulders back, Peter leaned forward ready to pounce if Kate read him correctly. "But not to their ways. I respect her and you with your moral standards. Please, sir, it is only for a few weeks."

"Would she still work at the palace like Kate?"

"Yes, during the days, but not at night any more. She has a lot to learn from you and your family. I wouldn't want her to be any other place."

Her father stood again, causing Peter to rise. "I will do this for Kate and for your sister. And for you, Mr. Reresby. I misjudged you. Somewhere along the way, you managed to stay above the lure of the court and the den of vipers."

Peter shook his hand. "Thank you, Mr. Sinclair." He glanced at Kate, and she winked at him. Peter used his humility and wit to win her father in this issue.

She walked him out to the alley. He took both of her hands in his and kissed her fingers, then her palms.

"Thank you," Peter said.

What did she do to deserve his kisses? She'd helped her friend in a time of need.

He leaned his head back and chuckled. "I expect the next time I confront him it won't be so easy."

"The next time?"

Peter grinned and stroked her cheek before adding a feathery kiss. "I must go and get the wheels moving for my departure. I envy Becca's few weeks with you. Bye for now."

"Goodbye." She placed her hand over her warm cheek as he rounded the building onto the street.

Chapter Twenty-Three

The king's urgency was not one of the fate of the realm or major peace treaties, but a desire in Peter's personal opinion. Did his advice ever sway Charles anymore? True, on the continent they all seemed to exist on an even plane—one of survival. Although a future kingdom drifted in and out of focus, no one claimed it as surety. Then Peter's word or Geoffrey's or any other in exile carried the same weight as exiled Charles.

Now was a completely different scenario, for Charles surrounded himself with ministers and nobles who carried power and wealth. Peter offered the presence of a friend, hardly an advisor. He'd listen to every word as needed and comment when asked.

Charles poured out his dilemmas, having most likely already sought the advice of his ministers. "Besides my nuptials and addition of Portuguese wealth, my ministers are wanting something done about the discrepancies within the Church of England. It seems each is doing its own thing, adding a little Puritan flair or whatever the priest wants. I say everyone worship how he deems appropriate—Puritan, Church of England, or Catholic. I'd like the state out of the church's business. My brother James is Catholic, as is my wife to be, and I'm Protestant because I'm afraid I'd be run out of the country if I declared myself anything else."

"So what are they proposing?" Peter knew he couldn't bring the priests of the realm together to agree on a single style of worship, but he could listen. Charles worked best surrounded by his spaniels. Already, Peter missed the open spaces of Hampton Court. The gravel and stone courtyards and pathways offered little freedom to roam. At least Charles suggested a brief walk around the gardens. They had time privately away from the listening walls, avoiding the court gossip.

Charles halted his quick pace and reached his hand out to Peter's arm. "Can you imagine? A book with common services, Scriptures, prayers. A set of rules for conducting worship."

"And the purpose?"

"Uniformity—The Act of Uniformity. If a priest or a church refuse to abide by the rules, then they leave the Church of England."

"I'd hate to be the one writing the book or the bishops deciding who is following the rules." Kate's Church of England recognized some Puritan ways as certain subjects were avoided out of respect for the Puritans who wandered back into the former church. No mention of theaters or extravagant holidays or elaborate fashions escaped from the pulpit. The minister watched his actions and words in front of newly reconciled members, like Kate and her mother. What would a book of rules do? For a priest like Reverend Turnard, he'd be forced to conform or to leave. His members, too, would have to follow the same guidelines as all other Churches of England.

Leaning his head back to catch a breeze, Peter decided his opinion wouldn't sway his friend turned king. "I can understand why you are a bit nervous. And when do the ministers want this feat completed?"

Charles laughed. "By May, the same month that I marry a Catholic queen." Charles bent to collect a stick from Rollo and threw it far down the path. The puppy's short legs scurried on the gravel for his trophy.

"Tell me, Peter. You have contact with this Puritan sect. Isn't little Kate, the puppy rescuer, gardener, cook, girl of many talents, from a Puritan family?"

"Yes. Her father refuses to go to the local Church of England, but his family attends. The priest is sympathetic to the villagers' plight. I think he handles the differences with patience and Christian love. Remember all of these citizens, whether priests or commoners, lived through the years with Cromwell where the Puritan doctrine ruled."

"Could that church and priest conform and use the new book of uniformity?"

"Depends on what's in the book."

"Yes, I see. Now you know my major project proposed by my ministers, not me."

In the past, the king would have a strong voice. Now parliament would win no matter what the opinion of the king. But the citizens wanted the king and parliament to agree; therefore, the hours of debate and compromise.

Peter wondered how the blending of beliefs would work in a marriage. Charles as Anglican, Catherine as Catholic. Kate as Puritan and Anglican. Peter as…what? Right now, God was his sole source of belief. The rest would have to fall in place.

They turned around and found the back of St. James Palace. The king's hour away from his ministers drew to an end. Their personal conversations would hold for another day.

Charles turned his head slightly before entering the halls. "One more thing. Lady Castlemaine is to return to London in a few weeks. I want to hold a ball in late September to welcome her and to open the London season. We'll use the great ballroom at Whitehall. I'd like you in attendance."

Peter hesitated. Two weeks in London, a week to pack up and close down Hampton Court and back to London for how long? He had plans that didn't include London, but now his plans had to give way to the king's. Perhaps with his mother's help, he could mesh his plans. The key to his success fell in Kate's lap. Would she comply?

MOTHER HAD the drawing room to herself. Her dark-green satin dress complemented the austere, elegant upholstered chairs and sofa.

Peter kissed his mother's cheek. "I need to talk to you. So much has happened since I saw you," Peter said.

"I can only hope by your smile and contagious spirit that it is good news, although I can't imagine what."

Peter noticed immediately the rose-colored cheeks and shiny healthy gray-black hair of his mother. Her health and disposition had improved once out of the dismal home in Sheffield where she surrendered herself to haunting memories.

He pulled a chair in front of her. "I found Rebecca."

Silence. He knew no other way than to just say it.

"I found Rebecca at Hampton Court."

"My Rebecca, alive!" She placed a handkerchief to her eyes.

He let her sob for a few minutes, waiting until the rapid jerks became gentle sighs. "She is a seamstress for Lady Castlemaine. Mother, she is beautiful. I was looking for a child and found a confident, green-eyed beautiful woman."

"Does she…does she for—?" His mother choked on her words.

"Forgive you?" He shrugged. "It took her a while to forgive me. But there is enough love in her to do the same for you. She does want to see you."

"When? Where? What would I say?"

"The first two I can handle. Your motherly heart and soul will have to handle the words. I made a mess of mine."

"Is all this true, Peter? Really, my little girl is all right?"

"Yes, Mother. This is not something I would joke about." He

recognized her doubts and unbelief because he had just gone through the same emotions.

"Would Lady Malcolm be willing to house two young ladies for two weeks? I want to bring Becca and her friend here. Obviously, for Becca to be with you and for the opening ball of the season."

"Yes, of course. I'll ask right away. Will she come, Peter?" The doubt shone in the wrinkles of her forehead.

"If I can persuade her friend to come, then yes. Becca will too." But how to persuade Kate to venture to London, much less to a ball?

The letters propped up against her writing box begged to be opened. "Here's one for you and one for me." Kate handed Becca the cream-colored paper with the blue wax seal.

"It's from Peter. I don't know if I want to open it. He's talked to Mother, I'm sure. Am I ready to face her?"

"You won't know what he's suggesting unless you read it." It made sense for Peter to write his sister. Kate still had his other letter, not expecting another one. She headed to the window and sat on the seat. The wax lifted, revealing Peter's neat hand.

Kate,

Thank you for your service to my family. Your friendship is immeasurable. I hope having a guest in the house has been a pleasant experience.

I wish I were there with you, wandering the grounds of Hampton Court. I will be there soon for a very brief visit. I must prepare Lady Castlemaine for her departure and close up the palace for a season.

Kate let the letter drop to her lap. She stared at the trees bending to the whim of the wind. She knew the time was coming when he would leave. When had she considered Peter a personal part of her life, her daily routine? Did she think he'd give up the court and live on his farm right away? Perhaps he'd decided to attach himself to Madeline.

She continued to read: *Please listen and understand what I am asking. I desire for you and Rebecca to come to London for a few weeks. You would stay with my mother at Lady Malcolm's house. With you there, Becca will always know she has a friend if Mother, or I, pose too much of a burden to her. Please don't refuse. I need you. Becca needs you. I want to show you the city. You will stay until after the opening ball of the court. Please convince Becca. I'm sure she will not come without you.*

I look forward to your positive response.

Peter

London? A ball? Although London was only twelve miles from East Molesey, Kate had never had any reason to visit. Could she do this even for Peter and Rebecca? He seemed to think she could give his sister confidence she lacked.

Becca walked to the window seat and sat opposite Kate. "What do you think, Kate? I guess your letter says basically the same thing." If her smile was any indication, her friend wanted to go to London.

Kate fingered her dark blue skirt. "I don't know. Do you really want me in the city social scene? What would your mother think?"

"It doesn't matter. Anyway, how could she not love you? Peter and I do. I'll fix you up with a couple of dresses—the yellow one you like and a green one that will go great with your hair."

Mrs. Reresby? Lady Malcolm? Dresses? Kate placed her hands on her flustered cheeks. "And what about my parents? They like you, but a stay in London?"

"You ask your mother, and I will talk to your father. He likes me." Betsy winked at the sneaky suggestion.

Did Rebecca have a way with her father, enough to convince him to allow this?

"That's because you talk to him at every chance you get. You make him laugh. You've helped Father rediscover his less serious self. I have a feeling you'll succeed."

"I've loved this time with your family. May I be honest with you?" Rebecca took her hand as Kate nodded. "I'm nervous about seeing Mother. It will be as if I'm meeting her for the first time. I need you by my side or I'll not even venture into the room."

"That is my reason for going. Otherwise, I would never set foot in Lady Malcolm's house."

"You need to give yourself more credit. Lady Castlemaine comments on your poise, grace, and extreme beauty. And Peter can't take his eyes off you. At the ball, all the courtiers will want to dance with you."

"Oh, I won't be going to the ball."

"We'll worry about that later."

Chapter Twenty-Four

Before Peter entered East Molesey, he turned Samson down a lane lined with trees. After scoping out the area, searching for a suitable manor to lease, Peter decided Mother and Rebecca would enjoy the proximity to town and the palace. It was an easy walk or carriage ride. The stone low-level house had wide steps leading to the entrance. Seconds after Peter let the knocker down, the property manager opened the door.

"Mr. Reresby, I've been expecting you." Mr. Townsend gestured him inside. "I think all is in order, and your requests completed."

"Thank you. I think this will meet my mother's needs. Have you made inquiries about a cook and housemaid?"

"Yes, sir. A mother and daughter from town. They have both worked at the palace in the past during the war." Mr. Townsend cleared his throat as if apologizing. Peter knew most of the town —including Kate, Mrs. Downs, and Mr. Payne—were employed by Cromwell. He was not one to judge. If Charles could forgive and move to the future, he could likewise.

"We'll set a time and meet later once I talk to my sister."

The man reached out his hand. "Here are the keys. I will

continue to care for the property for the owners and will do anything you need."

"Thank you." The men shook hands.

In the months to come, he could envision his mother and Rebecca making the house a home as they reconciled.

He unhitched Samson and breathed a sigh of relief. Pieces of his complicated life were falling into place. Four months ago, Peter had only himself to think about, if he didn't count Charles. Now, his singular existence increased by two women, or three. He had no responsibility for Kate, but she factored in to all he decided. His family attached by blood could not sever the ties easily, but Kate, she could disappear and refuse to be a part of his life.

Peter laughed. "Let's go, Samson, and see these women. I hope they don't plan on giving me much trouble." He dared not guess what the two had conspired during his two weeks' absence.

JANE RAN through the garden trellis, drooping with roses, straight to Kate, almost toppling her over into the bed of marigolds. Catching herself in Jane's outstretched hands, she managed to find her footing. "What has happened?"

Jane spun Kate around. In all their years together, Kate had never seen Jane so animated.

Shy Jane shouted the news. "Edward asked me to marry him."

"Oh, I'm so delighted." Kate stopped the spinning to embrace her friend. *It worked. My matchmaking worked.* To make it better, she believed they truly loved each other. "Give me the details."

"He asked me in front of the Hampton Court gates, for that is where we began to talk and to notice each other."

"I remember. I left you there to take the children into the gardens. I've always wondered where you got off to so quietly."

"Well, I'm glad we kept walking and talking. Anyway, we'll post the banns for the next three weeks and get married in late October after the harvest festival. Will you be there?"

"Of course. We should be back from London the first of October. Plenty of time to help with food."

"Do you think Betsy—I mean, Rebecca—oh, why did she do that? I'll never get it right. Well, do you think she'll help me with my dress?"

"Ask her, here she comes." The two girls waved at Rebecca strolling toward them. The afternoon sun bounced off her hair and added a gold shimmer over her yellow dress.

Kate watched as her two best friends met, blue eyes peering at green ones. At that moment, Kate realized how blessed she was for their friendship.

"Of course, I will." Rebecca answered a question Kate had missed. "Now, if only Kate could find the same happiness." Her tilted head, pointed at Kate, held an unspoken question.

"And you, too, Betsy." Coming from Jane, Kate knew her words to be honest. Jane could never be selfish, wanting this obvious happiness to be just for her. She'd not mind having a triple wedding if everyone could be as lucky.

Kate stopped the insinuations at once. "Let's handle one wedding at a time. And since you are the only affianced, the attention is on you, Jane."

Jane couldn't stay still longer than a squirming puppy. "I need to get back to Mother. We'll plan before you leave." She hugged her friends and left with the same energy as her entrance.

"I want that kind of ease of courtship," Rebecca said. "It seems like Peter would approve of Geoffrey since they are friends. Oh, well, I don't have time for a romance right now." She shrugged and looped her arm in Kate's. "Now you, on the other hand, might have a chance like Jane."

Kate jerked her hand, causing her friend to stop. "With whom do you see a courtship with marriage at the end?"

"Peter, of course."

Kate's mouth dropped open and her eyes popped open wide.

"Don't be so surprised. He'd be crazy not to grab you up."

Kate knew her earlier look was suspicious but not this awkward, unrealistic notion. "It's not so easy, silly girl, look at the class difference."

"Posh, he could care less. He's about given up on court life anyway."

"But your mother, my parents, the king. Surely, they have strong opinions beginning with 'no.' And you are forgetting. Peter has never mentioned anything about courting."

Her green eyes probed while her fingers drummed her chin. "Yet, he has kissed you."

How? Who told her? "How did you know?" Heat rushed up her neck to her cheeks.

"I didn't. But I'd guess by your color it might have happened more than once."

Why did she have to betray her secret? Kate turned toward the garden entrance. "Peter," she whispered, the topic in person walking toward them, smiling. He couldn't know he was the one occupying their conversation.

He embraced them together. "Ladies, this couldn't be more perfect."

"Are you always so prompt? You said today, and here you are," Becca said.

He gave the garden a sweep before letting his eyes rest on Kate. "London is relatively close. The garden looks complete. Is it?"

Kate scanned the area, trying to see it as he did with new eyes. "Just upkeep now. I can't force myself to stay away." This spot held such beauty, she dared a peek every time she could without interrupting the courtiers.

His smile lifted his dark eyebrows. "You shouldn't. You can

have access as a gardener any time." He offered his arms to the ladies. "Now, how about tea and biscuits?"

Peter seemed eager to share his plans. Kate and Becca had discussed issues over and over. Both concluded a few weeks in London would settle many unanswered worries and put some anxieties behind them.

"I'm sure Mrs. Downs would share the table in her kitchen," Kate said.

"It's already handled. Refreshments await." He guided them through the side entrance of the palace.

To Kate the room, small compared to the rest of the palace, was elaborate and ornate with tapestries, high beams, high-backed chairs, and a blue and gold rug. In the center someone had set a table with an assortment of cakes and tarts and three cups. She wanted to protest even entering the room, but realizing she was an invited guest, she determined to enjoy the occasion. After all, Peter and Becca were not the king and the mistress.

Peter leaned forward with his elbows on the table. "Don't keep me in suspense any longer. Are you two coming to London with me or not?"

Becca winked at Kate. "Do we have a choice?"

Peter appeared surprised and worried. Kate stifled a giggle. Why did his sister goad him? He sat up straighter. The confident Peter seemed less so if his wrinkled forehead and drumming fingers were any indication.

He looked back and forth between the two. "So, who do I have to convince?"

Kate's laughter escaped. "I can't stand to see you so anxious. We're going. Your sister has a knack for persuasion. You left her with a most difficult task—to convince my father and even me. I'm still not sure this is the best decision."

"Trust me—it is." Peter relaxed and bit into a small blueberry cake.

Becca sat back with her arms crossed. "How is Mother? Does she want to see me?"

"Of course, she does. She's in shock. She regrets all she did. She has no excuses. Her mistakes have stayed with her every minute." Peter reached for Becca's hand. "She wants your forgiveness."

"I don't know, Peter." Tears trickled down her cheeks. "I have seen how others forgive. Mr. Sinclair is an example in progress. As I've tried to forgive Cromwell for causing a war, he is working on forgiving royalty. With our conversations, we've met in the middle somewhere."

"She's right. I'm surprised at Father's attitude since Becca's been around. Father smiles and laughs as if he's finally put the past behind him." Kate didn't know how she'd act meeting her mother after ten years. Her friend put on a strong front, but inside she was broken.

"Perhaps, in time, you can, too, Becca. I know I had to forgive those who beheaded our king and sent Charles into exile. I think if Charles can pardon and forgive the rebels, I can also. It's not easy when I think of all the pain and death, but it is the right thing to do."

"And the Lord Jesus says to do that in Matthew: 'Forgive us our transgressions as we forgive those who transgress against us.'" Silence followed Kate's words.

Rebecca stood. "All I can say, Peter, is I will try. I have to help My Lady pack for her journey. When do we leave?"

"In a week. Lady Castlemaine already knows you will not be attending her while in London."

His sister bent to kiss him on the forehead. "I know I don't appear grateful, but I am. I appreciate what you are doing for me."

Peter blushed and watched her disappear into the Great Hall. For some reason Kate didn't feel like an outsider. In fact, she knew Peter and Becca better than they knew each other. Soon though, she would step out of their world back into hers. Their friendship would be a thing in the past.

He crossed his arms and frowned. "Why so gloomy?"

Did it show? Quickly, Kate smiled. She and Peter had a plate of goodies and tea to drink. He took her hand and turned it over. Tracing the lines on her palm, he let out a deep breath.

He sighed. "Tell me how you've fared during all of this. I had other plans for us this summer before I found Becca."

"You know I loved having your sister with me. For my family she was a needed burst of brightness." It was hard to concentrate as he drew pictures with his fingers on her palm, sending tingles to her toes. "I think she is nervous about seeing your mother. I know I would be after so many years."

"Are you nervous about London, my mother, or me?"

"Never about you." Did she sound too bold?

He laughed and kissed her wrist. She gently pulled her hand away only to have him capture the other one.

"Peter, I can't think straight when you hold my hand."

"I'm glad. That means perhaps you like it." He didn't let go. "Now, are you nervous about my mother?"

"Yes, because I want it to go well with Becca, and I want her to like me."

"Why wouldn't she like you?"

"Look at me. I'm nothing like your sister."

"I am looking at you, and I don't want you to look like my sister. You are beautiful." He moved to the chair closest to her, never dropping eye contact. "And what is most important is your love of God's creation, how you work with your hands, your love for your family and friends, and how I think you care for me."

"Peter, you don't know what you are saying. You have a whole kingdom of girls who could love you."

"So, you don't care for me? You couldn't love me?"

"Peter, stop it." *What does he want me to say? Yes, I love you and care for you and could for the rest of my life.* "I do care for you. As a…a friend…a very dear friend."

"I'll have to work on that. While we're in London, I'll have to see if my charm can sway your feelings."

"Your charm is not in question. It is me. Have you forgotten? I am the daughter of a baker and you are the son of a gentleman, courtier to the king."

"And you are the prettiest, most captivating gardener I've ever seen."

"Now you understand why I am concerned." She looked at the china cups and teapot, other symbols of their different status. Why would Peter choose a common villager over an elegant lady? He wouldn't, so she didn't want to compare herself to a refined beauty of the court. "Becca has tried to tell me what to expect from London, although I don't suppose I'll be out much."

"I wouldn't say that. I'll take you wherever you want to go. There are some well-maintained gardens, though nothing comparable to yours at Hampton Court. I'd like to take you to a play and to the ball. And you need to attend services at Westminster Abbey."

"Oh, Peter, some of that I'd love to do. Becca fitted two of her dresses for me and found me a pair of boots and slippers from one of the ladies-in-waiting. I'll be presentable enough for walking through gardens and going to market and possibly church. I can't go to the ball." She drew the line there, for she didn't care to be embarrassed in front of the king and royalty.

Peter bowed his head before once again staring at Kate. "Please wait to make your decision. I'd love to be your escort at the ball."

"What would I wear? Anyway, all the guests have been dancing since they were children. I don't know the first thing about dancing."

"Becca and I will teach you."

"Peter, let me just be there for Becca. Ventures out into society were not her stipulation for me joining her."

Peter held her hand as he walked her from the palace. "We'll drop it for now."

Kate tied her bonnet back in place. "Thank you for this opportunity. Father sees this as my one chance to see London, but my promise remains to not participate in the wayward ways of the world."

He kissed her cheek. "And I promise to protect your purity. The court will not get its hands on you. You are more important to me than anything the wealth of the court offers."

As she walked toward the vegetable gardens, she turned to him. "Remember, Father wants to speak with you."

Peter nodded. Most likely he wasn't looking forward to that talk. Father would have to be convinced of her safety in his care.

Chapter Twenty-Five

The day before the royal caravan left, Peter took Kate and Becca to see the manor house he had leased for his mother and Becca.

"Has Mother acquiesced to this move?" Becca asked.

"Yes. She thinks she will like it better than London." Peter opened the front door. "And she wants the time to get to know you."

Kate ran her hands along the hall table where the housekeeper had placed a large vase with roses. Peter would have loved to be in Kate's mind as she processed the manor. Although simpler and smaller than his childhood home, this house was large and ornate compared to Kate's. His own cottage behind Hampton Court did not equal this one, even though it had potential for expansion.

While Becca peered in every room, Kate stood at the foot of the staircase, mesmerized.

"What do you think?" Peter asked. "I wonder if my mother will like it."

"Peter, it is perfect for them, plus four or five additional people."

"Well. almost. It does have four bedrooms. And I think Becca has found one she likes."

"Come upstairs and look at the view," his sister yelled from the balcony.

Kate followed Peter up the flight. He wanted her to be comfortable around his family. He noticed she took her time, touching the furniture, the curtains, the fabric. Through her eyes, the house and furnishings would seem elaborate and unusual. Whereas to Rebecca and his mother, they would be normal, everyday items. How could Kate keep her love of simplicity while dwelling in the ultra-dramatic lifestyle in London? He'd give her time to absorb each particle of London, and hopefully, he could see it anew through her. Already, she allowed him to savor the beauty of this house, releasing it from mundane and used, to inviting and new.

From an upstairs bedroom window looking toward a stream and a forest, Peter reviewed the procedures for the next morning. "We leave by the ninth hour. Are there any questions?"

Kate half-giggled. "Do I have to go?" Was she serious at this point of the plans?

He stomped his foot. "Don't even think about backing out now, Kate."

"I'm not. I just wanted to see your reaction." She smiled, laughing with Becca.

Peter didn't mind being teased, but it occurred to him the sooner he left East Molesey with his wards the better. Kate could probably convince him to stay behind. An empty palace with a few essential servants, and the chance to see Kate every day on the grounds tempted Peter to forget London. If not for his mother and his sister, Peter would be free to concentrate on a life here.

Dropping the ladies off at the Sinclair's, Peter emphasized once again the departure plans.

"We know, at nine in the morning," both girls answered together.

He bowed to them and returned to the carriage. He'd deserve a few days' rest after the safe delivery of all the women. At least he had a handful of guards and courtiers assisting him on the journey.

THE CARRIAGE RESTED in front of a stately, white two-story mansion with an iron fence surrounding a manicured lawn. Kate surmised everything about the place, and the residents, to be properly formed and situated. Not even a piece of grass dared to wave in a different direction. Kate deemed the word "uniform" appropriate for this abode.

"Kate, you must exit the coach," Becca encouraged. "You promised to be at my side for this ordeal."

"Perhaps it won't be an ordeal." Kate remained positive about the reunion. She glanced at Peter rolling his eyes. Nothing he had said negated the fact of the meeting being painful and dreaded. Yet, Kate knew Becca wanted to see her mother. The suspense of unanswered questions made it awkward. Would the mother and daughter have anything to discuss? Would their past love heal their present situation? And, the most important one to Kate, could Becca forgive her mother?

Wanting to be the last one at the door, Kate tried to hide behind Peter. She grabbed his coat tail as Becca pulled her to her side. For the journey Kate wore a plain gray dress and her crisp white cap. Her new dresses were for daily audiences, not travel. *What will Mrs. Reresby think of me in this colorless dress?*

It's not about you.

She smiled. Of course, the only important thing right now was Rebecca. In that light Kate needed to be as invisible as possible. Her acceptance into the Reresbys' lives didn't matter at the present.

Peter squeezed her free hand before he let the knocker announce their arrival.

The butler ushered them into the drawing room. Chandelier, tall ceilings, huge fireplace, china, crystal, gold, and silver. The dazzling colors and sparkles blinded her for a second, until she focused on an elegant woman rising from the sofa. Beautiful, just like Becca. Her dark hair streaked with gray was pulled back in a loose bun. Her green eyes pooled with tears, glistening in the afternoon light. Her hands clasped in front of her emerald dress opened up wide. Kate saw the picture of a mother longing to embrace her child. The God-given relationship begged for love and comfort.

"Rebecca, my child. You are finally here. You are alive and well." Mrs. Reresby took two steps forward.

Becca looked at Kate for guidance. Kate nodded, squeezed her hand, and let go, releasing her friend to the one who had carried her, nursed her, and loved her the longest.

As Becca almost collapsed in her mother's arms, Peter moved to Kate, taking his sister's place.

"God's grace," he whispered.

"That's all it could be. I'm glad you see it as I do." An answered prayer.

"Perhaps we should step into the hall." Peter placed his arm behind her back, steering her to the door.

Becca reached her hand out for Kate's. "Wait. Don't leave. I want you to meet my mother. This is Kate Sinclair, my dearest friend. Without her I would not have come here."

Kate curtsied and dipped her head. Mrs. Reresby looked from her daughter to Kate. Instead of sizing her up, noticing Kate's attire, or criticizing her lack of social esteem, the older woman once again opened her arms and embraced Kate.

"Welcome, and thank you. What you have done is a miracle."

"I think credit should go to God. He is the author of reconciliation," Kate said.

Mrs. Reresby placed her hands on Kate's cheeks. "You are wise as well as beautiful."

"Yes, she is." Peter moved toward his mother. So far, he had not been acknowledged.

Beautiful? In this room of priceless treasures, full of light and riches? The Reresbys had a strange definition of beauty.

As Peter received his kiss from his mother, Kate began to inch her way out of the family circle. She was a friend, not a part of this reunion. Her disappearance didn't progress as planned. Both Peter and Becca held out their hands to her, beckoning her to remain.

"But this is family time, and I'm not family." Kate tried to give them their freedom to be alone.

Peter winked and laughed, the deep laugh of someone full of confidence. "You might as well be." Why did he insist on her presence? And Becca too? Was she truly needed here anymore?

A friend of the family. Almost family. She understood now what Becca felt the last few weeks. Kate's family, even her father, accepted Becca as if she were a family member, a daughter, and a sister. But Kate thought this would be different. Throwing Kate into this social stratum brought many dilemmas. Could she fit into this world even though briefly? Or should she leave on the next available coach to East Molesey?

Chapter Twenty-Six

The two dresses Becca had adjusted and made for Kate became Kate's wardrobe for the two weeks, alternating days. Not once did she put on her gray or dark blue dresses. Most days Kate walked about without her cap, letting her ringlets frame her face.

While Peter spent hours at St. James Palace with the king, and Rebecca and her mother talked of the past and of their future plans in East Molesey, Kate wandered the small garden in the back of the house. Often, she would take a book from Lady Malcolm's shelves and claim a bench with a black and white cat at her feet or in her lap. Garçon and Kate were fast friends.

Lady Malcolm took Kate under her tutelage. With no daughter of her own, the lady "adopted" her for the two weeks. Although Kate had no intention of going to a soiree or a ball, Lady Malcolm taught her all she would need to know just in case.

"A lady always needs to be prepared," Lady Malcolm said.

"But I'm not a lady, madame. I'm only a village girl." Kate protested her hostess' assumption that she would mingle with the elite.

"Sure, you are. You have more knowledge and beauty than

most of the court. All you lack is the mannerisms and dress. We'll take care of both of these before the ball."

It didn't seem to matter that Kate said she wasn't attending the ball. Becca assured her she didn't have to go. Though Kate was firm in her decision to stay away, she desired to learn all she could about being a lady.

She turned the book toward the cat purring beside her. "Look, Garçon, at this picture of a lady walking with books on her head, or this one with a lady batting her eyes over a fan. I'm supposed to glide into a room, not walk, never dance with one man too many times, and take tiny bites of a pastry." Kate had practiced with Lady Malcolm and in front of Becca and Mrs. Reresby. She ate all her meals in the dining room with the family, showing off her recently acquired table manners. Peter winked and nodded at her when she sought his help or approval, a secret language to get her through the meals.

Peter had taken them to a play in a newly opened theatre house and to friends' houses for tea or dinner. This afternoon he wanted to take Kate to Whitehall to see the preparations for the ball.

As Kate settled in the carriage, she voiced her suspicions. "Do you hope to convince me to go to the ball?"

"Always. I hope you are getting closer to saying 'yes.'"

"Why is it so important?" She would be no match for the ladies presented to the king. What if they laughed at her?

"I want you on my arm for one special night. I want the world, or at least Charles' small world, to admire you. Then, I want to claim every dance, and let every gentleman be envious."

Kate giggled at this unrealistic speech. "Lady Malcolm says a lady should not dance with only one gentleman."

"All right. You may dance with the king and Geoffrey. That's all."

"Peter, I don't have a dress, and I don't know how to dance all the drills."

"But Becca has an appointment for you tomorrow for a dress

fitting, and I've heard Lady Malcolm has brought someone in to give you some dance lessons."

"She has, but I'm not as good as you deserve."

"You'll have to follow my lead."

Silence hung inside the carriage with unspoken questions and very few answers. Kate knew she would not be gagged and carried to the ball so she said no. But what if she relented and went? Would it be so bad? A few dances with Peter and the rest of the time watching the guests and the king. She had done it before from the balcony at Hampton Court. Instead of seeing the top of heads, she would see their faces and gowns close up.

God, would it do any harm? Everyone has been so kind to me. I think they want to do this for me.

Their carriage joined others in the courtyard of Whitehall to gaze at the gardens or palace abounding with workers. After the splendors of Hampton Court, Kate was a bit surprised at the different architecture. Gone were the Tudor turrets and towers. Instead, the palace had high white walls hosting large glass windows on multiple levels. The familiar red brick of the only other palace she had seen could be seen on a building close to Whitehall. It held an arch as an entrance from the street.

Peter leaned toward her. "I know what you are thinking under that crinkled brow."

"What? That there doesn't seem to be a master plan?"

"Exactly." Peter sat back. "It has a random appearance unlike Versailles or Hampton Court. Whatever it lacks in grandeur on the outside, its interior is stimulating."

"Is this palace not as old as Hampton Court?" If anyone knew the history, Kate surmised Peter did. After all he had filled her in on the background of Hampton Court, dispersing the rumors of ghosts and skeletons.

He helped her out of the carriage and asked the footman to wait at the end of the courtyard. Before entering the building, Peter looped her arm in his and rested his hand over hers as if he wanted to make sure her hand didn't accidentally slip.

"Whitehall has a long history. There has been a residence here since the fourteenth century when archbishops possessed the site. Henry VIII gained the property from Thomas Wolsey, Archbishop of York. When Henry died, York Palace, which he renamed Whitehall, had twenty-three acres and was the largest royal palace in Europe."

They entered a large hall in the prominent, impressive building facing the courtyard. Kate had no words for the grandeur she faced. Her forward progress halted on its own force. Her jaw dropped as she tilted her head heavenward. Her abrupt action loosened Peter's hold and jerked him to a stop. His gaze followed hers. The ceiling, reflecting the afternoon sunlight from the many high windows, contained nine panels of painted cherubs and figures, each panel encased in a gold frame.

"This is the Banqueting Hall."

"I've never seen anything so beautiful." Blues, yellows, pinks, whites—angels floating on clouds above her head. God's heaven on display for her. Someone had a grand imagination—images she would never forget.

She glanced at Peter who watched her instead of the ceiling. "I agree, nothing so beautiful."

"Peter, I mean the ceiling." He couldn't be talking about her, not with the masterpiece over his head, beaming down on him.

"Oh yes. Those were painted by Sir Peter Paul Rubens for Charles I. Some of the cherubs are three meters tall. The central panel alone is over fifty-eight square meters. He painted them in Antwerp and had them shipped to London. The scenes depict the achievements of James I." The space continued on and on. "We could put Hampton Court's Great Hall in here three or four times."

He pointed to the windows with his free hand. "This two-story building with the seven bay windows across the façade is one large room used for court festivities and entertainment by the royal family. It had an austere beginning when it was burned down. But James I was determined to have it. Charles has many elaborate plans for the palace, plans previously halted by the Civil War."

No one else was in the Banqueting Hall except a few servants moving furniture, bringing in plants and statues, and setting up the stage for the king.

Kate lowered her eyes from the ceiling to Peter. "Why did you bring me here?"

He reached for her hands and looked at her through his thick lashes, one eyebrow raised. "In order for you to not be overwhelmed the night of the ball. I don't want your attention on the ceiling but on me, your escort."

She blushed. Could he be serious? "You are making this very hard for me to say 'no.' I still don't think you want me as a dance partner."

"Let's see. I'll hum a tune, and we'll try out the shiny floor." He hummed something she didn't recognize. But it helped her take her mind off her royal surrounding and concentrate on his lead.

He placed one hand in hers and his other guided her at her waist. She never missed a step. Closing her eyes as he twirled her around the room, she imagined herself in a silver gown in his arms at the ball. What were the chances that he'd be her only partner and what about the drills with the complicated steps?

Concentrate on now. This is my reality for the moment.

"Kate. Kate." She opened her eyes. They had stopped at the other end of the hall. "That was perfect. I have one more thing to show you that we might not see the night of the ball."

Could her mind stand another building with gold trimmed paintings or crystal chandeliers?

"Why the frown?" Peter tilted her head up towards his.

"I don't know that I can take anymore opulence."

"Don't worry. I want to show you one of the gardens."

Kate didn't want him to release her chin. He bent his head toward her, then backed away and whispered, "Not here. Not now."

There was a promise in his words. The room had placed romantic notions in her thoughts, or was it just Peter's closeness?

"All right. Let's see the king's gardens."

"I think you will be surprised."

They walked out into the sunlight onto a gravel path edged by well-manicured grass. As far as she could see each plot of grass had a statue in the center. She covered her mouth concealing her laughter.

Peter winked at her. "I think you are surprised."

"Confused. This is not much of a garden. Where are the flowers, the color, and the trees?"

"This garden has sixteen of these plots framed by gravel paths."

"Oh, not very impressive." Kate saw many people using the paths for an afternoon walk.

"Not compared to what you've done at Hampton Court. You should be proud of your work. Charles has yet to make changes here, but he will."

"Monsieur Mollett will have his work cut out for him."

"Yes, he will."

At the sundial Peter stopped and put his arm around Kate's waist to turn her to face the Banqueting Hall. "Please, Kate, I don't want to beg. Will you come to the ball?"

His green eyes implored her to go against her own desires and to fulfill his wishes.

"Yes, I will," she whispered. He smiled and squeezed her hand.

Chapter Twenty-Seven

"Becca, I can't go. I can't." Kate protested as Lady Malcolm's maid pulled Kate's new dress over her raised arms and torso. It was as if no one could hear her cry muffled in yards of material.

Her friend peeked around Kate's shoulder and straightened her sleeves, putting them in the proper place. "You can, and you are. Peter would be devastated as would Lady Malcolm and Mother."

But what about me and my feelings?

Kate looked at the yards of silver and white fabric covering her body. She checked the neckline, relieved again that she'd insisted on a modest square cut unlike Becca's scooped, lower-cut bodice. She might be going to the king's ball, but she didn't have to look and act like the other ladies of the court and realm. Even Becca fashioned her own dress without revealing too much.

"Now, I have brought in the long glass from Mother's room. I want you to have a look and tell me what you really think." Becca turned Kate around to see her reflection.

Kate started at her feet in silver slippers and made her way up the shimmering silver skirt overlaid with white gauze to her bodice with tiny faux pearls around the neckline and tapered sleeves flowing free at the elbow. Once she viewed her whole image, Kate waited to cry and laugh at the same time. Who was this lady?

"I look like a person from a book. I had no idea I'd look so different." She touched her long ringlets, tamed by the maid. The rest of her shining hair was loosely pulled back with pieces pinned in waves.

"You are beautiful. And yes, you're right. Very different from anyone else at the ball. Your freshness and simple, elegant dress will outshine all the young ladies."

"Even Madeline?"

"Especially Madeline. Do not worry about her. She has about ten courtiers following her around. She's only waiting for the best offer."

Becca stood next to Kate and admired her own dress in the glass. Becca's pale yellow and orange satin dress contained more ornate trimmings, buttons, and sparkles than Kate's. Her green eyes danced in the light reflecting from the gold heart shaped charm on a ribbon around her neck. Kate reached for it and raised her brows in question.

"It's from Peter." Becca caught Kate's eyes in the glass. "He gives me gifts all the time, making up for the past. He doesn't have to do that. I know he loves me, and I'm beginning to accept that Mother does, too, in her own way."

"She does. Please forgive her for her awful mistake or misjudgment. You are safe and whole and loved. And the entire time you've been loved by God, a better Father than any earthly father." Kate swiped her eyes for wayward tears.

"Enough of that. We don't want our faces blotchy for the ball." Grabbing Kate's hand, Becca twirled them around. Their skirts flowed lightly and freely around their legs and ankles. "Are you ready?"

"No, but let's go anyway before Peter and Geoffrey leave without their ladies." Kate as Peter's lady for one evening. One romantic, fantastical night. *A princess in a silver dress on the arm of a prince.*

~

PETER PACED the length of Lady Malcolm's drawing room, back and forth in front of his mother and her hostess. He knew it was inappropriate for a man dressed in the king's livery to shake sweaty palms by his side as if in fear or guilt. What was he doing exposing Kate to the vicious, merrie court?

"Get a hold of yourself, Peter." His mother used her deep authoritative voice, the one reserved to snap a boy, or a grown man, back to his senses. "Goodness, this is not your first ball. In fact, you've told me of grander balls in Versailles. What could be the matter?"

Lady Malcolm winked at Peter and patted her friend's hand in reassurance. "Can't you see, Mrs. Reresby? The only reason men act like this is about a young woman."

"Is she right, Peter? Is your total loss of decorum because of Kate? She is a baker's daughter, not a princess of England." His mother's sharp words halted his steps.

"You are mistaken. To me she is more special and valuable than any princess." He knew her words flowed out of years of snobbery passed down through generations of proper etiquette and rules. He was the one breaking the traditions and norms, not her.

"But what about, oh, what's her name? Madeline, is it? I assumed…"

"You assumed in error. You've not even met Madeline, although she would fit your design for a daughter-in-law."

Lady Malcolm, Kate's mentor and surrogate mother in London, cleared her throat. "Calm down. I'm sure Peter has no intention of relegating dear Kate to a permanent position in society. Let him have his amusement for the evening."

She was correct about exposing Kate to court life daily, but as for permanence in his life, that would be up to Kate.

"By the way, Peter," Lady Malcom continued, "you've no reason to be nervous. Kate will not embarrass you tonight. I've made sure of that."

He nodded his head to Lady Malcolm's insights and helpfulness. "Believe me, I'm not worried about her embarrassing me, but of the courtiers doing her an injustice." He noticed his mother remained speechless. She had enough on her mind with Rebecca. In time she'd figure out her role in Kate's life.

The faint swish of satin against satin paused Peter's rapid pulse, but only for a second. Two visions of pure light entered arm in arm. Propriety aside, he stared at Kate from top to bottom. Encased in a silver globe, she radiated beauty, not a false decorative cover but a shine that only purity could convey. As he bowed, he didn't take his eyes from hers, amber with pinpoints of silver.

"Peter, I can tell what you think of Kate, but what about me?" Rebecca twirled around out of focus for a few seconds giving Peter time to pull his eyes from Kate.

"Ladies, you both are stunning, pictures of perfection." Becca ran into his arms while Kate walked slowly towards him. He reached for her gloved hand extended before him and kissed her fingers. He dared not linger or he'd be drawn in by her lips and rosy cheeks, doing damage beyond repair in front of the watchful eyes of their present chaperones.

Lady Malcolm rose, inspecting each young lady. Indeed, Becca in her masterpiece would stand out among everyone, except Kate, although he guessed Geoffrey would take the opposite view.

"Do you approve?" Kate addressed his mother, the only one who remained seated and sedated, at least on the outside.

Startled, she looked at Kate. *Please be gracious, Mother.* For some reason Kate desired her approval, if not acceptance.

"Turn around, my dear." As Kate turned, his mother wiped

one eye and rose. "Yes, Kate, you are truly beautiful. You don't need my approval though. Neither of you ladies have anything to worry about. I trust Peter will take care of you as all the men will vie for your attention."

Without warning, Kate stepped towards his mother and kissed her cheek. "Thank you."

As his mother touched her cheek, Peter wondered if Kate's humble action melted his mother's hierarchal wall enough to let a baker's daughter in closer. In truth he didn't seek his mother's approval or anyone's, but if there were a chance of Kate having a relationship with his mother, he'd rejoice. Peter sighed remembering Charles' approval of Kate. Now, if only Kate could see a way across the barrier or a way to meet in the middle. The ball and dress were definitely steps forward.

The Banqueting Hall glowed as if the sun somehow shone through the dark skies. Sconces on the outside walls welcomed guests. Torches lined the drive, walkways, and steps leading them to the entrance of the enormous hall illuminated by thousands of candles in chandeliers and candelabrums. Peter imagined every inch of the polished surfaces reflected the golden pinpoints of light. After he handed Rebecca to Geoffrey, he turned to Kate claiming her arm in his.

"I see the beams of light radiating from your eyes. I hope what you see pleases you." From her grip and her stare, Peter hoped she wouldn't remain in a state of shock for long.

"It's so different with all the people and the intense light. With all the colors of the dresses, there's no reason to look at the ceiling." When she laughed, he felt her hand relax as did the furrows on her brow. "I'm glad there are so many people here."

"Why?"

"I can fade into the crowd."

"Before you do that, let's greet King Charles and Lady Castlemaine."

"Must we?" Her amber eyes increased in size. Fear? Sometimes, he forgot this world of royalty was foreign to Kate. She saw the King of Britain. He saw a friend, a man from exile.

"We must. He asked to see you especially, as did his mistress. Rebecca and Geoffrey are right behind us. And I promise to protect you from harm." Peter grinned and winked, for Charles had a kind, generous heart. "Anyway, never would he hurt the rescuer of his dear puppy. You are an angel to him."

Her gloved fingers went to her lips. "Oh, I had forgotten about Rollo."

On the stage at the far end of the room, the king sat on a red velvet throne greeting guests, with Lady Castlemaine at his side. Peter handed a card to the heralder who announced them.

"Mr. Peter Reresby and Miss Kate Sinclair."

Peter bowed and Kate curtsied. Instead of the usual bowing of Charles' head in recognition, Charles left his throne and stepped down to Peter shaking his hand and draping his arm around Peter's shoulders.

"You did it," Charles whispered. "How did you manage to convince Kate to come to my ball?"

Kate rose from her curtsy and glanced at Peter then the king. "Your Majesty, I don't want to appear ungrateful." She blushed and hung her head.

"My dear, I understand. I'm intimidated too." Charles touched her cheek. "Enjoy yourself." He returned to his lofty chair. Why was Peter still surprised by his friend's humanity?

Before the dancing began, Peter introduced Kate to a few friends and acquaintances. He made sure Rebecca stayed close. A part of him feared Kate fleeing for one notion or another. This was a lot for her to accept, even though she looked the part of a courtier.

The moment he dreaded arrived in a whirlwind of sapphire. Big white plumes fanned around her shoulders, allowing Madeline's blonde hair to cascade down the front. Of course, she would not miss the opening ball of the season.

"Peter, darling, I'm so glad you are here. It's been a long

time." Madeline laced her arm in his and hugged her body close to him. If only Kate had been attached to his other side, perhaps Madeline would not have pressed herself so close to him.

"Madeline, I'd like you to meet Miss Kate Sinclair. Madeline is an old friend."

"Nice to meet you." Kate dipped her head and smiled, but her smile never made it to her eyes. Didn't she know Madeline was part of his past?

"What a sweet little thing. Where did you find her?" Peter surmised Madeline had not changed her opinion of her higher status against the lower status of most everyone in the room.

He managed to dislodge Madeline's arm as he took a step toward Kate. "If you will excuse us, I think the dancing is about to begin."

"Please save me a few of the drills." Madeline's icy tone chilled him. "You know what great partners we are."

Peter followed her exit with his eyes only for a few seconds. His past fascination with Madeline had been brief. Fortunately, he had seen through her extreme beauty. She sought the glorious life of title and wealth, returning to Peter for a warped sense of approval. Even if he desired a permanent relationship, she wouldn't choose him.

On his righthand side, Kate waited, her eyes trailing Madeline too. He laced his fingers with hers, wanting confidence to replace her nervousness. "After the king opens with the first dance, will you join me on the dance floor?"

Her amber eyes sparkled, and once again he felt her smile true. "Yes, but remember I am new at this, and you are not my usual dance partner."

He laughed. "No, I'm not Becca, Lady Malcolm, or that flamboyant instructor. You'll have to suffer with a less proficient specimen."

Squeezing his hand, she said, "Thank you, Peter, for this experience. I'll never forget it."

As he stepped with her across the Italian-tiled floor with

Ruben's angels above, and gold and silver trappings on the walls and furniture, Peter realized he held the hands of the greatest prize. All faded from his vision except Kate who had not turned her gaze from him and never missed a step. His dream was to have her in his arms every night in East Molesey in a cottage with wooden planks as the floor and ceiling. They needed none of the glittering objects and expensive paintings and tapestries. Kate was priceless, and he didn't need tonight to convince him. She'd done that months ago in Hampton Court's gardens.

The music stopped and he pushed the reverie aside but wasn't ready to release Kate until Charles presented his hand for Kate's. She walked to the floor with her head facing Peter, pleading for an escape. He smiled, hoping to encourage her.

As Kate left with the king, Madeline placed herself at Peter's side, linking her arm in his. Did Kate notice Madeline's possessive pose? Etiquette demanded different dance partners, but was this one a good choice? He might as well put his obligation behind him in order to concentrate on Kate for the rest of the evening.

"This dance, Madeline?" She placed her gloveless hand in his, her long manicured fingers unflawed by work. She'd never knelt in the dirt and nurtured a plant to life. He held her loosely as they glided among the other dancers. Dancing came easily to them, a routine lacking sentiment, unlike the feelings he felt with Kate nestled close to him.

"Surely you are not thinking of something, or someone else, while I'm in your arms." Madeline searched the immediate area. Peter tried to keep Kate and the king in close proximity. "It's your village girl, isn't it? Come now, Peter, you're taking your country life a little far. What can she do for you?"

"That's enough. She has more to offer than you know."

"Don't you know everyone sees right through her? I don't see why the king is giving her his attention."

"Possibly because she does not pretend to be who she is not.

Charles trusts her. Maybe being honest and true to yourself is something you should practice."

"I see you have made your choice—the wrong choice." Madeline left Peter alone before the music halted. He stepped back into the crowd relieved, for she wouldn't pursue him again. Peter waited for Charles to return Kate to his care.

Flushed and winded, Kate leaned closer. "I'm so glad that's over, but I did enjoy the conversation. We talked of his dogs, the gardens here, his hopes for Hampton Court, and even of his new queen. He listened to me as if my opinion mattered."

"I told you that Charles is harmless. He sees you as a friend, not a threat."

"You and Madeline make a perfect pair. Such beauty and grace." She scrutinized him through her lashes.

"Well, that won't happen again tonight. Madeline has a larger goal in mind."

The first drill of the evening began, played by four and twenty musicians. Charles favored the light fantastical style of the French. He had thrown out the solemn pieces of the past decades. With Charles noise and frolic became the primary character he sought with his dances.

Peter presented his hand. "Join me? Rebecca emphasized your expertise."

After three such drills, Peter suggested refreshments. He left Kate on a velvet cushioned bench under an open window in order to catch a fresh breeze. The evening progressed as he had planned. Kate held her own in the face of the king, courtiers, the dances, and the music. He understood this wasn't her place of comfort, but her bravery and confidence put her on the same level as anyone in the room. Even though she did this for him and for Becca, perhaps she enjoyed the entertainment and variety the king's ball offered. He still preferred her presence in the more natural environment of Hampton Court. Filling a plate with an assortment of food and adding two cups of cider, Peter expected to relax with Kate, sharing the night and their surroundings.

Where was Peter? Kate fidgeted with her purse string wrapped around her wrist. The empty bench seemed to swallow her as the music and noisy crowd muffled the slight sound of rustling leaves outside the window. As she looked up, a figure in a blue billowing dress parted the crowd. At first blurred and in slow motion, Kate didn't recognize the woman until she motioned to the vacant seat beside Kate. *Madeline, the same goddess-like image as earlier. In fact, could she be more beautiful still?*

"May I join you, Miss Sinclair?" Already seated, Madeline probably knew Kate wouldn't refuse. What was she to say to Peter's former love? Did he ever mention loving her? *Maybe he did or still does?*

"Of course." Kate could think of nothing to say. Afraid of staring too long or hard, Kate forced her gaze in front of her where the dancers twirled in a rapid fog.

"I see you've been left alone. That's what Peter does best. He might pay attention to you for a while, but he has no intention of prolonging the time with you. Peter and I have an understanding. He has promised to wait for me." Madeline leaned in close to Kate, who couldn't resist the woman's intense dark eyes. They pulled her deeper into Madeline's story, holding her rigid, unable to move. "You see, I turned down his proposal because I want more than the love he offers. He's a pauper compared to what I want. Actually, he and I are the same—we both need a wealthy partner. And when we find these, we can still have our dalliances on the side. Excuse me for seeming so crude. Let's just say Peter and I are not willing to give up our physical attraction to each other."

Kate's insides twisted, her lungs pressed to explode and her hands twitched to make contact. Control won the battle. "I wish you both the best. Excuse me."

Released from Madeline's presence, Kate searched for Becca, finding her sipping punch with Geoffrey. If Kate didn't speak soon, her shaking and fear might turn to shrieking and words she'd regret. "Becca, I need to leave *now*."

"Why are you flushed and sweating? Are you ill?" Becca's arms went around Kate's waist. With no explanation from Kate, Becca took charge. "Geoffrey, please call the carriage. I need to get Kate home."

Kate's shaking didn't stop, but she felt she could control her speech, if not her confusion and anger. Her thoughts remained her own. How could she tell Becca what a rogue her brother was? She couldn't believe it entirely herself. Perhaps away from the ball and Madeline, Kate could concentrate on what was real. In fact, the whole evening had appeared a dream before it became a nightmare.

"I'm sorry to ruin your evening. Perhaps you can just send me back alone."

"Don't be silly. Geoffrey is coming with us. He's sending a messenger to tell Peter that you and I will be going home. Anyway, I've had enough of the glamorous court." Becca led Kate to the carriage with Geoffrey following behind.

Chapter Twenty-Eight

Becca sent a note to note to her mother when they arrived last night. "Kate needs to return to her home as soon as possible."

Kate couldn't put into words her own feelings, much less explain them to her hostess. She doubted Becca understood. At least she didn't know Peter's role in her desire to escape. Everyone believed Kate had embarrassed herself on the dance floor or said something inappropriate. No one knew her heart had been broken by her unrealistic view of Peter's intention and attention. Of course, she didn't belong in the king's presence or dancing with Peter while wearing a dress fit for anyone but a gardener or baker.

The day after the ball, over a light meal of bread, fruit, and cheese, Mrs. Reresby and Lady Malcom asked the questions Kate didn't want to answer. Lady Malcolm had arranged for Kate to accompany an elderly couple to East Molesey. Kate didn't feel like a burden, for Mr. and Mrs. Brown were headed to a cousin's manor about an hour beyond Kate's village.

Kate put Peter's note in her pocket, a note she had not answered when it arrived early this morning. What would she say? *I'm leaving you in the hands of Madeline, or even a warning that*

Madeline was playing with his feelings, or simply I love you and understand you won't ever love me. Instead, she decided answers would not come. While Peter was ensconced in London, she needed to find solace at her home or in the work at Hampton Court.

The older couple tried for the first hour to engage Kate in small talk, prying her with questions or telling her stories of their children and grandchildren. No longer did she look the part of Lady Malcolm's houseguest, for Kate donned her own clothes of gray with a white apron and a bonnet. All remembrances of her glamorous attire she left in Becca's care. Someone else should have better luck in the court wearing a silver dress with silver slippers. And someone else would claim Peter as her own.

As the carriage stopped in front of her house, Kate would not have traded it for all the palaces. She knew the people inside loved her, and for the moment, she needed their reassurance. Her mother raced to the open door and hugged Kate as soon as her feet hit the ground.

"Mother, it appears you received my message. You weren't worried? We are right on time." Kate made sure the embrace lasted long enough for her to gain control of her tears.

"It was so sudden. Are you ill?"

"No, just homesick. I had enough of London." And the court with beautiful ladies and intrigue. With Madeline's help, Kate saw through the secrets. Yet, part of her could not accept Peter wanting Madeline as a wife. What about his dreams, his house, his horses? *The Peter Madeline mentioned was not the same man I love, or used to love. The problem with love is I can't stop loving, even with the information I have. Could it be I'll never release my feelings for him?*

"Well, then welcome home."

The Browns disembarked to meet her parents. "Please stay for refreshments. We appreciate the safe deliverance of Kate."

Mrs. Brown shook her head, then turned and accepted her

husband's hand to reenter the carriage. "We must continue our journey. Perhaps we'll meet again."

Margaret and Robert crowded around Kate with an overload of questions. The only one practicing silence was her father. He hugged her and squeezed her shoulders. Of all her family, it seemed he understood that her turmoil had nothing to do with sickness of any kind. Did he know it was her heart? He would blame it on the court when actually her pain only involved Peter.

"I'll answer some of your questions tomorrow. Right now, I need to rest in my own room."

Her mother shooed her siblings aside. "I'll bring you some refreshments."

"WHERE IS SHE? REBECCA? MOTHER?" Peter tired of being denied entrance to see Kate. "I'm waiting for a believable answer."

Becca placed her hands on her hips. "All right. She returned to her home. And before you try to pry information from us, we don't know why, at least not from her mouth."

He knew that look. His sister accused him of something, but what?

"Son, perhaps this experiment ended how it should. She is comfortable in her position in East Molesey and not at court or here with you."

Peter shook his head. Something had to have happened between the time he left her on the bench and minutes later when he returned. What, or more precisely who, turned Kate away from him, from an evening she was enjoying? She would never leave without him unless he was involved in her fear and flight.

"I must go to her." He threw his hands in the air and let them fall against his sides with a clap. "I need to understand if I pushed her too far. I want to apologize."

Becca touched his arm and with her gentle fingers turned his face to hers. Her eyes pleaded with unyielding strength. "Give her a few days. Wait until Mother and I are packed. Go with us then as planned. I'm sure she will talk to you and explain. Anyway, she and I are both expected this week to help with Jane's wedding."

Peter snapped his eyes shut to release him from his sister's hold. He'd write Kate a note about his concern and even apologize for—he had no idea for what—his possible role in her leaving.

The rest of the afternoon Peter spent with Charles confirming his assignment for Hampton Court. As long as progress was made on the renovations for Catherine, the Privy Garden, and Lady Castlemaine's wing, Peter could use his time at his newly purchased property. Until he found out what ailed Kate, Peter didn't want to make decisions about his house. After all, he dreamed she'd be a part of the planning.

As he groomed Samson, he realized his mistake or mistakes. Suppose Kate thought he wanted her to change and be a part of the court? Suppose someone or something made her feel uncomfortable or inadequate?

Peter rested his forehead against Samson's. "Samson, I'm dimwitted when it comes to Kate." His horse lifted his head up and down agreeing with him. "I've taken a perfectly lovely girl and thrown her into an ugly court, for what purpose? Pride? Arrogance? Stupidity? I need to make it up to her, and I need to do it right."

Help me with a plan, God. I'm messing this up on my own.

THE BEST THING for Kate was to occupy herself with Jane, her dearest friend, and it was the perfect solution to forget her own woes. For in a mere three weeks, Jane and Edward would say their wedding vows in the parish church and start a lifelong journey together a few streets from Kate's front door.

I refuse to let her married state interfere with our friendship. I'll just have to rejoice in her love match and fit in where I can.

Although the wedding plans emphasized her own matchless state, Kate appeared as giddy as the bride. Flowers, colors, presents, dresses, food, and the making of a household consumed Kate's free hours.

Becca arrived at Jane's soon after Peter's letter. In a way Kate felt sorry for her two friends, who wore their perplexed looks about her removal from London on their faces with raised brows or stolen glances at each other and at Kate. Perhaps she should tell them about Madeline, but in truth Madeline was the confirmation that Kate had placed herself in the wrong world. Deep down Peter had to know that fact as truth.

Late in the afternoon, Becca laid Jane's wedding dress on Kate's bed, a shiny light-blue satin creation fit perfectly to Jane's form. "It's almost complete. Do you think she'll like it?" Becca spread out the full skirt, releasing any wrinkles.

"Even in her starry-eyed state, she will know what a treasure she'll wear. Thank you for making this so nice for her."

"I might have become her friend only a few months ago. Yet, I feel a part of her life because of you. I just wish…" Becca cut her green eyes in Kate's direction and smiled, a halfhearted attempt not quite reaching a truly convincing one. "All right. I'll say it since no one else will. I wish you and Peter were marrying as well."

"Rebecca Reresby, where did that notion come from?" Kate folded cloth napkins she'd made for the bride.

"From the way he looks at you, and he can't stop talking about you. And you are an open book, even though you try to hide it."

"But we, he…"

"Don't you throw excuses at me. I've lived a life of lies and hidden excuses. I know you think my brother, Mr. Peter Reresby, from the respected landowners of Reresby Manor, friend of Charles II, has no business marrying Miss Kate Sinclair, the daughter of a baker in East Molesey. In my opinion, you are perfect for each other. He can do anything he wants in the way of marriage. He already has the king's consent, and you've worked on Mother's heart without even knowing it."

Kate's mouth gaped as her friend discarded many of Kate's barriers. "You forget about Madeline. She said…"

"Oh, no. I hope you haven't been listening to her. Is that what all of this is about?"

"Partly. You are forgetting a major part of your argument." Kate mimicked Becca's stance, hands on hips, posed for battle, minus the swords. "Peter has not mentioned marriage or love or a future with me. All he has done is share his dreams about his future home and property. He's creating a perfect place for a family. He asks for my opinion, but not for me to share in his life there."

"My dear Kate, this whole time he's been afraid of drawing you from your Puritan world of family and rules into his world of merry court life with people living noisy, pointless lives. Think of how he views his presence in your life. He doesn't want you to lose your purity, your belief in God, your joy of the day, creation, and family."

"How do you know this?" Surely, Peter hadn't divulged all this information to his sister.

"I watch him. I listen, and if both of you would do the same, you'd know. I'm not wrong in this."

"I don't know if you are right about him, but you are right about how I feel. I do love Peter, and I trust God with the obstacles." Kate raised her arms in surrender.

Becca crossed the room and embraced Kate moments before the door opened. Margaret bounced in with Jane at her heels. Stimulated by God's ultimate control, Kate refocused on the true love story of Jane and Edward.

A path emerged as if by a secret lever allowing Jane to view her dress. "Oh." The only word Jane uttered explained her awe. She held the soft, elegant material next to her and swayed.

"Go try it on." Becca encouraged Jane by turning her toward the screen in the corner. No one said a word as if sound would disrupt the magical moment. What did anyone expect? A princess? Anyone other than Jane to emerge?

Kate spied Margaret sprawled on the bed on her stomach with fists under her chin, staring at the screen. Becca played with a ball of yarn, focusing on the movement of the trees outside the window. *If Jane doesn't hurry up, we'll all be hypnotized by the suspense.*

From behind the screen, Jane glided to the center of the room. "Beautiful." "Perfection." "Romantic." All four formed a circle and held hands.

Kate squeezed her friend's hand. "Jane, you are the first in this circle to find your true love and face an exciting future." Kate knew by age she should have been first, yet she was not envious of her best friend's fate. "In less than a fortnight you'll be Mrs. Edward Payne. Jane Payne." The girls giggled at the rhyme and embraced the bride-to-be.

"Who will be next?" Jane broke away and stood back with her finger on her lips, searching their faces.

"Well, it can't be me," Margaret said. "Father would as soon lock me up. And Kate's too old, so it must be Becca."

"Your sister is not too old." Becca seemed to scold. "I think she might surprise us sooner than you think. Anyway, I'm far from committing to any man. I need to get to know my mother and brother first. There is so much to do at our house. Mother might never let me leave."

The three congratulated Jane on her dress and left her to change. Pastries and lemon water waited for them in the family room.

"Thank you for saving me from Margaret's childish words upstairs," Kate whispered.

"It's true. I can promise you." Becca winked and bit into a sponge cake.

Me married next? Becca really does not see the obstacles.

~

OVER THE PAST FEW WEEKS, Peter had seen Kate as often as before. Something was different ever since the night of the ball. He guessed, and Becca confirmed, it was Madeline. She had put her claws in the veins of an innocent. And, he was left with salvaging Kate's opinion of him and even of the King's Court. He needed everyone's help—his mother, Becca, Jane, and most importantly, Mr. Sinclair. Confronting her father was his mission for this mid-October afternoon while Kate sequestered herself in the Hampton Court gardens.

Surprising to Peter, his mother's acceptance of Kate stemmed from the fact of spending two weeks with her in London. "She has the grace and wit of a refined lady and the fight and knowledge of a worker. The combination is irresistible. Peter, I have no objection to your Puritan maiden."

His mother's words boosted his will to confront Mr. Sinclair. Becca and Jane assured him the rest of Kate's family supported Kate.

Why did he worry about his attire for the meeting? Would the man care if he wore complete livery or filthy pants? Either way Peter expected to be thrown out of the bakery door. Did he blame her father? Why would a man holding strict Puritan beliefs want his daughter to associate with a Royalist employed by the crown?

If I don't think more positive about both of us, the interview is pointless. I must set aside labels and assumptions.

Pray, Peter.

Now? Right here?

Yes, now.

Peter felt no need to argue. Prayer for the most important decision of his life, one with barricades and obstacles. The only option was prayer. On his knees by his bed, no words spilled forth at first. God knew the situation.

"What is my role?"

Surrender.

"At this point, I surrender my wishes and desires for Yours. You know what I want. Help it not to be selfish desire, but Your lifelong will. Mold my heart and if You want, bend Mr. Sinclair's too."

His march across the bridge took seconds while his trudge to the bakery seemed to take half an hour. He found Mrs. Sinclair at the counter. If only he could speak to her instead.

"Ma'am, is Mr. Sinclair available?"

"Well, Mr. Reresby, what could you possibly want with him?" She smiled, nodding an encouragement to proceed. Could she know his mission? "In the sitting room with his feet up. Go on in and say your peace." She patted his arm after she unlatched the gate between the counters.

Mr. Sinclair sat in a well-worn cushioned chair with a book in hand, eyes closed. Peter cleared his throat. "Mr. Sinclair, may I have a word with you?"

The man sat up straighter, placed his book on the table, and motioned for Peter to have a seat. "Mr. Reresby, I assume this is a matter of the king's business."

"No, sir. It is personal."

Mr. Sinclair leaned forward and looked at Peter. "Go on, young man."

"It concerns Kate." He paused and rubbed his hands together. "And me."

"And you? What has Kate done?"

"Nothing is wrong, sir. We've spent a lot of time together and…the fact is I love her and want to marry her."

"That's not possible." Mr. Sinclair rose and walked to the window. He didn't yell or turn in anger. He just stared, away from Peter.

"Why, sir?"

Mr. Sinclair laughed and faced Peter, pointing his finger. "You are a courtier from a different class. You, I gather, are not a Puritan, maybe not even a religious man. Kate has no lineage worthy of a gentleman's son, no money. She is simply a baker's daughter, a girl with deep religious conviction. She promised me that life among the gardens of Hampton Court would not draw her into a life of impurity. Now this."

"I have no wish to change Kate. All these differences you mentioned mean nothing to me. We will live close to here on property I have purchased. We'll raise horses. I plan to only service the needs of the king here, not in London. And Kate's love of God has influenced me to renew my faith."

"Does Kate want this life with you?"

"I don't know for sure. We've spoken of dreams and plans. If you will give me permission, I will ask her and let her decide if a life with me is what she wants. I pray it is."

"Kate is old enough to make her own decision. I have nothing against you personally. Times are changing, and I suppose I must accept a few of the new ideas. If Kate loves you, I will give my permission for your union."

Peter extended his damp, shaking hand to Mr. Sinclair. "Thank you. Now, perhaps I can have confidence that she will accept me."

Chapter Twenty-Nine

Jane stood as a regal princess in the church. Kate wondered if a true princess could be any happier. Her friend's love of her life waited in front of the church, eager to complete his vows. Princess or not, wasn't that every girl's dream?

Becca adjusted the trailing veil one more time. "Relax, Jane. You might break from stiffness."

"I don't want to be in front of everyone. I just want to be married to Edward."

"All those people are your friends and family, not foreigners or dignitaries." Kate felt Jane's nervousness through her damp palms. "Time to put your gloves on."

After rolling the soft long gloves up Jane's arms, Kate handed her a bouquet of the palace's sweetest smelling roses—yellow and white.

"This should be you, Kate. You and your Richard."

Richard. Kate hadn't thought of him as a groom in a long time. Her young love for him was relegated to her youth. Another had come permanently to rest in her heart, but hardly as a groom. He held her heart with no promises. She knew Peter would be in the congregation among the guests. Their moments together had been few over the last two weeks. On purpose? Her fault for being busy? His for lack of interest?

Becca pinched Kate's elbow. "I saw Peter. He was looking for you. I haven't seen him much lately. I think he is very preoccupied with his new house."

"Really?" That would answer a few questions.

"He took Mother and me to see it last week. Peter listened to Mother talk on and on about decorating ideas. Then he calmly said he's not ready for those decisions yet."

"When does he expect to move?" Kate closed her eyes for a second and saw the cottage down the hill by the river surrounded by green pastures and trees on the border.

"He won't say. He told us 'it depends.'"

"On what?"

"Or on whom?" Becca winked at Kate, opened the parlor door, and ushered Jane into the foyer.

It depends on whom? Why does Becca like to leave me with more questions than answers? I need to concentrate on Jane, not Peter.

After Kate caught Peter's glance once, she determined to divert her attention to the ceremony. The words of commitment, faithfulness and love, children and home led her thoughts to Peter again instead of away from him. As Jane and Edward said, "I do," Kate opened the vulnerable part of her heart, wondering what she had missed by not being more honest with Peter, more responsive. Yes, the obstacles might have prevailed, but they might have been moveable.

Now, Kate would never know. She had been so wrapped up in her circumstances, she had let a possible love slip away. Were they past a point of no reconciliation or return to their earlier budding relationship? If she were a different sort of person, she'd present her open heart to Peter and accept the outcome—his love or rejection.

Jane turned with her new husband to face the audience. "Mr. and Mrs. Edward Payne." The minister released the couple to the well-wishers. Jane grabbed Kate's hand as she swept down the aisle. A squeeze and a thank you from her best friend gave Kate the hope of more good times together—good, but different.

Kate searched the grounds but never connected with Peter after the ceremony. Was her summation correct? Had Peter had enough of small-town life and Kate's persistent beliefs and actions? Her mind wanted to escape the wedding party, yet she physically and mentally remained, for Jane, Edward, and her family expected her presence. In truth, for this moment, God placed her in a situation where others came first.

Stop being selfish. Peter made his choice to leave. Anyway, I'm free now to concentrate entirely on Jane's pleasure.

HAMPTON COURT GLEAMED in front of him. The polished brass ornamentations blazed in the sunlight. With his hands stuffed deep in his pockets, Peter stood feet apart, shoulders back, glaring at the edifice.

What made him flee the wedding after the last "I do"? Was he scared he couldn't trust himself not to take Kate in his arms and propose right there? Or did he realize she was out of his reach? He had all the peripheral approval, but not the one who mattered—Kate.

The walk over the bridge was lonely. The Thames offered no comfort to someone who purposefully left a crowded church in order to be alone. Kicking gravel as he walked, Peter found himself in the Privy Gardens, a true masterpiece after months of design and care. Kate's fingerprints marked countless spots—the poignant herbs, flowering pansies, late blooming roses, and cascading ivy. He sat in an alcove, bent over, resting his elbows on his knees.

Lord, nothing makes sense. Six months ago, Peter had a career as the king's man and no care to change anything. *Now look at me. I want to change my career, my home, and take on a wife and a family of my own.*

Peter glanced at the scene around him—beauty and order, even in the transforming of seasons. *That's it—the answer. Change doesn't alter the purity or the goodness, whether the creation is a plant or a person.* He knew what he should do. Why not now?

He raced through the garden gate, across the lawn to the gravel drive, past the statue of the lion and the dragon. The huge iron gate would lead him to his future. Not wanting to miss a moment, he ran as if the Thames called him forward.

At the foot of the bridge, he stopped. A figure enveloped by the afternoon sun crested the top. Kate in her yellow dress appeared in a golden glow. When she halted, he found his feet moving to join her, to make sure she was really there.

"Peter, I was coming to find you."

"And I, you." He placed her hand in his and kissed her gloveless fingers. "Will you walk with me in the Privy Garden?"

She smiled and didn't pull her hand from his. As they descended into the palatial grounds, his joy left him silent. His hand encasing hers spoke the words he couldn't say. She belonged with him, at this time, in this place.

"I missed you after the wedding," she whispered.

He couldn't reply, not with the truth anyway. He trusted the silence more than his faltering words. It took effort to steady his pace and hold his peace.

"Tell me of the fete following the ceremony." He only cared about hearing her voice—the details didn't matter. If only her words would turn into a declaration of love for him.

"A true celebration with food and music." She sighed. "I am so happy for them. Sad for me, though."

"Why?"

"Now that she is married, things won't be the same. I can't interrupt her day or chatter for hours, for she'll have a household to run and babies to care for. But I wouldn't trade her happiness for mine."

They passed through the Privy Garden wall. "Where is your

favorite part of the garden? I want you to sit there." Peter watched her head turn to the right.

"That is easy. That bench under the willow tree."

Peter parted the long willow stems and asked Kate to sit on the bench. "Why is this your favorite spot?"

"Because of the animals that claim the nearby shrubs as their home. I've seen rabbits and squirrels, a fox once, and Sunshine had her kittens close by."

Sitting beside her, Peter touched her chin gently and guided her face with his fingers so that their eyes met. He took both of her hands in his. He knew there would be no better place or time than now in this peaceful oasis, alone, transplanted from the outside world.

"Kate." Just saying her name gave him courage. She stared at him with her big amber eyes. "Kate, I love you, and I have for many months." Her lips quivered but she didn't break eye contact or squirm away from him.

"I don't know if…" Peter didn't have to wonder long.

"Peter, I love you too. I thought it would be impossible for you to love me."

"How could you think that? I have never seen anyone more lovely or kind. You have talents immeasurable, and a heart so pure and wholesome. You have completed me. I'm now a believer in God again. I have the capacity to forgive and extend love to others."

"You didn't need me for that."

"But God put you in my life to show me what He desired for me. He gave you to me. Kate, will you marry me? Will you live with me every day? I want to go through the rest of my life with you."

"Yes, but…"

"Yes is enough. All the obstacles are gone. I never had any personally. I wanted you no matter what. But to make it easier, you have the blessings of the king, my mother, and your parents."

"Father?" Kate raised her eyebrows, which made him laugh.

"Easy. He said if you will have me, he will bless your decision."

Kate laced her fingers behind his neck, moving in as close as possible. Peter embraced her and bowed his head for their first kiss, not stolen or forbidden, a true sign of love, commitment, and of passion. Peter pulled away first and rested his forehead against hers.

"This will not be the easiest time to start our lives together. Soon the Act of Uniformity will stir up the land, Charles will marry, and peace in the kingdom will be challenged. But through it all I promise to put God and my family first. You before the king and country. I promise my love will remain pure and steadfast until I die."

Kate wiped a tear from her cheek. "You will never have to doubt my love. I will stand by you at our home, Hampton Court, and even in London." Her smile pierced his inner being. The same Kate but more confident and trusting. "I'm not scared anymore of the world. It cannot take away what is right and strong and pure."

The cool evening breeze reminded them the season was changing. They embraced it and each other as they returned to their families in East Molesey, with Hampton Court nestled behind them, harboring secrets in its gardens and halls for another day.

The end

Author's Insights

Thank you for reading Kate and Peter's story. I lived in England for a few years, enjoying the rich history and great manor houses and palaces. My sisters and I played in the gardens of Hampton Court. I've returned a few times as an adult, including a visit in the summer of 2022. The red brick palace with its meandering halls and mismatched architecture fascinates me and drives my imagination to ask questions. The beautiful gardens inspire me to wander and dream among the colorful layouts and intricate designs. Hampton Court Gardens rank as some of the most impressive in Europe. This series encompasses some of the things that I love: gardens, palaces, Europe, history, and travel.

If you enjoyed this novel, I hope you will continue the Gardens in Time series with the third standalone book, *Whispers of Wisdom*, releasing in 2024.

Follow me on social media and please leave a review on Amazon, Goodreads, and BookBub.

Newsletter Sylvan Reads: http://eepurl.com/gF-3I1

Website/Blog: https://margueritemartingray.com/

BookBub: https://www.bookbub.com/authors/marguerite-martin-gray

Goodreads: https://www.goodreads.com/author/show/14836211.Marguerite_Martin_Gray

Amazon author: https://www.amazon.com/Marguerite-Martin-Gray/e/B01ASA16RC?ref

Discussion Questions

1. Kate is a teenager during a Civil War. How do you think that influences her as an adult?
2. The question of religion dominates the 17th century in Britain. Church of England, Catholic, and Puritan beliefs are a few of the prominent thoughts. Would it be difficult to bend to the will of a state religion?
3. Kate loves the color of nature. She also wants to have color in her physical world like in her clothing. Would it be hard to live in a colorless world?
4. Peter decides to follow Charles in exile. Does he regret that decision?
5. What influence does the court have on Kate?
6. What influence does the court have on Peter?
7. Do you think a person can live in close proximity to the world (the court) and remain pure?
8. What role does forgiveness play in this novel?
9. Kate makes a promise to her father and God to remain pure. Does she hold true to that promise?
10. The Hampton Court Gardens are gorgeous and breathtaking. What role do they play in *Promise of Purity*?

Historical Facts

King Charles II reigned as king of Britain from 1660-1685 during the era of Restoration. His father, Charles I was executed in 1649, sending his son and family into exile during the volatile, chaotic Civil War with Cromwell as the head. While on the continent Charles and his "court" studied the royal courts of Europe, returning in 1660 with ideas of government and politics as well as palaces and gardens. Known as the Merrie Monarch, Charles II had many mistresses and children, though none through marriage. That posed problems for the royal line of inheritance, but that is a story for another time.

The building and expansion of Hampton Court Palace spans a few centuries. It is on the River Thames outside of London. Probably most famous as a residence of Henry VIII, it also housed other kings such as Charles II. During the 1660s, Charles updated the palace, adding rooms and furnishings, as well as expanding the gardens. His detailed and informed interest in garden planning began in Europe. Some of the impressive designs seen today are the result of his plans.

With the entrance of Cromwell, a civil war between religious beliefs emerged. He was a devout Puritan, highlighting an emphasis on simplicity in dress, words, actions, and beliefs.

Gone were the days of bright colors, festivities, singing, dancing, and pleasant carefree activities. When Charles II regained the throne, he brought life back to the court and the country, although the Puritan influence remained strong. The religious element would not be solved during his reign, yet he tried to accept different beliefs and worship preferences. Convincing a nation to widen her views on religion and the church was a constant problem for many kings after Charles II.

List of References

Harris, Tim. *Restoration Charles II and his Kingdoms.* London: Penguin Books Ltd., 2006.

Longstaffe-Gowan, Todd. *The Gardens and Parks at Hampton Court Palace.* London: Frances Lincoln Ltd., 2005.

Plaidy, Jean. *The Loves of Charles II: The Stuart Saga.* New York: Three Rivers Press, 2005.

Scott, Susan H. *The French Mistress.* New York: New American Library, 2009.

Thurley, Simon. *The Official Guide Book: Hampton Court Palace.* England: Historic Royal Palaces Agency, 1996.

About the Author

Marguerite enjoys the study of history, especially when combined with fiction. An avid traveler and reader, she teaches French and Spanish and has degrees in French, Spanish, and Journalism from Trinity University in San Antonio, Texas and a MA in English from Hardin-Simmons University in Abilene. She has two grown children and currently lives with her husband in north Louisiana. She writes historical fiction.

facebook.com/Marguerite-Martin-Gray-261131773910522
instagram.com/margueritemgray
bookbub.com/authors/marguerite-martin-gray
goodreads.com/margueritemartingray
amazon.com/author/margueritemartingray

Also by Marguerite Martin Gray

The Revolutionary Faith Series

Hold Me Close

Surround Me

Bring Me Near

Draw Me to Your Side

Wait for Me

Gardens in Time Series

Labor of Love

Promise of Purity

The Time Between

Promise of Purity Bonus Story!

Rainbow of Colors

East Molesey, 1647

Skipping ahead of her parents, Kate Sinclair veered toward the massive iron gate of Hampton Court Palace. She glanced behind at her ambling mother with her big belly—Kate hoped for a baby sister—she received the nod to approach her favorite view of the burnt-orange brick façade with the lions standing guard on high pillars.

Where were all the beautiful ladies in their flowing gowns of yellow and purple and blue? It had been a while since King Charles had resided at the palace. How could anyone stay away so long? She yearned to step through the gates into the gardens where the villagers had once been invited to stroll.

Her head rested between the cold iron rods as her eyes scoured the grounds. "There. There are the roses Mr. Payne planted. Father, can we go in? I know the way. Richard showed me." Kate covered her mouth quickly before more confessions flowed.

Her father leaned to the side of following the rules. His burly form hovered beside her with his arms crossed. "Kate, what have you done?" His gray eyes wavered between curiosity and condemnation.

Standing a little straighter, wondering if it would help her cause, Kate offered controlled speech. "I promise that we had permission. Mr. Payne let us in to play with Edward. The gardens are ever so pretty. Or they were."

"Do I need to be concerned about your whereabouts? Suppose the king had found you playing in his gardens?"

She giggled. "Perhaps he'd want to play too. He has children and dogs and horses."

He draped his arm around her shoulders and leaned close. "Kate, I love you too much to have you swallowed up by the images of the court. I promise you there is more value in the simple things of God than in the flattery of mankind."

"Like the flowers. God made them sparkle with bright colors and designs. Mother has her roses and lilies."

Her head turned with his as they sought her mother. She had found a bench among the willow trees. *So pretty and so very round. When will the baby arrive? Will she like me*?

"Yes." Her father smiled. "Look at the difference from your mother, who needs no adornment, and the ladies of the court, who drip with jewels and satin. You, my young daughter, have the same beauty. You don't need the fancy clothes."

Kate nodded back, facing forward, studying the bronzing effect of the sun across the palace's façade. "But I love the colors. Yellow is my favorite. I'm glad my Sunday best is yellow."

"That's all well and good. You are young and a child. One day the court will try to change you. But I'll not let it." He turned, challenging her lack of response. "Don't let your play and fascination with beauty turn you from God."

"Oh, Father, it's only Richard and Edward. What harm can they do?"

What did his raised brow and wide-eyed gaze mean? Did he not trust the boys? Or her?

Her hands gripped the iron bars. Glancing toward the

gardener's house, Kate saw Edward run through the hedge in her direction. "Kate, can you come inside?"

Bouncing on her toes, her grin spread. "Hello, Edward. I don't know. Is your father home?"

"Yes. Please ask. I've found a rabbit's den. And we have a new litter of kittens."

Before he finished his plea, Kate skipped to her parents. Mother might release her sooner than her father, especially after his speech about her friends.

"Mother, Edward wants me to see the kittens. Mr. Payne is home."

As her mother sought Kate's father's approval, Kate realized her faith in her mother's decision was misplaced. Father would have the last say anyway. The slightest nod and a wink accompanied the permission.

Her hand resting on her belly, her mother added her own smile and nod. "Yes, you may play for an hour. But stay out of the way. And remember that Edward is only five years old. Watch out for him and stay in sight of Mr. Payne's cottage."

Kate pivoted while waving goodbye. Once inside the small gate to the right of the massive ones, the air dispersed and mingled with the herbs and roses. Freedom? Color? Was any of it wrong? Something in her father's concern hadn't made sense. How could pretty dresses and brilliant flowers lead to a path of disobedience or destruction? She shrugged, adding it to a list of things she didn't understand about adults. Perhaps one day.

The whiffs of rosemary, basil, and lavender floated around her, slowing her steps. "Show me the kittens first."

Edward took off toward the stables. "Follow me."

What would her days be like living on an estate so grand? A quarter of an hour away, she lived with her parents over the bakery with one old male cat. A good mouser. A few fragrant flowers, but mostly the smell of fresh bread and herbs.

"Come on, Kate. I'm here." Edward's blond head peered around an end stall.

Shivers shimmied down her back and legs. The large brown, black, and white heads peeking over several stall doors spooked her into slow, awkward steps. Were the stalls locked? Could their hooves reach her? She loved cats and dogs. Horses, not at all.

Edward stood in the middle of the stall with his hands on his hips. "Why are you still so scared of horses?"

"You know why."

"But that was a long time ago, right?"

"I was your age. After the cart turned over, the horse neighed and reared and leaped toward me. If father had not pulled me aside, I would have been trampled."

Her friend waved his hand in the air and grimaced. "I know, but these horses are tame."

Inching her way across the hay, Kate peered into a box full of fresh yellow hay where a golden orange mother cat nursed six babies of all different colors. Even the animals, God's creatures, wore shiny colors—sleek, smooth patterns.

Kate clasped her hand tightly for fear she'd reach out and disturb the brood. Crossing her legs under her blue skirt, Kate relaxed forward. "Have you named them yet?"

"Well, they're not really mine. Are they?"

"If the king isn't here, whose are they?"

Edward petted the cat's head. "I guess the stable hand is in charge. He has these six horses, a few dogs, and chickens. I'm glad the pigs and sheep are out on the farms."

"I like pigs more than horses."

Jumping up, Edward tapped Kate's arm. "To the rabbit den?"

"Ah, yes." Racing her friend through the wide stable doors, Kate entered the vast orchard with pear trees. They approached a knoll with a wide hole under a grassy overhand.

"How do you know bunnies live here?"

He pointed to three smaller holes. "I've seen them come out when I'm very quiet."

Whispering from their perch on a stump, Kate searches the area. "Are they brown?"

"Oh course." Quizzical eyes popped in her direction before returning to the quest. "Have you ever seen any others?"

"Well, no. But I've read about them—white, black, multicolored. Why don't we have them?"

Edward jumped from his lookout post on to the next adventure. "You ask too many questions. Anyway, it would be more for Father to scare away."

Too many questions? Did her parents or Richard think that of her? Perhaps that explained her love of reading. When her mother began teaching her how to read, Kate had heard her father express his concern about his daughter's education. But Mother had won. After all, her mother came from a more educated family who believed in all children having a basic level of learning. Who knew that Kate would take learning to the limits, reading everything in sight?

Glancing one more time for elusive rabbits, Kate ran after Edward. "Have you ever seen the ballroom in the palace?"

His jaw dropped as he rolled his eyes. "I've only ever been in the kitchen. You'll never be invited any further."

No, she wouldn't, but she could dream of the places she would go in there.

"SIT STILL, KATE." Her mother pulled a comb through Kate's long, tangled hair. "If you'd wear your bonnet and avoid the windy banks of the Thames, I'd not have to battle this mess."

And if we didn't have to go to a boring church meeting, I could let my hair behave how it wants.

"Tell me again why I have to go. You know I can stay here by myself."

"Normally, yes. Today, there is to be important news about the king."

"So, no church service." That might be all right. "Just uninteresting adult conversation." Kate still didn't see her purpose.

Her mother gently tugged the long braid down Kate's back. "You, my dear, might just learn something."

"Will it be good news?"

Something shifted in her mother's usually calm features. A shadow. A grimace. Uncertainty? Kate didn't want to know. Her little corner of the world was good enough, growing more colorful every day. She hoped no one would decide to disrupt the budding brilliance, especially with a little sister on the way.

Walking between her parents, Kate spied all the villagers joining the crowd. Village meetings tended to be scarce. The growl-like mutterings from her father took the spring out of Kate's step. She refused to frown and spoil the clear-blue-sky promises of the day.

Jane Washburn, her best friend, only a few years younger than Kate, hopped to her side. Her friend's cheery disposition beamed with hope. Would they be able to play later after this meeting—or gathering—or whatever it turned out to be?

Her friend's big eyes pleaded for Kate's attention. "Will you be able to sit with me? It would be ever so much more fun than seeing you across the room."

Kate spied her father shaking his head and frowning. "I can't today. For some reason, I have to sit with my parents. Perhaps later."

"All right. I'll see if Edward can." Jane skipped away.

How can a six-year-old's world be less serious than hers? Kate studied the old stone church in front of her. She believed God cared for her, but would He want to know her concerns—about the baby, her father's moods, and her desire for bright colors? He should. He made the pretty colors. For some reason, He forgot to let her father know it was all right.

Her family found a pew in the back. Soon, standing room only existed. Kate rose on tiptoes while her mother settled her awkward form on the pew. Spotting Richard, Kate waved. How she'd love to be fishing with him or walking through the fields to the highest hills in the area. His smile confirmed she might have a friend for life.

Father gripped her arm. "Have a seat by your mother. I'll stand at the side."

If only she had that option. Or better yet, the freedom to remain outside. Why did she need to know what men in London decided? *I thought that's why we have a king. Let him make the decisions.*

Instead of using the pulpit like Mr. Galloway did every Sunday, the magistrate for the parish used a lectern placed in the center and a big gavel. Kate imagined that men in parliament knew about gavels and lecterns and how to make their voices boom.

Kate's body swayed as she sat on her hands to stop her fidgeting. A good book would have occupied her, but still her mind would have drifted to the kittens in the stables. Even the big horses with their giant hooves would be better entertainment.

"Hear ye. Hear ye." The gavel fell as the magistrate, clothed in black, startled the crowd into silence. Kate's sway ceased as her back straightened. Under no circumstance would she move unnecessarily.

"Citizens of East Molesey and the surrounding area. We are gathered here today to partake of some grave news that will affect your future. Many aspects of our lives are changing and soon East Molesey will feel the results. Two factions exist in our country—the royalists and King Charles and the parliamentarians. They both want change. I will share with you some things to watch in the coming days."

Change? Problems? Kate lost interest or didn't understand. Something about rulers and laws, religion and sinners, and high prices and no food. *The way he is talking, we're all going to starve and not go to heaven.* Kate glanced at her mother, stoic in her unblinking stare. Surely, her mother could make sense of it all and tell Kate later.

A man, red in the face, stepped into the middle aisle. "Will there be war?"

The magistrate lowered his head and cleared his throat. When he raised his head, his chin higher than before, his eyes blazed a path to the man, capturing other stares along the way. "There are already skirmishes around the country. The king is calling for his army to be on the ready and is accepting volunteers."

Another man stood. "And the parliamentarians? Do they have an army?"

The magistrate squinted, bringing his lips into a grimace. "Well, yes."

"If they're recruiting, I might join them."

The blaze pierced hotter than before. "Be careful what you say, young man. A civil war would not be a good thing. I don't think it would solve our problems." The magistrate adjusted his shoulders, pulling to his full height. "Choose wisely. Going against the king will have its consequences."

Someone in the audience laughed deeply and drawn out. "We know what side you're on. A true royalist."

Kate's head volleyed as the crowd bantered back and forth. Some for the king, some for change. As much as her mind could understand, change meant a rigid structure for religion and government. Would the changes hinder her from visiting the gardens or playing with Jane and Richard?

Finding her father's figure, Kate wondered at his pinched lips. Was he upset with the magistrate? Could he possibly want the strict changes without a king? That would explain his rants against the palace and anything fancy.

After half an hour, her father extended his hand toward her mother. "I want you to take Kate home. I'll be there soon."

Kate watched and absorbed her mother's shivers and shudders through her close proximity. Her mother's shaking voice confused Kate. "Are you sure you need to stay? What do they need with a baker? What can you possibly do to influence these men?"

His voice ground like gravel. "You don't understand. The king has to realize what his decisions have cost him."

Her mother pulled on his sleeve and pleaded with wide eyes. "Please, stay out of this conflict. Think of Kate and your baby. And me."

His smile didn't quite reach his eyes. Kate had observed his expression before when dealing with disgruntled customers. She knew he would try to please her mother while doing what he believed was correct and good for the family.

His nod dismissed them. Kate gained confidence, hoping her mother would allow her to join Richard and Jane outside.

"Run along, dear. I know you want to join your friends. I'll go on home and prepare the meal. Stay away from the edge of the river. It's still cold and very swift."

Kate kissed her mother's cheek. "Thank you, Mother. I'll be home soon." She shuffled through the crowd, rounded the building, and plunged toward the river bank under the bridge, a favorite meeting place for her friends. She had no idea if they were able to escape their parents.

The Thames in the spring roiled over the stones, forming foamy ripples against the bank. Richard stood close to the water with his arm pulled back, releasing a small smooth stone to skip across the water's surface. Skimming rocks occupied first place in their games. Jane sat on a large rock away from the swift current. Kate waved, but turned toward the river to join Richard.

Sitting posed the safest option, but less interesting than skimming rocks. Kate's direction veered toward Richard. The lapping waves deterred her from the edge, the warning ringing in her head. But with Richard there, Kate inched to his side, picking up a smooth stone. "Hello, Richard. Care for a game of pebbles?"

"If you are ready to lose." His brown eyes winked at her while his hand gestured for her to go first.

With a slight twist of her wrist, she tossed her stone and

watched it skip on the surface five times. Grinning, she bent down to pick up another stone. Out of the corner of her eye, she caught Richard's congratulatory grin. "What do you think about what the magistrate said?"

He leaned to the side and followed his stone as it skidded across the waves—six times. "I think I'd have to fight for the king. At least his rule is familiar."

She frowned at her loss and his comments. "I don't believe fighting is the answer."

"True. Unless your home is attacked."

"Attacked?" She released her pebble too soon. One, two, plop.

Richard chuckled and smiled like he always did when he won their games. "I don't think the soldiers will attack your home, but they will demand that the citizens change and believe as they do. I don't trust the parliamentarians."

She peered up at him. His eleven years must give him such opinions. She just didn't understand. Oh, to be older. "How do you know so much?"

His pebble almost made it to the middle of the river—six, seven, eight. *How does he know how to skip pebbles so well too*? "I listen to my father and uncle. They are too old to be soldiers, but they would if needed. I guess I feel I could do my part if older. But don't worry, my little friend. I won't be going anytime soon. Who would want an eleven-year-old boy?"

No one, she prayed.

Her next stone performed better, giving her another five points.

"Kate. Kate." She shaded her eyes and spotted Mrs. Washburn on the hill. "Come quickly. Your mother needs you. Jane, you come home too."

Lifting her skirt, Kate ran toward the road. "Richard, we'll finish the game soon."

~

A few hours later, the midwife announced the birth of Margaret, the sister Kate had dreamed about for years. She didn't mind boys, not really. Edward and Richard were all right, though she had more in common with Jane and the village girls. Margaret would be her special baby. She'd teach her how to read and work in the garden. Kate could share her love of bright colors with her in God's creation. The yellows of the flowers, butterflies, and fields in the spring. The orange and blues of summer dresses. And the greens and reds of trees.

I'll not let anyone take that beauty from me. Nature will not stop showing off the myriad of colors—not for the king nor parliament.

Shades of Black and White

1654

After replacing her dirty white apron with a crisp, clean one, Kate checked her bonnet and straightened her black skirt. The black showed streaks and puffs of stray flour as much as her gray or brown dresses. How she missed the blues and yellows of her childhood. Like the dandelions in the wind, her colorful garments disappeared with the changing of the leaders. Cringing at the cruel beheading of King Charles, Kate wondered at the influence the Lord Protector Oliver Cromwell had over the kingdom. Closer still, the influence on her father.

Crumpling her skirt in each fist, Kate anticipated her secret meeting with Richard. Ever since the Civil War had begun and battles raged across the country, her father despised everything having to do with the monarchy and the royalists. Richard, once a favorite household guest, was shunned. As a royalist soldier, his presence signified all things negative to her father.

Oh, Richard. How can we manage?

His note appeared at their favorite spot by the river in a

crevasse in a big rock. "Meet me Tuesday afternoon under the bridge. R."

Richard. My Richard. If not for the war, they'd be married. Kate had known for years, even in her girlish dreams, that Richard would claim her heart. Her father had approved of Richard then—not now. Not in an upside-down world where young men are coerced from their homes to join a dying cause.

In the family room, her mother sat with a few open readers, trying to teach Robert and Margaret how to decipher their numbers. Margaret had a hard time because she wanted to grab her sewing basket and make a new dress for her doll. Robert's six-year-old legs ran their own race under the table. Like their father, he didn't see much point in education.

Margaret sprang from her seat. "Kate, where are you going? I want to go."

Before Kate could answer, her mother caught Margaret's arm. "Not today, Margaret. Let your sister have some time alone."

"But..." her sister whined.

Normally, Kate would welcome her sister's company. Did mother know somehow? Had Kate's secret not been much of a secret? Glancing at her mother, Kate recognized the nod of understanding.

She knew and...approved?

"Be careful."

Kate mouthed, "I will."

Walking as nonchalantly as possible, Kate passed the village church, a separatist one since the establishment of Lord Cromwell as ruler. The lack of ornamentation and colorful flags or emblems startled Kate, even though the stark plainness should have replaced her memory, by now, of festivity and praise.

The flower containers and gardens remained barren with lack of attention. The windows drooped with an invisible black veil. Kate ignored them, screaming for light. Her dresses in her wardrobe served the same purpose—deflecting the light. Day in and day out—drab, dark, and hopeless.

Please, God, let the misery end. Cannot purity exist among the colorful variety of Your creation?

The track leading to the river bank portrayed lack of use. Not many family and church gatherings. People preferred to stay away from the crowds. Any celebrations were frowned upon.

"Over here." Richard exposed his presence in his uniform, covered by an oversized coat—out of place in the warm afternoon. But a royalist soldier's attire in East Molesey would never do. Richard's family had left with the first round of immigrants to the Americas, refusing to participate in the senseless Civil War. Richard's choice hurt many people.

Tripping on a stone in the overgrown path, Kate fell into his arms.

He laughed. She had missed his laughter. "Well, that is a nice welcome.

Heart pounding, Kate sank into his touch. "I've missed you. Please tell me you can stay."

"My sweet Kate. You know my commitment. I refuse to let the false ruler preside without a fight." He laced her fingers with hers and brought her hands to his lips. "Let's not waste this hour. I have something important to ask you."

She rested their laced hands on his chest. "Anything."

In one swift move, Richard lifted her onto a low wall under the bridge. The Thames swirled over the rocks, distorting the visions of her pebble-skipping days. Richard held a serious gaze fastened on her. Would she give away her undying devotion to him? Her love? She'd told him before—three years ago, when he joined the royalists and their cause.

Richard secured her left hand in his and squeezed. "Kate, I love you." He pushed out a heavy sigh. "I want to marry you. Will you commit to be my wife? Will you wait for me?"

"Yes! Yes! Let's not wait. We can find a priest of the old religion. We won't tell Father. Let's do not wait."

Her plea of desperation rang in her ears, piercing her heart.

He loves me enough to marry me. Does it really matter that Father will disapprove?

Whether a nudge out of her own desire or from God, Kate couldn't decipher.

Now.

Richard's lips grounded her to the present. The sweet kiss of innocence, of promise, of purity, and of love. All bundles up in urgency.

Gentle fingers caressed her cheeks. "My dear, Kate. We must wait. When this war ends, one side will be victorious. The citizens will find work and contentment again. We cannot rush the process."

A stream of warm tears trailed down one of her cheeks. "All right. Then you have to come home when it's over. To me."

"I promise. It can't last much longer." His smile crinkled his eyes. "As long as I carry your promise, I can face the enemy with courage."

Face the enemy. For Richard, the enemy is my father and citizens like him who have accepted the new regime and all its darkness with barely a glance back to their country's grandeur. Someone has to win. What if it isn't the side of the exiled king? What will happen to Richard? Will he be executed too? And…will I follow him?

I would.

Richard reached into his jacket's inner pocket and presented his closed fist to Kate. As a rosebud in bloom, his fingers opened, revealing a silver band. "My mother left this for me, knowing about my desire for a wife one day. She will be glad it is you."

He slipped it on her finger. Her vision blurred as tears dripped onto her hand. "Thank you, my love. I'll have to wear it tied around my neck, hanging close to my heart." She stared at the perfection, glistening from a recent polish.

"One day, you can wear it for the world to see. You are mine, sweet girl. Forever."

Two hours later, with a future loosely mapped out as Mrs.

Richard Douglas, Kate clung to Richard's neck. A spark alighted that her father and Cromwell could not put out. In her black and white world, a little sphere of brilliant colorful stars ignited.

Pivoting one last time on the path, Kate placed her hand over her heart. "Goodbye, my love, for now."

"We'll meet again soon, God willing."

THE SUN POURED through an upstairs window, landing on a large table covered with material scraps that Margaret had collected. "It's your turn, Kate, to take Mrs. Pew her basket of bread. I have to finish this dress."

Kate peered over Margaret's brown curls. "You know your dolls are better dressed than we are."

"I know. It's rather sad. Mother gave me these beautiful scraps from your old dresses. I don't really understand why we can't wear anything like this anymore."

Kate fingered a yellow and blue striped piece—an old church favorite. "When, I was your age, I wore some of these happy colored dresses. Then one day, Father came home with fabric in the dullest shades and had Mother make new dresses. I do miss the cheery hues."

Margaret placed a dress decorated with lace on the auburn-haired doll. "Do you think times will change?"

"Perhaps the pendulum will swing toward the light and bring back softer shades."

"With flowers and butterflies on the dresses?"

Kate imagined the doll dress material on Margaret. "Hmm. I'd be happy with a solid yellow or blue one."

The eight-year-old, nimble with a needle, created a simple frock out of the old fabric. Compared to the drabness of Puritan style, Margaret's doll clothing would be fit for a princess.

"I'll let you finish. When I get back, let's go to the banks to read and play."

Margaret threaded her needle again. "Lovely. I just have to add the lace."

Kate found the basket of baked items for Mrs. Pew. Her father pounded dough, sending puffs of flour toward the ceiling. "I'm going to Mrs. Pew's."

"Thank you. I'll have a basket ready for the reverend and his family when you return."

Kate disliked how the minister made her feel. His scour deflated her usual optimism. But that would be later. She'd enjoy her first visit immensely.

The widow Pew lived at the edge of the village past the dominating Hampton Court. Her cottage faced all the action. Kate giggled as she let the knocker fall on the front door, picturing Mrs. Pew stationed at her window, observing the town's drama.

A petite woman of sixty-something invited Kate inside. "I'm so grateful for your visit and the pastries and bread, of course."

Kate set the basket on a side table. "Would you like me to put these in the kitchen?"

"Later. I have news to share. Sit."

A sofa positioned in front of the window allowed for a comfortable view. Kate fingered the elegant brocade on the cushion. Somehow, Mrs. Pew had avoided the mandate of the Puritan rule. Her dress sparkled with tiny silver flowers on a light-green background. Beautiful. Kate's black marred the delicate scene.

Kate turned her body toward the older woman. "What news do you have? There's not much doing on at the bakery."

The woman's eyes concentrated on the huge brick palace. "Have you been to the palace lately?" Kate shook her head. "Cromwell and his family are returning for a short stay. You know what that means?"

Kate did. Lots of work for the few servants remaining on the palace grounds. Mr. Payne would need help with the gardens and Cook with the meals. Mrs. Pew followed a gossip chain all the way from London, so Kate pried some more. "Who is he bringing with him?"

"That's the interesting part. Some important parliamentarian members, his family, and personal household."

Mrs. Pew ran her gaze up and down Kate's form, causing increased jitters about the dreary fabric that Kate's father insisted she wear. "You will fit right in, dear." The woman smiled. "In my opinion, that is unfortunate."

Mine, too. I don't want to fit into the drab, formal, boring group where little distinguished one from another. "I'll be sure to ask at the palace how I can help. You know how I love the gardens."

The walk back to the bakery with an empty basket proved as heavy as before. Shouldn't Kate be excited about the protector's visit? How could she when Richard fought against the man and his rule? If Kate were a man, she'd fight for the king too. Or would she? Yes, she noticed more each day the freedoms she had lost. If not for her father, then the new church, harked on rules, a long list of "do nots." If God gave her eyes to see color, why not spend a bit of time admiring His beautiful creation in His people, scenery, animals, a single flower, or a tantalizing meal.

Her imminent call on the minister hung morosely over her. After Mrs. Pew's news, she wondered if her father needed to know. Surely, he'd appreciate a warning, even though Kate's opinion rested opposite of his.

She entered into the living area through the back door. Margaret and Robert had exchanged their books for helpful activities—Margaret mending cloths from a huge basket and Robert snapping beans.

"Hello, do you know where Father is?"

Margaret didn't lift her head from her tedious task. Why a sock needed perfect stitches, Kate failed to know. "Where he always is in the late afternoon, asleep in his chair."

"And Mother?"

"Preparing the minister's basket." Margaret set aside her walk. "Why can't I go with you?"

"I'd love that." Anything to distract the minister from over-preaching about Kate. She never seemed to reach his high standards of rigidity. Even her stride and posture caught the attention of some broken rule. "Ask Mother."

Margaret pouted. "I did. She said no. Either she doesn't trust me or she doesn't like the minister. I don't like him much either. He looks down his long nose at me and points at my bonnet or apron. One is askew and the other dirty, every time."

Kate giggled. "The same for me and I'm eight years older. Well, I'll take you both to see the new kittens at the palace. Edward says there's another orange one like Marmalade." The male cat had lived in the stables for years, leaving images of himself every season.

Treading down the dirt paved road, dreading her encounter, Kate focused on Richard, his handsome face and bright eyes, feasting on his memory. Just out of reach. "Oh, Richard. Where are you? When will this stupid war end?" This war—a manmade debacle, springing from the ground floor of parliament. Sighing and regretting hadn't changed Kate's world. Richard was still gone, facing danger every day, and she still did her father's bidding.

Before her hand hit the door, it opened, revealing a wide-eyed round housekeeper, Mrs. Martin. "Come on in, girl. Himself is expecting you." The fake grin warned Kate of things to come.

The dark hallway led to an even darker sitting room. Heavy curtains let in little light through the separation in the middle. Standing in the entrance, Kate contemplated spinning on her heels in retreat. But at the other end, her father would chastise. This way she'd receive the usual reprimands and return to a semi-content home.

"Come in, Miss Sinclair. Set the basket on the table. Mrs. Martin will see to it later. Thank your father for me."

Kate nodded as she stepped the few feet toward the table. Without the weight in her hands, she experienced an imbalance, a desire to float away as a mist. Lacing her fingers, she forced herself not to sway or fidget. Ready or not, the lecture breathed itself into the room.

The dark-clad man growled his words. "I'm glad you are here. I have something to say to you. Listen well and heed my words." The wolf cornered his prey.

At least he said his words and not God's words. Pulling in a deep breath brought her shoulders back, poised for battle. Her only armor was God's protection and promise to be with her.

"I'm concerned about your continued affiliation with Richard Douglas."

Her heart froze, missing a few beats. Richard? What would the man know of him? Of them?

His pinched scowl bellowed as an omen, warning her of condemning words. He leaned with locked elbows on his austere mahogany desk. "That soldier lover of yours is of the devil himself, taking arms against God's chosen people. The church forbids you to cavort with him anymore."

Oh, she had words for this man. Words to challenge his "lover," "devil," "cavort" vocabulary. Instead, she stared as his features transformed into a pale, grim blob, more comic than scary.

Trying hard to suppress her mischievous grin, Kate bowed her head, drew in a lungful of air, and prayed her words would honor God and Richard. "I am an obedient child of God, pure in His sight. My love for Richard is good and pure as well. I have done nothing to cause you or the church's condemnation. You have chosen to label and disregard another child of God because of your beliefs."

The minister's eyes squinted, shooting out fiery warnings, and his mouth pursed, creating deep crevices around his lips. Anger? Hatred? Had she overstepped the boundaries. So be it.

Kate exited without an empty basket, but her heart heaved relief. She'd defended Richard, God—who didn't need defending—and herself. Her father would hear about her misconduct. But repent? She would not, until God showed her a different way. Love in the midst of chaos could not be an evil thing. Although she'd rather the war dissipate and all the soldiers come home and live together in peace, she accepted her plight, which did not include disregarding Richard and his decision.

A peace descended on the way home. Her soulful burden lightened, though she'd pay for her assumed misdeed.

Richard, the gardens, Jane, and her siblings were enough color in her life to keep her believing in God's plan. The day would come when He'd make everything right again, clothed in yellow and orange, blue and green, purple and gold.

COLORFUL DAYDREAMS HALTED as Kate approached her yellow stone house. Margaret paced the stone walkway from the road to the door. Upon seeing Kate, Margaret's hands lifted to her mouth. She hiccupped words Kate could not decipher.

Grabbing Margaret's wrists, Kate pulled the girl's hands to her sides. "Slow down. What is the matter? Catch your breath. It can't be that bad. Is it Robert or Mother or Father?"

Margaret shook her head.

Good. Then what?

"It's…well…Oh, Kate, I'm so sorry."

What crime could Margaret have committed to cause the stress and shaking? "Tell me." *Do I want to know*? Something akin to dread rested as a mantel over her shoulders.

"Mrs. Douglas. Richard…Kate," Margaret paused and slowly emitted the words Kate never expected to hear. "Richard is dead."

Kate's world faded to the darkest black.

Not Richard. Please, God, not my love.

Glimpses of Pastels

1660

If she never heard the name of Cromwell again, that would be fine with Kate. If not for him and his like-minded parliamentarians, the world wouldn't have tilted so much. So many things she held dear fell apart during his regime. His takeover. His agenda. As pure as Cromwell claimed to be, God had other plans. Either that or the new king claimed his throne at an opportune time—the death of Cromwell.

Slowly, new life and growth crept back into the town of East Molesey. Kate's frozen heart thawed as the years passed.

"Oh, Richard. If only…" No, she couldn't go there. "If only" never returned or came true. Richard was dead. Taken down by one of Cromwell's men. He took her heart with him, at least the romantic part. Determined to live her days without a husband or children of her own, Kate tried to be the best sister, friend, and daughter.

After lightly scratching on her bedroom door, Jane let herself in and pounced on Kate's bed. "Well, are you ready? If we don't go soon, Anne will be married and half way to Devon."

Kate giggled at her friend's exaggeration. "All we have to do is show up. Let me find a ribbon for my hair."

"Are you truly going to wear it down? No cap? I'm surprised at you. Finally, not so much black and gray."

"It's only a ribbon." A yellow one.

"True. But your dress is not as dull. Blue becomes you." Jane tied the ribbon on Jane's long braid.

It was past time for Jane to find a husband. The pretty girl dressed in a pale-green dress could have the pick of the young men, though a lot of them never returned home, like Richard.

"Jane, who are you hoping to see today?"

Jane shrugged. "No one in particular. I'm happy for Anne and hope that it's my turn one day." Her brow crinkled. "Are you still determined to avoid courting?"

Kate sighed for the hundredth time when someone asked the same question. "Yes. I gave my heart to Richard. It's not available for anyone else. Not today. Not ever."

"But, what about children?"

"I will be the best aunt to your children and Margaret's and Robert's. Although, I can't imagine anyone wanting to marry Robert."

Jane snickered. "You better not let him hear that. He's taller than you are now."

"True." Her brother shot up over the summer. Yet, his boyish tirades and manners persisted.

"Jane, who can we find for you? The vicar's son, John? Or possibly Edward?"

Jane blushed. "Edward is like a brother. Anyway, he only has eyes for you."

"That is ridiculous. We work together in the gardens at the palace. That is all."

The unladylike *humph* sealed Jane's unbelief. Kate couldn't help his puppy dog attachment to her. He was too young and not Richard.

Kate grabbed a blue shawl from a peg. "Let's go. At least, one village girl has a chance at love."

Feigning lightness and joy, Kate shoved the hopeless subject of marriage back into its spot. If only she could bury it with her other dreams in the bottom of her hope chest. Now, her mother filled Margaret's chest with beautiful items. Should Kate give hers away? It would save her family extra expense and time. Yet, the presence of the chest and its contents soothed her heart, knowing she had a true love at one time.

One love for a lifetime. Only one.

The old stone church at the end of the road sat on a small hill with a large field surrounding it on all sides. Dotted with sheep, ewes with their lambs, the property had returned to the ownership of the Church of England. The Puritan hold had slackened, leaving only a few congregations scattered throughout the towns. Her father attended one about five miles away. He didn't require his family to join him.

The large red doors opened for the special occasion, offering a smile, as did the stained-glass windows, finally undraped from years as hostage to Cromwell's rule. What he had against light and colors, Kate failed to understand.

Once inside, Kate and Jane sat in the middle with a good view of the altar. The once-covered windows now let light stream into the church, making colorful patterns on the floor. Candles placed around the church served more for decoration than a light source. How times had changed back to the ways of her childhood. Hopefully, personal freedom to choose how to worship would take root, never to return to the strict one church policy. A dream. Why couldn't there be many different kinds of places to worship without the label of dissenter attached?

Jane poked Kate in the ribs. "You've been staring out the window for ages. I thought you were here for the wedding."

Kate glanced behind her. Anne stood with her father. The groom and minister at the front waited patiently. "It's all a bit unreal. The light. The colors. And here I am in dark blue."

"Give your father time. You'll be in a pretty, flowery dress soon."

Soon, as in months or years? Chances are I'll spend the next fifty years in similar attire.

Anne, though, beautiful in face, would be beautiful anyway because of the pure joy radiating from her form. The pale-blue dress flowed effortlessly, as if lightly draped over her. Angelic and pure. Love as God intended.

Kate fought down jealously and remorse. The war had ended but the price for her remained great. Bit by bit she continued to relinquish her hold on the past. Though Richard would never return and no one would replace him, the new regime and her place in it could spark a much-needed focus. This church had been transformed to a venue of light and life. Why couldn't she?

She'd make her own vow today. Not a vow like Anne to her new husband. But a vow to God.

I will put on a new garment of faith every day. My inner clothing will be of bright, shiny, pure fabric for the world to see, as befitting a child of God.

As they waved adieu to the couple, Jane looped Kate's arm with hers and stared at Kate. "I think that wedding did you some good. You have color in your cheeks, and knowing you, or the old you, you have a plan churning."

Kate giggled and patted Jane's hand. "I don't even think I can explain it."

A new hope? A rebirth? God's gift of newness. Free from a dark world.

~

"MOTHER, how can I make Father understand my new sense of excitement about everything happening." Kate measured flour for pastry dough, cutting her eyes toward her mother. "I see it as a time of possibility with new ideas. He sees it as…evil. Is that word too strong? Perhaps, sinful is better."

Her mother stopped her kneading and wiped her hands on her apron before placing her hands on Kate's cheeks. "Your father is doing the best he can. All the changes back and forth have left him stranded in the past. He finally found a position where he fit, and then in a matter of months, it was ripped from him." She sighed and lowered her hands. "He strongly believes in the Puritan ways. It is something he will have to work out on his own. He knows I am happier in the Church of England and allows his family to attend."

But…so many decisions he made for the family. When could Kate make decisions on her own? *I'm one and twenty and can't decide on what clothes to wear, except between black, gray, brown, and dark blue*. "But, Mother, I want so much more. Is there anything you can do or that I can do?"

Her mother pulled out the sides of her dark gray skirt. "I choose to follow what he desires. It would do me no good to present myself in a light-green dress, flaunting my wants and desires. This is my fate."

Kate needed one parent's approval. "You are his wife. I am a grown adult, screaming to make my own choices."

"Ah, my child, you are his daughter, living under his roof with his protection. You have no means to leave and set up house on your own. Until you marry…"

"I'll never marry." Kate jutted her chin out at the proclamation.

That didn't phase her mother. "When you marry, your husband will make the decisions for you. Who knows? You might be able to twirl around in your yellows and lavenders all day long. Until then, this is your lot in life."

Kate's hope deflated, bringing her shoulders to a stoop and her lips to a pout. "Do you understand at all?"

A twinkle of hope sparkled in her mother's eyes. "Yes, I do. My prayers for all my children render me to tears at times. I want you content, fulfilled, and being who God wants you to be.

If that is wearing colorful clothes, then I suppose God can supply that too."

Kate kissed her mother's cheek. "Thank you, Mother. It's not about the clothes. It's about all God's creation. It's beautiful and colorful. Purple eggplant, green, yellow, and red apples, yellow sunflowers, and orange poppies. Don't you see? He made those to brighten our daily lives—splashes of wonderful variety. I crave that."

"Then find ways to bring that into your life. You could create new recipes, cultivate a garden with flowers and herbs. Your ornamentations could be in the form of culinary treats and flower arrangements."

Hope tingled from head to toes. "That's it, Mother. Thank you." Pivoting, Kate ran out the door, remembering her cap at the last second.

THE HAMPTON COURT garden gate by the river Thames was unlocked once again. Her plan might not work, but it was definitely worth a try. Access to the gardens held her number one goal.

With no one in residence at the palace, Kate's confidence soared. Mr. Payne had been head gardener for years through the reign of Charles I and the rule of Lord Cromwell. Would he keep it with the new Charles? Someone paid him, so her guess was yes. Why get rid of someone who knew what to do?

The path led by the river and around the front of the gardener's house, a small two-level brick and wood structure—perfect for Mr. Payne and his son. Before Kate knocked on the door, she heard humming come from the gardens somewhere close. She followed the tune, knowing the source to be the gardener.

Peeking around a hedge that served as a wall, Kate found the man kneeling in an herb plot. "Mr. Payne, may I join you?"

"Good afternoon, Kate. Join me as in plucking weeds?" He gestured to the overgrown spaces.

"I would love to help. You know me. Ready to get my hands dirty."

"Here is a sack to kneel on. I'd hate for your skirt to be stained."

"It can't be any worse than flour dough."

"True." Mr. Payne stood and stretched his back. "What brings you here?"

"You. The gardens. A plan."

He chuckled, bringing his hands to his hips. "A plan? I like the sound of that."

Would he? After I told him? "Would you let me work in the gardens in exchange for a few herbs, fruit, and flowers? I want to create a few new recipes. I'm tired of the same old fare."

His pointer finger tapped his chin. "Of course, if you will share your treats with me."

"Perfect. You will be my official taster. You and Mrs. Downs."

"I can't speak for her, but I would love to help."

She stuck her hand out to him. "So, we have a bargain."

His firm shake sealed the venture. "We certainly do. When do you start?"

"Right now."

Dropping to his knees, she began the arduous task of uncovering abandoned herbs. All would benefit, including God's bountiful gardens. Though tended by humans, Kate saw God's hand in every sprout, even the weeds.

JANE LEANED on the counter with her hands, cupping her chin and digging in her elbows for support. "I haven't seen you as much lately. Are you ready to divulge your secret? Is it Edward? Do I hear wedding bells?" She said it without a smile.

Why couldn't everyone disassociate Edward from her future?

It didn't help with her working in the gardens outside his house. She gave them fodder to feed their make-believe scenarios. Was entertainment so dull in the village that she was the fuel?

"No bells. Yet, I do have some news. I don't mean to keep it from you. It has nothing to do with love, only my sanity."

"Do tell. It has to be more exciting than who visits my father's butcher shop. I'm glad I work for the seamstress. I can't stand the smell and blood when I work Father's counter."

One more blessing Kate had. Bread instead of dead animals. "Exciting for me for sure. I have been spending the afternoons in the palace gardens, helping Mr. Payne. Then at home or in Mrs. Down's kitchen, I create new recipes with herbs and fruit and berries from the gardens. Exciting news, right?"

Jane searched the baskets in the bakery kitchen. "Anything for me to try? I don't see how that inspires you."

Kate giggled, knowing her past times did little to ignite a spark in others. They weren't meant to impress or influence. "Try one of these. A rosemary, lavender flat biscuit."

The slight crunch, followed by a contented sigh, reinforced Kate's confidence. She raised her brows for confirmation.

Jane didn't fail her. "The best sensation. The lightness and the snap surprised me. And no crumbs. I think you should offer these to the villagers."

"Since they meet with your approval, I just might, though I'd have to convince my father."

Kate set the dough aside to rise and clicked her tongue. "I have an idea. What if I make a variety of my new recipes and have a picnic? I'll invite you, Mrs. Downs, Mr. Payne, Edward, Mother, and Margaret and Robert. Father wouldn't come, so no reason to include him. I could add cheese and fruit and some ham. We'd have a splendid 'tasting' meal."

"Please do. I'll wear my pretty new frock."

A new dress. Good for Jane. Kate would wear her newest blue dress, the closest she'd get to a light blue. Maybe she'd call it pastel blue.

While working in the gardens, Kate praised God for the colors all around her. The bouquets of wildflowers and cultivated bulbs sprinkled her room as a tiny garden. Her mother appreciated the stems of lilies or roses in the windowsill or on the table. Her father eyed them but never commented. She wished she could catch him smelling one or touching the petals. For a man who worshipped the same God as she did, he sure monitored his praises.

She closed her eyes for a second. *Thank you, God, for Your creation and for allowing me to toil in Your gardens.*

"Let's do this next Saturday on the river bank by the big boulder."

Jane clapped her hands. "I'll bring some sliced ham."

"Perfect."

Now that she'd committed herself to the picnic, Kate had decisions to make and invitations to extend.

EDWARD MET Kate in the road outside the bakery on a bright spring day. The trees bent with their buds of green. Bushes of lilac laced with honeysuckle vines reached toward the river. Birds dressed in their reds, blues, and yellows flitted and sang around them.

"I'll carry one of your baskets, Kate."

Kate handed him one of them. "Thank you. I might have filled them too full."

"Oh, not to worry. My father and I will make a big dent."

Kate snickered. "If you can stop Robert from feasting continually."

Her small clan of friends and family gathered on the old quilts faded with time. Kate arranged her breads, pastries, and pies as a meal fit for a king—well, a king who wouldn't mind sitting on the grounds without servants.

Rosemary and cheese tarts. Lavender and thyme bread sprinkled with caraway seeds. Savory cheese and basil rolls. Blueberry biscuits with crabapple sugar glaze. Apple and cinnamon tarts. Ham, cheese, and bread with garlic butter or ginger spread. A feast ending with a gooseberry, caramel, sponge cake.

Mrs. Downs, sitting on one of the chairs Mr. Payne provided, clapped her hands before she filled her plate. "My dear Kate, I'm hoping you'll remember these receipts for the king's feasts."

Kate blushed. "And when do you expect His Majesty?"

"Oh, whenever he has the whim to visit this residence. Rumor has it, he'll be here next spring."

Kate discarded her white apron and smoothed out her pastel blue skirt. Times were changing as light filtered out the darkness, exposing colorful possibilities.